A Different Kind Of Love

A Novel By
Nanette M. Buchanan

I

©Copyright 2008 by Nanette M. Buchanan
All rights reserved. This book is a work of fiction. All the events, places and characters are products of the author's imagination or used fictitiously. Any resemblance to actual events or locales or persons, living or dead, is purely coincidental. No part of this book may be reproduced, stored in a retrieval system, or transmitted by any means, electronic, mechanical, photocopying, recording, or otherwise, without written permission from the author.

Type of Work: Text
Creation Date: 2007
Second Edition: 2010
ISBN: 13-978-0-9793883-1-6
ISBN: 10-0-9793883-1-7
Cover Design: Terry Smith, CEO,
        Photographer, Smoove Productions
Cover Models: Aaron Brown, Mecca Brown

I Pen Books
www.ipendesigns.com

The Sequel to

Family...Secrets, Lies & Alibis

Acknowledgement

I would like to thank all of my family, friends and readers who supported and continue to support the success of "Family...Secrets, Lies and Alibis." I hope you enjoy "A Different Kind of Love" as the saga continues. You will never know how your support encouraged the publishing of both novels. To my husband James, your understanding is beyond what I could ever expect. We made it through this trying year on the wings of angels and God's mercy. Together we will continue to grow strong. To my children Tynicia, Katia, and Aaron life continues to be a blessing with the three of you in my corner. To Terry Smith, your work adds to this piece in more ways than you'll ever know. I thank you. Thank you all for your constant encouragement. It is a blessing to be at this point in my writing. I again ask you to travel with me as *"I Pen"*.

Forward

The thought of family has been on my mind since my childhood. I knew that I had two brothers, one older, one younger; sons that my father never thought to introduce to me. Their existence was acknowledged by my mother in conversations regarding family lineage.

These conversations often reminded me that I knew little of the life my father lived. I had the honor of meeting this man at the age of seventeen. I often wondered how my childhood would have differed had I known them. I never thought much about looking for them as an adult, nor did I stay in contact with my father. Since then I have had occasional thoughts about where they may be, whom did they marry, and do I have any nieces or nephews. Have our paths crossed without the knowledge of our connection? Will we ever meet?

My first novel "Family...Secrets, Lies and Alibis", sets the stage for the sequel "A Different Kind of Love". The characters, though fictional, can be anyone who is unaware of their family lineage. One may be able to cover the secrets, lies, and excuses for siblings not knowing each other, but what happens if they meet and unaware of their family ties, they fall in love? Is it easy to put that love aside and begin over as sister and brother? How do they cover feelings that they have grown to depend on?

This story is fictional.
But could it be one that has been told?
The secrets continue.........

Chapter 1

Mitch packed his briefcase with contracts he had to read before the next morning. He had a full day and taking work home had become somewhat of a habit. It filled in his time when he didn't have evening plans with his new love interest Marci. He hadn't heard from Marci much during the day, and he thought it was strange. He was falling in love with her. It had been four months since they got together. He planned on asking for her hand in marriage during the Christmas holidays. Darlene, Marci's mother, told Mitch she couldn't wait for them to be married because Marci only talked of him and the things they did together. He was ready for the commitment. He hadn't told anyone yet of his intentions, and he decided he would spring it on Byron and 'Rell while they were at the sports bar on the upcoming weekend. Football season had started and they had a date every other Sunday at the sports bar. The alternate Sundays they spent entertaining the females in their life. Byron was dating Tracey, a young lady who worked as a paralegal for Mr. Simpson, the lawyer for DQ Enterprises while 'Rell's relationship with Shai was still a secret to all except Mitch and Marci.

Mitch passed 'Rell's office and wondered what was going on. 'Rell never left early. He waited until he got to his car and called 'Rell's cell phone.

"What's up Rell? You never leave early."

"I left today to get my mother some flowers. It's her birthday tomorrow and she already said she would be going out of town so I took off to spend some time with her. Is everything okay with you?"

"Yeah, have you heard from Shai or Marci today?"

"They're spending our money man. They went to the spa. Shai passed some exam that had her stressed out, and she's celebrating. I don't think Marci even knew she was coming by to get her. Call her on her cell man. You missing her like that?"

"Man, don't start? You can't talk. If Shai didn't call you, 'Rell, you know you would break down."

"It's a different kind of love man. We've been dealing with each other for almost three years. Well, I guess we can't count the first two."

"Yeah, you can't count long distance phone calls. Anyway, I'll call her now. Thanks man."

Mitch looked at his phone. *Why didn't she call?*

Mitch's phone rang.

"Hello."

"Mitch? Hey baby. I know you guess I lost my mind."

"No, you made me lose my mind. I just wanted to know you were alright."

"I'll meet you at your place. This spa is closer to you. Shai drove so she'll drop me off at your house."

"Do you want me to pick anything up for dinner?"

"Okay, umm, pick up some Chinese food. You know what to get right?"

"Yeah, baby I know. Marci, call me if you're going to be later than you think. Those roads to the house get dark."

"I will. Love you."

"Love you too."

Marci went back to the room where she and Shai were waiting to get a manicure and pedicure. She noticed Shai holding her head.

"Hey, what's wrong girl?"

"I think that sauna heat got to me. I feel dizzy. My head is heavy."

"You probably need some air. We're not next. We can step out into the other room. I'll tell the girl where we'll be."

"Thanks." Shai had been feeling bad the past few days.

It was a weird sick feeling; she didn't know what it was. Marci came back and sat near her.

"You look sick. Shai are you alright?"

"Girl, I feel like, damn, I feel sick."

"Maybe you got a touch of the flu."

"I'm going to the doctor's office tomorrow."

"We can skip the pedicure and the manicure. Let me tell her you're not feeling well."

"Get a refund, I paid for everything already."

Marci got the reimbursement and told Shai they would reschedule. She walked her to the car and told Shai to give her the keys.

"I'll drive you home and tell Mitch to pick me up at your house. Do you want me to call 'Rell for you?"

Marci helped Shai into the car. Shai let the seat back and closed her eyes. "No, don't call him Marci. He's going to his mother's today. Her birthday is tomorrow and she is leaving town for the weekend."

Marci drove while Shai tried to drift off into sleep. They pulled in her driveway twenty minutes later. Marci tapped Shai and they both got out the car.

"Do you feel better? Maybe you need some Ginger Ale to settle your stomach."

"I have some in the house, 'Rell usually drinks that. Marci, this is the strangest feeling. I don't think it's a cold."

Marci's phone rang. "Hello."

"Marci, are you still at the spa?"

"No, as a matter of a fact, I was going to call you. Can you pick me up at Shai's?" Marci replied; glad Mitch called again.

"Well, it will be after seven. I have to stop at 'Rell's mom's house. He has a file I need."

"That's okay Shai doesn't feel well so we left the spa."

"What's wrong with her?"

"I don't know. She's going to take something for her head and stomach and lay down."

"Alright, I'll pick you up after I leave there."

"See you then."

Marci went into the house with Shai. She offered to make her a cup of tea. Shai told her she would try the tea instead of the ginger ale. When Marci returned to Shai, she had laid down on the couch. She was sleep. Marci turned on the television and waited for Mitch.

Chapter 2

"Ms. Mince, please follow me." Shai got up from her seat in the waiting room and followed the nurse.

"The doctor will be in to see you. Please take off your clothes and put on the gown on the table. There's a cup there for your urine sample. When you're done, place the cup through that little window on the right side of the counter."

"Thank you."

Shai hadn't told 'Rell she was going to the doctor. She made the appointment after she had missed her period twice. She was too scared to take the EPT at home. If she was pregnant she wanted to know how far along she was. Shai went into the bathroom and followed the nurse's instructions. 'Rell walked into Mitch's office laughing with Byron.

"Man, Mitch didn't even give us a chance to change our mind. He just said he had things to do. We knew Marci had him under her control."

Mitch started smiling. He was sitting behind his desk. He looked up.

"Y'all got jokes. I miss one Sunday and you jump right on it. Marci had made plans that I didn't know about. It happens."

"She got you man."

"Byron, who got who?"

"Man that's 'Rell talking. You didn't hear me saying a word. I know I get caught up sometime. So I know the feeling."

"Oh, Byron, you taking sides?"

"No, man, I'm just saying I get caught doing things at the last minute. Wait 'Rell you do too."

"Not lately man. I haven't missed any of our outings."

"No, 'Rell, it works fine for you. You set the dates."

They all laughed. The intercom caused them to be silenced.

"Yes, Ms. Berry."

"I'm looking for Mr. Mince."

"Yes, Ms. Berry, I'm here. What's up?"

"You have a phone call. Ms. Mince says it's urgent?"

"Transfer the call here please."

"Rell?"

"Shai, what's up?"

"Call me on your cell please."

"Alright, are you on your cell?"

"Yes, please call me right back."

"Okay. Hang up the line."

"What's wrong 'Rell?" Mitch was concerned. Marci told Mitch Shai wasn't feeling much better, and it had been three days.

"I'm not sure. Hello, Shai?"

"Rell what time are you getting off?"

"I can get off now. What's the problem?"

"I'll meet you at the house."

"Mine or yours, Shai what is wrong?"

"Yours, I want to tell you then."

'Rell hung up the phone. "Mitch man I'll call you guys back. I don't know what's wrong."

'Rell drove home thinking something had happened to Derek or Tonya. He couldn't imagine what, just that something had happened to them. *"Shai should have been at work. Maybe someone found out about us and she's upset about it."*

Tonya had not been back to the office since her visit two weeks prior. Mitch told her the name of the holding company and escorted her to the front of the offices. Mr. Simpson told 'Rell she should be calling him within a week to complain. *"Maybe Tonya complained to Shai."*

'Rell pulled into his driveway. Shai's car was in the garage. He used that entrance to inspect her car, just in case she had been in an accident. Shai was sitting on the couch with tissue on the table and in her hand. When 'Rell walked in the room she looked up at him, he could see her eyes were swollen, signs she had been crying a long time. Her eyes were bloodshot.

"Baby, what's wrong?"

"Rell, I didn't think this would happen. I don't know what we're going to do. Say you love me 'Rell.

"Alright Shai, you're making me mad now. You know I love you. What is wrong?"

"I went to the doctor today. I hadn't been feeling well for about a week or two. I was sick in the stomach and dizzy and just sick."

"What did the doctor say Shai?"

"I'm five months pregnant. I thought everything was fine. I've had my period." Shai lied about the last two months. She thought if anything she would be three months pregnant, and she would have an abortion.

"Five months Shai? Your period came last month?"

"Yes, the doctor said that is possible. I had a little blood today. She said that is just because I am a little upset."

"You should have told her you were a lot upset. We can't have children Shai. How are we going to put this over on anyone? Damn, what about the baby? Will it be healthy?"

"Rell, there's something else. She said I am fine and so are they."

"They, they who?"

"They're twins, 'Rell. I'm pregnant with twins."

"Shai, oh no, baby what did she say about an abortion? I mean you can't want to go through this with their health being questionable."

"Rell, she said I was too far along for it to be safe to have an abortion. It's not safe for the babies or me."

"What about their health Shai? You know they say they could be born with deformities or mental problems when siblings are the parents."

Shai started crying again. 'Rell was pacing the floor.

"Baby, how are we going to do this? My own kids are going to call me uncle 'cause they can't call me daddy?"

"Rell, do you love me?"

"Shai you know I love you. Loving you got us into this shit. But, yes baby, I love you."

"I love you too. I love you and we'll get through this."

"Twins?"

"Twins."

'Rell sat next to Shai on the couch. He kissed her and pulled her into his chest as he sat back on the couch.

Chapter 3

arrell didn't sleep much and as the alarm rang, he knew he wouldn't be in the office until after eleven. He sat staring at a picture of himself, Dershai, and Derek, taken shortly after their father's death. They all agreed that the family should have a picture of the three of them together. 'Rell let his mind drift thinking of his pre-set schedule for the day. No meetings, no urgent phone calls, nothing that couldn't be delayed by a few hours. The clock sounded again as a reminder. 'Rell turned it off. Although he had not slept much, 'Rell couldn't sleep now that the morning light had touched his face.

'Rell and Shai talked until she fell asleep. He hoped she felt rested. Shai had a lecture to sit through that she couldn't miss. They talked until two thirty. *"Okay, it is what it is!"* 'Rell found that he used his aunt's saying more and more lately. He picked up the phone to call his mother and hung it up shaking his head. *"I can't call her until I know what I'm going to say. I'll call Mr. Simpson first. How did I get caught in this shit?"*

As he got dressed, he lost himself in memories of the past three years. His father, D.Q., and his mother, Nikki, were inseparable, or so it seemed. Inseparable but not married, that's where it all started. After 'Rell overheard their argument about marriage, he moved to Maryland leaving them to their secrets and lies. 'Rell was dating Monique then but Shai had all his attention. They met in a mall before his move to Maryland, and he stayed in touch, just in case he returned to Virginia single. They talked late many nights, sent missing you cards through e-mails. They never thought to delve into either of their families business. It was the next year when his life became a whirlwind. 'Rell was named one of the top CPA's in the state while working at Sheldon Finance. Derek Quincy Mince died in late May. That had been a little over five months ago now. It seemed like it was longer. Being with Shai helped the healing and the time was lived with a new love. 'Rell couldn't imagine living without her.

'Rell received a letter from Mr. Simpson, his father's lawyer and confidant. The letter declared Darrell as the executor of his father's will. That's' when 'Rell and Shai's relationship changed from a distant friendship to the best love either of them knew. He called Shai, told her he would be in town for a while for family business. Although Shai said she had death in her family, they were not prepared for what was to happen next. They spent hours of getting acquainted both physically and mentally. There was one problem. Darrell Quincy Mince was the eldest child of Derek Quincy Mince and Dershai Quinelle Mince was his youngest child. They both neglected to ask the others last name fearing their father's success would be to the other's advantage. Once they realized the other was financially independent it didn't seem to matter what their last name was.

As the offspring of D.Q. Mince they both were at the reading of their father's will. Marci, their first cousin and Mitchell, 'Rell's best friend and Mr. Simpson were the only people who knew they were seeing each other. They both advised 'Rell and Shai they should end the relationship, but they were in love. They couldn't just stop what took two years to develop. Besides they didn't want to lose the love they found. They were truly in love. 'Neither Rell nor Shai felt they were anything other than lovers. They hadn't met as siblings.

The relationship started as a friendship and had developed for two years before any physical contact.

Marci, Mitch and Mr. Simpson did agree, 'Rell and Shai were in love. The relationship continued, as a secret. Dershai moved from her condo that she shared with their other brother Derek to avoid the questions about 'Rell's frequent visits.

D.Q. spent a lifetime building D.Q. Enterprises. 'Rell acquired D.Q. Enterprises, a financial corporation with large profits in real estate and investments. D.Q. left his secrets untold, and as they unraveled, Darrell's life was becoming more complicated. Mr. Simpson applauded 'Rell as he handled each situation, as though they were of no surprise. He now knew why his mother and father were not married. D.Q. had been married for thirty years to Tonya, Dershai and Derek's mother. D.Q. told Nikki about Tonya but never mentioned his children. Tonya knew that D.Q. had an outside family but accepted his discretions thinking she would be rewarded eventually through their divorce or his death. Now that D.Q. was dead, she was furious with the world because she wasn't bequeathed anything. The stocks she owned were sold as D.Q's revenge from his grave. She was no longer connected to D.Q. Enterprises, and she continuously looked for ways to reestablish her ground.

D.Q.'s brother, Darryl and D.Q's son, Derek shared the bad habit of gambling. Darryl had a construction company and Derek had started his own web design company. 'Rell took care to monitor their accounting business files without their knowledge. 'Rell's Aunt Darlene, his father's sister, was becoming his favorite. She had qualities that reminded him of his father. Darrell told her he often wished they knew each other when he was younger, so she could have spoiled him. He smiled at his thought.

Shai was special, not because they were sister and brother, but because he loved her. He loved her more than anyone else he had ever loved. He loved her like his father expressed loving his mother. D.Q. died loving Nikki and expressed it on the taped recording of his will. That day 'Rell died inside. Shai sat across the conference table at Mr. Simpson's office and felt the same way. They were in love and had made love as lover's do. They couldn't accept being siblings. They continued to see each other as lovers secretly. They missed family dinners where Nana could look them over and catch their eyes staring at each other. Nana would often ask them if they were okay. They knew she suspected them, but they couldn't and wouldn't say it was so. Marci and Mitch kept their promise but warned them constantly.

"Well, Mitch, I guess I'll call you first before Shai tells Marci and you call me." 'Rell picked up the phone and dialed Mitch on his cell.

"Hey man, what's up?"

"Mitch, man, I won't be in until after eleven. If you guys need me call the cell."

"You do remember you are supposed to meet with Keith at ten this morning or am I telling him to call you later."

Keith Larson was still working at Sheldon Finance. Mitchell Carter, Byron Washington, Craig Masters and Keith Larson were friends since college. They all worked at Sheldon Finance together. When D.Q. died, Mitch and Byron were offered a partnership in D.Q. Enterprises where 'Rell was now the President and CEO. Craig was dating 'Rell's ex-girlfriend, while 'Rell was deciding they couldn't make the relationship work. He was also caught rolling over company accounts for personal gain. 'Rell gave him the option of resigning before Sheldon's management fired him.

'Rell was warned by Mr. Simpson that the existing partners weren't found of Craig or Keith. Keith had not shown his disloyalty but 'Rell had learned to believe Mr. Simpson's word. 'Rell wasn't sure he wanted to meet with Keith, but he had put off the appointment for weeks. Keith had called early the week before and Mr. Simpson gave him a nod of approval. Neither

Keith nor 'Rell mentioned partnership. Keith was looking forward to working with Byron, Mitch and 'Rell again.

"I did forget about it, but it won't be a problem. I can get to the office by ten."

"What's up, you sound out of it? Is Shai okay?"

The last Mitch heard Shai was under the doctor's care. 'Rell took the question as the opportunity to talk. He looked at the clock, which now read seven o'clock.

"Are you on your way to work or home?"

"What does that mean man? I go home at night? Mitch laughed. 'Rell and Byron teased him about staying at Marci's and never going home. 'Rell didn't laugh.

"I didn't know which way you were going. I need to talk with you before you see Marci again."

"Huh? I know there's a reason for you saying that. I just don't know if I'm going to like the reason."

"No man, it has nothing to do with Marci. It's about Shai. Well, it's about both of us really. Well, all of us."

"Rell, I'm on my way."

The phone went silent. 'Rell went into the kitchen and got a glass of orange juice. He decided to prepare Mr. Simpson. He had been a loyal friend of D.Q.'s and was becoming 'Rell's right hand man, just like Alfred was to Bruce Wayne. Where would Batman be without Alfred? Stanley Simpson was an important part of the puzzle that connected 'Rell and D.Q. 'Rell knew there were more pieces, and now he had his own pieces to add. Rell decided to call his new confidant before Mitch arrived.

"Good Morning Stan."

"Rell, good morning young man, you're up early this morning. I thought you would be sleeping until eight or nine."

"Excuse me?" 'Rell often thought Mr. Simpson had his home bugged.

"Nothing, just teasing, my sources could be wrong."

"Stan, let me find out you and your boys are snooping in my home."

"I love keeping you on your toes young man. What can I do for you this morning?"

"Shai's pregnant. Twins, the due date is July tenth. Probably before, I don't think twins go full term."

"Have you set a date to go through your father's belongings?"

"Stan, did you hear me? Shai is pregnant. I don't want to think about my dad's things right now. How will we deal with this?"

"I heard you 'Rell. Set a time and date to get to your dad's belongings. Until then talk to no one about her pregnancy."

'Rell had learned in the past months that Mr. Simpson knew all of D.Q.'s secrets but refused to tell them before time. *"What would be found in D.Q.'s belongings?*

"Stan, I am exhausted. I didn't get much sleep. Help me here. What is in my father's belongings that could possibly add light to this situation? I know there's a reason for you telling me to complete this task first."

"There is. Did Mrs. Mince contact you?"

"Who?", 'Rell was getting agitated with Stan Simpson's mind game, "Mrs. Mince?"

"Yes, Tonya Mince."

"Oh Shai's mom, no, should she be contacting me?"

"I would have thought she would have by now. Her past is catching up with her. I told her there were no funds or stock in her name through D.Q. Enterprises. She assumed there would be a quarterly report prepared for her."

"I am really tired. I don't understand what you're talking about. Stan, don't hold it against me, but my mind is on this family I am now responsible for, not Tonya Mince."

"She will contact you. She feels you are weak or have some secret she can ruin you with. This pregnancy if not handled properly could be a piece of gold to her. She is desperate, always has been."

"I can't believe she would ruin her daughter. What does she want to gain?"

"Rell, she feels you stand in the way of a fortune, her fortune. Even if she has to go through her children, she wants a large part, if not all, of D.Q. Enterprises. She'll use the pregnancy to her advantage. She may….well, I don't want to speculate. Just know that she will contact you. Your defense is in your father's belongings."

"Stan it's hard for me to believe she would use her daughter. It would kill Shai. She doesn't care for her mother's actions, but she still loves her mother. That would rip her apart."

"Believe me, Tonya Mince loves no one. That includes Derek and Shai. She loves only herself. Enough talk about her. Talk to no one. I know Marci and Mitch will be told by Shai. You should make arrangements to go through your father's belongings sometime this week if your schedule permits."

"Okay, I'll talk with Nana. I hope this is not as sticky as the reading of the will. My father, a real under cover man. Listen, I will be offering Keith a job. Are there any concerns?"

"No, Keith's problem is his family. I think that's why he wants to transfer. He was worried about his mother's health. She is living with her sister now in Philadelphia."

"You guys are amazing. What did you do, follow the man around? Never mind, I don't want to know. Just remind me to stay on your good side." 'Rell laughed at the thought of men in black hiding in his bushes outside his home.

"It's what you pay me for. Let me know how your meeting goes and when you will be dealing with your father's belongings."

"As usual I will contact you at some point today. Stan thanks."

"My pleasure young man, actually your father paid for this part of my services before his death."

"I guess he knew he was leaving a mess."

"He knew you could handle it. Call your grandmother and take your time reading the materials you find."

"Thanks Stan, I'll talk with you later."

'Rell hung the phone up and sat at the kitchen table thinking about D.Q. giving Stan orders to complete upon his death.

"How could he know this would come up? Another piece to my father's scrambled life revealed."

Chapter 4

itch pulled into 'Rell's driveway, expecting to find him sick in bed. He cut off his cell. He didn't want Marci to be able to reach him during this talk with 'Rell. Darrell Mince was the closest to a brother that Mitch had. He had three siblings, all girls. Mitch and 'Rell adopted each other during their college years at Maryland University. He respected 'Rell and his opinions. He hoped this wasn't a talk that would discredit Marci or Shai.

Mitch never rang the bell. It was a habit that the door was unlocked when 'Rell expected any of the guys. Mitch walked in and headed straight for the kitchen to grab a beer.

"I've got your beer in here man. I heard you pull up."

"Damn, it's like that? What's got you on edge?"

"Mitch, I thought I had my life together. That was about three years ago. I feel like I'm on a rollercoaster and I can't get off."

"What's the problem?"

"Okay, where should I start?"

"Rell, it is what it is. Start where you want, I'll put it together."

"Okay, thanks. Shai is pregnant."

"And we're just drinking beers?" Mitch laughed, "Shit, I mean okay, and?"

"We're having twins."

"Rell, twins? What do you mean **having**? You can't possibly think that this is okay. I mean you guys have a lot of problems to consider?"

"Yeah, man. I said the same thing. We're going to the doctor together next month to talk with her about the problems."

"Next month. C'mon 'Rell, you and Shai can't be thinking that you can have these kids. That's your sister, man.

What about their health? What are you going to tell your mother or your grandmother?"

"Mitch, the doctor told her it would be a risk to her and the twins if she had an abortion at this late date."

"Late, 'Rell how far along is she?"

"Five months, she's not showing much though. She said they checked closely for their development because it was twins, she's in her fifth month."

"Man, do you think she knew about it. I mean five months and you don't notice a change?"

"Mitch, she has gained a little weight but not pregnancy weight. Man, I don't know. She still had her period. At any rate, even if she knew we can't change the facts."

"They say their breast change. I know you would have noticed that."

"I don't know Mitch."

"So, what are you guys going to do? Announce it at a Sunday family dinner? She'll be showing real soon. I can't imagine you playing this off to some mystery boyfriend."

"Yeah that's what I said. We didn't get that far in the discussion. I think we both had an emotional shock. We talked until she fell to sleep. I called you and Mr. Simpson this morning."

"Mr. Simpson, our secret agent. What did he have to say about the situation?"

"Mitch there's more shit to uncover."

"What are you talking about? You're not the father?"

"I better be! No, he told me that I might find a solution to this matter in my father's belongings."

"What, 'Rell how would your father be able to help you through this?"

"He also added that Tonya Mince would want to use this pregnancy to regain her financial status in D.Q. Enterprises."

"So, Tonya is not finished?"

"No, Mr. Simpson asked had she contacted us. She didn't call you, did she?"

"No, the last time she was in the office she vowed she would get even. She mumbled some shit as she left the office. I didn't take her seriously though."

"Well, obviously she is serious. Stan said she would walk over both Derek and Shai to acquire a piece of my father's business. I wanted to talk about our dilemma, and he just told me to go through my father's belongings."

"Okay, so your plan is to search through his stuff first. And then if you don't find what may help you, what will you do?"

"I don't know. Stan sounded certain that the solution was there. Shai and I are inviting you and Marci to dinner to talk about this so maybe by then I can get to my father's things."

"Okay, so is dinner Saturday or Sunday?"

"I'll leave that up to Shai. She'll probably talk to Marci first. So you'll know before me."

They both laughed. Communication in their friendship circle was like this since Marci and Mitch started dating. Mitch and 'Rell would talk while Marci and Shai talked. Marci would tell Mitch and Mitch would then tell 'Rell. 'Rell would agree with Mitch knowing that Shai already knew about the matter.

"So if it's Sunday, Byron will talk about both of us canceling. This is our week out."

"You know what? Byron won't be here this week. I think he's meeting Tracey's family in Washington over the weekend. Sunday may be the best of the two days. After all you don't want to see your team get their ass handed to them."

A Different Kind of Love

"Who are we playing?
"You play St. Louis."
"Yeah, Sunday's good. The Eagles are in a slump."
"Mitch, wake up brother. They are slumped!"

<h1 style="text-align:center">Chapter 5</h1>

Mitch left 'Rell preparing his briefcase for his afternoon meetings. 'Rell called Ms. Berry and told her his schedule for the week would have to be revised. He knew he would need at least two days to go through his father's closet and storage trunks. As she gave him his list of clients he would be meeting with later in the week, 'Rell put their folders in his briefcase to remind him to go over the paperwork sometime during the day.

Shai called saying she survived her class and was on her way to work. Her shift would end at seven that evening and she would be at Nana's with Marci. They were meeting Mia, Marci's sister and their mother Darlene and a few others for their monthly book club meeting.

'Rell was glad the meeting was early in the week. He would need Shai to be available if he found disturbing news in his father's belongings. Shai's call reminded him to telephone his grandmother and see if she would be home later in the week. He had a key to get in; he just wanted her to know what he would be doing.

"Morning Nana, it's 'Rell."

"Hey Baby, how are you? I just spoke to your mother."

"Yeah is she home yet?"

"No, she decided she would stay until Wednesday, something about meeting some fabric supplier."

A Different Kind of Love

Nikki loved interior decorating and took a leave of absence from her job as a Secretarial Assistant, hoping her cousin Simone would be her partner in developing an interior design business of their own.

"Things must be going well with Simone. My mother was worried that Simone wouldn't take her up on her offer."

"I don't know baby. She didn't say whether Simone was there or not. But she said she would be calling you after she got settled this morning."

"My day started unsettled too." 'Rell wished he could tell Nana about Shai, the babies and their relationship.

"Nana, I want to go through my father's things, maybe, Thursday or Friday. Will that be okay with you?"

"Baby, what time you talking about starting on Thursday? Reverend Wilcox is coming to pick me up Thursday morning. We're shopping for Bible covers for the Bible study class."

"I have my keys but I wanted you to know I would be going through his things."

"That's fine, you can come by but lock up good if you leave before I get back. 'Rell there's a lot to go through. Your Uncle Darryl has been trying to get here to go through his things for weeks. Do you suppose your father has something worth some money in all those papers?"

"I don't know Nana. I just want to go through the papers, sort them if needed and put them up."

"Well you're welcome to it. Mr. Simpson asked had you gone through D.Q.'s things yet. I told him I didn't think it was of interest to you. But if you want to do it Thursday then fine."

"Yeah, I'll take off Thursday and Friday to handle that. I'll call the family members if they need to know any information that may be in his papers."

"Talk to Mr. Simpson first. You know family gets real stupid when they think they're owed something."

"Yeah, you're right." 'Rell thought about Tonya and what Mr. Simpson said about her.

"Nana, has Tonya called you lately?"

"She calls Darlene. 'Rell she don't want no parts of what I want to tell her."

"I can understand that Nana. I deal with her from a distance, when I have to deal with her."

"What is she bothering you for? I thought she wasn't connected with the Enterprises."

"Legally, she's not. She's just snooping. Trying to get close enough to find out what's going on."

"Well, what is going on that would interest Tonya?"

"Nana, Tonya wants to own a part, or what she can of D.Q. Enterprises. Mr. Simpson warned me to be aware of her."

"Yeah, and Mr. Simpson is right. Tonya is all for Tonya."

"Well, I've been warned and she will be warned too."

"Mr. Mince, I'm quite sure you can handle it."

"Thanks for the vote of confidence Nana."

Chapter 6

Nikki hung up the phone shaking her head. "Simone, tell me that you wrote the number down for the fabric warehouse in the village. There's no answer at the number I'm dialing. I'm beginning to think the office is closed."

"Why would they be closed? It's Tuesday."

"I'm not sure, but it's been at least two years since I used this warehouse. Maybe they changed their number, or they're no longer in business."

"Is that the only place you deal with? Maybe we should just go to the fabric district and walk around. We might find suppliers that we can make the same type deals with."

"You're right. Are you ready to go?"

Simone entered her livingroom carrying her oversized purse and her boots. She sat on her couch and sighed.

"Simone, are you okay?"

"Girl, it's just the thought. I didn't know what I was going to venture into next. I just didn't want to work another job that held no security for my future. I wanted to work for myself, but I didn't know what I would or could do. It was one of those re-occurring dreams. Then you call and say you're coming to visit and whew, dreams do come true."

"Listen girl, it's still a dream. We have a lot of hard work ahead of us. It will take a lot of unrewarded hours to get this thing off the ground. I want to make sure we have a strong foundation so if we fall, we can fall on a cushion."

"You're right. A lot of small businesses start out with a strong financial backing, experience, and knowledge of how competitive their field may or may not be."

"I've done the research. The market for interior designs is a growing field. We have to put ourselves out there though. That's where you come in. You have the ability to sell our service. I can teach you the rest. I'm going to talk with 'Rell and his partners about a sound business plan. That's why I need to know who would be our potential suppliers and what stock may cost."

"Well, sister-girl, I'm ready."

"Simone, I want you to know I love you. I'm glad you accepted my offer. This is a new beginning for both of us, and I'm scared to death, but knowing you're in it with me eases my fears."

"Nikki, don't start! We'll be here sniffing and blowing if you start. I feel the same. If you had started this venture without me, I would have been pissed!"

"Did you write down that number?"

They both hugged each other and laughed. Simone went in the kitchen and handed Nikki her note pad. She and Nikki had spent two days writing plans, contact information and a schedule for the next month.

"I think it's this number here. Are you sure you dialed it correctly?"

"I thought so but I could have been wrong."

Nikki tried the number again. She smiled as the phone call finally connected. Simone slipped into her bedroom to get her cell phone she left on the dresser. When she returned, Nikki was standing at the door with Simone's purse in her hand.

"Girl, you are in a hurry this morning."

"Mr. Denson said after all the years of working with me he would give us open credit. Let's get out of here before he changes his mind."

"Girl that's what I'm talking about, dreams coming true."

Chapter 7

The weather was showing signs of winter approaching, but there still was no need for heavy outerwear. Simone talked most of the way to the fabric district telling Nikki how they could set up a business account that could be easily managed from Virginia. Nikki didn't think much about what Simone was saying until she hinted that finding an apartment in Virginia would be difficult without proof of employment. Nikki couldn't understand Simone being so willing to leave her stable job in New York.

"Simone, I thought you took a leave of absence from your job?"

"I did, kinda. I left the job on suspension. I didn't go back. That makes it a leave. I'm still on their payroll. I just haven't been back."

"Simone, you were suspended? Suspended for what?"

"What? Does that mean that I can't work with you? Nikki it wasn't my fault. I had an argument with a coworker who filed a complaint."

"And you got suspended?"

"Yes, I got suspended."

"How long have you been out of work?"

"D.Q.'s funeral was in May, right?"

"What? Since May, Simone, why didn't you say something?"

"What was I supposed to say? You got mad at me after the reading of the will remember?"

"Simone, you made me feel like you wanted in on D.Q.'s money. Money I wasn't guaranteed and didn't have."

"No, money you didn't know you would have."

"Simone! How could you want to benefit from D.Q.'s death?"

"Nikki, you're taking this all wrong. I was in a financial crunch. I had just been suspended and rent was due. I guess in desperation I came off wrong. Things worked out for me though."

"I don't even want to ask."

Simone had a bad habit of borrowing money from ex lovers and boyfriends that she never intended to pay back. This caused problems in her relationships and problems with her and Nikki. Nikki usually paid them back to keep trouble from knocking at Simone's door.

"I didn't borrow money from anyone if that's what you're thinking."

"Okay, so you've been out of work since May, it is now October. How have you made your ends meet all this time?"

"Nikki, leave it alone. Believe me, it won't resurface, and you don't have to repay it. I'm just glad I can move on."

Nikki stopped walking. "Simone, if we're going to be business partners we need to be honest with each other. I would think our relationship was honest anyway. I just want you to be okay. I don't want shadows following you or us into this business."

"It won't believe me."

"Okay, I don't want to be making money and have to forfeit it because of you and some ex 'I love you' shit."

They both found the humor in the comment as they walked on. Simone kept her thoughts to herself knowing Nikki wouldn't like how she managed to get by the last six months. She had promised Darryl, D.Q.'s brother that she wouldn't tell

Nikki or 'Rell about his newly acquired frequent flyer miles that stopped quite often in New York.

Mr. Denson showed both, Nikki and Simone to his conference room. The larger window served as a wall that overlooked the eastside of the huge warehouse. The room was filled with sample swatches posted on the walls. Various spools of thread were stationed at what looked like sewing cubicles. Simone had never seen so much fabric in one area. Nikki met with Mr. Denson on occasion when she took on large jobs for new offices or homes. He always complimented her taste in materials and the pictures she showed of her finished work.

"Ms. Robbins, I'm so glad you haven't given up your passion. I was hoping your absence meant you went into business for yourself."

"Mr. Denson that's what I want to talk with you about."

"Oh, you are in business in, where was it that you lived?"

"Virginia. I haven't decided completely but if it won't dig a hole too large for me, I'm willing to give it a shot."

"Well, then the decision is made. You'll be fine, give it a shot. I think I mentioned to you on several occasions you have an eye for interior design. I hope our meeting means you have chosen me for your fabric supplier."

"Mr. Denson, I think you knew that."

"Are you thinking of moving to New York?"

"No, my cousin Simone and I will be business partners. She lives here in New York."

"I see. Simone is your eye for interior design like Nikki's?"

"I can't say that I am as good as Nikki, but I do have an eye for designing. I guess it's in our blood."

"Well ladies, let's look at what I can offer. Whatever I can do to help you get started, please take advantage of me."

"Mr. Denson we won't take advantage of you, so don't you take of advantage of us."

The three of them sat, talked and laughed for most of the morning. Nikki gave Mr. Denson her new business cards and they all shook hands bidding each other good-bye. Once they stepped into the winter air, they both turned up their coat collars and quickly crossed the busy intersection.

"Nikki, what is the name of the company again?" Simone felt slighted. She hadn't seen the business cards. Nikki didn't mention the company's name or if Simone's name was on the card at all.

"Interior Dreams."

"That is so different. I like it. Will I have my own business cards?"

Nikki stopped and looked in the side of her tote bag. She handed a stack of business cards to Simone. Simone looked at the card and smiled, it read 'Interior Dreams'; Nikki Robbins, Simone Marshall - Proprietors.' There was a toll free number and a fax number listed.

"Girl, we're really in business!"

"In business with an open line of credit, now we need to shop around for customers."

"Nikki, you didn't answer my question about me moving to Virginia."

"Simone there's no rush, really, you can stay in New York for a while if you can afford it. I mean, what is your financial situation? Are you collecting unemployment or what?"

"I'm collecting unemployment as of next week. I still have to file."

"Girl, I don't know what you're up to but just keep it in your personal file. I'm serious. I don't want it to ruin this dream I have for us."

"It won't, trust me."

The rest of their morning was filled with window shopping and making a supplier address list. Simone's thoughts drifted from the business to Darryl. Living in New York would be better for the business, but it would also allow her to meet with Darryl with no questions asked.

"This mess has to stop. Nikki won't go for it if she finds out I'm sleeping with D.Q.'s brother. Besides, he's not leaving his family and I'll be damned if I wait."

"Simone do you think you would want to live in Virginia. I mean we could travel to New York when we needed to. You could stay with me until you got stable and then find your own place."

"I'll stay put for now. I have a few loose ends to tie up before I move."

"Simone, tie them in a knot."

They both laughed and moved on looking to the next window display.

Chapter 8

onya answered her phone and paused as she listened to the voice on the other end.

"Tonya, I'm so glad I caught you before you left for work."

The man's voice was one Tonya was not prepared for. After dealing with D.Q.'s death and funeral, she had hoped her dealings with Karlton Harris were buried too.

"Tonya, say something baby."

"Good morning Karlton, how are you?"

"Just fine, trying to catch up with you these last few weeks has been a chore. Did you forget to return my calls?"

"I have been trying to cope, you know. D.Q. is dead now and it is taking a while to get a handle on things."

"Does that include my money? I haven't received an envelope since June."

"Karlton, I know you don't think our agreement is still on. D.Q. is dead."

"Tonya, what does D.Q. have to do with this? I made an agreement with you. I never asked him for nothing. He didn't owe me anything. Hell, the man didn't even know me like that. That's the way you wanted to keep it remember? My business is with you. Just the way you wanted it."

"Well, Karlton, that was fine when D.Q. was living. As I said he is dead. There is no business left between us."

"How's Shai and Derek?"

"Why are you asking about them?"

"I just thought I would ask. How are they managing since their father died?"

"Karlton, what are you getting at?"

"Tonya, we ain't ever been able to play around with each other fairly. Why start now? I want my money. You're overdue. Let's say I allowed you to miss because your husband died. You've had more than enough time to grieve. I'll expect to be paid next month."

"Karlton, we really need to talk about this."

"We just did. I hear Shai is doing well at Richmond Medical Center. A Medical Technician and studying in the field of… What is that again, Research Biology? You should be proud. Derek is holding his own now too. They both have their own Condo's and he owns Quintech Designs. I'd say they have been set up well."

"Karlton, you promised to keep them out of this."

"So I did. Tonya, check your caller ID. Keep my number. I don't want to make this call turn into a visit. I mean, unless you want to invite me over for dinner or something more comforting."

"Is that what this is about? D.Q. is dead and you want to know if you have a chance?"

"Don't flatter yourself baby. We're done, unless you want to play around a night or two. I want what was promised to me. Tell Shai and Derek hello for me. They probably don't remember me, huh?"

"I don't have any money Karlton. D.Q. didn't leave me anything. I work to make my ends meet and that's it."

"Wallet can't cover your expenses? Baby please, I wasn't born yesterday. D.Q. was sitting on a gold mine. You were his wife. Shit me my golden egg on a regular and I'll be gone. If not, I'll wreck your happy nest."

The phone clicked. Tonya put her cordless phone in its cradle. *"Shit, what was I thinking? D.Q. your family will pay for this shit. If you had done me right this would not be happening. Damn!"*

She decided to go to work would not be an option. There was business to be dealt with. She would have to speak with the associates at D.Q. Enterprises. They would have to understand her financial situation. She would put up an argument and threaten the company with embarrassment in the media. Tonya knew they avoided scandals at all cost, but she would put one in their lap if they didn't give her a lucrative share of the company's stock. She only needed something to maintain her living expenses and enough to get rid of Karlton Harris, one way or another.

Chapter 9

'Rell arrived at D.Q. Enterprises at ten thirty. Ms. Berry greeted him with a pleasant smile while handing him his morning messages. As he entered his office, he remembered Keith's appointment was on the agenda. He decided to get situated before asking Ms. Berry if Keith called or was waiting in the reception area.

"Mr. Mince, Mr. Larson is in Mr. Carter's office. Should I let him know you are in now?"

"No, Ms. Berry, that's okay, I'll call Mr. Carter."

The secretary was ahead of his thoughts as usual.

"Mr. Mince, Mrs. Mince called this morning requesting to speak with you. When I told her you weren't in she insisted you call her when you arrived. She left the number for you to call. It's with your morning messages but I wanted you to know she stressed it was urgent that she speak to you this morning."

"Not a problem Ms. Berry. I was expecting her call. Thank you. Is there anything else?"

"No, I think I covered it all."

"Thanks. Ms. Berry, hold all my calls until I meet with Mr. Larson."

'Rell called Mitch's office to let both Keith and Mitch know he was in his office. He told them he would come down in about ten minutes to talk with Keith. He wanted to return Tonya's call.

"Good morning, Mrs. Mince?"

"Rell, thank you for returning my call, I thought you were avoiding me."

Tonya got comfortable with her pen and pad ready to make notes of their conversation.

"Why would I do that? I'm quite sure my secretary told you I was out of the office. Unlike others, if I didn't want to talk to you, I don't have to make up any excuses. I simply would have refused your call."

'Rell wanted her to understand there was no reason for either of them to disguise how they felt. He didn't care for her or her intentions. He planned on letting her know what he felt. He was waiting for the appropriate time. First, he needed to know what she wanted, or what she was going after.

Tonya didn't care for his response, but she needed to keep her thoughts to herself, for the moment. She knew she wouldn't get far if she came across harsh. 'Rell was in command for now, but it wouldn't be long.

"I didn't know what to think, but let's not dwell on that. I would like to sit with you and talk over a few matters that your father left undone."

"Such as?"

Tonya could feel tension in 'Rell's voice. *What does he know?* 'Rell seemed well prepared for the battle.

"Some of the stocks that were sold were not just D.Q. Enterprises' to sell. Since they were sold, I am entitled to a percentage of the sale. I am quite sure we can come to some agreement on the amount owed. I also invested in a few of the vacation homes. I have searched D.Q. Enterprises property's web sites and the owners, my name is not listed."

"What would be the purpose of meeting with you? I have employees who can research your concerns. If necessary, my lawyer can look into them for you and contact your lawyer with the findings."

"Rell is there a reason you prefer to keep a distant relationship with me. It seems that you don't want to deal with me directly."

"Mrs. Mince this is business. I prefer to keep business as business. I don't have to deal with you directly for the matters you wish to discuss. Besides, these matters were arranged prior to my involvement in D.Q. Enterprises. You may have to make an appointment to see Mr. Scott or Mr. Franklin to look into the original documents."

"I see, so talking with you about this is not the way to a solution?"

"If you should have a problem after talking with the people who can help you, I will be more than happy to assist you. It's just that I don't know the entire picture. I don't like dealing with bits and pieces."

"Hmmn, I wonder if you would treat anyone else this way. I can't help thinking that for personal reasons you don't want to sit with me."

"What reasons? Mrs. Mince you seem to forget my position in the company. I employ people to solve problems for our stockholders and investors. That would include your claims to being either. Even if I did sit with you and get all the information I would still have to go to these employees and the partners to get answers for you. I am actually saving you time. I'm quite sure you want this resolved so you can get on with your life."

"Rell, D.Q. Enterprises is my life. Until your father and I separated, I was a part of D.Q. Enterprises. I want to remain just that."

"It was my father's decision to sell your stock and pay off your investments. Whether or not you have more stocks or investments is a matter to be researched. I respect my father's wishes, and I have no intentions not to carry them out. If after discovery we should find that you do have stock or investments we will buy your shares. Mrs. Mince you will not be a part of D.Q. Enterprises as long as I own it."

A Different Kind of Love

"They said you were blunt. I can respect that. Your father was quiet about his razor sharp deals. As long as you own D.Q. Enterprises you should stay alert. Watch out for shadows and what they may reveal. You might find yourself needing to deal with me in the long run. I think our relationship should remain cordial, you never know."

"I have no problem with a cordial relationship. However, for what you need to resolve, you need the staff of D.Q. Enterprises not the CEO. Mrs. Mince, don't hesitate to call if you should need my assistance. Would you like me to connect you to Mr. Scott or Mr. Franklin?"

"Rell, seriously, can you and I clear this tension I feel is between us? After all, you are related to my children. There may be family gatherings where we are both in attendance. We shouldn't have a wall between us."

"Mrs. Mince, my relationship with Derek and Dershai does not need your guidance or involvement. I doubt if anyone at a family gathering would notice the relationship you and I share. Most of my family as well as you and your family know who I am, and what I represent. I don't like secrets, and lies. I will not pretend that I like the circumstances in which we met any more than you. It is what it is. My father left many secrets and there may be more. I intend to have a clear mind to sort out the pieces of his life. I don't expect you or anyone else to feel comfortable about the way I handle myself. I am my own man. I don't need your approval or relationship to handle the "shadows" you feel may be revealed."

"So you say Mr. Mince. So you say. Well time will tell. Live in comfort now. You've got big shoes to fill. I knew how to lace those shoes for years. I'm just offering a cordial relationship. You may need someone to lace yours."

"Enough with the underlying threats, what do you really want?"

"Just what's mine? What I was promised by your father. If he had done the right thing we wouldn't be having this conversation."

"I see. Again, would you like me to make an appointment for you to see Mr. Scott or Mr. Franklin?"

"Neither, I can make my own appointments. Thanks for your time Mr. Mince."

"If you don't get what you need from Mr. Scott or Mr. Franklin, please call."

"It won't be a phone call 'Rell. It will be in person."

"Have a good day Mrs. Mince."

Chapter 10

The intercom beeped as 'Rell was leaving the office. "Rell, are you still busy?"

"I'm on my way to your office. I had to wrap up a phone call."

"Okay, Keith is still here. I have a lunch appointment. I'll send him down to your office."

'Rell looked at the clock. It was eleven thirty. Tonya had taken up more time than he expected. He waited for his office door to open. Keith and Mitch could be heard talking as Keith entered the room.

"Thanks Mitch. I'll catch you later. I think I'll take you up on that tour before Friday."

"We can meet later if you want to see the unit I live in. I can check with Marci about the spot near her job. Call me and let me know what you want to do."

Mitch waved his hand at 'Rell indicating he would return at two o'clock. 'Rell nodded his head and gave him a thumb up signal.

"Keith come on in man, sit down. Tell me what's going on." 'Rell stood to greet his friend.

He led Keith to a larger room, which was attached to his office. The room, which served as a conference area had a beautiful mahogany bookcase that extended around the walls from the floor to the ceiling. Keith was impressed as he looked around the room smiling. He walked in the room turning in a complete circle admiring his friend's wealthy taste. Keith proceeded to a bar where three leather stools sat near the large window that overlooked the mini park, which was a beautiful scenic view any time of the year. He pulled out the stool and nodded his head giving 'Rell a sign of his approval. 'Rell walked to the bar and held up a bottle of Grey Goose offering Keith a drink.

"No man. The doctor told me I could drink and have complications or stop drinking all together. I'll have a glass of Ginger Ale, please."

"What kind of complications?"

'Rell was concerned. He didn't know Keith had any health problems. Mr. Simpson said it was his mother's health that had been failing. The two men left the bar area after 'Rell poured himself a drink. They took a seat at the long conference table that sat in the middle of the floor. The plush chairs, on wheels, moved with ease as Keith pulled out his seat.

"My heart man, I had clogged arteries. I had surgery two weeks after your dad's funeral. My mother was having seizures that led to a stroke and paralysis on her left side. The next thing I knew I was in the hospital looking into bright lights. 'Rell I had a heart attack. They attributed it to stress, bad diet, you know a combination of things. So I was in the hospital unable to help my mother."

"Man, why didn't you tell someone? We could have been there for you."

"'Rell you had your own crisis going on. Especially after the reading of your father's will, you had enough to deal with."

"Man you're family too. You could have called and said you were in the hospital."

"I'm on medication and I am following the doctor's orders. My mom is with my aunt in Philadelphia. Have you heard from Craig lately?"

'Rell took a drink from his glass as Keith thumbed through a Black Enterprises magazine waiting for an answer.

"Did Mitch tell you about Craig's outside ventures?"

"Yeah, 'Rell, I thought by now he would have contacted you. He's blackballed in the industry. Shut down man. Investors don't take that shit lightly. I guess if you hadn't seen him in the mall, he would have gotten over."

"I don't know I didn't speak to him because I saw him in the mall. The client called and said the figures didn't look right. We went over them and he was right. There was a huge difference. Craig offered him better returns on investments with the company he was dealing with. He would have made his commission with us for the original deal and then a second commission when the client transferred to the other investment firm. The guy didn't even question his commission, he just wanted to know if another company could low ball our numbers, offer better returns and be legit."

"How low did he go?"

"He put the client's firm into the same money market investments at lower rates. Craig fixed the numbers and the paperwork. By the time the client would have realized he would was paying more for shaky investments, the client would come running to Craig complaining. Craig would sell the client on returning to Sheldon Finance to recover some of his firm's monies. Embarrassment would keep the client from telling anyone he fell for a bad deal."

"So, Craig would make two commissions. Save a company from totally losing out and make a fee from Sheldon for regaining a lost account."

"Exactly; I gave him an option, leave or get caught. It would have been investigated, and he might have been arrested on criminal charges. I didn't quite find out how much he would have made on the deal, but I know it wasn't the first time he had done it."

"Craig was working it on both ends? What about the outside firm? How did they make out in a deal like that?"

"There was a contract drawn up indicating how long the client would be with the company. If the client wanted an early out, they would have to pay a fee for breaking the contract."

"Yeah, that smells criminal. What was up with him dating Monique? Weren't the two of you still dating?"

"Man that was weird. I was debating whether or not she and I were going to continue the relationship. We had an argument and everything was still shaky. I told her we needed space, I told her it was over. I needed to know her hand wasn't just in my pocket. I go to the mall and see the two of them hand in hand. I spoke with Monique earlier. She wanted to work things out, or so she led me to believe. Anyway, they couldn't have just gotten that wrapped up. It was going on a while; then this client calls. It just all fell into place."

"Damn, well, his lost. This is a real nice building. Your dad did his thing. The good thing about it is there's room for expansion. Are all the offices in the building occupied?"

"There's twelve floors and each floor is a division of D.Q. Enterprises. Not all the offices are filled but will be. My father figured out how many secretaries, associates, directors, etc. would be needed to run this entire operation once the building is completely filled. There is a ten-year business plan set to be implemented, and it follows the plan we currently are operating under. As each business goal is met, we take on the next."

"Well thought out process."

"I don't plan on deviating from it if all the elements are there to carry out what my father's intentions were."

"He seemed to be well educated in business."

"That's something I learned after his death. Enough about D.Q. Enterprises for now, where are you staying?"

"At the Holiday Inn on Route 95."

"Keith, I know you've been seeking to become a part of D.Q. Enterprises for a while, how soon are you able to move to Virginia?"

"You say when. I'm ready."

"How about the end of the month, that will give you time to wrap up things at Sheldon Finance?"

"It can be sooner than that. I haven't signed with them yet."

"Good, don't. We can welcome you officially at our twenty fifth anniversary celebration with Byron and Mitch."

"When is the celebration?"

"November seventeenth I think. You'll know in ample time."

"Thanks man."

The intercom interrupted their conversation. Ms. Berry's voice was the next sound they heard.

"Mr. Mince you have a call from Mr. Simpson on line one."

"Thanks, Ms. Berry; Keith where will you be later?"

"Well, since the job is secured. I might take a flight to see my mother and then go to Maryland to get ready for the move."

"Makes sense, listen I have to take this call. Do you know your way out?"

"Sure, no problem, if I get lost, I'll call it a tour."

They laughed, stood, shook hands and embraced. Keith left 'Rell picking up his phone.

"Stan, yes are you in your office?"

Chapter 11

*T*onya poured herself another drink. Time had passed; it was now close to three o'clock in the afternoon. She had been drinking since she hung up the phone at eleven thirty that morning. She didn't know what to do next. Her plans were falling apart step by step. Tonya was prepared to fight 'Rell and D.Q. Enterprises, but she wasn't ready for Karlton Harris. She hadn't thought much about Karlton. When D.Q. died, she felt that she was released from their agreement.

"D.Q. they think I'm scared of them. I fought for your love, your attention and my rights as a wife as long as you lived. I damn sure ain't about to give in after your ass is gone. I stood by your ass in all that you did. I deserve to live easy now. I'm going to get what is mine. And I'm going to get it from that bastard son of yours. And I ain't sharing it with Karlton Harris."

Tonya had begun talking to herself and mumbling curses between each thought. The phone rang startling her. She reached for the phone and dropped it. When she leaned over to pick up the phone she knocked her glass over causing her drink to spill on the table and onto the floor.

"Shit, hello!" Tonya answered sucking Vodka off her fingers.

"Mom," Derek called. "Are you okay?"

"Hey, baby, I knocked a glass over and spilled stuff over the table, hold on."

"Mom, are you okay?"

Derek held on listening to Tonya babbling and cursing about spilling her drink. She returned to the phone repeating Derek's question. His mother loudly into the receiver making sure he heard her.

"Are you okay? I said yes, now damn it; hold on!"

Tonya got a dishcloth and blotted the table. She checked her glass to make sure it wasn't chipped. She picked up the phone again while she got a sponge out of her mop closet.

"Now, I'm sorry I wanted to clean that mess up before it dried."

"Hmmn, have you heard from Shai lately?"

"No I can't say I have. As a matter of a fact, she didn't call me this week at all. I guess she was busy with her classes. I think she said she had a few exams, or was that last week. Anyway, she calls you more than she calls me."

Derek chose to ignore her last comment. He was concerned about Shai, but now his focus was on his mother.

"Well how is your day going and why aren't you at work?"

"I didn't go today. I had business to attend to. I did get some rest though."

Tonya knew Derek was questioning her as usual to find out if she had been drinking. He annoyed her with his constant questions as though it was a sobriety test.

"Why aren't you at work?"

Derek shook his head slowly. That question answered his suspicions. He told his mother that he would be working from his home office while they added the final touches to his building. Although he went in every morning to check the progress, his Uncle Darryl sent one of his top foremen to oversee the work. After months of blue prints and ground breaking, Quintech Designs had a home of its own.

"I went to work and came home early. They're finishing the final touches on the building."

"You should have gone to your old office. You don't want to get into the habit of bringing work home. Your father used to do that until he started taking his work to that winches' house."

"Ma, Ma, cut it. I'm not getting into that today. Listen, would you like to go out to dinner later? Think of what you want to eat and either, we can order in or go out."

"I thought about it. I'm busy. I've got some things to look into over the next few days, and I can't get it done later. I'm already late. Shit! Later than I thought!"

"What is it that you're late for? Listen, I'll stop by later, and if you're there we'll deal with the food then. Okay?"

"Derek, call Shai. I'll be busy. I don't think I will be home later. Really, I'm fine. I'm just under some pressure to take care of this business."

"Okay, as long as you're fine."

The phone went dead. Tonya held it to her ear until the operator began to ask her to 'please hang up'.

Tonya decided to call for an appointment with Mr. Scott or Mr. Franklin. She poured another drink to replace the one she spilled and dialed D.Q. Enterprises for the second time that day.

"D.Q. Enterprises, good afternoon."

"Mr. Scott, please."

"I'm sorry Mr. Scott is on vacation until November tenth Ma'am. Can someone else assist you?"

"Uh, yes Mr. Franklin. Is he in today?"

"Hold on Ma'am. I will connect your call."

"Thank you."

Tonya wanted to talk with Mr. Scott, but she couldn't wait until November. There were still two weeks left in October.

"Hello." Mr. Franklin's voice came through the phone cracking, as though he had a cold.

"Mr. Franklin, this is Tonya. Tonya Mince, D.Q.'s wife."

"Yes Tonya. How are you?"

"I'm fine, thank you. I wanted to make an appointment to see you. Would you be available, say, early next week?"

"Hold on, let me check my schedule."

"Tonya Tuesday would be fine. What time would you like to come?"

"The afternoon would be better for me, around three or later if that's okay with you."

"If you prefer later," he paused looking at the calendar on his desk, "how about five o'clock?"

"That would be fine. Would we meet at your office or elsewhere?"

"The office is fine. Tonya, if you don't mind me asking, what is this meeting about?"

"Mr. Franklin, I believe I am entitled to monies from my stock and investments in D.Q. Enterprises."

"I see. Do you have your paperwork, your proof of ownership or anything to validate your shares?"

"I should, but it's been so long I wouldn't know where D.Q. kept them."

"Tonya, we can check for you, but you really should find your papers. You can't make a valid claim without paperwork."

"If I have the paperwork or not your company knows I own the stock!"

"Tonya, it's your proof of validity. As a friend of yours and D.Q.'s I wouldn't take what's legally yours. But whew, baby there is plenty who would."

"Robert, is that why they're giving me a hard time?" Tonya took his tone to mean it was safe to drop the formalities.

"No, they don't want to violate D.Q.'s last wishes. We were all asked to respect his final decisions. That included stocks, investments and claims. I will check everything for you and by Tuesday, I will have information for you to read and discuss. Tonya, does 'Rell know you're seeking this information?"

"Yes, I spoke with him this morning. What you can't look into anything without him knowing?"

"Not when it comes to D.Q. or 'Rell's family. He's his father's son. 'Rell is handling D.Q. Enterprises as though D.Q.

is still here. No rules have changed and he is strict about keeping them."

"I think he's arrogant and a little too blunt."

Robert Franklin chuckled. "Tonya, he's D.Q. all over. D.Q. was that way in our younger years. He's pleasurable but he can be cold and nasty too. I'll look into it for you. You do have all your court papers, right?"

"Court papers! What do you know about court papers?"

"Tonya, I handle litigation paperwork for our law division. I have copies of all settlements that pertain to D.Q. Enterprises. That includes what you were given at your separation, what he left you in his will, and what you would have gotten at the time of your divorce."

"So why are we playing this game, Robert? You know what is mine. What are you checking for? Give me what belongs to me.

"Tonya, let me check. I don't remember you owning anything except the house you live in. All else you are to pay for. There is no longer a need for D.Q. Enterprises to handle your personal allowance. You will get a monthly check to maintain the home only. Now if you have paperwork that disputes what I just told you I will need to see it."

"Damn it, Robert! Damn it! My husband dies and I have to show proof of my financial involvement in his life?"

"If you want what he left behind, Tonya, you need those documents."

"Will D.Q. Enterprises provide me with a copy of what they have?"

"I'll see. I'm not sure about giving you copies of paperwork. Listen my other line is ringing. Tuesday is fine. I'll talk you through it slowly so you will understand."

"Thanks Robert." Tonya hung up the phone and went to get her coat. She got in her car, turned her on ignition and headed toward Stanley Simpson's office.

Chapter 12

Karlton stopped at the entrance of D.Q. Enterprises debating whether he should call and make an appointment to see the new CEO, go to his office unannounced, or wait for Tonya to make another mistake. He hoped he got his point across when he and Tonya spoke, but if not he would be visiting Shai, Derek and Darrell. He was sure with the problems he could cause, someone would pay him.

He arrived in town two weeks prior and made sure no one knew he was around. Karlton followed D.Q. Enterprises stocks, investments and loved their vacation properties. Tonya spoiled him with the extra finances, the perks one needs to be content with life. Karlton lived in Baltimore, Maryland where he met Tonya. He would leave once she understood that they were connected for a lifetime.

Tonya told Karlton she was not left anything after D.Q.'s death. He didn't believe, as the wife, she didn't inherit any of D.Q. Enterprises or a large sum of money. He had time to kill. There were two weeks left in the month. Karlton would use the time to meet Shai, Derek and Darrell. Tonya wouldn't decide not to pay him again. He would get closer to her children, and what she loved the most, D.Q. Enterprises.

Karlton pulled over as he headed for the site of Quintech Designs. He stopped there earlier only to learn he had just missed Derek. He would leave his card and request to meet

Mr. Mince. As a potential client he could sit in person with Derek without be suspected. Meeting with Shai would take some arranging. There was no reason to meet her at her job. Karlton thought about it often. He could meet Shai at the college. It would take him a minute to find out her schedule. Darrell was another problem. He had been following articles in business weekly papers about the new CEO of D.Q. Enterprises. Karlton knew speaking with Darrell would put him in a good position to speak bluntly about Tonya if she decided not to pay him.

Karlton turned right at Cantor Street. Quintech Designs was in the opposite direction. He changed his mind and decided to go to the hotel to make a schedule.

Chapter 13

Shai posed in the mirror. She turned to the left and then the right, sizing up her stomach. Marci said she wasn't showing too much, but you could tell she was gaining weight. It was verified at the book club meeting the other night. Mia and Darlene agreed, saying she looked as though she put on a few pounds. Nana said her face was fatter. Other members laughed and teased, suggesting she was pregnant. Shai heard their comments, whispers and giggles. She could only smile. *"Suppose, just suppose, if they only knew. 'Rell we need a plan to tell this story quickly."*

Saturday, while eating dinner, they planned to ask Mitch and Marci to be the Godparents. 'Rell knew Shai told Marci she was pregnant, but they both agreed not to tell them they chose to keep the babies. 'Rell discussed the complications with Mitch but saved most of the details and plans for dinner.

Shai's schedule for the day was light. Since 'Rell was spending the next two days going through D.Q.'s belongings, she decided she would make a stop to see the progress of Quintech Designs and visit Derek. Until she and 'Rell could think of what they would say to the family about the pregnancy, Shai didn't want to be around people who would ask questions.

The doorbell rang and Shai looked at the time. It was eight o'clock. *"Who's at my door?"* Although she wouldn't be attending any classes, everyone knew on Thursday morning she left early for her nine o'clock class.

The doorbell rang again. Shai didn't rush to answer and peeked out of the foyer window before reaching the front door. There stood her mother.

"Not today, not today! Why didn't Derek warn me? He didn't know. What does she want?" Her thoughts ran rampant as she opened the door.

"Hey Mom, come on in. What brings you this way without a phone call?"

"If I called you, would you have said you had class? I see you're still here."

"No classes today, some type of administration, staff and teacher meeting."

"I see. Well then I chose the right morning to drop in. You don't call, so I thought I would kill two birds with one stone. I'm here to see you and talk awhile."

"Well sit down in the living room. I'll get us something to drink and munch on. Is coffee okay?"

"Juice will be fine. Can you bring my glass now?"

"Sure is orange juice okay?"

"Yes baby, that's perfect."

Tonya checked her handbag. She cracked the top of her Vodka bottle and waited for the orange juice.

"Your place is beautiful. I know I tell you that every time I visit, but I just can't help myself. It looks like a page from the magazines. Did you pay a designer to come in?"

"No, Darrell's mom does interior designing full time now. She's really doing well with it."

"Oh, well let's not ruin our morning with talk about him or her. When did you get the picture of your father enlarged?"

Over Shai's fireplace was D.Q.'s picture, the one that was used on the program for his funeral. Derek, Shai and Darrell each had the copy enlarged for their homes. It was Shai's favorite picture of him, and she felt safe in her home with its presence. 'Rell teased her about D.Q. watching them, whenever they got frisky in the living room.

"I love that picture, so I enlarged it. It adds a touch of him in my home."

"I don't see a touch of me anywhere."

Shai entered with a serving tray. She brought the orange juice in a pitcher with two glasses. Shai smiled at her mother.

"You're here to add your own touch. When you pass, I'll have one of you done. What would you like, toast, bagels or a full breakfast?"

"Toast is fine. Come, sit and talk."

"Let me get the toast. Keep talking, I can hear you."

"How did you make out with your exams?"

"I passed them all. I may take a semester off after this one. I think I burned myself out. I really haven't decided though, but it is a definite thought."

Shai wanted to be with the twins for the first two years of their lives. She didn't want them to be in a day care or with any babysitters. She hoped after their first two years Nana would assist in that department. There was a daycare for toddlers at Nana's church.

"Why would you take off a semester? I thought you wanted to finish within the next two years."

"I do, but I want to be at my best going through the course. I think I need a break."

Shai returned with the toast. Tonya had poured her mixture and was drinking a second glass. She handed the pitcher to Shai.

"Whew, baby, I was thirsty. Before you sit down get more juice dear, please."

"Sure, have you heard from Derek?"

"Derek called a couple of days ago looking for you. I told him I hadn't seen or heard from you. I thought he would have called you."

"No, I e-mailed him last night. He didn't call or e-mail me, so he must be okay. I was going by Quintech this morning.

Why don't you and I go together? Have you seen the building lately?"

"No, did he get it done the way he wanted it?"

"It's beautiful. Uncle Darryl's company did the work. It's nice. He's got the top half of the building, and he'll be renting out the bottom as office space."

"Why? Didn't he need the space for his offices?"

"The last I spoke with him that was the plan. Anyway, I guess he could have changed his mind."

"I think he did. He didn't mention renting out any space. He wasn't even working the other day because they were completing the office space."

"Hmmn, well we ought to plan for his grand opening."

"Oh, that's so common. Why do a grand opening for a graphic design shop?"

"It's a way of letting people know you're ready for business. I'll talk to Derek. I think that would be a great promotional tool for him. A nice evening; opening with his designs on display, some food and drinks. So, you want to ride with me this morning?

"Shai, I came to visit you, not go to his office. I'll come to the reception when you set it up."

"We, you and I, should set it up for him."

"That's not going to happen. I'm too busy to set up some party in lime lights. I didn't like that type of shit when your father did it."

"But you loved dressing up and showing off."

"That's what one does when they can afford it. You can pay someone to set up a grand opening."

"I want to be a part of the arrangements. I want to invite people who thought he would fail. There's nothing like climbing a ladder without steps and knowing those who removed the stairs are waiting to see you hesitate to climb. I want those people to know he didn't stop climbing."

"Hmmn, you do what you need to do sweetie. I don't need to prove I've made it. How is your grandmother and Aunt Darlene?"

"Everyone's fine, I saw them at my book club meeting."

Shai readjusted herself in the reclining chair. She hoped her mother hadn't noticed her pulling down her t-shirt.

"Girl, you must be eating well. You look like you gained a little weight."

"That's another thing, stress makes me eat. The last classes stressed me out. I studied, ate and slept."

"How's your love life?"

"Mom, what made you ask that?"

"You didn't include it. You said you studied, ate and slept. I know you must have a male friend you're seeing."

"Periodically, we see each other when we can. He works odd hours at the hospital."

Shai lied and knew she would have to tell Marci and 'Rell the same lie, so they would know how to respond if they were asked.

"Well, if you don't have a man, you'll get rusty."

Tonya laughed. The drinks were beginning to get her light headed. "Don't forget to get a tune up every now and then."

Shai shook her head. She looked at the clock, got up and cleared away the butter, toast and jelly. She smiled letting her mother know she understood her joke.

"Do you want anything else from the kitchen?"

"No, this is fine dear."

Tonya was glad Shai went into the kitchen. She could fill her glass again before leaving. Tonya had no intention on going with Shai. She was headed to talk with Nana. She needed to know if anyone found paperwork in D.Q.'s belongings that she should have known about. Tonya knew Nana wouldn't talk to her if she was drunk, but she would use that as a play for her sympathy. Tonya's plans included her playing the depressed, drunk, widow. As pathetic as it sounded, she would try to appeal to Nana. Shai returned from the kitchen before Tonya could put the bottle back in her bag.

"Mom! Tell me you're not drinking. It's before noon. Are you okay?"

"Are you okay? Are you okay? You and your brother; yes, am I okay? I'll get through this my way."

"Get through what?"

Tonya quickly downed her drink and gathered her things.

"Thanks for the minutes, Shai. I've got to go."

"I guess you would. The bottle is running low. What do you do, carry it so you don't have to stop at the local bar?"

"Shai, I don't have to explain it to you. I'm okay and I will get through this."

"Get through what? Drinking before twelve and carrying it with you; you're not okay."

"Your father's dead Shai and no one is helping me. You guys got a boost towards your future. I got what? I got trouble."

"What trouble? Do you need money? Everything you own is paid for. What is the problem you'll get through? Why are you drinking like this?"

"Shai, I need my stability too. I don't want to have to work a lifetime. I shouldn't have to. I put in years with your father. I should own part of D.Q. Enterprises."

"Mom, you got more than the average wife who was separated from their husband at the time of his death. I'm not trying to get into your business but what happened to the money you got when the separation was final?"

"Shai I have obligations that have to be met every month. I used my pay from my job on my personal stuff and the money from your father on those other obligations."

"Well, I don't intend on playing guessing games. You're talking around the problem without saying what it is. Obviously, you don't want me to know. If you need money, I can help you out for a while. I can't say I will do it the rest of your life though. If dad lived you wouldn't be getting his money the rest of your life. You have to "get through it" and get on with your life."

"Thanks for the lecture. I needed that like I need another drink. Perhaps I will have another. What difference does it make? I'm going to get what is mine. I won't need your money or your brother's."

"Well, if you do, don't hesitate to call. You don't have to drown your financial burdens in a bottle. Now if you just want to drink because you're still grieving you may need more than a drink."

"What, do I need counseling, grieving? Why would I be grieving over a man who slept with another woman all the years of our so called marriage?"

"Mom, call me if you need any money? Leave the rest of that alone. Daddy's dead, so is that topic. We can't change the past. I don't plan on living in it."

Tonya reached the front door without stumbling. She turned the knob, as she adjusted her coat while repeating, she would talk to Shai later. She wasn't drunk. She had enough to give her the backbone she needed to deal with Nana.

Chapter 14

t was close to nine o'clock and 'Rell was behind schedule. He had planned on being at Nana's house by nine. He opened his briefcase and realized he had unfinished paperwork and notes to be added to a client's file. It took longer than he expected but the file was updated and it was work he wouldn't have to do over the weekend. Shai's face crossed his mind, and he decided he would call her before he left. 'Rell looked at the clock again. Nana wouldn't have to wait for him, he had his keys. He picked up the phone and dialed Shai's number.

"Hey Sweetie."

"Rell, good morning, I thought you would be at Nana's by now."

"Got a late start, I thought about you and decided to call. How are we doing this morning?"

"You would have known if you let me come home last night." Shai was teasing 'Rell. They both laughed.

"You know you can come home anytime. How was your night?"

"It was fine. I caught up with some girl gossip with a few friends. I wanted to tell them I was in total bliss; in love and pregnant, but I didn't. I'm trying to keep this secret, but I think we need to come up with a story. Monday at the book club meeting comments were made about me gaining weight. I played it off. This morning my mother asked who my lover was?"

"Who was your lover? What made her ask that?"

"She said I must be spending time with someone and if not I needed to."

"Hmmn, so what did you say?"

"I told her I was dating someone at the hospital."

"I see."

"Rell, I know you're not mad at a lie."

"No, but I just wish this shit wasn't so, you know. I said from the door how I felt about our love. I want to be able to yell from the highest mountain. I love Shai. This is hard babe. Anyway, did you give this dude a name?"

"No, she didn't ask any other questions, so I dropped it. I decided I would only feed the information when asked. 'Rell, I'll be showing more soon. We need to know what we're going to say."

"Whatever you want; I'll follow your lead. Just let Marci know and we'll all be on the same page. There's got to be a way around this."

"Well, until then I'm dating a brother at the hospital. We've been dating for a couple of months. I guess we'll stay together until people start asking why he doesn't come around. I'll say we broke it off, and that I'm keeping the twins."

"Okay sounds good. I'll play the proud uncle."

"C'mon baby, we have to do it this way. There's no way around it."

'Rell was getting depressed. His first-born and he couldn't claim them. He wanted to tell his mother about the dilemma. He wanted to talk to Nana about it. He needed someone to understand his feelings. Shai was ready to play this lie out. She sounded as though she had accepted parenting without 'Rell.

"Rell, you're quiet baby. Are you alright?"

"No, I don't like it Shai, I never will, but it can't be any other way."

"Are you on your way to Nana's?"

"Uh, yeah, I better be on my way. I don't know how much paperwork there is to go through. I'll need to read it all through. Your mother seems to think there's something hidden in his belongings that links her to the company. I hope not."

"Well, take your time. I know it has to be done but do only what you can."

"So far dad seems to be ahead of all of us, Mr. Simpson told me don't discuss the pregnancy before I go through his belongings. It's as though he knows what I will find. I hope it's a solution."

"I don't think daddy was prepared for you being the father of my children. We weren't prepared for it."

"I was. I wasn't prepared for you being my sister. I had already imagined us together, married and raising a family."

"Wow all that before the reading of the will?"

"All that baby, and more enough of me pouring my heart out; that's why it hurts to sit back and live this lie."

"Rell, I love you."

"I love you too. Listen; let me go to Nana's. What are you doing for lunch? Can I interest you in a lunch date?"

"I'm going to Quintech to see the progress and Derek. I would love to have lunch with you."

"Tell Derek what's up for me. Call me when you're ready to eat."

"All right, I'll talk to you later."

'Rell put the receiver in the cradle. He wanted to cry. His emotions had him twisted in knots. Parenting in the shadows would be hard. He didn't know if he could handle the role of an uncle to his own children. He didn't want them to be confused. 'Rell would have to live the lie that Shai explained in detail.

'Rell grabbed his jacket, put his cell phone on his belt and searched the room for his keys. He remembered his keys were in the kitchen as the doorbell rang. He went to the door hoping it was Mitch or Byron.

"Good morning, Mr. Mince?"

A man in a dark suit and leather jacket stood at the door with papers in his hand.

"Yes, I'm Mr. Mince."

"You've been served sir. Have a good day sir."

The man walked down the walk to his car parked at the end of the driveway. 'Rell looked at the paper he was handed. The word Subpoena stood out in bold print. 'Rell closed the door and returned to the living room. He decided to call Nana and tell her he would be there in the afternoon, if he got there at all.

Chapter 15

Simone packed her clothes in what would be her second piece of luggage. Since Nikki's visit to New York, Simone had been busy making appointments with prospective clients in New Jersey and Atlanta. She would be spending the next few days meeting with them. After the appointments in New Jersey, she would be flying from Newark Liberty Airport to Atlanta where she would meet others. The clients insisted meeting with her immediately. All were opening new offices and were impressed with the "Interior Dreams" brochures. The prospective client list was growing. Neither Simone nor Nikki limited themselves on where they would go to design offices or homes. They decided to split the appointments and the travel. After Simone's meeting in Atlanta, she would spend a couple of weeks with Nikki, who had appointments in Maryland and Washington, D.C., to go over the new contracts and follow up calls.

Before leaving, Simone promised Darryl she would call him. They planned to meet at some point during her travel. Quintech Designs would be ready for the grand opening within the next two weeks and Darryl would be in Virginia for the celebration. Although Darryl wanted to satisfy his appetite to be alone with Simone, Darryl told her that Francine, his wife, may come for the celebration. There would be no way he could spend a lot of time with her without the family noticing.

Simone played her role as the other woman but if Francine slipped up, she wouldn't mind being a Mince. Francine could keep the kids. Simone wasn't about to play Mama to someone else's kids.

She was more interested in his loving both in and out of the bedroom. The man was passionate, good looking, and he filled the empty space in her bed perfectly. He also happened to have money, a plus in any girl's book. Simone watched Nikki play the role of the other woman for thirty years. She didn't need Darryl to live with her to reap rewards. He showed her he was willing to spend his time and money.

Shortly after D.Q.'s death Darryl called her using the excuse he was concerned about Nikki. Simone told him Nikki was doing well but he could call anytime and that's what he did frequently. It took him two months to ask her if he could visit. They met, had dinner, and entertained each other the rest of the night. Now it was a habit that neither of them wanted to break.

Simone wanted to tell Nikki about her relationship with Darryl but she wasn't sure about Nikki's loyalty. Nikki was close to Francine and Nana. She didn't want to come between them.

Simone made a mental note to call her neighbor once she reached New Jersey to have her gather her mail while she was away. They were the only single residents in their complex and they looked out for each other when one was out of town. She was ready to leave when she remembered again to call Darryl.

"Mr. Mince, how are you?"

Darryl laughed. "Mr. Mince was my father. How are you lady? Are you packed and ready to leave?"

"As ready as I'm going to get. I don't think this first meeting will be a success but its all gold after that."

"Well, don't think negative. You may change their minds. You never know."

"Anyway, you sound out of it. Is everything okay?"

"Actually, it's not. I will be in Virginia for two reasons."

"Really, you sound disappointed."

"I've been served a subpoena. I have to appear in court."

"Court for who and about what?"

"For Derek and I'm not sure. I called to speak to him, and I got his answer machine. I called 'Rell, and he said he just received the same thing. He was on his way to Mr. Simpson's office when I called."

"Mr. Simpson. Who is Mr. Simpson?"

"I'm sorry babe. He is the lawyer that works for 'Rell. He was D.Q.'s lawyer. 'Rell didn't know what was going on with Derek, but he was sure that Mr. Simpson knew or could find out."

"So what do you have to do now?"

"I don't know. I planned on being there by this evening, unless something else comes up. The proceedings start Monday morning."

"Darryl, will you need to talk to a lawyer?"

"No, I think me and 'Rell are just witnesses."

"Darryl, witnesses to what?"

"I'm not sure. I think it may have to do with Derek's last job. I'm not sure."

"Darryl, be careful what you say and to whom. Maybe you should talk with Mr. Simpson too."

"Simone, that's one of the reasons why I'll be there this evening. The other was to see you."

"Darryl, can you meet me in Atlanta? I mean will there be time for us before the weekend?"

"My plane lands in Newark this afternoon. When are you flying out to Atlanta?"

"Tomorrow morning, I'm meeting the clients at eleven. My flight leaves Newark at eight in the morning."

"Atlanta, you'll be there for a day or what?"

"Just Friday."

"Okay, let's play that by ear. I will meet you after your meeting in Jersey. Where are you staying tonight?"

"I was going to make my reservations when I got to the hotel. I'll choose one close to the airport."

"Simone, why did you wait? You should have had the hotel locked down babe."

"I'll call you when I know the one I'll be in."

Simone wasn't about to listen to a lecture about her travel arrangements. "Is Francine coming later?"

"No, I don't know about this court thing or how long the proceedings will be. So that means I'm yours for a few days."

"We'll see about that."

"What do you mean? I won't be busy all day everyday. Besides this court thing will push the grand opening until a week after it's over."

"And then your wife will be in town."

Simone sighed, a sign Darryl recognized as anger building.

"Simone, look, don't start that shit. You knew I was married."

"I'm not starting. Anyway, you have a safe trip in. I'm going to get going. I will call you when I book the room."

"Listen, Francine is not making this trip at all. So don't get an attitude. We have to be careful around family."

"Darryl, I understand. It's just harder than I thought. I didn't want to get caught up in this married man thing. It's just hard."

Simone didn't want to think of the games she would have to play around Nikki and others. She was becoming less willing to play those games.

"Darryl, while you're in Richmond, let's just meet in the evening where we don't have to worry about who is around. Maybe you can book a suite or something instead of staying with your mother."

"Simone, baby, you make your way to Jersey. I'll deal with my family. I can't change my plans like that. Everybody would be suspicious. The suite idea is good for our little rendezvous'." Darryl smiled knowing that would be all he had to say for her to agree.

"Okay, we'll talk about it later I guess. You're right, I have to go. I'll talk with you later."
"Later babe."

Chapter 16

Darryl hung the phone up as Francine entered their bedroom. She walked over to him and massaged his shoulder. He stood and faced his wife.

"I have to go to Richmond. I'm leaving today. Derek's case is starting on Monday."

"Does 'Rell know about it?"

"Yes, he has to be there also."

"Also, what do you mean has to be there? Who else has to be there?"

"Francine, I will have to testify as a witness for the prosecution and so will 'Rell."

"For the prosecution; you're not testifying for Derek?"

"Apparently not; when Derek called, he said his lawyer didn't need us to testify. I guess the prosecution feels differently."

"Darryl this can't be good for Derek. What is he charged with?"

"I don't know how long he was doing it Francine. Derek would design logos and sell them without his company's knowledge to other companies. I guess they would call it Trademark infringement. I don't know the correct terms."

"Hon, you mean he would sell someone's logo to another company?"

"Something like that. I don't know how he did it. I'm glad I don't know. Anyway he got caught. I don't know whether or not he has to pay a huge fine, or it carries jail time."

"Did you talk with Derek? Doesn't he know?"

"I talked to him, but for some reason this doesn't seem to bother him. Francine, this could bring trouble to his company. Who would want to deal with a logo design company whose CEO has this indictment in his folder?"

"I understand, maybe it will work out."

"Anyway, I booked a flight for this morning. It has a stop over in Newark. I was thinking about talking with those contractors at Schulman's about a few of the developments on the table. They can talk with me this evening. I'll get to Richmond in the morning."

"Darryl, I think Mr. Schulman called. You better call him before you leave."

"When did he call?"

Darryl was worried. If Schulman called it would throw a curve in his excuse to stay over. He had been speaking to the Schulman brothers for months going over plans for their Jersey developments. It was the excuse he used when he visited Simone.

"It must have been late last night. He was on the company answer machine this morning. What time did you leave the office?"

"It was about seven, no eight. I don't know how I missed that call."

"I think the machine said the call came in later than that. He thought he would catch you. He said he would talk to you today. If you're meeting with him, maybe that's what he meant."

"I'll call him to be sure. Maybe he can't make it. Which brother was it?"

"I couldn't tell. Anyway, call him."

"Thanks babe. Are you going to the office today?"

"I guess I'll leave when you leave. Do you want me to take you to the airport?"

"No, I have to make a stop. I'll have Michael drop me off."

Francine moved closer to Darryl, close enough to kiss him gently on his lips.

"I guess I won't see you for a few days then. You should have let me know. We could have said our intimate farewells. Now I won't see you until the grand opening."

"Fran, I don't know when that will be. I'll have to call you. It may be postponed for a few weeks."

"Darryl, you're not staying in Richmond that long are you?"

"It depends. I don't know how deep this boy is in this shit. He'll need my support. My brother's not around for him. I think I need to be there."

"I guess you're right. Maybe I can fly out and come back on the weekends if it will be a while."

"We'll see. I hope things will go well, but I've got a bad feeling about this."

Francine backed away from Darryl and looked the other way. The bad feeling she had for a few months was resurfacing. It had nothing to do with Derek. It was about their relationship. It just wasn't the same. Darryl spent more time in Richmond than he had in years. He had begun opening more business deals on the east coast and neglected to keep appointments in Detroit. If anyone told her there was another woman in the midst, she wouldn't disagree. Francine had seen the signs before. She didn't want to be the paranoid wife, especially after she had accepted his past indiscretions. She promised herself she wouldn't put up with the secrets and lies again. If Darryl didn't want their marriage, he could stay in Richmond.

Chapter 17

everend Wilcox rang Julie Mince's doorbell waiting for her pleasant smile to brighten the doorway. She opened the door smiling with the phone to her ear. Waving her hand she signaled for the Reverend to enter her home.

"Baby, I understand. These things will be here whenever you get to them…No. I won't let anyone go through them… Uh, I haven't heard from him… I guess if you say he's coming, he'll be here…okay, I'll tell him… Now is Derek going to talk with Mr. Simpson too?.. What? Why would he do that?. . . Well, he ain't never had common sense. Okay baby I'll talk with you later. Yes, he just came in… I will… Call me and let me know how you made out hear…Alright, bye now."

Reverend Wilcox made himself comfortable in the den sitting in the recliner chair using the remote to find a channel worth watching on the television. Nana came into the room, and he stood to greet her.

"Good morning Jewels." Reverend Wilcox kissed her cheek.

"I don't know how good it is Wallace. Derek has been indicted and 'Rell and Darryl have been subpoenaed to be witnesses for the prosecution. What kinda mess is that?"

Nana took a seat. Reverend Wilcox used the remote to cut off the television.

"Indicted for what?"

"He was selling logos he designed for other folks companies. I don't know what that boy was thinking. It was back when he was gambling so heavy."

"The logos were sold and he resold them?"

"I think so. 'Rell said he knew what he was doing, but it's not just one company. He did this for some time. I guess to pay off his betting debts."

"Jewels, that boy had to know it was against the law. You can't take the Pepsi logo and sell it to another soda company and rename it."

"Well he did. 'Rell said he would make minor changes and claim it was different. I guess he figured the companies weren't as large as Pepsi, and they wouldn't find out about it."

"So what is Mr. Simpson saying?"

"That's the funny thing about it. Derek isn't using Mr. Simpson. He's using the lawyers from the company he worked for. I think it was Carson Designs or something like that. I don't know why he would think they would give him a better defense than Mr. Simpson."

"Maybe the indictment includes the company."

"Maybe, but Wallace, that boy could lose this new company and all he has worked for since his father's death."

"Jewels, he knew that. He should have talked with Mr. Simpson about this before he built his own company. Maybe there was a legal way to settle it before he got to this point. Maybe he will just have to pay a fine."

"Derek has money now; money and a company. They waited until he had something they could take away."

"So Jewels why the prosecutors want 'Rell and Darryl to testify?"

"I don't know and I don't think they do either. 'Rell didn't even know Derek then. Now Darryl may know something, but who knows what that may be."

"So 'Rell is not coming to go through his father's belongings?"

"No, he's going to talk with Mr. Simpson, and then he's going to catch up with Derek. I think he's a little upset."

"I guess he would be. He's done nothing but helped Derek. Derek is his brother and in business this will look bad for 'Rell and D.Q. Enterprises. I can understand his concern."

"Well as Darlene would say, 'it is what it is.' Did you contact Sister Wright about the bible covers?"

"Yes, we can pick them up from her this morning. Then I want to take you to pick up a gift I purchased for you."

"A gift for me, Wallace what is that about?"

"I bought you a gift, and I want you to have it today."

"What time did Sister Wright say for us to come?"

"We can leave when you're ready my dear."

"Well Rev, let's get going. I can't wait to see this gift. It's been a while since I've been surprised."

Nana went to her closet and got her coat and hat. Reverend Wilcox helped her in her coat and followed her to the door with his coat in hand. They left the house talking about the design they would have engraved on the covers.

Chapter 18

Tracey, Mr. Simpson's assistant, hung up the phone as 'Rell came through the reception area's doors. She could tell from his expression that he was there on business and had not stopped in just to say hello.

"Good morning 'Rell."

Since Tracey had started dating Byron, she had dropped the formal use of his name. Byron introduced her to Mitch and 'Rell as his friend but they both knew it was getting serious when he wanted her to meet Shai and Marci. Byron kept most of his relationships away from their inner circles, especially if they were just women he called every now and then. Tracey was his first serious relationship, since he relocated to Virginia.

"Morning, Tracey. Is Mr. Simpson free? He's expecting me."

"I think so. Let me check."

'Rell took a seat and decided to call Shai. He would let her know his morning plans had changed.

"Shai, listen, I'm not going to Nana's this morning. I'm with Mr. Simpson. Can you make sure Derek comes with you when we have lunch?"

"Sure baby, why?"

"I'll explain then. Thanks, love you."

'Rell hung up the phone. He knew this would leave Shai wondering, but he didn't want to talk to her about the situation over the phone.

Stanley Simpson came out of the large doors, the entrance to the conference room. The last time 'Rell sat behind those doors it was for the reading of his father's will. He didn't want to talk to Mr. Simpson in that room. Mr. Simpson must have felt 'Rell's displeasure with the room. He walked over and shook 'Rell's hand.

"Good morning young man. Let's go in my office."

"Thanks Stan."

"I guess this morning's visit caught you off guard."

"Well, to be honest Stan, it did. I didn't know Derek had been indicted for Trademark Infringement. This is all news to me, and I'm wondering why I wasn't told."

"You'll have to ask him that question. Derek has not called my office about this matter. I have checked with our lawyers handling the Quintech Designs account, and they weren't aware of the indictment."

"Why not Stan? I told you to watch my family, which included Derek. Do we have any idea if this indictment holds merit? He could lose a lot here."

"That is understood. I have placed a call with the law firm from Carson Designs to see what is in discovery. I don't know what their strategy is."

"Stan we have today and tomorrow. The case starts Monday. Can it be postponed?"

"I don't know. I will need to talk with them and Derek."

"Okay, how much damage does this do to our stocks and Quintech."

"The stocks should be safe; however, Quintech would need a damage control plan for what would be released through the media."

"Do we have a plan in place?"

"As I get the information I will be talking with those who need to get the ball rolling before Monday. 'Rell I know what your concerns are, we'll handle them."

"I'm going to meet Shai and Derek for lunch. I'm going to advise him to see you after our talk. Will you be in this afternoon?"

"Yes, if my plans change, I will call you."

"Okay, keep me updated on the information you get from Carson's lawyers."

"Rell, when will you get to your father's belongings?"

"After the dust has settled, right now, it can wait."

"How are you making out with Shai and the pregnancy?"

"She's got a story she'll tell about the father. She seems to be happy with it, so I guess I'm okay. No, I'm not okay, but what can I do? Shai's healthy and I don't want her stressing about what to say. She can't stay in hiding and then appear with two babies. I just hope no one gives her that single parenting speech."

"Single parenting speech?"

"Yeah, the one that makes women marry the next man coming along. I think I would have to stand up and confess then."

"I guess you're right. Let's get you through this drama first. You and Shai can handle the questions for now."

"Alright, call me as soon as you get a grasp on this thing, and what they could want me and my uncle to say that would help the prosecution."

They both stood and walked to the office door. Mr. Simpson's phone rang as he shook 'Rell's hand and waved bye.

'Rell stopped at Tracey's desk.

"Hey lady, how's your day going? I know I seemed like I didn't want to be bothered with you before I went in the office."

"Rell I know you better than that. Things are going well. I'm waiting for your boy to call to see if we're having dinner tonight."

"Hmmn sounds good. Enjoy. I'll talk with you later."
"Thanks, tell Shai hello for me."
'Rell walked out the door heading for Quintech Designs.

Chapter 19

Nikki hadn't spoke with 'Rell since she left Washington, D.C. He congratulated her accomplishments and promised he would visit her and Simone during the weekend. She couldn't wait to tell him how well the telemarketing campaign was going. 'Rell was pleased that she decided to use D.Q. Enterprises' telemarketing department to promote her business for a month. Nikki was against it at first, but she promised herself that in a month she could set up her own telemarketing line. It hadn't been quite a month and the calls generated from telemarketing had proven to be profitable.

In two weeks, they had five new customers and six potentials. Interior Designs was a dream come true. Nikki was glad Simone shared in her dream. She hoped their endeavor would be a financial success.

She looked forward to them traveling and working together. Nikki got home, unpacked and prepared to go over new contracts when 'Rell came in the front door.

"Hey Mom, I didn't know you would be home this early."

"Actually, I'm later than I thought. The traffic was backed up this morning on the expressway."

"You drove through the morning traffic?"

"Yes, my mistake. I should have waited but I thought I would hit the lunch hour traffic. I wanted to be here by this afternoon. What brings you here in the middle of the day?"

"I was on my way to see Derek and Shai at Quintech but no one is there yet. They're operating on a skeleton crew due to the construction."

"I thought they were done. Your uncle said they would be finished by tomorrow at the latest."

"They are finished but no one's working in the offices. Shai and Derek were supposed to meet for a tour of the facility. I think I got there before they did."

"Oh, I see."

'Rell wanted to open up to his mother. He had so much to talk to her about. This was the first time, since he was a child that he felt shy about talking with her. When he was thirteen he wanted to tell her that he found out sex was great, but that too was a secret he couldn't tell her. He didn't want her to begin to read his expressions. Nikki and Nana had a way of telling when he wanted to talk. He went to the den and sat in the reclining chair and called his answering service at the office. As he expected there were no messages. He told everyone he would be back on Monday. Mitch was handling his calls and any immediate problems. He knew 'Rell would be at Nana's and could be reached on his cell. He closed his eyes to relax a moment. It wasn't long before he fell asleep. Two hours passed, Nikki tapped 'Rell to wake him.

"Rell, are you hungry? I'm making a little something to eat, and I wondered if you wanted something too."

"Thanks, but no thanks."

'Rell looked at his watch. It was two thirty. Shai hadn't called. Something was wrong. 'Rell looked at his cell phone. No calls or messages.

'Rell called out to his mother as he was putting on his jacket. "Mom, I'm going to go over to Quintech. I'll call you later."

"Alright, come back by later. Simone will be here tomorrow."

"Okay, I'll call you if I don't come by."

'Rell hurried out the front door, as though he was late for an appointment. Nikki didn't think much of it. Maybe he stayed longer than he wanted to. She was surprised, she hadn't heard from Simone. She got up to find her cordless phone when her cell phone rang.

"Hello."

"Hey, Nikki, this is Sam."

"Hi, how are you?"

"I should be asking you that question? I hadn't heard from you since last week. Are we on the outs and I don't know it?"

Samuel Smalls was a Deacon at First Chapel Baptist Church where Reverend Wilcox was the pastor. He and Nikki had been a couple for the past three months. Sam was falling in love with Nikki and hoped she felt the same about him. Nikki had feelings for him, but she told him she wanted to take it slow. He didn't quite understand because her body told him different when they were together, and he was addicted to her loving.

"I'm sorry Sam. The week went by so quickly I didn't have a chance to call you as often as I would have liked."

"So what's up? How's the business going?"

"It's going well. We have a total of three jobs lined up and potentials. Simone is coming into town, so we can purchase the supplies for the first job. The place is here, so we can knock it out quickly. The next job is in Baltimore and Washington D.C. is to follow. They're all interior office jobs. They won't be difficult to complete. No wives to change their minds."

They both laughed. Nikki's first two calls were a decorator's disaster; wives that changed their minds every step of the way. Nikki got frustrated and told each of them what they needed to do was make up their minds and call her back. She didn't get a call from either of them.

"I'm glad everything is going well. How's the telemarketing working for you?"

"That's where most of our calls are coming from. We've sent out at least one hundred brochures. It's growing fast. I think Simone is going to have to move closer. We work well together splitting up the calls, but it's difficult for her to see what each job spec is from New York. It's the same for me when she lands a project."

"Give her time. She'll move when she's ready. Are you up for company later?"

"Your company is welcomed anytime. Come early, I'll cook dinner for you."

"I hoped you would. I'll see you around six."

Chapter 20

Shai didn't know what was taking Derek so long. He called her at one-thirty and said he was on his way. It was two-thirty and he still hadn't arrived at Quintech. 'Rell called saying he was on his way and no one in the office had seen or heard from Derek. Shai was worried, this wasn't like Derek. 'Rell's car pulled up next to hers in the parking lot where she sat waiting. He got out of his car and walked to her window.

"My lady, I'm glad to see you."

"Have you heard from Derek? He's still not here."

"No, he didn't know I was coming. I don't think he would have called me."

"Rell, I'm worried. He wasn't himself this morning and when I spoke to him about an hour ago he sounded unsure about meeting me here."

"Open the door." 'Rell walked around the car and got in on the passenger side. "Shai, do you think Derek's gambling again?"

"I don't know. He kept that from me. I didn't know he was gambling until he was so far in debt, he needed me to bail him out."

"Baby, I don't think he can bail out of it this time. Derek has been indicted for Trademark Infringement. I think he's still gambling, but I'm not sure."

"Indicted? 'Rell how long have you known this?"

"I was subpoenaed this morning, his case starts Monday. I don't know when he found out, but I'm sure it was long before today. Uncle Darryl was subpoenaed too."

"So you're going to testify and say what, if you don't know anything?"

"That's just it, Mr. Simpson seems to think it started when he was with Carson Designs. He resold trademarks and logos that he designed for some companies. I guess he used the money he made to pay off his gambling debts."

"So what can you possibly say to help him?"

"Shai, we were subpoenaed by the prosecutor's office. I guess they'll ask me about his financial status when I took over. The mess I cleaned up and how he got Quintech. Uncle Darryl will probably testify about his gambling. I'm just guessing at this point."

"So is Mr. Simpson going to be able to help him? Why didn't he tell you about this?"

"Derek is not using Simpson. He's using the lawyers for Carson Design. I guess the company was indicted as well. Simpson didn't know until I called him this morning."

"I thought he was watching us. Where could Derek be then?"

"I was going to confront Derek while we had lunch, just to see where he was coming from and what plans his lawyers had for him. If they don't have a plan, I was going to suggest he switch law firms. I can't see them not selling him out since he now is a competitor in the business."

"You're probably right. He'll be their fall guy. I'm worried now. Suppose Derek still owes a large amount of money?"

"I was going to sit with Uncle Darryl to find out what they've been up to. They both have the same habit. They could be gambling in the same circles."

"So what, do they bet on horses, cars, what?"

"I don't know. I just know he's in with the big boys and he may owe them big money."

"Do you think they found out he was indicted?"

"Depends on who "they" are; did you call his cell number?"

"I called about fifteen minutes ago, no answer."

'Rell's phone rang. It was Mr. Simpson.

"Darrell, you need to go to the Medical Center. Derek's been in an accident."

"What type of accident?"

"A car accident, 'Rell it's suspicious. I think he was run off the road. He's in ICU."

"Who called you?"

"The police found my card in his billfold. There was only his license and my card. Nothing else, someone went through his clothing and the billfold looking for whatever. The police are considering it an attempted homicide, if he dies murder."

"Is he that bad off?"

"Yes, 'Rell you and Shai need to get there. Call his mother on your way. I'll wait for you to call me."

'Rell held the phone. He didn't say a word.

"Rell, what's wrong? Who was in an accident?"

"Derek; baby switch seats. I'll drive, you call your mother. He's in ICU."

"Rell, let's get there first, I can't deal with this and my mother."

Chapter 21

Shai and 'Rell arrived at the hospital emergency room twenty minutes after 'Rell received the call from Mr. Simpson. The police were still present talking with the medical staff. A nurse from the triage room noticed Darrell Mince when he came through the door.

"Officer, there's Mr. Mince coming through the door." An officer approached Shai and 'Rell as they reached the information desk.

"Mr. Mince. Would you come with me sir?"

"This is my sister; she'll be coming with us."

"Sure, let's go into a room where we can talk a minute."

"I'd rather find out about Derek. 'Rell you go with him while I check on his condition."

"Ms. Mince, is it? He's been rushed into surgery. He sustained a serious head injury and has internal bleeding in the head and the abdomen. If you need to talk with someone you may, but I do have a few questions to ask for our paperwork if you could help me."

"If there are any questions Darrell can't answer I will answer them after I talk to someone about Derek's condition."

Shai turned to the nurse's station before the officer could say anything. 'Rell followed him to a small room down the hall.

"Mr. Mince, I'm sorry. I'm trying to wrap up this preliminary paperwork, so we won't have to bother you later. I was the officer who called Mr. Simpson, the attorney. We had no other numbers to call. It appears your brother's car was hit both from the rear and the side. The vehicle was pushed into oncoming traffic in the opposite lane. Derek's car was traveling south and the tractor trailer coming north had no time to break when it approached the curve in the road, and it hit your brother's car head on. The driver wasn't hurt as bad, but he was injured. The call came in from a third party. We think it may have been one of the drivers of the other cars that ran Derek into the other lane. We arrived at the scene and other than the cars that arrived after our initial call, there was no evidence of any others. We know it was two other cars involved because the paint on the fender and the side are different colors. The driver's door to his car was open. Someone had gone through the car and his clothing leaving his billfold in plain sight. We have an investigation team at the scene of the accident gathering evidence. His car is being held."

"You've given Mr. Simpson this information?"

"Yes, Mr. Simpson said he was the family attorney. We will send him a written copy of our findings."

"What are your questions?"

"Are you able to answer the questions now or would you prefer to wait?"

'Rell felt as though he had been sucker punched. He was drained. He was riding on an emotional roller coaster and was getting sick. This was a lot to deal with in less than a year's period; the death of his father, a new love that turned out to be his sister, the inheritance of one of the most prestigious companies on the east coast, those who wanted to undermine his position as the eldest Mince and the new CEO at D.Q. Enterprises, the pregnancy, twins, the indictment, and now what could be a fatal accident. 'Rell took a deep breath and sat back.

"I won't say I understand what you're going through because I've never been in your shoes. If you need me to talk with you later, I'll understand."

"No man, ask your questions if it'll help you catch the bastards that did this."

The officer began asking questions about Derek's last couple of days, his business and who might have a problem with him or his business. The officer said it was thought it might have to do with the case that was to begin on Monday.

'Rell listened to his questions as it seemed that the police knew more than the officer was telling.

"How long have you been following my brother?"

"The prosecutor's office has an open investigation on him. They had a few investigators at the accident site. Your lawyer may want to contact them."

"Do you need to speak with my sister?"

"No, I think we're almost done. We can get the rest of the information later if we need it. Thank you for your cooperation."

"Sure man."

'Rell remained in the seat to gather his thoughts. Someone tried to kill Derek. *What for? Certainly not a gambling debt, there's more to it than that. Damn.* 'Rell heard Tonya scream from the emergency room waiting area.

"Oh, God no!"

"Mama calm down, he's still in surgery."

'Rell made his way down the hall to where he saw Shai trying to hold her mother's weight as she was falling to the floor. A man sitting in the waiting room ran as did 'Rell to assist Shai.

"Lord, don't let him die. Please, don't let him die."

"Shai, step back baby, we have her."

'Rell and the security officer in the area picked her up and sat her in a nearby chair. A nurse brought her a cup of cold water. Shai thanked them all as she sat next to her mother and took her hand.

"Why didn't you call me Shai? You called Darrell and not me, why?"

"Mama, I didn't call 'Rell, he called me. He got the call from Mr. Simpson, the lawyer. The police contacted the lawyer. That was the only number in his wallet."

"Shai, it's on the news. I heard it on the news. They just said the late D.Q. Mince's son was in a head on collision. I knew it wasn't 'Rell because of course, he is the new CEO of D.Q. Enterprises. They said that enough times too. Shai how bad is it?"

"He's in critical condition. They're trying to stop the bleeding in his head and in his abdomen. They don't even know what's bleeding."

Tonya hung her head and tears rolled down her face. 'Rell stood near the door. He was giving Shai time to talk with her mother without Tonya being distracted by his presence. Shai looked up and he noticed her tears. There was nothing they could do but pray.

Chapter 22

our hours passed. No one spoke to Tonya, Shai or 'Rell about Derek's condition. He was still in surgery. 'Rell called his mother, Mitch and Marci. They heard about the accident on the news. Mitch and Marci went to Nana's house to sit with her. She and Reverend Wilcox had not returned but Marci assured 'Rell, they would be there when she came home. At six thirty a nurse asked for the Mince family to follow her.

They walked down the hall and followed the signs to ICU. The nurse didn't say a word as she led them through the hospital. Tonya walked ahead of 'Rell and Shai. 'Rell placed his arm around Shai, who was beginning to cry again. The doors to ICU opened as the nurse pushed the large silver circle on the wall. The atmosphere changed to what reminded 'Rell of the television show "ER". The nurse led them to a small room with chairs and a television.

"Please have a seat here. The doctors have called to say Mr. Mince is out of surgery and on his way to this unit. No more than two of you will be allowed to be at his bedside at a time. The doctor will come in to answer your questions and tell you about his condition. Please wait for a nurse to tell you Mr. Mince is ready to receive visitors."

The nurse left without allowing anyone to question her. Tonya sat across the room from Shai and 'Rell. They sat in silence for what seemed to be more than fifteen minutes. The doctor entered the room in his green scrubs with his head still covered with the matching surgical cap. He showed no expression. His somber mode didn't reveal whether he would be delivering good or bad news.

"Good evening I'm Dr. Pittman, I was the surgeon who operated on Derek. He suffered severe damage to his spine. We have repaired the damage and there's a fifty percent chance he will be able to recover from that injury. He has three broken ribs and a fractured arm. One of the ribs punctured areas in the abdomen causing internal bleeding. We successfully stopped that bleeding. He also fractured his skull. This fracture caused his brain to swell and leak. We won't be able to tell what damage he has had until the swelling reduces, and he wakes up. He may have permanent damage. We have stopped the leakage, but he is being monitored for this, the leakage could start again. Are there any questions you may have for me?"

Tonya was wiping her tears. She opened her mouth to speak but nothing came out. Shai shook her head as tears flowed from her face.

"When will we know that he's out of danger? What is his critical window?" 'Rell posed his questions not knowing what they may have wanted to ask.

"If he can make it through tonight, he stands a chance. We will continue to monitor him. No test can be done to determine the damage until his strength builds. That will mean rest."

"What is the likelihood of the brain leaking again?"

"Mr. Mince, I am sorry to say it could start at anytime. That's the purpose for the monitors you will see in the room. We don't know at this time."

"Will he need more surgery?" Tonya and Shai raised their heads to hear the doctor's response.

"He may need more surgery on his spine. That would depend on how this injury heals. It's too early to say if he will need more surgery for the damage to his brain."

Tonya stood up and started pacing. "Where is he? Has he come downstairs? I want to see him."

"Mrs. Mince they are cleaning him up, he will be in his room area shortly. If you should have any other questions, please tell one of the nurses, and they will contact me."

"Dr. Pittman, who will be the doctor checking on him? You said you're the surgeon."

Shai wasn't comfortable talking with just anyone on the ICU floor.

"I will continue to check on him while he's in ICU along with Dr. Collins. She should be here shortly to talk with you."

'Rell shook the doctor's hand. "Thank you for all you've done Dr. Pittman."

A nurse came into the room. "Mrs. Mince, Tonya Mince?"

"Yes, that's me."

"You have a call Ma'am. You can pick up the phone near the nurse's station. If you like I can give you the number in this room for people to reach any of you."

"Thank you. Thank you very much."

Chapter 23

onya hadn't called anyone to tell them of the accident, and she couldn't think of who would call her at the hospital. She went down the list of family that would be concerned enough to call, but she knew they would wait until she called them with details. Since Shai told her where Marci was she thought about the call coming from Darlene or Nana. She even thought it may have been Darryl.

"Hello, this is Tonya."

Tonya turned her back to the nurse's station so no one from the desk would be looking in her face. She waited for a familiar voice to answer on the other end.

"Tonya, is he okay?"

It was Karlton. Tonya had not even considered he would call. She could feel anger and then fear came completely over her. *"Did Karlton try to kill my baby? Why would he be calling?"* Tonya's defenses kicked in. She hung up the phone.

"Excuse me, nurse?"

A nurse behind the desk put a chart in front of her and began writing. She raised her eyebrows responding to Tonya as she repositioned the phone.

"Yes Ma'am."

"If any other calls come in for Tonya Mince, I won't be taking them. I don't want to be away from my son until I'm sure his condition is stable."

"Not a problem Ma'am."

"Thank you. I wouldn't know what to say to anyone right now. I know you understand."

"Yes, I think I do. It won't be a problem Ma'am."

Tonya returned to the waiting area. Shai and 'Rell were talking softly to each other. Tonya was puzzled. For a moment, she would have thought they were talking as a couple would, definitely not a brother and sister. She put the thought to the back of her mind remembering Shai could have been upset.

"Who was calling Mom?"

"It was a bad connection. I don't know who it was. They'll call back."

Tonya said the words but she didn't want Karlton to call back. Her mind drifted back to the conversation they had on the phone earlier. He mentioned introducing himself to Derek and Shai. Tonya didn't think he would hurt her children. Maybe she should have talked to him. The thought of calling him back was now nagging her. His business card with his number was on the counter at her home. Now after giving it some thought, Tonya wanted him to call again.

"Was it someone who knew Derek? Mom, Mom?"

Tonya was deep in thought. *'Karlton wouldn't want the children to suffer over our agreement, would he?"*

"Mrs. Mince, are you okay? Can I get you something to drink?"

Tonya looked up from her seat. 'Rell was leaning over her rubbing her shoulders.

"Did any of the doctors come back to say anything about Derek?"

"No Ma, they didn't. Are you okay? Let 'Rell get you a tea or coffee."

"Rell can't get me anything." Tonya moved her shoulders shaking off 'Rell's touch. "I'm fine, thank you 'Rell. Shit ain't changed 'cause you're here for Derek. You and I are not family or friends. Don't make it seem that way because Shai is here. As a matter of a fact, if you want to do something, you go and check what's taking them so long."

Tonya repositioned herself in her seat. She wasn't about to allow him to get close to her. She still had plans for D.Q.'s first born.

Shai was embarrassed by her mother's rejection of 'Rell's attention. "Rell, that's a good idea, they said it would only be a few minutes. It's been forty-five."

'Rell didn't argue and although he could have given Tonya an overdue piece of his mind, he decided against it. He remembered to give her that dose of sugar that Nana would say "your enemies always hate".

"Are you sure you don't want anything, how about you Shai?"

"I'm fine. I don't think my mother wants anything either."

"I'll be back after I talk with a few of the attending nurses."

"Mama who was on the phone? You lied about it because 'Rell was around. You know who it was. Tell me. Is there something going on that I should know about?"

"If it was something for you to know they would have called you to the phone. Now I said I couldn't tell who it was so leave it at that."

"Do you know anyone who would want to hurt Derek?"

"Why would someone deliberately want to hurt him? Shai, I don't think it was deliberate."

"The police do, and I do too. They said his car was hit on the side and in the back. It sounds like they pushed him into the other lane. They pushed him into oncoming traffic."

"Who, who was there? Who saw this? Shai, let's just deal with your brother first."

"Okay, but as the days go on you'll want to know too."

Shai was wrong, it wouldn't be days. It was now. Tonya knew there were a few who had threatened Derek over the years. He owed money that was lost in all kinds of bets. He didn't bet small and he lost big. Then there was Karlton. Tonya shook her head. She couldn't see Karlton doing something criminal for the money she owed him.

"Mrs. Mince, Shai, come with me. They've brought him down. We can stand at his bedside."

'Rell led them to a room directly across from the nurse's station where Tonya had taken her call. The nurse told them that only two could be in the room at a time. One of them would have to wait in the sitting room on the unit. 'Rell told Shai and Tonya he would wait.

"Rell, could you call Marci and update her? I know she's on pins and needles by now."

"Sure, I'll call on Nana's line, so I can talk with her also. Mrs. Mince is there anyone I can contact for you?"

Shai hurried past her mother into the room.

"No…did you hear me? We are not on the same page. I am not your friend. As a matter of fact, did you get my letter of intent to sue your ass for what's mine? That's where we stand."

"Have it your way Mrs. Mince. You don't have to like me. Our problems are small in comparison to Derek's, so your venting is nothing right now. I understand, stand your ground. Just beware not to soften your foundation and sink into the very place you think you stand firmly on today. You may need assistance from me in the next few days. Your son, my brother, has a lawsuit and a grand opening for Quintech that must be handled. Even if it is postponed it may take a wand to be waved in his favor. Be careful how you talk to the one who may be the only one that can help."

"If that's some sort of threat…"

Tonya's words were interrupted by Shai hollering for them both to come inside the room that Derek occupied. Tonya rushed in while 'Rell stood back and watched from the door. The nurses had reported to the room as well as physicians and others.

"Shai, what's happening?"

"Mom, I think his body or his system may be rejecting the medication he's on. They said he would not be able to recognize his surroundings."

Derek seemed to be having a mild seizure. His body was jerking as though his nerves had been stimulated. A nurse came to where Tonya and Shai were standing.

"We'll need to stabilize him. Would you please wait in the waiting room? We will allow you to see him shortly."

'Rell answered because he knew Shai and Tonya couldn't. Their attention was focused on Derek.

"Thank you, we'll wait there."

As promised, within ten minutes a female doctor was the first to come out of the room. She held a clipboard with Derek's chart in her hands. She was flipping through the pages as she approached them.

"Are you the family here for Mr. Mince?"

"Yes, we are the family." Shai answered before her mother could say otherwise.

"I am Dr. Collins. I will be working with Derek while he is in ICU recovering. He has had a traumatic accident. The next twenty-four hours are critical. He needs to rest. I know it is hard for you to limit your visits, but I must insist. Although he's not awake he's not in a coma. He will need time to regain his strength. Do you have any questions for me?"

"I don't know what to ask. There are so many questions about his condition going through my mind. Shai you ask the questions, you're in the medical field."

Tonya feared the answers, so she avoided asking the questions she knew would bring her tears.

Shai looked at Tonya and 'Rell. "Dr. Collins, his chances, I mean, are they good considering his age and health?"

"His injuries are critical. The chances are just that, chances. We're going to do all we can to assist his recovery. However, he will need his rest to gain strength to fight."

"Did he have to have a transfusion?"

"Yes, he was given blood during the surgery. We are hoping all the internal bleeding has been found and handled. We will watch his vitals for any drastic changes."

"Dr. Collins he could die, couldn't he?" Tonya asked hysterically, "No, No, No, don't tell me."

"Mrs. Mince, at this point we really don't know. If he makes it through the twenty four hour mark, we will be able to check his injuries, his vital signs, and his response before moving toward his step of recovery."

"When will it be okay to sit with him?" 'Rell felt this question wasn't meant for him. He decided to let Shai and her mother sit with him. He would go to Nana's and wait for Shai to call him.

"You can sit with him now. It's alright. Please don't sit for longer than ten to fifteen minutes. Give him an interval between each sitting. If you should need a nurse, please call the desk."

"Thank you, doctor. I am sure we will have more questions tomorrow. Mom you go in, I'll be right there."

Dr. Collins walked over to the nurse's station and surrendered the clipboard. Shai walked over to ask 'Rell if he was okay. They faced each other and spoke without opening their mouths. 'Rell took Shai's hands.

"Listen, I'm going to go to Nana's and update them on what is going on. Call when you are ready to leave. I will come and pick you up."

"Do you think my mother will be suspicious if you come back just to get me?"

"You're probably right. Call if she won't drive you home for some reason. Otherwise call me when you're home, I'll stay with you tonight."

"Thank you. Call Uncle Darryl. He should be landing shortly. He probably doesn't know Derek is in the hospital."

"No problem. I'll call him."

"Rell, be careful."

"I will, I will."

They separated for the first time since they had been together without a farewell kiss.

Chapter 24

Nana rode home with Reverend Wilcox in silence. They picked up the bible covers as planned. The covers were maroon in color with First Chapel Baptist Church embroidered beautifully in gold lettering on each of them. They said their thanks and left in good spirit. After lunch they walked, made small talk and laughed. As they stopped at the window of Zale's Jewelry store and looked in the display cases for a gold necklace and cross for Nana. Reverend Wilcox told her to ignore the price tags and choose one that she liked.

"Jewels please pick out the one you like. Consider it a gift from me to you." Nana looked at him knowing that her accepting the gift would mean so much to him. She didn't want to seem anxious.

"Oh Wallace, I'm not one who's much on jewelry around my neck. I have a cross that I used to wear regularly, now I keep it in my jewelry box with my family heirlooms. I've had it close to thirty years. It was given to me by my Aunt Ellen when she passed on."

Reverend Wilcox nodded his head smiling at her comment. He still insisted she make a choice. Nana made her choice, a beautiful diamond cut necklace and cross. The man behind the counter smiled as he asked if they would give him a moment to put it in a box. They left the store with the gift boxed and wrapped.

"Jewels, would you let me put the cross around your neck? I'd like to see how it looks on you." Reverend Wilcox seemed more excited about the gift than Nana.

"Wallace, we're going to the house. Can it wait until we get there? I've wrapped up 'round my neck for the wind outside."

"C'mon Jewels. Well, just hold it against your face for me."

They took a seat on a bench that sat near the exit in the mall in front of Zale's. Nana took the box out of the bag and shook her head at the wrapping. She put her handbag on her lap as she began to open her gift. Reverend Wilcox moved closer to Nana and waited, like a child, in anticipation. Nana looked at him and decided not to ask him what he was so excited about.

"They sure know how to sell you something. Look at this, I picked the gift and they still wrapped it tight. It's pretty wrapping too. Almost makes you not want to open it, it's so pretty. Don't you think it's pretty Wallace?"

"Jewels it is beautiful wrapping. I want to see how beautiful you are with the cross on."

Nana enjoyed teasing Reverend Wilcox. She took off the wrapping and opened the box. Her eyes got large and filled with tears. In the box was a beautiful set of wedding rings. The diamonds glittered as the Reverend started his proposal.

"Jewels, I know this is late in our lives. I've always believed that love has no particular time to come calling. It has come to me that I am truly in love with you, and I would be honored if you would be my wife, my first lady, and accept me as your husband."

"Wallace, I don't know how many times I wanted to say this. I love you, and yes I would be honored to marry you."

They kissed a sweet passionate kiss. Reverend Wilcox sat back and smiled. He stood and took Nana's hand in his, helping her to her feet. Nana gathered the wrapping paper and folded it neatly for a keepsake.

"Wallace? Does this engagement mean I won't be getting that beautiful necklace and cross?"

They both laughed and returned to Zale's. The salesman shook the Reverend's hand as he gave him another bag.

"Congratulations, Ma'am, Sir, I wish you both the best and thank you for shopping at Zale's."

"Thank you, young man, you made this easier than I thought."

Reverend Wallace and Nana waved goodbye as they left the store. They walked to the car holding hands smiling at all that passed them. They felt like young lovers, pleased with their new commitment. Just as they got into the car headed home, Nana's cell phone rang. Reverend Wilcox started the car and Nana touched his hand to stop him from shifting the gear into drive.

"What? Where was the accident? Oh my God! Is he alright? Yes, I'm on my way. Reverend Wilcox is with me. Yes, he'll come with me home. Okay, I'll see you there."

"Jewels, what's wrong?"

"Derek has been in a terrible car accident. Seems that he was hit head on while he was driving on the expressway, and he's still in surgery. They don't know how bad he is. Marci and Mitch will meet us at the house."

"Jewels, let's pray."

Reverend Wilcox bowed his head and began to pray for Derek's soul and recovery. At that moment, Nana didn't know what or how to pray. She was too emotional to think.

"Lord, the boy just got it together. Stand by him, Lord. Watch over him."

They rode in silence until they reached Nana's block. Reverend Wilcox thought about the bible covers as he turned the corner.

"Jewels, I'm going to go in with you, but I will need to contact the church so these covers can get to the junior ushers for tonight's meeting. They planned to cover the Bibles tonight."

"Wallace, you can drop them off and come back if you want. I'll wait here for you. I don't think I'll be going to the hospital until sometime after his surgery."

"Okay, we can work it out, I'm sure. 'Rell's car is in the driveway, maybe he has more information. Let's go inside."

Nana opened the front door. She could smell coffee brewing. Marci was in the kitchen and could see her grandmother coming through the door.

"Nana, I didn't think you would be coming home this early. I thought you would be coming in later."

"Girl what you yelling about, who you trying to let know that I walked through my own door?"

"It's just me Nana." 'Rell came into the kitchen.

"What is going on? Y'all sending signals up in here. What's going on I said? Is Derek all right?"

"Yeah Nana I guess. Shai didn't call back yet to say there were any problems."

Marci was nervous and Nana could tell. Nana pushed her way past 'Rell with Reverend Wallace following close behind her. She walked into the living room and the rest of the house, as though she expected there to be someone else in the house.

"Where's Mitchell, Marci?"

"He went to get some soda and beer. If you need something else I can call him and tell him to bring it."

"What I need to know is what the two of you was talking about that you had to yell for 'Rell to stop talking."

Marci and 'Rell couldn't tell Nana their conversation. They were talking about Shai's condition and how she was going to handle dealing with her mother, Derek's accident and being pregnant. 'Rell wanted to tell her, but it wasn't the time and Marci was following his lead.

"Nana, come sit a minute. I'll explain as much as I can. Marci, why don't you get Reverend Wilcox and Nana a cup of coffee or something to drink?"

Marci looked at 'Rell, as though he lost his mind, but she followed his lead.

"Nana, Reverend Wilcox, what can I get you?"

"I'm fine child, Wallace you want to hear this or do you need to drop those things off to the church now?"

"Jewels, I will get them there before six, it's just a little after four now. Marci, I'll take a cup of coffee with crème and two sugars please."

"Rell, what is going on? You know I don't stand for no whispering and foolishness." Nana's tone showed she was agitated.

"I was explaining, well discussing with Marci, Derek's condition. The police don't think it was an accident and that brings up a lot of questions. I didn't want you to worry about that, and Derek's condition too."

Marci listened from the kitchen. *That damn 'Rell, whew, I see why Shai fell in love with him. Fast thinker, sharp and can handle any situation. Damn, I hope he can smooth things over when he speaks of being in love with Shai. How is he going to explain the pregnancy?*

Marci brought out the coffee for Reverend Wilcox and herself. "Nana, are you sure you don't want a cup? I can get you tea if you like?"

"No baby, sit down. Let's get this all in the open, so I'll know what we are faced with. First off, did Derek have the surgery?"

"Yes. He's in recovery. The next twenty-four hours are critical. They'll be able to tell us more after testing him when his strength pulls him past this critical period. He's not in a coma, but he's on strong medication that will keep him sleeping a while. The doctor's are watching for internal bleeding. He's had serious head trauma, and he may have brain damage."

"Oh my God."

Nana began to rock in her seat. Reverend Wilcox got up from his seat and sat next to her on the couch. He put his arm around her, and she allowed herself to rest in his chest as tears rolled down her cheek. The Reverend took out his handkerchief and handed it to Nana. Marci and 'Rell looked at the two of them and then at each other. They both wanted to ask questions, but they decided it would wait.

"Rell, where is Shai?" Nana was concerned about her being alone.

"She's still at the hospital with her mother. I told her if she needed a ride home to call me."

"So, Tonya's there. Has she been drinking?"

"Yes, I can't tell how much though, but she has been drinking."

"Lord, Shai don't need that. Well, what is this mess about it not being an accident?"

"The police called Mr. Simpson. They found his card in Derek's billfold. No money, no ID, no other papers. That's strange. They also saw signs of the car being hit from the back and the passenger side. It seems as though someone was pushing Derek's car into the other lane while he was on the expressway."

"Nana, they think he was pushed into the oncoming traffic. Right around that curve you say is so bad."

The bell rang just as Marci spoke. She went to the door, opening it for Mitchell.

"So did the police say they knew who did it? Were they injured in the accident too?" The Reverend's voice showed the depth of his concern.

"No, Reverend they didn't get hurt. They never even stopped, other than to search through Derek's car. The truck driver that crashed into Derek is in the hospital too. But he'll be released if he hasn't been already. He didn't get hurt too bad."

Reverend Wilcox reached for his coffee cup as Mitchell came in the room.

"Hello, family. They're going to release the driver of the truck. He suffered some bruising and a broken wrist and leg. He probably won't go home tonight though. I think they said he was going to be questioned by police later. I heard them talking about it just now on the radio."

"Mitch, did they say anything about the other cars?"

Nana and Marci sat listening as the men took over the conversation. Mitch took a seat as he handed Reverend Wilcox his cup of coffee. He hesitated before answering the question. He noticed Nana and the Reverend were sitting closer than usual.

"No sir, they didn't say there were any other cars. 'Rell they told you there were other cars involved?"

Mitch asked 'Rell the question but his underlying question was reflected in the look he gave Marci and 'Rell about Nana and Reverend Wilcox. 'Rell ignored Mitch's look continuing the discussion.

"Man, they said there was paint from other cars on the passenger side and the back bumper of Derek's car. I'll wait and call Mr. Simpson and see what information he gets. If we have to, I'll send some guys to check out a few things."

Nana hadn't heard 'Rell be so rigid or firm. She was impressed. He sounded like his father. D.Q. would have had men on it already, no doubt a few of the officers he knew. Nana didn't know that Mr. Simpson had already put the investigators at D.Q. Enterprises on alert.

"I'll call Shai and find out how things are going. My cell is in my purse. Reverend, that's it near you, can you pass it to me please?"

"Marci, you can use the house phone."

"Nana thanks, I don't know the number by heart."

"Eight, five, six, nine, four, one, two, two, six, five."

'Rell rattled off the numbers before he could catch himself. The room was silent. Everyone looked at 'Rell.

"I call her often I guess. She's the sister I never had."

Nana got up from the couch. "I guess there are some other secrets going around."

Marci cut in before anyone could answer.

"Thanks, 'Rell. I always get it confused with Aunt Darlene's. The numbers are similar."

"Speaking of secrets, Nana, I don't know when I'm gonna get to dad's stuff now. I mean with Derek's trial on Monday and this accident."

"What trial?"

The phone rang. Reverend Wilcox picked up the receiver answering, "Hello".

Marci stopped dialing, Mitch and 'Rell looked toward Nana as she walked toward her bedroom. This brought the trio's attention to Reverend Wilcox.

"Jewels, pick up the phone, it's Darryl."

Marci, 'Rell and Mitch all had the same thought. Rell shook his head saying aloud, "It is what it is!"

Chapter 25

arryl hung the phone up and looked at his watch. It was four forty five. Simone hadn't called to say what time she would arrive at the hotel. They talked shortly after Darryl's plane landed. She told him her room was reserved at the Courtyard Suites near Newark Airport. She booked the suite for the night. Darryl called Nana from the lobby. She explained he needed to get to Virginia, as soon as he could. After hearing the news about Derek, he felt an urge to leave after a drink. He would call Simone with the explanation later. Just as he decided to go to the bar, he spotted Simone walking through the front door.

"Hey baby, I'm sorry. I thought I would have gotten here by four o'clock. Have you been waiting long?"

Darryl smiled at the sight of Simone but wasn't going to greet her the way he wanted to in the lobby. Her appearance distracted him momentarily, he needed to tell her about Derek and explain they would have to alter their plans.

"We need to talk, Simone. Let's get a drink at the bar."

"Darryl, what's wrong? We can check in and then have a drink."

"C'mon baby. I don't want to explain here in the lobby, besides this may affect you too. My overnight bag is being held at the front desk. We'll put yours there too. We'll decide what to do and where to go from there."

"Darryl, what's wrong?"

He didn't want an argument to start. He kissed her on her cheek and took a step back to look at her again. Simone's response to his kiss was a full kiss on the lips. Darryl placed his finger on her mouth and whispered, "Follow me."

They went into the bar and found a seat at a table that sat away from the lobby traffic and the chatter of the other customers. Darryl looked across the table at Simone, longing to be in her arms again. Their rendezvous' were arranged around his business meetings on the east coast. It had been a few weeks since they had been together intimately and their teasing talks had promised that this weekend would satisfy his desire for her. The bar maid came over to their table and placed napkins in front of the two of them.

"Can I take your orders?"

"What do you want hon?"

"I'll have an Iced Tea."

"Make that an Iced Tea and a Vodka and Cranberry Juice. Can we see a menu please?" Darryl reached across the table and touched Simone's hand.

"Sure."

The bar maid left the table to place the order for the drinks and get the menus.

"So Mr. Mince, what's so pressing that we needed a drink?"

"I don't know if you needed one, but I did. Have you talked with Nikki or 'Rell since your meeting?"

"No, I didn't have any messages either. Should I have?"

"I thought one of them may have called you by now. I called home to tell my mother I would be to see her over the weekend. She told me to get there as soon as possible because Derek had been in a terrible car accident. He had surgery and could have some brain damage. They're waiting twenty-four hours before they do any more tests. He's in ICU."

"Darryl was anyone else hurt?"

"The driver from the truck was injured but it all seems suspicious. My mother is worried. I don't know if 'Rell called

Nikki, but you can't tell Nikki you know about it before she tells you."

"Okay, so you're going to Virginia tonight?"

"Don't you think I should? I mean, Fran will speak to my mother, and know I'm not there. If there was no accident she probably would think I was in New Jersey with a client and stayed over night. But with D.Q. gone and Derek being his son and all, she'll expect me to be in Virginia with the family."

"I see. So we won't be with each other until this crisis is over."

"No that's not what I'm saying."

A waitress came back to the table with a menu and the drinks.

"I have one Iced Tea and a Vodka with Cranberry. I'll give you a few minutes, and I'll be back to take your order."

Darryl moved the drinks over to make room for the waitress to lay down the menus.

"Thanks. Do you know what you want to eat or do you need a minute?"

Simone looked at the menu. "I'll look this over, thank you."

The waitress moved to the next table to fill another order.

"Don't misunderstand what I'm saying. I just don't want to be questioned about why I didn't care enough to be with my family during a crisis."

"So I guess if you were still in Detroit this would have been a family trip huh?"

"No, I would have still come by myself. I just wouldn't have stopped in New Jersey."

"I see. Well, since you did stop, and we don't want anyone to become suspicious, I will check in now and I won't change my arrangements. I'll still get to Virginia tomorrow. I'll catch my plane as scheduled in the morning. But you don't have to leave right away. I mean you said they won't be running tests until later. You can still fly out late tonight."

"My thoughts exactly, I'm booked on the last flight out tonight."

"And until then?"

"Well let's finish our drinks and order from your room."

They both smiled knowing satisfaction was minutes away.

<h1 style="text-align:center">Chapter 26</h1>

arci and Mitch left Nana's promising to call when they got to the hospital. They volunteered to stop at the hospital and check on Shai. Her mother, Darlene called to ask would she and Mitch mind picking up Mia. Marci told her it wasn't a problem at all. They would go to the hospital together and speak with her later. Darlene was waiting for a shipment of products for one of her salons and couldn't leave until it arrived. Once she knew there was a crisis she told Marci she would be at Nana's as soon as possible. 'Rell promised Marci he would be with Nana until Darlene got there. Mitch and Marci talked about Derek's condition. They went over the list of associates and friends, they knew Derek dealt with regularly. They couldn't think of anyone who would want him dead.

"Marci, do you think what 'Rell was saying could be true? I mean, do you think someone would really want to kill Derek?"

"I don't know Mitch, but it could be true. Derek had a bad gambling habit. Suppose he owed someone a lot of money?"

Marci pulled her Expedition into the parking lot of the Christian Academy where Mia worked. She looked around and shut her truck off after she realized she was ten minutes earlier than the time Mia would be getting off her job. Mitch turned down the radio and let his seat back a little.

"So you think it has to do with his gambling?"

"Mitch, I really couldn't tell you. Derek is kinda secretive. No one even knew he was gambling until Shai got mad about the money she had to shell out to save his neck a few times. I don't think my mother knew how deep he was into it either. And I know Nana didn't know."

"Well that indictment isn't about gambling. It's about Trade Infringement. A whole different ball park and I think Derek didn't know all the rules of the game."

"Wow, so you think someone tried to kill him to keep him from testifying?"

"Marci, I think that's what 'Rell is thinking too. I mean as much money as he stood to make at Quintech, he would have easily paid off any gambling debts. But if he could tie others into this trade thing, well, that could be a problem."

"Mitch, I hope you're wrong, but it does sound possible."

"More possible than I would like to believe."

"So who else might be involved?"

"Your Uncle Darryl and 'Rell were served to testify for the prosecution. I don't know how that would play out. I mean, they would have to answer the questions that could snag Derek. I hope they're not mixed up in this without their knowing."

"Do you think they knew what Derek was doing?"

Marci couldn't believe that her uncle would be involved in an infringement of some sort and knew about it.

"I don't thing your uncle did, and I know 'Rell didn't. Derek and 'Rell aren't really close enough to talk about anything other than business. I don't think they got that brother thing down yet."

"Really, you don't think they talk outside of business?"

"Marci, 'Rell is in love with Shai. They're expecting a baby. Shai is Derek's sister. 'Rell just found out they were related when their father died. 'Rell is still trying to sort those feelings out. He's confused about his love for Shai as his woman and Shai his sister. Having a brotherly relationship with Derek would just throw more fuel into the fire. Nah, they don't have much of a relationship outside of 'Rell helping him set up Quintech and small talk now and then.

'Rell's been keeping it that way so if he and Shai should decide to leave, that wouldn't be another relationship he would have to kill."

"I didn't think of it like that. I guess 'Rell would have to be distant in a way. Uncle Darryl and Derek are close though. They used to hang out at times when Uncle Darryl came into town."

"Hmmn, I wonder what your uncle may know."

"Mitch, do you think Uncle Darryl's life may be in danger too?"

"That may be. I mean, they gambled quite a bit together. That was one of the problems with the debt in his business."

Mia tapped on the window smiling and signaling to the locked door. Marci hit the lock release letting her sister in the truck and the cold outdoor air.

"Hey guys, it's getting cold out there. Thanks for the ride. What's up people? How was your day?"

Both Marci and Mitch gave her a look that indicated the day was not going well at all. They explained in detail as they rode to Richmond Medical Center. Mia listened without any response. Tears rolled down her face as she thought of the possibility of Derek's death due to his injuries.

"Marci, does Mom know what's happened?"

"Yeah, she's going to sit with Nana after her delivery comes."

"Does anyone have a clue who may have done this to him?"

"That's what Mitch and I were discussing while we waited for you. It could be a deliberate attempt because of the indictment."

"Indictment?"

Mia was confused. She didn't know about the pending court date. Mitch explained the charges and how they may have caused someone to want Derek dead.

"Trade Infringement? In the company where he worked? What the hell was Derek thinking?"

"Mia, I can't answer that. We don't know. Right now we're just speculating. Maybe we're wrong. I hope we are."

Mitch thought the situation over from beginning to end a few times. Each time it seemed to be clearer that whoever ran Derek into the other lane wanted him dead. The question was for what?

"Mitch, let's not mention this thought around Shai and her mother. I mean I don't want it to cause them to become rattled in the hospital. We can talk with Shai when she's not with my Aunt Tonya."

"Marci, are they together at the hospital?"

Mia could only imagine her aunt's conduct waiting for updates on Derek's condition.

"Girl, all I can say is be prepared; Mitch do you want to drop us off?"

"Babe, it's up to you. If you want me to come back, I will. If you want me to stay with you, I will."

"Such a sweet man that Mitchell Carter."

Mia teased and laughed at her comment. She really liked Mitch. She thought he and Marci made a beautiful couple.

"Marci, listen, call me when you are ready. I'll stop by Byron's for a minute, and then I'll head to my house. Just call when you're ready."

Marci pulled the truck up to the main entrance. The sisters got out into the cold and made gestures to Mitch about the difference in the weather. Mitchell walked to the driver's side and kissed Marci telling her to be sure to call when she was ready.

"Mitch, the cell phone may not work in the hospital. It's about six-thirty now. Come back about seven forty-five we'll be ready by then."

"Alright, I'll be back by then. Love you and send my prayers to Derek."

"Later Mitch thanks."

A Different Kind of Love

Mia and Marci waved goodbye and entered the hospital looking for the directions to ICU.

Chapter 27

Nana was in the kitchen preparing dinner while 'Rell dialed his mother's home for the second time. He tried her cell phone but couldn't leave a message because her voice mail was full. After another ring, he hung up.

"Nana, have you heard from my mother lately?"

"She went to D.C. earlier this week. I think she's due to return today or tomorrow. She may be back already. Did you leave a message for her to call you?"

"No, I tried her cell, but I didn't really know what message to leave her, after that I figured I'd call her at home."

"She could be with Sam. They've been keeping company on a regular now. Could be she stopped over to the church or his place first."

"She really likes that guy, huh?"

'Rell's voice had a disappointed tone. He couldn't explain why. *"She deserves to be loved. Can she get on with her life now that dad's gone? No, she would have told me if she was in love again. He's just a cushion for now, can't be serious."*

"Rell, you really don't know Sam. He's a nice man, a Deacon at the church, a sound man. I think he's into Real Estate, that's what attracted the two of them. You know, your mother getting into interiors and Sam selling property; they talked for hours. I'll let her tell you the rest if it's anything deeper than friendship. I think she enjoys his company, as well as he enjoys hers. They're good for each other."

"He's not married?"

"No, he's a widow. His wife and child were killed in a car accident. That's what brought him to the church. He always says it was his last hope, God or insanity. That was about five years ago."

"I guess I've been too busy to catch up with the goings on with her. I'll have to sit and talk with her about this thing with Derek."

"Rell, you have to slow down too. You've been working on everyone's problems. You got Shai a home, Derek secured in his business, your uncle in his, your Mom in hers. What have you done for you? You didn't even pause after the funeral. You need time to sit back and take all this in. It's a lot. Even if you do have the wit to handle it all, it can take a hold of you emotionally and physically."

"Nana, you're right. I just think that once everyone is stable on their own, I can rest. I can rest knowing that what my father wanted was for everyone to be alright financially, and it was handled as though he were still here."

"That's just it baby, he's gone. You can't fill those shoes he left. Do what you can, for sure, but don't try to be the answer for everything and everyone. You have enough of your own to sort out and live for."

"I know it's just like a burning inside. I mean, it feels as though he's pushing me to finish what he left undone. After I go through his belongings, I think I'll be able to stop. Not until then though."

"Well baby, I'm watching you. I don't want you to be in no hospital bed suffering from mental exhaustion. It ain't easy being D.Q.'s number one."

"Tell me about it.

"I see you and Monique didn't get back together. Is she still seeing your friend Craig?"

"Nana, I don't know. I don't talk to Craig that much anymore. He was doing some shady things on and off the job. I don't call Monique at all either. I think the last time we spoke was shortly after the funeral. She sounded as though she wanted me to invite her out or over, but I ignored her hints. It would be the same. She wasn't interested in me as much as she was interested in my gain since my father's death."

"Well, I'm sorry you and Craig don't talk. You were such good friends, you know, the four of you; Craig, Mitch, and Byron. It's a shame. You all grew up together into manhood. They say all it takes is a woman."

"Nana, I don't think that is what caused Craig to do what he did to the business. You know, now that you said that, I don't know what would have made Derek do what he did? Does he have a girl?"

"Baby, that I don't know. But you know Derek had it bad for that gambling. That probably was his weekend lady. Now during the week he might have been seeing someone else. But if there was a bet to be made at that race track he was betting. It got so bad Shai had to pay his debts. Your father gave me his college money. He was scared he would kill him if he found out, he gambled it all away. I kept it but Lord, Derek would beg for it."

Nana chuckled to herself and went to the refrigerator for iced tea. She got herself a glass and gestured to 'Rell as she laughed.

"Thanks, Nana, do you think someone would want him dead over his gambling? Were there debts that may have not been paid?"

"Derek was careful after the threats he got the last time. Shai paid all the debts off, and some she had to pay in payments. That was another reason he was living with Shai. So she could keep her eyes on him. When she pulled the reins, he could feel it. I thought he was getting better. I don't know though, to tell you the truth."

"Did Uncle Darryl gamble in the same circle?"

"I don't think he did until maybe a year or two ago. Your father caught him begging me for money. D.Q. was against that and they argued and cussed up a storm in here. Anyway,

Darryl got the money from D.Q. and promised he would get out of it. Your father was keeping Derek out of real trouble, some lie about him and Derek beating the man out of his money. He paid the entire bill off and threatened to beat the brains out of both of them."

"So they weren't just gambling at the track then?"

"Rell, now you know better. They was messing with the man, the man and his money. Well, when the man wanted all his money they didn't have it. D.Q. paid it. That happened one or two times before D.Q. and Darryl went head to head. If anyone knows if Derek owes any money or is still gambling it would be your Uncle Darryl."

"I hope he wasn't involved with this mess. I mean, if he is, he could be next."

"Rell, you don't think those people would kill them like that for money do you?"

"Depends on how much, it could be for more than we know. I don't want to speculate, but it seems that they would retaliate if they thought Derek or Uncle Darryl was ducking them."

"But Derek doesn't know anything about that Trade Infringement thing."

"He knows something Nana. They indicted him."

"So, 'Rell what do you know?"

"It's not what I know; it's what they think I know. They know I'm Derek's brother. They may figure I may turn my back on him, or join the prosecution to put him in jail."

"Humph! I know if he has his hands in the wrong pot, he's going to jail. I ain't bailing out nobody who can't follow the law."

'Rell smiled in spite of the serious attitude Nana took on. 'Rell loved his grandmother. He realized his feelings for her, whenever he visited. This visit was special. Nana hadn't talked to him in a while, and he thought it would help them both to share time together. As he listened to her talk, he noticed her beautiful aging features and her hands.

"Nana, that's a nice ring. I don't think I saw that one before. It fits your hand perfectly too."

Nana felt her ring with her other hand. She didn't want to seem like a girl waiting to be asked to the junior prom. She smiled proudly.

"I'll tell you and the family about it soon as we know definitely that Derek will make it. Right now there's too much going on."

"So is it some kind of announcement that goes along with the explanation. I mean, why should the family have to know about the ring?"

"Rell, Reverend Wilcox asked me to be his wife. I accepted."

"Just like that, Nana, did you give it any thought?"

"What was there to think about? We don't have a lot of mess between us. We're mature adults who love God and each other. I think it can work, and it's obvious he does too."

"I guess that's what really matters. So when is the big day?"

"We hadn't talked about it. We got the message about Derek as we were leaving the jeweler. I don't want to talk about it until I'm in the right frame of mind. He's not going anywhere and neither am I. We have to talk about it more. Derek needs us, our attention and our prayers now."

'Rell's cell phone rang. It was Marci calling from the hospital. 'Rell listened for what seemed to be too long to be a two way conversation. Nana started questioning his silence.

"What's wrong 'Rell? Who's on the phone?"

'Rell covered the phone with his hand to speak with his impatient grandmother.

"It's Marci. She's talking to me and Shai at the same time. I think Shai and Tonya got into an argument and the hospital staff asked Shai to leave since Tonya is the mother. Shai's not happy with that at all."

"You tell Marci I said bring Shai away from there with all that yelling over that boy. That ain't gonna help him none. Tell

Marci either take Shai home or bring her here if she's not going to Marci's house with her."

'Rell relayed the message and shortly after said goodbye. Nana didn't say a word but her expression said she wanted to know the outcome.

"Marci is taking her home. Shai was crying and saying she hated her mother. I could hear her through the phone. She doesn't need this extra stress."

"Well, anytime you get Shai around her mother, and she's been drinking, there's trouble. Tonya is just a sad excuse for a mother and Shai can't help but to tell her. I guess it's just the way things are between them. They have never got along. Derek truly loved his mother until the last few years. It seemed like it happened overnight. But for the past eight or nine years he's been real distant to her. D.Q. used to say he was just learning about the woman he called "Ma"."

"Did Shai know how Derek felt?"

"Baby I don't know. You want something to eat? It's getting near the dinner hour now. I've got spaghetti left over. I was gonna heat it for tonight. You're welcome to it if you're hungry."

"No, Nana I think I'm going to try to catch my mother. She still didn't return my call."

"I bet she's with Sam. Wait, I have a number I can call."

'Rell's phone rang again. He looked at the number and smiled. It was Shai.

"Baby, are you alright?" 'Rell spoke softly while his grandmother went toward her bedroom to get the number for Sam.

"That woman can aggravate the dead. I don't want to talk about it though.

I'm just mad that the hospital chose her to be with Derek. He's liable to wake up see her and refuse treatment while she's there. He's not going to talk to her."

"Well Shai, they don't know that. Don't worry, they know who you are, and they will contact you if he refuses treatment. She'll probably leave soon. Where are you?"

"With Marci, Mitch and Mia; going home."

"I'll give you two hours, and then I'm coming. Is that okay with you?"

"Why two hours?"

"You call it then; how long?"

"They're just dropping me off. By the time you leave Nana's, they'll be gone."

"Is Mia in your area? You're talking like you can't wait."

"Alright so you'll be here in about an hour?"

"About that, I just want to reach my mother first."

"I love you."

"I love you too, relax."

Nana stopped in the hall leading to the living room. She didn't know exactly who 'Rell was talking too, but she had removed his mother from the list. She couldn't put the first part of his conversation together with the last part. At first she thought 'Rell was talking with Shai. Even so, with the ending of "I'll be there" and "I love you", she was confused.

There was a strange silence in the room where 'Rell sat. Nana entered the room thinking to herself, *"D.Q., seems like you're not the only that has secrets."*

Chapter 28

Simone walked into the bedroom of her hotel suite and noticed Darryl was hanging up the phone.

"Did you call your wife, so she won't call you?"

"No, I called the hospital to check on Derek's condition. The nurse said he's sleeping, but he'll be closely monitored through the night. I guess Tonya and Shai left. They didn't mention whether he had visitors or not. I called Shai but she didn't answer. I left a message."

"I'm sorry you didn't get her. I think she could have put your mind at ease. I mean, if they're not at the hospital then he must be stable enough for them to feel comfortable about leaving. Did you try 'Rell's phone?"

"I don't need to talk to 'Rell. I don't know who I should call."

"How about if you don't call anyone else for now, unless her name is Simone?"

Darryl smiled as he thought of how he called her name when they had sex. *"That's exactly what I need to calm my nerves; a stiff drink and satisfaction."* Darryl stood up and crossed the room to meet Simone at the foot of the bed. They embraced and kissed. Darryl began to run his hand down Simone's back until he reached her waistline. He slowly began kissing her on her neck as his hands fondled her breast. Simone had been waiting for the moment, and prepared to make it the best sex they ever had. She backed herself to the bed and pulled Darryl on top of her. They teased each other with kisses and massages.

Simone unzipped Darryl's pants as he unbuttoned her blouse. She had on a black bra with lace covering her nipples. Her nipples rose to the gentle strokes of his hands. She began to massage his manhood. Her touch caused his shaft to respond, as it enlarged in her hand.

Darryl felt different having sex with Simone. Although Francine was a good lover and wife, Simone made him want her. He couldn't remember a woman making him as hard as she did. Just the lingerie she wore would arouse him. Darryl tried not to become accustomed to them getting intimate every time they got together but Simone just wasn't the same as Francine. She never complained about oral sex, and they made love in more than one position. Francine had forgotten about the thrills of making love, and it was obvious it had become more of a "wifely duty".

Simone kissed Darryl's chest and began to lick his nipples as his hands got busy taking off both his and her clothes. Simone had her wants too when it came to good loving. She let Darryl know her desires during their first escapade. She didn't hold back anything. She felt if he didn't like to perform, he didn't have to waste her time. Although Darryl seemed shy to some of her wants at first, he did it all, gently and thoroughly.

Simone's kisses had caused Darryl to get harder quick. He kissed her breast and used his hand to massage her inner thighs. His mouth found hers and their tongues played teasingly while their hands explored the other's body. They both were ready but loved the foreplay. Darryl took the lead and put his fingers inside Simone's vagina.

"Ooooh Darryl yes." Darryl moved his finger back and forth using the other fingers to massage her clitoris. Her juices began to flow.

"Mmmm, is that good baby?" He wasn't ready for her to climax so he slowed down the rhythm of his fingers. This made her moan more. He mounted her for the first round.

Simone took all of him in, moving with him in anticipation for him to explode. Darryl pulled out his penis and turned her over. She loved the position and didn't realize how much she enjoyed it until he put his penis in place again and massaged her clitoris as they moved. She could feel her temperature changing. He began to moan and saying her name.

"Simone, baby. Oooo Simone." Justas he began to pick up the pace Simone pulled away from him and turned over. "Baby, what? Oooh Simone."

She had his manhood massaging it with her breast. Each time his penis would get close to her mouth she would slowly kiss the head and tease it with her tongue. Darryl was done. He hadn't felt like this with a woman in years. His body began to quiver. Simone had to conquer him totally so she continued. She rolled him on his back and gave him her breast to suck as she mounted him. The rhythm picked up instantly. Simone broke him like the cowboys did their bronco. He exploded and she did too. She didn't stop; she sat him up and kissed him slowly. She could feel his penis rising and she smiled like a villain.

"Simone, let me…" Darryl's words faded as she pushed his face toward her navel. Darryl kissed her navel and continued on until he found a familiar area. He loved Simone's body, her smell, her skin, and her essence. It was more than sensuous. He wanted her to enjoy him as much as he enjoyed her. Using his fingers and his tongue he gave her the pleasure she needed to explode twice before his penis returned to please them both.

"Darryl, do I satisfy you?" The question came only fifteen minutes after their lovemaking session.

"Yes, you don't know? I know I must show you that you do. I don't usually talk while I'm having sex. You make me talk I just can't help but tell you it's good. You're good. I feel good. Damn, I'm getting hard just thinking about it."

"Well, we can't get busy again without it going into the time you have to leave."

"Girl, let me worry about that. I can't go through the airport quivering either."

Darryl put his hand on Simone's. He wanted her to feel his penis getting hard again.

"I don't know Simone, you got me going girl. At this rate I won't be leaving tonight."

Simone opened her legs, repositioning her body for a continued night of ecstasy. *"You won't be leaving tonight Mr. Mince. No not tonight."*

Chapter 29

arrell walked in on Shai crying hysterically into the phone. He stood, pausing, waiting for her to notice his entrance into her bedroom. Shai looked his way but continued to talk.

"Nana, I can't take much more of this. I don't know how to treat her or what to say. I ignore her remarks and I don't comment when I know I should. She's bitter, and she wants me to be as bitter as she is. I won't Nana! I won't put up with her treating me like she does!"

'Rell knew from the sound of the conversation that his appearance wasn't enough to calm her feelings. He went into the den and called his mother again on his cell phone.

"Hello."

"Ma, where have you been?"

"Well hello to you Mr. Mince. How was your day?"

Nikki responded to 'Rell's question with a hint of sarcasm that 'Rell didn't acknowledge, which told Nikki something serious was going on.

"What's the matter baby?"

"Ma, Derek has been in a real bad accident. He's at the Medical Center in the ICU Unit. They say if he makes it through tonight he may stand a chance of living."

"Oh God, is Shai and Nana alright?"

"Shai's shook but I think it has more to do with her mother. I'm at her house now. I stopped by to check on her.

She got thrown out of the hospital and told not to return while her mother was there. Nana's talking with her now on her phone."

"Goodness, what could have happened between them at the hospital? What in the world was her mother thinking, having her thrown out?"

"That's Tonya Mince for you."

"I wish I had got to her when I had the chance but God protects fools."

"I was trying to call you earlier. Did Simone come in yet?"

"No, she'll be here tomorrow. I left early and came in from Washington around three this afternoon. I had a meeting with a supplier at five. I just got here. I stopped to tell Sam I had got back and….yeah that was it."

"You stopped to see Sam and didn't tell me you were back, or that you had gone. What's up, am I in second place now?"

"You're never second. I wasn't sure if I was going, and then I didn't have a clue of what time I was coming back. At first I was going to stay until tomorrow but the client wasn't ready for the prices. I hate those meetings. You show them everything and they seem interested then they want to Jew you down on the price. I promised myself I won't take a cut in prices. The work is worth the prices that I charge. Anyway, Simone will be here first thing in the morning, so I needed to come home early."

"So is Sam visiting this evening?"

"Are you?"

"Ma, c'mon tell me about this Sam guy."

"Tell me why you're at Shai's so much?"

'Rell was stunned. He didn't think it was "so much". If his mother suspected something his grandmother had mentioned it to her.

"I asked you first."

"Well I decided to get my life in order. You know my business, my esteem and worth, my social life. Sam is a part of my social life. We have a friendship for now."

"Are you trying to convince me or yourself? Ma, don't get me wrong, I'm happy for you. I just hadn't been introduced to him like that."

"Like what? We're not getting married."

"Okay, it's cool."

"Now why so much time at Shai's?"

'Rell thought about telling her everything. He couldn't without talking to Shai about it. This wasn't the right time. He would have to tell another lie to cover his secret.

"Never had a sister before; I kinda like it. We get along well and we understand each other. She's told me a lot about dad that I didn't know. I guess I've done the same for her. Today she's been through a lot. I'm here if she needs me."

"Such a man, Darrell it sounds good but there's more to it and I know it. Does she have a friend you like or something?"

"Ma please, I can't tell you." 'Rell thought to himself as he had in the past with others who questioned their closeness. He would have to get his mother to talk about something else.

"She does but I don't see her much, so much for my love life. I'm not ready to deal with a relationship right now. My life and time is surrounded by a lot of unfinished business. As you know, it takes a lot to maintain a new relationship. I still have to go through dad's belongings. Who knows what that may turn up?"

"You're right about that. 'Rell, hold on baby."

'Rell walked into the bedroom to peek in on Shai. She had stopped yelling into the phone, although she was crying and listening. She motioned for him to come closer. He gestured for her to give him a minute.

"Rell, I'm sorry. That was the other phone. Your Uncle Darryl told your Aunt Francine, he would be here tomorrow morning. She wanted to know if I knew where he was staying. I tell you, Darryl and your father, and their mess."

"Ma, do you know if Uncle Darryl is still gambling?"

"I don't think so baby. Fran would have said so. I think the last time you and Nana bailed him out he vowed to quit."

"Me and Nana; what did he get from Nana?"

"Close to ten thousand dollars, that was right after your father's funeral."

"Did Nana say what he needed it for?"

"No, she was heated though."

"Ten thousand; for what and why would he get money from me and her?"

"Rell you think he's still gambling?"

"Yeah but his life and Derek's has become the wager."

'Rell didn't want to think the worst but for a payment of that size it couldn't be anything less than trouble. He had set all of his uncle's business debts in order and advanced the company's account for pending projects. There wasn't any need for ten thousand dollars other than personal use.

"He'll be here tomorrow. I'll see if I can ask him in a vague way what's up. Maybe he'll tell me something that would give you a clue. 'Rell I hope Derek will be fine but what about Darryl, do you think he's going to face any danger."

"Ma, I don't know. I know we were supposed to go to court on Monday. I'll call Mr. Simpson in the morning to see if the court date has been changed since Derek is in the hospital."

"I would think they would postpone it. They can't expect you and Darryl to testify at all with the boy still in the hospital."

"I'll call Simpson and see. I do need to know if Uncle Darryl is still gambling though."

"Well, when he comes by, I'll do my best to see how he's been spending his free time."

"Okay, thanks Ma. I'll see you either tomorrow or Saturday. I'll be checking on Derek and Shai for the next few days though. You know the big brother look out thing."

"Yeah, big brother, you take care of yourself as well. I'll call you."

"Later Ma."

A Different Kind of Love

Shai was standing in the bedroom looking out the doors leading to the adjacent deck. The light from the moon was shining in on her face. 'Rell treasured the moment. Shai's beauty was enhanced with the light and the small bulge from her stomach indicating she would soon be a mother. He smiled to himself as he walked up behind her. Their bodies made a shadowed silhouette on the deck. 'Rell could feel Shai's tension.

"Baby, you need to relax."

"I'm scared 'Rell. Why would someone want to kill Derek? What could he have done to cause someone to want him dead?"

"Shai, baby, Derek owed a lot of people money. It could be any one of them. Mr. Simpson is looking into the infringement case filed against Derek. It could be a connection to the accident. We don't know what it is. I do know you need your rest. I can't tell you not to worry, but you've had an emotional day. You need to rest, if not for you, for the twins."

"Rell, what is wrong with my mother? I know you don't know but your opinion may help."

"Your mother, I don't know. I don't think there is anything wrong with her. I mean, she has issues, but I don't think they have to do with you or Derek. I think she had them before you and Derek were born."

"You do? Tell me what you think."

"I don't know. Maybe she didn't want children. I mean not that she didn't want the two of you; just the fact that she didn't want any children. I think dad did and she had you and your brother as an effort to keep him.

Obviously, she wasn't happy with her choice. When he died, she saw a new beginning with his money. You both would grow up, and she would be in a "win win" situation. But dad threw a loop into her plans by leaving her nothing to claim, or live on. Now she hates the world."

"It's funny Derek said the same thing right after dad died. He said our mother couldn't love us. She wouldn't allow herself to. I guess you're both right. But how does she expect us to live with her hatred for us or who we remind her of?"

'Rell hugged Shai and slowly began to massage her stomach. He wasn't looking to go any further than a loving touch. He wanted her to relax and let him take her mind off of her mother and Derek's condition. He whispered into her ear.

"Come to the bed and rest."

Shai followed his lead and eased her self across the bed. 'Rell pulled back the comforter and undressed her. He asked her was she comfortable as he took off all his clothes, leaving on his boxers.

"I'm better. I just wish I could get the scene out of my mind. My mother and I disagreed about what to do if Derek should be declared brain dead. I told her I didn't think we should talk about it until we were told that was the diagnosis. No, she wanted to talk about pulling the plug, not letting him be a vegetable, and she went on and on. I screamed 'Shut the fuck up'!!'; 'Rell I couldn't take it anymore. How could she talk like that right over Derek, right in the room with him listening? We don't know if he can hear us or not. She's just a bitch."

"So she had you thrown out for telling her to shut up?"

"No she had me thrown out because I told her this was another opportunity for her to pretend she cared."

"And…."

"And she responded by saying how she was his mother, and I didn't know how much she cared. I told her I hoped I didn't have to be near death before I found out. She slapped me and I slapped her back."

"That's when she had you thrown out."

"No she waited a while in silence. I thought I slapped her tongue out. She told me I should have been the one in the car, that I was as dead to her as dad bwas. I told her she had been dead to me long before dad died. She jumped up to hit me again, and I told her I would kill her if she touched me again."

"That's when she had you thrown out."

"Yeah, that did it. On my way out, she told me I would need her to hold on to before it was all over. I told her don't hold her breath waiting. Security came up after she spent five minutes or more at the nurse's station. You know she told them I was hysterical and couldn't make rational decisions about Derek. That's when she requested that I not be allowed in the room visiting when she was there or by myself."

"Baby, again, I don't understand your mother. You have to get through this with strength enough for our children. Lay here and relax. I'll get you some tea and lemon."

"Thanks Rell. Can you call the hospital and check on Derek's condition? I'll sleep better knowing he's well on his way to recovering."

Chapter 30

*T*hursday seemed like it would never end. Shai had gotten on Tonya's last nerve, and she downed two strong drinks before sleep took over. She never had a chance to talk with the nurses before she left Derek's side, but she would definitely talk with them today. Tonya didn't know if Shai would try to ignore her wishes, but she meant what she said.

"Shai is not to visit her brother while I am here or by herself. She is hysterical and must not be allowed to make any decisions concerning his health or his care." The words repeated over in her head. She would take care of Derek. He would need long term care, and she was his mother. Who else would be expected to care for him? *"Well, D.Q. I'll have my hands on your money anyway. Derek won't be able to make financial decisions and his portion will be handled by me. When he passes it will be left to me."*

Tonya gave it no other thought. That was the way it was meant to be. She now had another way of accessing D.Q.'s fortune. Derek being in the hospital and needing care would require her to quit her job and be available for him. Upon his death 'Rell would have to see things her way and provide finances for her loss of work and her son.

However, the thought of Karlton Harris jarred her soul. He would definitely have to be paid off, or he could be trouble. He didn't deny that he caused Derek any pain. Tonya was sure that if he had hurt Derek or had someone hurt him, he would

133

want her to acknowledge his involvement. That was her agenda this Friday morning. She would call him and have that face to face meeting before he could cause any other trouble.

She phoned the hospital checking on Derek's condition. Tonya was told he was stable and had made it through the night without any incidents, and he would be going down for testing by noon should she want to be there. She told the nurse thank you, and she would be there during his test.

Tonya got dressed taking care to wear an eye catching outfit with a matching Burberry bag and shoes. Her hair was attractively done and her makeup glistened, as though she was ready for a models runway. She took one last look in her bedroom mirror, picked up her cell phone and dialed the number that would connect her to Karlton Harris.

"Hello Karlton?"

"Good morning, my love. How are you?"

"How else would I be with my only son in ICU? But then you couldn't ask yourself the question. You put him there."

"Tonya, I think you should think about that accusation before saying it again. I wouldn't hurt Derek or Shai. They haven't done a thing to me. However, you have. If I wanted to harm someone it would have been you."

"I'm calling a truce Karlton. Meet me in two hours downtown at the diner across from the park. Do you know the one I'm talking about?"

"Yeah, I know the one. You amaze me Tonya. What are we talking about at this meeting that we can't say over the phone?"

"Just be there Karlton. It's time we discuss our issues and not involve anyone else."

"If you insist my dear."

Karlton hung up the phone with one thought on his mind, Tonya had become his bait. He had a choice, let her continue to think he was ruthless enough to harm her son or allow her to control the situation. The latter held danger for Karlton, whenever Tonya was in control things didn't go his way. He got dressed carefully picking a suit Tonya would love to see him in. Her taste had not changed anything that appeared expensive, would capture her attention. Karlton played the part. He selected a shirt and tie that would compliment the Demantie suit and his accessories were white gold.

Karlton Harris was a handsome man with sharp features. He looked as though he could have been from Brazil. His skin tone was bronze in color with jet black and gray silky hair. He kept it cut close to avoid having a head full of curls. He was not what one would consider muscular but his body held no fat or flab. He stood about six two and weighed about two hundred and thirty five pounds. He had that manly look, one that made most women gaze and wonder. Karlton never had a problem attracting women, and Tonya always sparked his interest.

He left the hotel with the feeling he was winning a game, and Tonya was his competition. His intent was to have her or her money. Either way he would be well taken care of.

Chapter 31

Shai called her job and told them she would not be in. She let her supervisor know about her brother's accident and told her that she would keep in touch over the next few days. She got up to get dressed. She wanted to get to the hospital early to avoid meeting her mother during her visit.

She could smell the bacon cooking and the coffee brewing. 'Rell was in the kitchen preparing breakfast. Shai felt bad that she had not given him any of her attention, since they found out about Derek.

"Rell, are you okay?" Shai shouted toward the kitchen but didn't receive any answer. Shai couldn't hear any music or the television. Her curiosity peaked. She put on her robe and walked into the living room. There she found 'Rell putting together a bassinet. Just the thought of him putting together baby furniture touched her emotions.

"Oooo 'Rell, when did you get it? It's beautiful. Are they both the same?" Shai had noticed the second bassinet in the box waiting to be assembled.

"Yes, they're the same. I bought different bedding though. You're in your fifth month. Since we are expecting two, I figured I better get started working on their nursery. I'll do the nursery here first. I didn't know if I should do one in my home. Family may wonder, you know."

"Rell, this is so sweet. When did you get all of this?"

"When you decided to keep the twins; I wanted the first thing in the nursery to be from their father. You can decorate the rest. I just wanted to be a part of their beginning."

"Baby, you are their beginning. Without you, they wouldn't exist. I love them. They are beautiful. The room next to my bedroom is theirs. I haven't thought of the décor though. I wanted to ask you if you would think it would be awkward to ask your mother for her input. I would love for her to decorate the room for her grandchildren."

"Shai, she doesn't know they are her grandchildren."

'Rell lifted the assembled basinet and took it in the room. He didn't wait for Shai to respond to his comment. The room was colored in a soft mint green; it had been a guest room. The double bed and dresser would soon be replaced with a changing table and cribs. The room was large, it had plenty of room for the babies growth. It gave them plenty of playing space. Shai's home was built for children. 'Rell smiled as he thought that was her intention when she selected the house. He loved her home and what she had done with it. They agreed that if they could live together he would sell his home and move in with her. Shai walked into the room pleased where he placed the bassinet. She pressed herself gently against his back.

"Rell, I love you."

"I love you too, Shai. Whew, did you check the bacon? I forgot it was on."

"I turned it off. You must have gone into deep thought. It's going to be alright. You'll see."

"I know. I know. It's just hard. Did you tell Marci about dinner tomorrow night?"

"Yes, they will be here around six. Is that a good time for you?"

"Six is fine. You need to eat before you leave here. You'll probably be running around all day."

"I need to get to the hospital before my mother, after visiting Derek I don't know what I'll be doing."

"I was thinking about talking to Mr. Simpson about what he uncovered. Why don't we go together? I'll call the office and tell them I can be reached on my cell phone."

"Okay, thank you."

"Thank you, for what Baby? That's why I'm here; to love, protect and support you."

Chapter 32

arryl and Simone waited at Gate 21 for their flight to come in. They decided they would fly into Virginia together. Darryl would go to his mother's from the airport, while Simone would stop to meet a client and then go to Nikki's. Simone would be in town for two weeks. Actually, her departure would depend on the pending meetings and client needs. Darryl made no immediate plans to leave. Now that his visit would include more than just the court case, he couldn't pinpoint a date for his return flight. He would have to talk with Darrell and Mr. Simpson before leaving. There were some things that they would need to know before he could leave for Detroit.

"Did you want something from the gift shop?"

"No, I'm fine. You look worried though. Is everything okay?"

"No, Simone. We need to talk. I can't tell you here. Not now. When you get to Nikki's, call me. We will meet for dinner or a drink. I need to talk with you tonight though."

"Darryl, why didn't we have this talk last night?"

"Simone, this is on a different level, topic, I mean, this is about something else."

"Flight 729 is now boarding at Gate 21. All passengers please show your boarding pass to the flight attendants."

As the intercom announced their flight, they moved closer to the gate doors for boarding.

"C'mon, we'll talk later, when we're alone."

Simone followed Darryl and the other passengers as they showed their boarding passes to the stewardess prior to boarding the plane. She was interested in what he had to say and didn't want to wait until later. Their tickets were across the aisle from each other and conversation would be limited. Simone found her seat and adjusted it to her comfort. She waited for Darryl to do the same.

"Darryl, is there a problem? I don't want to wait to get to Nikki's to find out I did something to annoy you."

"You didn't. It has nothing to do with you. I need to talk to someone who will listen, and I think you will. I just can't talk about it here on the plane."

"What about when we land?"

"You have a client to see. Besides, Darlene is picking me up to go to my mother's."

"Why did you ask Darlene? I'll have a rental car. I could have dropped you off."

"Simone, you can't take me to my mother's house. We have to keep this relationship between us a secret. I don't want to lose you or my family. If I'm forced to make a choice it won't be you. Let's not get too frisky. We can't flaunt this relationship in front of my people."

Darryl's voice was raspy as he whispered his words of warning. Simone just stared at him. She understood what he said, but she was confused. *What could you possibly want me to listen to if it's not about us?*" As she leaned back in her seat, she closed her eyes to let her anger die.

The flight landed and Simone realized that she slept through the entire ride. Darryl stood, got their carry on luggage and extended the courtesy for Simone to walk ahead of him. He didn't say a word to her as they walked the length of the plane.

Simone looked for the signs that read car rentals and found that she had to go in the opposite direction of the arrival gate.

"Darryl, I'll call you. Hopefully, this will be the last time we'll have to separate this way. I wish you would trust me enough not to have to make a big deal out of sharing your feelings with me."

"Feelings, listen Simone, I don't have a problem sharing my feelings. I like you a lot. Don't push it girl. I will tell you what I feel when the time is right for me. I'm going to ask you again, please call me from Nikki's later on. We will meet and we will talk then. Not before."

"Darryl, I don't understand. Just tell me why."

"Why, what Simone? I just wanted to vent. I've got things on my mind; the court, the accident. Do you want to be my sounding board, my shoulder of support or what?"

"Alright Darryl, we'll do this your way, but I don't like you starting to tell me something and leaving me in suspense. You should have just waited until later."

"Maybe so, but I said it as the thought crossed my mind. Listen, babe, let's not argue. I want to see you later. I need to see you later. I don't need you to make me feel like everyone in this airport is watching us. I will talk to you later hon, okay?"

Simone turned heading for the sign that said car rentals without a goodbye. Her thoughts ran rampant as she listened to the rhythm of her heels tapping the waxed floor. *"What will he do now? I'll make him want me. I'll make him beg for me. If he does, Francine can kiss her sweet thing good bye."*

Darryl had his own thoughts watching Simone turn and walk away. As the sound of her stilettos began to fade, he picked up his luggage and headed for the sign that said, "Arrival Passenger Pick-Up".

"She can't possibly think with all the shit that's going on I'm going to play games. If she doesn't call, oh well. She's was good lay."

<h1 style="text-align:center;">Chapter 33</h1>

arlene spotted Darryl and began to wave. He recognized her immediately, smiled and picked up his pace.

"Hey Sis; thanks for coming to pick me up. I would have rented a car but that nephew of ours was against it."

"Rell told me your car was waiting in the parking lot at D.Q. Enterprises. I can take you there on the way to Mama's house so you can pick it up."

"That will be good. How's Derek? Have you been there to visit with him?"

"Darryl, I can't. Not yet, I want to remember him as he was if, well you know. Marci was there yesterday with Shai and Tonya. They had it out. Words got pretty bad between them, so I heard. I guess I'll be the buffer for this one too. Tonya doesn't want Shai visiting Derek alone or when she's there. The hospital is abiding by her wishes. Marci was with Shai yesterday, and I guess I'll go with her today. Darryl someone tried to kill that boy."

"The problem is they almost did. Do the cops have a lead?"

"None, I'm parked over here."

They went to the car in silence buried in their own thoughts. Darlene never wondered if Darryl stopped gambling. She knew he hadn't, although he promised her and Nana, Darlene could tell. She also knew he spent a lot of time gambling with Derek. She wanted to ask him if Derek's debt could have been paid off another way. She was still in shock that someone tried to take his life. She pulled into the parking lot of D.Q. Enterprises. It was still early enough to catch 'Rell before lunch.

"Darryl, are you going to stop in to see 'Rell. If you are, I'll meet you at Mama's house."

"No, I don't think I'm going to stop. I'll follow you to the house. I really want to see Derek and talk to Mr. Simpson about this court case. Does anyone know if it was postponed since Derek got hurt?"

"Rell would probably know that. I don't know. I didn't get the news about that until late last night. Marci told me about it, and she didn't know much. So what are you going to do? Are you going to Mama's now? I have to make a stop before I go there though."

"Well you go ahead. I'm still going to the house first. I'm going to drop off my luggage and make a few calls. I can see 'Rell later."

"I'll see you at the house then. Tell Mama I'll be there shortly."

"Hey Darlene, do you really think someone tried to kill him? I mean, maybe it was just an accident."

"I'll see you at Mama's, we'll talk there. I don't think it's over Darryl. They wanted something. Him dead, his debt paid for that damn gambling y'all do or something. It ain't over and they know it and so do you."

Darryl didn't realize that Darlene was angry. He knew she wasn't mad at him, but he didn't expect the answer he got. She was right. Darryl knew it wasn't over. That's why he needed to talk with 'Rell and Mr. Simpson.

"I'll see you there."

Darlene pulled off leaving her brother standing in the parking lot. He went to the security desk on the main floor of D.Q. Enterprises. 'Rell usually left the keys at the desk whenever Darryl's rentals were secured by him.

"Mr. Mince, how are you today?"

"I'm fine Kenny. Did Mr. Mince leave the keys for my car?"

"No sir he didn't. He said I should tell you that he and Mr. Simpson were waiting for you upstairs. I'll take your bags sir, if you'd like. I can put them in the vehicle for you."

"Oh well okay, thanks."

Darryl left his luggage and made his way to 'Rell's office.

Chapter 34

Ms. Berry greeted Darryl as he entered the reception area. Darryl always wanted to talk to her outside of the office but Ms. Yvonne Berry wouldn't give him the time to ask her out. She would make sure her conversations with him were always professional and never personal. Darryl told D.Q. and 'Rell, she was a fine 'red bone', and that they should put in a good word for him. Neither of them took him serious and didn't think twice about his flirtatious gestures. Ms. Berry was indeed a good looking woman. She was in her mid-forties and well taken care of. Her skin was flawless and she didn't wear much makeup. Although she wore glasses, they fit her face, as though she was modeling them. Her clothes were always complimented by her handbag, shoes and accessories. Ms. Berry was what 'Rell and Mitch called a golden dime, and they protected what was gold. Darryl didn't stand a chance.

"Good morning Mr. Mince."

"Good morning Ms. Berry. How have you been?"

"Just fine thank you. Please have a seat Mr. Simpson will have to be informed you've arrived. It may take a few minutes before he comes to the office. Do you want to see Mr. Mince or Mr. Carter while you wait?"

"No, if you don't mind, I'll sit here where the view is beautiful."

"Can I offer you coffee or tea? There is a fresh pot in the office."

"No thank you. I'm not much of a coffee drinker. I don't see your cup. Haven't you had your morning coffee yet?"

Darryl hoped to be able to change the subject shortly. He wouldn't make it too personal yet. He was grateful she was talking to him. Usually she would leave the area until 'Rell came out.

"I'm not fond of coffee. I drink more tea. I've had a cup this morning though. You should try it. It's herbal but it is rather good."

"One of those relaxing teas?"

"No this one is just an herbal blend. Those that say they're for relaxing, tend to put me to sleep."

"Oh I see, is 'Rell in his office?"

Darryl wondered what was with the small talk. She never carried on any conversation. He wanted to think he had her interest, but he couldn't be sure.

"He's in with Mr. Carter. They are aware you arrived. The security desk called."

This was a new procedure. He never was announced before.

"Is that something new?"

"Yes, Mr. Mince requested it as of today. Since his brother's accident, he wants to be aware of anyone entering this floor. Didn't you notice the security office is on this floor now? They moved up here this morning."

'Rell wasn't taking a chance of not knowing who was in the building or on his floor. Darryl couldn't blame him. This court case and the so called accident had him rattled too. The intercom sounded with the voice of a security officer.

"Ms. Berry, this is security. Mr. Simpson has arrived."

"Send him to Mr. Minces' office. He is expecting him. Thank you Kenny."

"Well I'm impressed. Two security checks and then you; he's taking things a little serious huh?"

"Mr. Mince is always serious. He reminds me of his father. It's easy to work for him because you know what he tolerates.

If he doesn't tolerate it, it will have to go. I like that about him."

"Ms. Berry, may I ask you a question?"

Mr. Simpson came through the reception area door interrupting Darryl's question.

"Good morning Yvonne. How are you sweetie?"

"Good morning Mr. Simpson, I'm fine, how about you?"

The intercom sounded again. This time it was 'Rell.

"Ms. Berry, please send in my uncle and Mr. Simpson. I am in my office."

"Certainly Mr. Mince, gentlemen, you know your way. Have a good morning."

Darryl sighed and stood ready to proceed to 'Rell's office. He shook Mr. Simpson's hand and the two entered the glass doors leading to the offices on the floor. They walked down the hall in silence. Darryl had no idea what would be discussed in 'Rell's office, but he was glad someone had the foresight to call a meeting. They walked into the office where 'Rell was sorting papers. After putting the pile in the desired order, he placed them on the conference table. It reminded Darryl of a crime scene layout. There were four or five pictures of what appeared to be dead bodies with the articles to match.

"Rell, what is this about?" 'Rell continued to lay out articles and photos.

"Uncle Darryl, how was your morning flight? I took the liberty of renting you a vehicle and having it brought here. I hope you didn't mind having to come to my office. I figured before you got swamped with family issues you would want to talk to clear up a few things."

"I'm not understanding, maybe I'm confused. Do you think I'm involved in these murders?"

"No Uncle Darryl, these were sent to me in an envelope marked confidential. When I opened it and read the cover sheet I thought we needed to have a serious talk."

'Rell handed his uncle the sheet that served as the cover sheet for the envelope. Darryl read the paper and put it on the table. He sat in the chair and waited for 'Rell and Mr. Simpson to take a seat.

"Rell, we didn't know what we were getting into. We just got in too deep. At first we were winning regularly. Then we met this guy who said he knew a joint where the stakes were a little high but the turn around money was good. 'Rell, you have to believe me man. This started long before we knew you or had a chance to stand on our own. I don't think these guys would kill someone though. It was all about paying the turn around money back. Derek set up a few guys. We used their money and promised to get them double, sometimes triple back. It would have worked if we won. I gave up some of my stocks in my company and some of the pension funds that I had. I gave all I could."

"You mean you paid these guys their money?"

"Yes, 'Rell we had to. They wanted to tell D.Q. what was happening. We owed big money. I got money from Mama and Darlene. When you came around, we were trying to pay off the last guys that we cut a deal with. Derek paid them with money he got from…"

Darryl's voice drifted off as though his thoughts faded into fear. He stared at Mr. Simpson and 'Rell, not saying another word. They both waited for him to speak.

"Mr. Mince if you know something that would help us catch these men who harmed your nephew, I hope you would tell us. It may mean a lot to the trial and to the family's security."

"Security, what do you mean? We paid them their damn money."

"And they paid Derek back."

"Are you sure they're the ones?"

"Who else Uncle Darryl; is there someone we don't know about?"

"What about the people who got paid with Derek on this logo scam thing?"

'Rell and Mr. Simpson looked up from the table where the three sat. 'Rell began to collect the pictures and put them into the envelope.

"Hold it 'Rell. I'm serious. Derek had to pay those guys too. I think it's one of them that ratted Derek out. They knew I was his side kick, and he was mine; at the tables, the races and during this logo thing."

"Uncle Darryl, you were involved in the scam?"

"I knew enough about it to be involved. I knew the operation, you know, how it went. 'Rell, those guys have connections and they move without anybody noticing. They don't want Derek to take the stand and neither do I."

"But they called you and me for the prosecution."

The intercom sounded with Ms. Berry telling Mr. Simpson, he had a call from Judge Thorne's chamber. The intercom clicked and the phone rang. Mr. Simpson picked up the phone.

"Good morning, your honor. Yes. I see. Yes. No sir just the uncle and the brother. Yes, thank you sir. I'm not sure he has. I will. Thank you again sir. Good day."

'Rell and Darryl sat patiently as Mr. Simpson put the phone onto its cradle. He returned to the table in silence.

"Stan, what did he say?"

He said, "In light of your relationship with Derek, the defendant, the case would be postponed until Derek's condition is better. It will give us time to do some research. We need to start with what the prosecutor thinks you guys know."

Chapter 35

It was twelve thirty before Darlene got to her mother's house. As she pulled into the driveway, she thought it was strange that she didn't see any signs of a rental car in the driveway; which meant Darryl wasn't there. Darlene really wanted to talk with him before he started running around visiting and taking care of what he would say was business. She was concerned about Derek's condition and the mess the two of them were involved in. Darlene parked her car in the driveway leaving room for Darryl to park and her mother, to pull out if she chose to.

As Darlene turned her key in the door, she could hear her mother laughing softly. She couldn't imagine what would make her giggle, but she could tell she was in good spirits. Darlene just knew she would find her mother on the phone or watching a program on the television.

"Hey Mama, I hear you. Where are you? What's got you laughing so?"

As she turned toward the hall leading to the bedrooms, Darlene bumped into Reverend Wilcox. His face was full of shaving cream.

"Hello Sister Darlene, excuse me a moment, I need to clean my face."

Darlene looked at Reverend in disbelief. *"I know Reverend Wilcox didn't get dressed here with Momma. Where's his car? What's going on?"* Questions continued in Darlene's mind as Reverend

Wilcox scurried on to the hall bathroom. Darlene didn't know whether to continue to her mother's bedroom, check the other rooms or to return to the living room and wait for her mother to come out. She chose the safest of the three options and returned to the living room and waited. After five minutes or more, Nana entered the living room smiling.

"Hey baby, I expected you earlier than this. Darryl called saying you were on your way. You got hung up?"

Darlene wanted to ask her mother about Reverend Wilcox but decided to wait for her mother to explain it when he entered the living room.

"I stopped at two of the shops. I have a new girl in one and need to fire a girl in the other. As usual, it's good on one side of town and drama on the other. I need an older group of employees, but it's a young girl's field. I don't know what I would do if all the shops went into a drama mode together."

"You would handle it. The drama is always the same. Women are the same. Have you been to see Derek yet?"

"Mama, to be honest, I don't know if I can do it. I mean, just burying D.Q. and all. I don't want to see Derek until he's out of CCU. Did you go?"

"We were going up there this afternoon. That's what Wallace was doing. We thought you and your brother would have been here by now. Wallace needed to shave and get cleaned up."

"Now if that don't sound like the Rev spent the night. Mama and the Reverend? I need to call Nikki."

"Oh, I was wondering what I walked in on."

"Nothing, chile, nothing; he had to shave and get cleaned up. He wanted to shape his beard and that's all."

"Mama, why are you explaining to me? Both, you and the Reverend are grown. You don't owe anyone an explanation. I'm not one of your congregation members."

"I know you're not. I've tried to get you to join the congregation for months. And I don't owe them an explanation either. We have to deal with them and the rumor mill, you know."

"Tell them the truth. It's none of their business. You and Reverend Wilcox have been friends, since he came to the church. You've gotten a lot closer since D.Q.'s sickness and death. That's all they need to know. If you want to tell them more that's up to the two of you, not them. They can think what they want. And that's the kind of drama that I avoid by not being a member of the congregation."

"Well thank you Darlene, I guess I needed to hear that. Believe me, they're going to talk. And I might as well get used to the fact that it ain't all gonna be nice. But I don't owe them the satisfaction of knowing my business; I will let you and the family know when we're ready."

"Know what?"

"I said when we're ready Darlene. Where's Darryl?"

Darlene learned at a young age that when Nana said when she was ready it could be longer than never. So the subject was quickly changed.

"I guess he's meeting with 'Rell and Mr. Simpson."

Reverend Wilcox entered the room. Nana rose from her seat and went into the kitchen but continued talking to Darlene. Reverend Wilcox sat on the couch across from Darlene.

"Darlene would you like some lunch? We were going to eat here before we left for the hospital. I don't know what time the meeting at the office will be over. I want to get to the hospital before Tonya gets there. I really don't want to deal with her. You know she put Shai out of the hospital yesterday. That child is a nervous wreck. She was by here this morning before she went to see Derek. She wasn't sure how she could duck her own mother to see her brother. Tonya is sick."

"You don't have to fix me anything. I'll wait here for Darryl. I'll get something if I get hungry. Has Tonya called here at all?"

"No, you know she and I don't get along. All that mess she did during and after the funeral. Tonya would use this to get back at us. She's just that spiteful. Did Darryl know you were going to wait here for him?"

"Yeah, I told him I would be here. Reverend you and Mama go on and eat, I'll be okay. I just find it funny that Tonya calls me regardless, this time she didn't."

"Wallace you want iced tea or lemonade?"

"Iced tea will be fine Jewels, just fine."

"Darlene come on in the kitchen with us."

That was Reverend Wilcox's cue. He got up and made his way for the kitchen. Nana looked at his face and ran her hand around the trim of his beard. Darlene couldn't wait until they left so she could call Nikki. Nana and the Reverend ate as they talked about Derek's condition. More than a half an hour passed during their meal and discussion.

"Well Darlene, I can't understand why Darryl hasn't called yet. Wallace and I are going to the hospital for a while. Are you still going to wait for him?"

"Yes Ma'am. With all that has happened, I think we need to talk. I really think Darryl knows something that may help us understand what or why this happened to Derek."

"Do you think Darryl knows something that the police don't?"

"Yes I do, but I hope he doesn't. But I won't know until I talk with him."

"Well, if you should decide to leave before we get back, lock up and leave the light in the living room on. We'll probably be at the church until eight this evening."

"Okay, Mama. Reverend, have a good day."

Darlene waited until she heard the car drive off. She went into the kitchen and got a glass of juice. Returning to the living room she didn't hesitate to get comfortable with the telephone.

"Nikki, I sure hope you're home. There's a few things a sister needs to know."

Chapter 36

*T*onya chose a window seat in the restaurant while waiting for Karlton to arrive. She went into deep thought about the days that followed D.Q.'s death. Those days had been the hardest for her. She had not come to grips about his death, although her outward appearance didn't show it, or so she thought. She started each day with a strong drink before going to work. In her position as the Director of Programming at Richmond Cablevision, she could come and go. Tonya chose to go every lunch hour to have a drink to keep her going for the afternoon. After a day at work, she would go home open a beer and sit on the couch for what would seem like hours. The only outside interest that Tonya Mince acquired was how to get financially attached to D.Q. Enterprises. 'Rell proved to be a bit difficult. It became apparent that he wouldn't be easy to win over, but she wouldn't let that stop her. Tonya was determined. She had a plan to follow but for now she had to get Karlton either on her side or out of the picture.

Karlton parked his car in the restaurant's parking lot. This meeting with Tonya was unexpected, and he really didn't know what it could be about. He knew Tonya didn't want him to reveal any information about her that would ruin her image. He could care less about her image. Since D.Q.'s death, he hadn't received a dime to keep his mouth shut. He lived the last twenty-five years on what he called the D.Q. stipend. If he couldn't have Tonya's love, he would settle for the money. Three thousand dollars a month was used to aid his plans to get Tonya to love him again.

He worked from his home as a consultant for an insurance company in Pennsylvania. It wasn't that he needed the money; he needed the connection with Tonya. If she collected from D.Q. Enterprises it would be because of him. Without him, she had no link financially to D.Q. Enterprises. He would ruin it all for her if she didn't include him in her life. Karlton knew Tonya wouldn't give up her claim to her dead husband's estate. He spotted Tonya, who smiled signaling for him to come and join her.

"Good morning, Mrs. Mince. You look better than I expected this morning."

"What does that mean Karl? What did you expect?"

"The tone of your voice on the phone didn't leave me to believe you would be smiling. I'm glad my assumption was wrong. You look good Tonya."

The two had not seen each other in years and Karlton always told Tonya if it had not been for D.Q. he would have been her husband and love for a lifetime. She looked him over. He was the 'Billy Dee' type for sure and hadn't lost a touch of his charisma. She could definitely use a night to persuade him to see her point of view. She couldn't be sure he would go for it. He had always been money hungry and usually didn't work hard for it; that was his downfall. The women he enjoyed the most were those who took good care of him. She refused to take care of a man. Karlton had used her for the past twenty five years, it had to stop.

Tonya would convince him that joining her to get finances from D.Q. Enterprises would be a winning situation for them. Her secret would be safe, and he could continue living the life of luxury. She didn't feel she had much to lose and a relationship, even though it would start as business, with Karlton Harris wouldn't be bad. D.Q. died in May and it was now November, people wouldn't think twice about her being seen with him. They would assume that she got on with her life. If she could convince 'Rell that she had changed and wasn't bitter, the money for Derek would be in her hands. She would then give Karlton his portion for playing the role and say goodbye if she needed to.

"You look well yourself. How have you been and how are things in Baltimore?"

"Things are well. So to what do I owe the pleasure of the forbidden face to face?"

"D.Q. is dead Karl. We don't have to dread face to face meetings."

"Well it was always your rule. No more face to face meetings."

Tonya smiled. She remembered the argument they had when she told him she couldn't see him anymore. She felt that her husband had someone following them. She met Karlton Harris two years after she and D.Q. were married. Although she didn't intend to have more than an innocent drink with a good looking man after work, it lasted for longer than five years. Karlton was indeed someone she loved. Things went sour when she said she wanted to see him less because of D.Q.'s suspicions. When she told him that she wouldn't see him anymore he decided to put a noose around her neck.

Karlton made several threats to tell D.Q. about their relationship. He would tell her husband that it lasted five years; he would mention that she stayed married only for his money; and all their other intimate secrets. Over the years, the price raised. Three thousand was the current fee and Tonya had paid it every month or every month and a half. Anything past two months and Karlton would call threatening to visit D.Q. at the office. She gave in every time.

"I see. So since D.Q. is dead, revisiting the past is allowed?"

"I think it needs to be revisited, maybe even renewed. If we face the facts Karl, neither of us forgot the past."

"Oh, you wanted to. I insisted you didn't. Tonya, you probably think bad of me for having you pay hush money for the life and love we had. That money kept my memory fresh with what we had and how deep down, you still loved me."

"Karl, you really are stuck in time."

"Am I? Prove it. Walk away and don't turn around, don't call me, beg me to leave you alone."

"Do you think I would be sitting here if you didn't have me paying for our past?"

"Yes. I didn't just do it for the money. I did it for us. I have a beautiful home in West Virginia for us. I built it just the way we described the home we wanted together. I go there often but it's empty without you. I always thought D.Q. would leave you for his woman. What was her name?"

"Nikki Robbins, you knew about her too?"

"Yeah babe, I knew. Anyway, I thought he would have let you go earlier than when he did. The timing was wrong. I was out of the country for a year and a half and I wanted to be close to you when I came into your life again. When I heard he was sick, I waited until he died and picked up on how you were. I called you hoping to end our little charade. Now Derek is hurt and I'm willing to stand in the shadows and wait again. I must say, I'm glad you called."

Karlton threw out the bait and waited for Tonya to grab it. He knew she couldn't resist. She wanted to play the game as bad as he did. Tonya was never good at being one step ahead, that's how she wound up with nothing in the will. She didn't play hard against men. She put up a good front. He liked that about her, she had spunk.

"Are you hungry, we can order if you'd like?"

"I'll have Tonya."

"Karl, this is, I mean, do you think we can just pick up what we had again?"

"Where did it go Tonya? Tell me you never thought about us. Even if you did tell me that I don't think I would believe it. We have a different kind of love, a solid love. You were married to money. As you said, D.Q. is dead and the money died with him. It can be about us now."

Tonya smiled. Just what she wanted, Karlton would be in for it now. She would tell him later about her plans to conquer D.Q. Enterprises through Derek.

"I haven't had an appetite for months. I'm starving. Can we order now?"

"Can pleasure be the desert?"

Karlton smiled slowly. Just what he wanted, Tonya would be a part of his life now. There was no one between them. And if she hadn't given up her stocks at D.Q. Enterprises, he would share the profits with her.

Chapter 37

Simone made calls and appointments most of the morning after her arrival. Nikki spent the morning typing out proposals, thank you notes and confirmation letters. Interior Dreams was well on its way to making a great start. After working most of the morning and the early part of the afternoon, Nikki and Simone decided to order Chinese food and watch movies. They both agreed to keep their conversation off work. They were determined to spend the rest of the day and the weekend relaxing. Monday would be a full day of business.

"Girl, that food tasted like it was made just for me. I must have been starving and didn't know it."

"Nikki, we both were starving. Pass me your tray. Do you want anymore tea? I'm headed for the kitchen."

"Yes, please. I don't think I can move."

"What's up with Sam? He didn't call for you this morning, that's unusual."

"He's handling some church business for Reverend Wilcox, he called earlier. The Reverend went with Mrs. Mince to the hospital. Derek was in a bad auto accident. Girl he was almost killed."

Simone did as Darryl told her she pretended it was all news. She would let Nikki tell her all the information before she would join in with her thoughts.

"He's supposed to have more tests done. According to 'Rell, they're hoping that he doesn't have brain damage. It's a mess. They think it was done deliberately. 'Rell and Mr. Simpson think it might be connected to Derek and Darryl's gambling. Darryl is due in town this weekend. They're going to have to tell this man that his life is in danger. I'm kinda glad they didn't have to fly out to Detroit to get him. I can't imagine how that would affect Francine."

"You mean the people who tried to kill Derek may be after Darryl too?"

"Simone, I'm only repeating what 'Rell said. If the accident was due to some gambling debts, Darryl could owe some of the same people."

Simone was quiet. All she could remember was Darryl sounding helpless at the airport. *He said he needed to talk. What was I thinking?* Simone needed to know where Darryl was.

"Do they know when Darryl is coming in town?"

"I don't know if 'Rell said today or tomorrow. They'll get him when he lands. I don't know the plans from there though. I guess to question him and tell him what they suspect. I just hope he's okay."

"Yeah, that's some scary shit, Nikki. I mean they have proven their point with Derek. Wow! Darryl's family could be in jeopardy. What about 'Rell and Shai?"

"Rell seemed to believe they just want their money. Derek and Darryl gamble a lot. It's just scary."

The phone rang and Nikki picked it up smiling.

"Darlene. Hold on girl; let me get the cordless phone out of the other room. Simone hang that one up. I'll be off in a minute."

Simone was glad for the minute to call Darryl from her cell phone. The phone took forever to connect and then his answering machine picked up.

"Darryl, this is Simone. Call me. I'm really scared for you baby. Call me."

Simone hung up the phone only for it to ring while in her hand.

"Hello, Darryl? Oh baby, I'm so glad to hear from you. Oh, you're still with them. Okay good. Yes, call me when you're done. I'm better now that I heard your voice. Thanks for calling me back. Yes, I'll be fine. Call me and let me know where to meet you. Okay, bye."

Nikki was on her way back to the den when she questioned herself about what she heard Simone say as she spoke on the phone. *Did she say Darryl? Did she say baby? What the hell is Simone up to now? I hope she's not sleeping with Darryl. Aw shit!*" Although Nikki knew her thoughts usually didn't lead her wrong, she would keep them to herself until she had concrete proof.

"That was Darlene, she's coming over. She was waiting for Darryl, but he's still with Mr. Simpson and 'Rell. I told her come on over. I hope you don't mind the company."

"No, besides Darlene is family. You know being D.Q.'s sister and all. I'll be glad to see her.

"I bet you would. Simone, I better be wrong, cause if you're messing around with Darryl, all hell is going to break loose."

<h1 style="text-align:center">Chapter 38</h1>

Shai, Nana and Reverend Wilcox left the hospital when Derek was taken down for tests. The nurse informed them that it would be at least four to five hours before he would be back in his room. Tonya didn't come to the hospital, which meant she probably would be there for the evening visit. Nana's suggestion to leave and call later sounded best for all of them. Reverend Wilcox opened the passenger door of Nana's car and helped her in before taking his place on the driver's side. Shai stood by waiting to tell them goodbye.

"Shai, you take care of yourself, young lady."

"I will Reverend, thank you for coming and your continuous prayers." Shai felt good that the Reverend and Nana were with her during her visit.

"Shai, are you going to work at all today?"

"Nana, I took the day off. I didn't want to be there worried about Derek and the tests. I had no idea it would be four to five hours before he would return to his room. I guess if I had known that I could have gone to work."

"Well, if you'd like, you're more than welcome to sit with me the balance of the day. I think Marci and Mia are coming over straight from work. I'm going to cook something for everyone. Your Aunt Darlene will be back to meet your Uncle Darryl there and 'Rell, well, he'll stop by too I'm sure. You might as well come by."

"I'll talk with Marci and arrange to meet her there."

"I'll be there earlier if you want to spend a little time talking with me. I know your mother's attitude is a lot for you to take on Shai. You should be able to see your brother without worrying about Tonya's behavior."

"I'll be fine Nana. I've got a few things to take care of before coming to your house. I'll be there though, don't worry about me."

Reverend Wilcox closed his door and started the engine. Shai walked to her car and waved as they drove by. It was almost one o'clock, she was a little tired. She decided to go to 'Rell's house.

'Rell and Mr. Simpson finally convinced Darryl how it was possible that the men who attacked Derek could possibly attack him.

"Uncle Darryl let me have two of my security personnel with you until the police sort this thing out."

"Mr. Mince, I'll call the police with the information you've given us this morning, and I'm sure they'll pick these guys up this afternoon. There's enough information question them at least."

"Mr. Simpson I hope these are the guys, but what if it has to do with this logo thing. I mean we're guessing here. It could be anyone who has a thing for Derek, past boss, past client, someone he owes money. The list could go on. I agree it may involve me, but then again, it may not. Darrell, I'm not used to spending my days looking over my shoulder. No thanks, I don't want your boys with me, wherever I go. I have personal things to handle here too."

"Uncle Darryl, I wasn't trying to cramp your style or anything. When you don't want them around, tell them. They'll meet you when you need them. I'm just making them available for you to have them as needed. I want you to be safe and of course comfortable."

"Alright, give me their number. If I think someone is following me, or I spot someone around more than once or twice I'll call them."

"Well gentlemen, let me call the police and get this search started. I'll talk with you later 'Rell. Mr. Mince, as always, I'm glad to see you and don't hesitate to call if you should need my assistance."

"Thanks, Mr. Simpson. I will, and can you call me if the police should find those guys? I would like to know if they tried to kill Derek."

'Rell and Darryl stood to shake Mr. Simpson's hand.

"Thanks Stan. Call me when you get word on anything."

The intercom sounded off as Mr. Simpson walked out the door.

"Mr. Mince, line one sir, it's Ms. Mince."

"Thanks, Ms. Berry. Hello, Shai. How's Derek?"

"Rell, I'm going to your grandmother's. Will I see you there?" Darryl spoke as he was going out the door. 'Rell covered the phone's receiver.

"I'll be there later. I have a few stops to make. Don't forget to call the guys if you need them."

"Thanks man. I'll see you at the house." Darryl left the office.

'Rell returned to Shai's call, "Shai, yes, how is Derek?"

"They took him down for testing. They won't be done until about four or five. I don't think we'll have the results until tomorrow or the next day. Otherwise, he was resting. He never opened his eyes. He's not hooked to all the tubes today though. They only have the one tube connected to his head. It looks different though, and he's still hooked to all the monitors. I can't tell if he feels or hears me at all. The nurse said his response is weak, but they have had one."

"Has he moaned or anything?"

"No, they didn't mention it. Nana and Reverend Wilcox sat with me for a while. They've been spending a lot of time together. What's up with that?"

"I don't know but Nana was close to him before, wasn't she?"

"I don't recall it being that close. Anyway, my mother didn't show up so it was a blessing. Are you going to Nana's house later? She said everyone would be there then. I think because Uncle Darryl is in town. She'll be cooking. That's a big enough reason."

They both laughed. If Nana opened her doors the neighbors would be there too. 'Rell thought about it. He hadn't made up his mind totally when he told his uncle yes. He decided if Shai wanted to deal with the questions that may arise he'd be there for her.

"What are you going to do?"

"I don't want them questioning where we are, so I figured I would go."

"No, you figured it for both of us. I have to stop at the house first then I'll be there."

"Okay, I'm at the house."

"Good, I'll see you there."

Chapter 39

arci and Mitch decided to stop at 'Rell's house before stopping by Nana's. Marci called Shai to remind her they still hadn't talked with Shai and 'Rell alone about the pregnancy. She wanted to know about the dinner as well. Shai was glad she mentioned it with Derek in the hospital she almost forgot about their previous plans.

"Rell, Marci and Mitch are coming by before we all go to Nana's. We could have our talk with them tonight just in case things get crazy over the weekend."

'Rell was in the bedroom closet looking for a sweater to wear with his jeans and boots. He didn't answer Shai because he knew it was more of a statement than a question. She entered the bedroom and found him standing in his boxers.

"Baby, you shouldn't tease me like this. I might forget that we don't have time for the pleasure."

'Rell laughed. He slipped on his jeans and continued his search for the sweater.

"What's wrong 'Rell?"

"Just out of it, I guess. I don't know. It seems like things are out of sorts. I'm working on someone else's time line. I had plans on going through dad's things this weekend and finding out why Mr. Simpson said don't say anything about the pregnancy until I did; that's got me wondering. These guys trying to kill Derek; that's got me wondering. Then there's Reverend and Nana."

"That's got us all wondering!"

Shai interrupted and they both laughed. She walked closer to 'Rell and kissed him gently in the mouth. They both hugged and held each other for what would have lasted longer but the phone rang.

"Hello….Yes, this is he….Yes, Yes, 'Rell that's right…I see. Well, if you call me and let me know……Yes, I will…. Thank you…. Good bye…. Yes I will….Thank Thank you again."

'Rell hung up the receiver smiling. Shai didn't speak, waiting for him to speak.

"That was the nurse at the hospital. The doctor told her to call me. It seems like Derek began to mumble my name going in for one of the tests. They thought it would be good for me to be available when he came out of the testing. They're not going to give him a heavy drug to see if he'll respond to me. She said that was a good sign. He remembered my name."

"What did he say exactly?"

"She didn't say, just that he was mumbling 'Rell, 'Rell."

"I wonder what he wanted to say."

"Well she said she would call my cell when they wanted me there. They have both numbers Ms. Berry gave it to them. Shit. Suppose your mother is there. She won't allow me to talk with him."

"It's not you, it's me. I'll stay at Nana's and you go. Maybe he just needs to talk to you."

"You may have a point, we'll see. I'm just glad he responded in some sort of way. Hey, I never asked, does Derek have a girlfriend?"

"He did. I don't think they're together anymore. I think it was an on again off again thing. Anyway she lives near Ft. Lee. They broke up about a month ago. I don't know if he was involved with someone else. A few of his friends have been calling though, so if there is someone they would have told her."

"Okay, look babe, I'm looking for my black and grey sweater. I'm running late now. Don't tease me anymore."

"Only if you promise to tease me later."

"It's a promise I need that more than anything else." Shai smiled and turned to leave the room.

"Hey Shai, you're showing. Did you notice that?"

"Yeah, I went shopping this afternoon and picked up some maternity pants. I need the room."

"So what's this dude's name that you're dating?"

"I didn't think of a name?"

"I think Nana may ask you. She may even want to meet him."

"Rell, I hate this. I'll wear a really baggy sweater. She's seen it before; she won't think much of it. She calls it my slummin' sweater."

"Think of a name babe. It may still come up."

It was about six o'clock when the door bell rang. Shai opened the door welcoming Marci and Mitch inside.

'Rell went to the refrigerator grabbed the beers, ice, wine and soda. He arranged the beverages and glasses at the bar. Mitch walked in the den smiling as he greeted his friend.

"Hey man, I didn't see you all day. How was the meeting with your uncle, and Mr. Simpson?"

"Informative, but it's all got to be checked out. My uncle made a good point. It could have been a lot of people out to get Derek with this logo thing.

"Did he know who Derek was dealing with in Carson Web with the logo scam?"

He named those that he thought were involved. Stan will research it and get back to me. Hey, I got a call from the hospital. Derek mumbled my name while he was going for testing. They said they would call when they think he's coming around."

"Wow, 'Rell did he say anything else?"

"No Marci, just my name over and over."

"Well, that's a good sign though."

Shai was quiet while the three of them continued talking about Derek's progress. She left them in the den and went into the kitchen. Marci followed her.

"Shai, are you okay?"

"Marci, it's just weird. Derek begins to come around and speaks 'Rell's name and nothing about me or my mom. He's only known 'Rell for six months. Why the bond with 'Rell and not me? I can even understand not calling my mother's name but why not mine."

"Shai, let's be glad he remembered someone. This is a sign that there may be little to no brain damage. It's a good thing. You'll see."

"Marci, why am I taking it so hard then? I wanted to cry when 'Rell told me, and I wouldn't be crying because I was happy. I'm upset that I wasn't the one he called on."

"You're pregnant, they say when women get pregnant they get over emotional. You'll be fine. Let 'Rell talk him back to us all if he can."

'Rell called for them from the den where he was pouring soda for Marci and Shai.

"Ladies, what's up? We all need to talk before going to, Nana's and you know she'll be calling us if we don't get there soon."

Shai followed Marci back to the den. Mitch looked at Shai's sweater and touched the hem as she passed him to sit on the stool next to 'Rell.

"That sweater camouflages the baby well."

Marci and 'Rell laughed while Shai stood and modeled.

"I thought no one could tell with this on. I don't want to explain anything tonight. I think it'll work don't you Marci?"

"Yeah, Mitch is right. It makes a good cover. It's a good thing it's not summer."

"Well," Shai picked up her soda and took a sip, "Mitch and Marci that's why the two of you were being invited to dinner tomorrow. 'Rell and I have decided to keep the babies."

"Babies?" Marci still hadn't been told Shai was carrying twins.

"Yes, twins. We wanted you guys to know right away. The doctor said it would be a risk to have an abortion. A risk for both, me and the twins, I'm five months pregnant. Twins are not usually full term. I may have them within the next three months or so."

"But you're small. I can barely tell you're pregnant."

'Rell rubbed her belly. "That's a good thing. If we can get through this with the least amount of drama it will suit me fine."

"You're right, but Shai, what are you going to tell everyone?"

Mitch sat and watched 'Rell's reaction as she told them how the story would unfold from her dating an intern at the hospital, him being transferred and her not wanting to go with him to Seattle, Washington to live. She explained, she would say it was a once in a while dating thing, and she got pregnant. She would tell them she thought of abortion but waited too long, and once she weighed the odds, she chose to keep the babies. Shai had it all mapped out. They would just have to understand that she wouldn't be alone. Marci, Mitch, Derek and 'Rell would help.

"What's this guy's name? Am I supposed to know about him? Nana will pull me in the room by myself, and I'll be stuttering?" Marci wanted to get the story straight before Julie Mince began questioning her. She never could fool Nana.

"Marci, I said the same thing. Give the guy a name."

"Rell, are you upset again?"

"Yes, you're damn real I am. These children are mine and I want the world to know it. I know it's not your fault, and it's not mine either but damn, this hurts. What's the name babe? Don't worry about me. I'll be alright."

"Rick? How does that sound?"

"Okay, Rick who? Shai you know our grandmother. She'll want to know."

Marci was right. Nana was sharp. She might put out a search on him. Shai was scared for the first time in years. She didn't know what to do. She began to cry. 'Rell put his arms around her.

"Babe, whatever name comes up when she asks you that will be it. It's not enough for you to get upset and upset them. Stay calm. Marci, Mitch, we want you to be Godparents."

"Well we're not married or anything. Can we still be the Godparents?" Marci's was a little concerned.

Mitch looked at 'Rell then at Marci. He answered for the both of them.

"Is that a trick question? We aren't married? What does that have to do with it? Sure we will guys. I wouldn't let you choose anyone else."

"Thank you both, Shai and I couldn't think of anyone else we would want to have as Godparents to our children."

"Oh, twins, Shai I don't know what to say. Have you found out if they're girls, boys, or one of each?"

"Marci, I was so shocked I didn't ask anything. I don't really care as long as they're healthy."

"Rell, what do you want, boys?"

"Mitch, man y'all better hope I don't reveal the secret. I'm just happy Shai's okay, and they're doing fine. I guess we can find out when we go to the doctor."

"Shai, that's right. Are you going to let the doctor know who the father is? I mean, what if there may be some problems?"

'Neither 'Rell nor Shai answered. They hadn't thought of the doctor needing to know, but it was true. The doctor needed to know 'Rell was the father not someone Shai pretended to be seeing. Mitch went to the bar and poured 'Rell a drink and filled his glass as well. Neither of them knew what to say.

"When is the next visit? Maybe we have time to do some research ourselves."

"The appointment is in two weeks. 'Rell was going with me but we hadn't discussed what we would be talking over with the doctor."

"Mitch, what kind of research? I don't want to ask someone questions and get their suspicions up."

"Rell, you remember my cousin who lives in Cali, she's a G-Y-N, I bet she can answer my questions and not wonder a thing. I'll just call her and we can get a heads up."

"Mitch that may work, I don't think we should have the four eyes, two heads, and seven toes problems."

The thought of what 'Rell said took some of the tension out of the conversation. They laughed, in spite of the problem.

"Well there's one thing to your advantage. You and Shai have different mothers. I don't know how that may affect the genes, but it may avoid some genetic complications."

"Marci, how good were you at science." Shai smiled waiting for the answer.

"Well, alright I got C's in science, but it's true, you're step brother and sister. There's got to be a difference."

"Mitch, we'll call your cousin tomorrow. Dinner's still on for now unless things change again. Shai are you ready, you and Marci? Nana will call here, it's almost seven thirty."

"Is it that late? I wonder if Derek woke up again."

They all stopped moving and looked at Shai.

"I mean, you know, woke up after his tests. C'mon guys, I didn't mean it literally."

"Let's go. Mitch you want to ride with us or follow?"

"We'll follow man."

Chapter 40

onya stepped out of the shower feeling revived. She hadn't had a love making session like that in years. Karlton was what she missed in her life. He had agreed to fix their drinks and bring them to the bedroom. She could live this way for years. The only thing missing was finances. She didn't know if Karlton had a fortune one hundred job or not, but if he did, maybe just maybe, she could forget D.Q. Enterprises.

"Oh, my God Derek, I forgot his tests." Derek's tests were scheduled at twelve. She glanced at the clock as she entered the bedroom. It was seven fifteen, no one had called.

"Karl, did the phone ring while I was in the shower?"

"No, are you expecting a call. Maybe they called earlier before we got here."

"Maybe, the hospital was testing Derek at twelve, and they didn't call to say whether the test went okay or not."

"Get dressed. We'll go there Tonya, then you'll know for sure what's going on."

"I'll check the machine first."

While Tonya checked the machine Karlton jumped in the shower. Her machine indicated she had two messages. She pushed the appropriate numbers to retrieve them.

"Mrs. Mince this is Richmond Memorial Hospital. We are taking Derek down for testing. We are contacting you as you requested. Please contact the Hospital with any concerns or questions."

Tonya sighed as she pushed the button again to listen to the second message.

"Mrs. Mince this is the nurse's station at Richmond Memorial Hospital. Derek has been returned to his room. His test results will be read and evaluated tomorrow by the doctor. You can call the doctor then if you should have any further questions. Thank you."

"Karlton, you were right sweetheart, the call was on the machine. We won't have to go to the hospital at all."

Tonya had no intentions of going to the hospital if she could avoid it. As long as Derek wasn't dead there was time to get her hands on his portion of D.Q. enterprises.

"Did you hear me Karl?"

Karl stepped into the room wrapped in a large bath towel. "I heard you. Tell me what's going on. The hospital called and said what?"

"They said Derek had his tests and was returned to his room. I can call tomorrow for the results."

"So you're not going to visit him?"

"Karl, there will be plenty of time for me to do the bed watch thing. I haven't been pleased or relaxed in so long I just want to enjoy the moment."

"Well, lay back and let me lay my head on your thighs."

Tonya adjusted herself in the king size bed and laid back on the pillows as directed. Karlton took pleasure in kissing her thighs and inner legs. He already proved he was what she needed. His mission now was to prove to her, she needed to keep him forever close.

"Tonya did you want to go to the hospital? I mean, I would go with you."

"Not right now Karlton. I need to know that I fit into someone's pleasures, even if it's only for a moment."

"Oh, this is not just for the moment. We can have moments that begin now and continue forever. Tonya I don't plan on going anywhere, unless you want me to."

"Karl, you don't have to say that just to be with me for the night. But if tonight is all I'll have with you, I'll take it."

"Tonya, listen. Listen woman. I want you. I want to be with you. I still love you Tonya. I always have and my life has been splintered without you."

"Karl, we haven't been together in years. You can't mean you haven't been married or living with someone. You sound as though your love life was on hold."

"Never been married, as for my share of women, I've had some; none that touched my heart. I have always been committed to you. You told me once you thought you loved D.Q. and then found out you didn't. Well, I knew I didn't love any of them. I love you. You don't have to love me back. I was a financial pain in your ass deliberately. I didn't want you to forget me. I spent your money on a home. The rest is in a savings account."

"Karl, you always knew what to say but this is a bit much. Your words always fell at the right time."

"Let me please you and myself. Let it sink in. Or, excuse me, maybe I'm intruding. If you'd like me to leave, we can talk about it later."

"Man, don't play with me. It's just a change from money hungry Karlton to the Karlton I was in love with."

"I haven't changed Tonya. I waited a long time to love you. Let me have my way tonight. You'll have your way the rest of our lives."

"What about Derek and Shai?"

"You'll introduce me as your new lover. Someone I'm sure they will learn to love as you do. It will be fine. You'll see. We fit like hand and glove. Derek and Shai are grown, living their own lives. We need to enjoy what's left of ours."

"Karl they don't need to know anything about our past. That would put us in a negative light. They loved D.Q. and wouldn't think twice about hating you if they knew we were together when I was married to him. Also we have to consider Derek's condition. Derek may not be alright after this."

"We'll care for him together. It will be fine. I will care for the two of you. Shai and Derek don't have to know anything until you're ready to tell them. I'm fine with that. I would hope someday you could tell them. They know about Nikki and 'Rell. What could be worse than that? We loved each other about the same time as D.Q. loved Nikki. Listen, Tonya, I didn't come to you because I am poor and begging. I have love for you, a home and a job, but you're the missing link. I need you in my life. If Derek needs us, I will be there for him if you allow me to. I've always told you that, even after they both were born. I wasn't ready to leave you then, and I'm not ready to leave you now."

Tonya bent to meet Karlton's lips. They kissed and he returned to meet her pleasure spots and fulfill his night's wish. Tonya was pleased to hear he would be with her. She was pleased that he still loved her. This was easier than she thought. Her luck had changed.

Karlton moved up in the bed until his head rested in between her breasts. Her warmth and softness gave him a rise. He remembered their nights together. The warmth of her body and the taste of her lips always made him quiver. He understood why D.Q. wanted to marry her. She was beautiful. She was feisty, but beautiful. He never knew why she hadn't fallen for D.Q. the same way, but he didn't doubt that whenever they were together she truly loved him. He would get her to love him again. Maybe not in one night but she would love him again.

Karlton made love to Tonya like he had so many times in his dreams over the past few years. Tonya moaned in ecstasy over and over. Afterward they spent the rest of the night talking softly and caressing each other. They laughed about the past and the memories they shared. It was a good night for both.

Chapter 41

Darlene rang Nikki's bell and waited for her to reply. Simone answered the door with a smile and invited her in.

"Nikki, Darlene is here. I'll be back in an hour or two do you want or need anything while I'm out?"

"No, thanks, tell Charise I said hi."

"I will; Darlene good to see you again."

"You too Simone, take care."

"Darlene, come on in girl. I'm making some iced tea. Would you like some?"

"Yes, I'll take some. I brought those chips you like too."

Darlene walked in the kitchen and placed two bags on the table. The women greeted with a hug. They had become pretty close since D.Q.'s death. As promised, they developed a sisterly relationship. They shopped and went to the movies and shows together often. Darlene and Nikki cherished their friendship and regretted they didn't get to know each other years earlier.

"Great, I didn't cook dinner yet, but you're welcome to stay."

"My mother's having dinner at her house. I've got to go there to see Darryl, so I'll probably eat then."

"Oh, so Darryl is in town."

"I picked him up this morning at the airport. He's been with 'Rell and Mr. Simpson in a meeting since then I guess. I haven't heard from him. You think he would call me and tell me he'd be at the house later? No, just had me sitting waiting, like I didn't have other things to do. I'll talk with him when I get back over there. I guess everyone should be arriving by seven or seven thirty at the latest."

"Darryl came in from Detroit this morning?"

"No, his flight was from Newark. I think it was a stop over there or maybe a stop over from a flight he caught in New York. He does that a lot. I think he has a client or two in New York."

"A client named Simone Marshall." Nikki could feel anger rising as Darlene confirmed her suspicions. *"Simone suddenly had to go see Charise, a girlfriend she barely spoke to."* It was all beginning to add up. Simone was seeing Darryl. Nikki didn't want to lose her relationship with the Mince family. She didn't want to lose her respect for Simone or the new business relationship they had developed. Simone had put pressure on her once again. Nikki wasn't sure how Darlene would respond but someone needed to know that she didn't condone Simone's actions.

"Darlene, have you asked Darryl about his New York visits?"

"No, I think those clients came about after 'Rell found him new clients and associates, a couple of months after D.Q. died."

"Hmmm, I know. That's what troubles me."

"Why would it trouble you?"

"Darlene, you confirmed suspicions I had about Simone. I think she's seeing Darryl. I don't want anyone thinking I condone her actions, so I'm putting it out there."

"You're joking, right. I mean she knows he's married. Didn't she meet Francine?"

"Just the fact that he's married may not matter, or the fact that she met Francine, but what should matter is that I am close to his family. I mean today she even said you were like family. Well if that's the case, how can she be messing around with Darryl? If you're family so is he."

"What the hell was Darryl thinking?

They both thought it over for a moment and responded together.

"He wasn't thinking."

They laughed. Darlene thought about Darryl and all his extra marital affairs. There were too many to count, not to mention the ones that came to light nine months later.

"Nikki, I don't know if it will help ease your mind, but I wouldn't hold it against you. Simone and Darryl are grown. What they do is their business."

"Not when it can affect my business. Simone can't keep this mess up. Darryl can mess around with her in New York, not here. I don't want to have to explain her actions to anyone, especially your mother."

"I don't see how anyone can expect you to explain their actions. They're grown. Darryl has made a mess of his marriage since day one. There have been so many other women in and out of their marriage that Simone is just another...."

Nikki jumped in with her thoughts immediately.

"Slut, tramp. Nikki's cousin the home wrecker. Darlene, when D.Q. and I were seeing each other, I stayed in my place. I didn't flaunt the relationship. I didn't know about his kids or whether or not he and Tonya were together as a couple. Simone knows and doesn't give a damn."

"Nikki, Darryl doesn't give a damn. Simone can't make him meet her or go to her home. What you and D.Q. had is a different kind of love. Darryl and Simone aren't in love. It's just a thing, for the moment. Don't work yourself up about it girl."

"You know how rumors start. Just remember I spoke to you when I suspected this mess. I don't think I'll tell your mother. She won't take it as well as you, I'm sure."

"Girl she's wrapped up in her own rumor."

"What? What did you say Darlene?"

"That's why I wanted to talk to you. What's up with my mother and the Reverend?"

"Oh."

Nikki laughed. She stood up and got the tea out of the refrigerator.

"Girl, you want more tea?"

"C'mon Nikki, I drove all the way over here to find out. It's killing me. Are they dating or what?"

"Darlene, now you know they call it courting. Do you want some more tea?"

"Yeah, they are dating then. Wow, this is news. I'm happy for them."

Nikki opened the bag of chips and put them on a paper plate.

"So have they been dating for a while?"

"I don't know. They've been spending time together since D.Q.'s funeral. I don't know when it turned to dating."

"Nikki, it's been a long time for my mother. She seems happy though."

Darlene and Nikki laughed and talked for over an hour or more. Darlene told Nikki about her reaction to the Reverend coming out of her mother's bathroom. Nikki had a few encounters with the Reverend and Julie Mince before she realized they had to be dating. They talked about Derek and Shai and the problems Shai was having with Tonya. Darlene told her how lucky Shai was to have 'Rell by her side. Nikki updated Darlene on the progress of Interior Dreams and all the new clientele.

"Darlene do you think Darryl knows who had it in for Derek?"

"If he does I hope he tells Mr. Simpson and doesn't try to take them on by himself. Nikki, I'm scared for him. Darryl is arrogant when he's determined to do things his way. I hope he doesn't try something stupid."

"So, you do think he knows."

"Nikki, between me and you, I know he does."

"That's another thing that worries me. If someone is after Darryl what's to stop them from involving Simone or the rest of the family."

"Let's hope it won't get that far, but you're right. I just wonder how much they owe. For someone to want to kill a person over a debt it has to be a big debt."

"Girl, do you think Darryl will tell you what is going on. But then again, you being his sister, he may not tell you to protect you."

"I hope he doesn't have anything to tell. I didn't let my thoughts wonder that far."

"You're right. I'm letting my thoughts wander."

They talked later than they intended. Darlene never made it back to her mother's house that night. She and Nikki had dinner and watched television as they enjoyed each other's company. Simone stayed out the rest of the night.

Chapter 42

inner at Nana's was plentiful as usual. Everyone had more than they could eat and plates were wrapped in aluminum foil waiting to be carried out as leftovers for the next day. 'Rell, Shai, Marci and Mitch stayed with Nana talking long after Mia and Reverend Wilcox left. Darlene and Darryl called separately saying they would be over the next day to visit. Nana checked the hospital about eight o'clock to question the result of Derek's tests. She was told she could contact his physician in the morning for the results, and he was resting peacefully. The nurse was pleased to tell Nana that Derek mumbled words off and on for ten minutes but no one understood what he said. She told Nana not to worry it was a sign that his condition was improving. The nurse also confirmed that Tonya had not visited all day.

"Her only son is in the hospital, and she can't make her way up there. Yet, she bans his sister from visiting. I tell you that mother of yours is a gem, Shai."

"Nana, I don't understand her either, but it's easier to ignore her and her actions. I can only deal with her from a distance."

"Rell, did you and your uncle figure out who put Derek in the hospital?"

"Nana, we can only go on what Mr. Simpson finds out about the guys Uncle Darryl told us about. We can't say they were involved without some evidence linking them to Derek."

"Rell, you mean we just sit and wait. There may be someone waiting to kill any of the family. I hope it's just the debts and not the web designed logos."

Mitch was as upset as everyone else. His fear was retaliation that may include D.Q. Enterprises and its partners.

"Mitch, man, it is what it is."

"I know it is what it is 'Rell, but we can't forget everyone is in jeopardy as long as we don't know who these people are."

Shai, Marci and Nana left them in the room to continue their conversation of possible suspects. Leaving them to talk was the best thing for Shai. She had mixed feelings that had nothing to do with business. Marci and Shai tried to convince Derek his gambling was dangerous but Shai never imagined it could cost him his life. Nana set coffee cups on the kitchen table and brought out slices of cake for them to eat as they talked.

"Nana do you have any juice? I don't think I'll have any coffee."

"Shai, you love my flavored coffee, are you sure? Would you prefer tea?"

Shai thought about the caffeine. It didn't agree with her pregnancy, and she would be up all night if she drank it.

"No, juice will be fine. Do you have some? I'll get it."

"It should be some in there. I think I have that cran-apple and that berry flavored. They're pretty good too. I got them on sale. Marci is coffee or tea okay with you or have you changed your habits too."

"Oh no, Nana, I'll take the coffee. I love the mocha flavored."

Shai returned to the table with the cran-apple juice and the mocha coffee. The tea pot whistled and Nana brought the hot water to the table.

"Well ladies, help yourself to the cake and pie. This one is coconut crème. The other is a pound cake. I try to stay away from them so have as much as you like."

Marci was the first to cut the coconut crème. Shai watched her and shook her head, pointing to the pound cake.

"I'll just have a slice. I'll have to make up my mind which I like better though. Marci cut me a slice of the pound cake."

"Shai, you can try them both if you like. I know you're not still watching your weight?"

"Nana, that was so long ago. I got to the size I wanted to. It was last summer before I went on vacation, remember Marci?"

Marci looked at Shai questioning her inclusion in the discussion about her weight. She caught on as Nana started laughing out loud. Marci and Shai looked at their grandmother not quite understanding her reason for the laughter.

"Shai, I don't mean to laugh baby, but I can remember you running around here just 'bout every summer losing weight for your vacations. But Lord, sure seems like you gain it right back girl. What size are your pants now? You can't possibly still wear eight pants."

"No, Nana they aren't eights. They're a little big"

Shai couldn't believe she walked into this conversation about weight. She knew her grandmother would want to touch her waist, butt, and thighs to make the point that Shai had indeed gained weight. *"Shit here we go. Shai you did gain weight? Girl, if I didn't know better, I'd say you were expecting?"*

Nana didn't get the chance to say it. Her finger began to glitter and caught the attention of both Marci and Shai.

"Nana, where'd you get that beautiful ring?"

Marci grabbed her hand before she could answer the question. The ring sparkled, catching the light in the room as she turned her grandmother's hand from side to side.

"Is this an engagement ring Nana? How long have you had it? It's beautiful."

Shai walked around the table to get a better view. The women were huddled over Nana as Mitch and 'Rell entered the room.

"What's going on?"

'Rell saw the ring and looked at Mitch. They both smiled.

"Nana, that's a beautiful setting. The jeweler cleaned it nicely."

Shai assumed that she had cleaned her old wedding set.

"Shai, I don't think I wore that set you're thinking about since you graduated from high school. Yes, it's an engagement ring. Reverend Wilcox asked for my hand in marriage."

Marci and Shai kissed her cheeks from opposite sides. 'Rell and Mitch waited for their turn. They all told her congratulations.

"I wanted to have dinner with all of you to tell you together. Darryl and Darlene never showed, and well, Derek is in the hospital. Wallace and I were at the jewelry store when we got the call about Derek. It threw everything off."

"I can imagine. My mother will be glad to hear you and the Reverend are getting married. She thinks he's a nice guy. I'm glad for you Nana."

'Rell kissed his grandmother again. Nana hugged him tight to show she was glad he shared in her happiness.

"Now that don't stop Shai from letting me see how fat she got."

"Aw Nana, I'll lose this weight in no time you'll see."

Marci and Mitch saw Shai needed help. Marci interrupted Nana's comment with her own. Mitch went to the closet to get their coats.

"We're going to leave you good folks now. Shai, 'Rell we'll talk with you guys tomorrow or Sunday."

"Don't forget we're on for dinner, if there's any change we'll call you."

Shai caught herself before telling them she would be at 'Rell's house. Nana would be suspicious for sure if she wasn't already.

"Nana, do you think Aunt Darlene will be calling you later tonight?"

"Rell, I don't know, your uncle said he would see me tomorrow. He must have called her on his cell phone. They were supposed to meet here. Boy I don't know whether I'm coming or going, let alone knowing what they're doing."

"Rell, I'm ready when you are, you can drop me off and then catch up with Aunt Darlene if you want."

That was 'Rell's cue that Shai didn't want to stay much longer. He cut a slice of cake and wrapped it in aluminum foil.

"Shai get you a piece too while 'Rell is there cutting. Y'all better take this cake before your uncle comes and eats it all. 'Rell I don't guess you'll get to your father's belongings this weekend. Maybe you can do a little at a time until you get through it all."

"Nana is it all together. I mean I won't have to dig through a lot, will I?"

"What is it you hope to find?"

"I don't know. I just know I need to sort through a few things that may need to be back at the office. I also want to make sure there's no lingering business I need to know about."

"Well if you don't get to it, it will stay right where it is. You can look in that closet in his bedroom. That's all his stuff. The closet has a lot of papers, pictures and other items. I don't know why he kept it."

"Well Shai needs a ride home, and I don't need to start that task tonight. So we're both leaving."

Nana stood facing Shai. She looked Shai over and as she did Shai realized Nana knew she was pregnant. She hoped she couldn't predict the father. Nana nodded her head and smiled. Shai didn't know if it was a smile that said, *"I know"* or *"We'll talk about this."* Shai returned Nana's look and smile. They said their goodbyes with no further questions about Shai's weight.

Chapter 43

*T*hree weeks had passed since Derek's accident. He regained his ability to speak, but he chose to limit his conversations after he received the news that he was paralyzed from the waist down. There was hope he would regain feeling after surgery and therapy. Derek convinced himself that he wouldn't be able to walk again, although he continued his therapy and whirlpool treatments. Tonya visited daily pampering him until he would beg her to leave. Derek woke up on day twenty-four determined to make contact with his brother and sister without Tonya blocking his calls and visitors. He could feel she was up to something, but he couldn't tell what it was. Derek knew he needed to be steps ahead of his mother if he was to keep his inheritance.

Derek waited until breakfast to speak to his morning nurse, Leeza. Derek and Leeza talked often after breakfast and Derek found himself longing for her visits. Leeza was Brazilian and her complexion looked like a permanent tan. She had big brown button eyes and dark colored hair. Derek wished he had met her prior to the accident. She informed him his mother expressed her worry about him getting his rest, so she requested the staff block his calls and screen his visitors. They were to call her if the caller or visitor insisted. The staff honored her request after all she was his mother.

Leeza would try to limit her visits with him but Derek encouraged her to stay every morning. She was beginning to

187

hold a special place in his heart and he hoped she wasn't nice to him out of pity.

Leeza came into the room and opened his curtains letting in the morning light. She prepared his wheelchair for his transport to therapy. She checked his water and placed his meal on his tray near the bed.

"Good morning Mr. Mince. I know you're not asleep I saw you smile when I came in the room"

"It was an automatic reflex to your perfume. It smells different today."

"Thank you for noticing. How are you feeling today?"

"I'm okay, how are you?"

"I'm good, would you like the whirlpool first or therapy?"

"It doesn't matter. They both wear me out."

"Well if you decide after you eat let me know."

"Leeza, don't go yet. May I ask you a favor?"

"Sure Mr. Mince, what do you need?"

"I need to get in touch with my brother and my sister today. Would it be hard for them to visit before the normal visiting hours?"

"I can call your brother and sister but so can you. I don't know whether or not they will let them in downstairs."

"Listen, tell the other nurses that my brother is bringing my sister and see if it would be okay to avoid any conflicts with my mother. I need to see them before my mother gets here."

"Do you think you'll have time for therapy?"

"The whirlpool first and if they come before the next session I'll make it up later. I have to speak to them today, if I can."

"Did you need anything else?"

"No thank you, Leeza. Really, thank you."

"You're welcome, Mr. Mince."

"Will you please call me Derek?"

"Derek, okay Derek." Her accent made him grin. He hoped her reaction meant he could get personal.

"Leeza, are you married? I know it's not my business, but I would like to know."

"No, I'm not married."

"Seeing someone?"

"No."

"I'm getting too personal?"

"Well, I'll tell you when to stop."

Leeza returned a devilish grin and walked out of the room. Derek rolled over toward the door to watch for her return. She would be back to see if he ate. Her routine was like clockwork. He wanted to be a part of her routine. The hospital was slowly coming to life. Nurses and doctors busied themselves checking on patients and answering phones and pages. Derek turned on the morning news and reached for the phone. He dialed 'Rell's number hoping to catch him before he left for the office.

"Hello, 'Rell."

"Derek, good morning are you okay?"

"Yeah, man I need to see you and Shai."

"I told Shai, I was going to visit you today. I should be there about three this afternoon. Is that okay?"

"No, can you and Shai get here this morning. I need to talk with you both at the same time and my mother usually comes and sits most of the day. Shai won't stay if my mother shows up. It's important that we talk before another day passes."

"Well, I'll have to go to the office and change a few appointments. I won't get a chance to change my first meeting. It starts at nine. It should be over by ten thirty. I can come to you right after that. I don't know what Shai's schedule is though."

"So, you'll be here about eleven?"

"Yeah, eleven is good for me, I guess. Derek, are you okay?"

"We have to discuss a few things. Is Shai working today? She said she was taking a few days off."

"I don't know. I can call her for you, if you'd like."

'Rell was aware of Shai taking off a few days. She wanted to shop for the twins with Marci. They were preparing the nursery in her home, and she would be off the rest of the week. Marci was on vacation and was using the time to help. Shai still hadn't told anyone about the pregnancy and stayed away from the family blaming it on a busy schedule. She told 'Rell, she planned a family dinner at her house to spring the pregnancy on everyone at once. Darryl announced he would be in town for another week, but then he would be going back to Detroit. Shai wanted him to be included.

"That would be a good idea. I mean if you get the chance. Just tell her we need to talk."

"Do you need me to bring you anything?"

"No, they said I may be able to go home at the end of the week. I may need your help then."

"Alright, I'll see you at eleven."

"Rell thanks man."

Chapter 44

Karlton was reading the morning paper when Tonya entered the kitchen. She noticed he was dressed in casual attire, and he was definitely on his way out. They had spent the evening discussing their concerns with Derek's condition and his financial connection with D.Q. Enterprises. Karlton did most of the listening. Tonya convinced Karlton it would take a while for them to tap in to any of his money because he needed to trust both of them. Tonya's relationship with her son was in need of repair, and it would take time before she would suggest she handled his money. She didn't think Derek would be receptive to her new found relationship right away.

Karlton needed to find out how 'Rell, Shai and Derek really felt about Tonya. Karlton wanted to meet them, hoping they would believe Tonya truly moved on with her life and was committed to rekindling their family relationships. Karlton wanted the two of them to believe she was involved with him and was satisfied. They had to be convinced Tonya was willing to help Derek as much as she could but didn't know how they would accept her. Tonya wanted them to look at her as a loving mother. Karlton's theory was to kill them with kindness, and they would be more than happy for her to handle Derek in his condition and eventually his end of his business. She walked around to Karlton and kissed him on the forehead. As she kissed him, he pulled her down sitting her on his lap.

"I've decided to visit 'Rell this morning. I made a nine o'clock appointment with him."

"An appointment, what are you doing?"

"Don't get so worked up. I just want to meet the man. I need to meet Shai and Derek too. I mean we've got to let them see me as the good guy. I'm the one who changed you around. If you go to 'Rell's office, that would tip them off. Let me go and see if I can wet my feet. If they buy the fact that you're satisfied and moving on with your life, they won't think you're after Derek's money. We need to act fast though. When are they releasing Derek from the hospital?"

"I guess you're right. He has tests to take this week and then if all is well he'll just return for therapy as an outpatient."

"We don't have a lot of time. So today I meet Mr. Darrell Mince. Maybe tomorrow or the next day, I'll meet Shai and Derek, any objections?"

"No, now that you put it that way. It just seems strange. How will you explain your visit?"

"I'm an investor. You recommended I look into D.Q. Enterprises. Seems simple enough, what can the man say other than he doesn't want my money?"

"Here, take some of these brochures. It will help you look the part. Tell him you're interested in vacation properties."

Tonya went into the hall and got the brochures from the magazine racks. She had plenty of them lying around the house, and it would make his story logical. 'Rell would have his guard up, but she had confidence in Karlton.

"What do you have planned for the rest of the day?"

"I'm not sure. What did you have in mind?"

"Well if you want to meet Derek, we can visit him this afternoon."

"That will be fine. I'll call you after I leave Mr. Mince."

"Okay, I'll wait for your call."

Karlton put down the paper and sipped the last of his morning coffee. Tonya cleared the morning dishes and followed him to the door giving him a simple kiss and smile.

She watched as Karlton pulled off in his Audi. She felt a rush of warmth watching him leave the driveway. Karlton Harris, on her side after all these years, if she could just be sure it would stay that way.

Chapter 45

$\mathcal{T}$onya picked up the phone expecting it to be the hospital calling about Derek's testing. She couldn't remember if it was in the morning or the afternoon. She did know that she would visit him after the conclusion of the test and not take the chance of getting there before the tests were done. Derek wasn't talking much and she knew he would be annoyed enough with the nursing staff. She would wait until he rested an hour or two.

"Hello." Tonya put on her pleasant business voice.

"Tonya, this is Mr. Franklin, Robert, from D.Q. Enterprises. I was calling you back to tell you I did look for those papers you requested a few weeks ago."

"Oh, yes, Robert. How are you? Did you find out anything?"

"Well, Tonya, I'm afraid I was right. There is no paperwork that confirms that you have any holdings in D.Q. Enterprises. I can send you the copies of the file if you like, or if you want, I can bring them to you."

She listened to Robert talk. If Karlton had not been a part of her bedroom pleasure, she may have taken Robert up on his offer. She knew that was what he was hinting to.

"No, Robert that won't be necessary. Be a dear and put them in the mail. I'll be in and out the next few days, and I don't want to miss your visit."

"Okay, I'll do that. If you should need anything else, don't hesitate to call me. Let me give you my cell number. You don't have to call the office."

"Damn, who's next? I don't need another man. I need a man with guaranteed benefits."

"That will be fine. What's the number, Robert?"

"It's eight seven five, four three five, eight nine four zero. Call anytime. I'll be happy to help you."

I bet you would… Thank you for your time, Robert. I'll call you if I need to."

Tonya hung up the phone smiling. *"If Karlton doesn't watch himself, I just may call you baby."* Things were indeed turning in her favor. She looked at the clock. It was close to nine o'clock. She went into her home office and got on the computer. She logged into D.Q. Enterprises vacation homes and laughed thinking about Karlton investing only to own a part of D.Q. Enterprises later. He would start with the vacation homes and work his way up. It was only a matter of time. The two of them would have a partnership in what D.Q. thought he could keep away from them.

Karlton slowed signaling to make the turn into the parking lot at D.Q. Enterprises. He gave his name to the security guard in the booth. He watched, as the guard checked his name off and issued him a visitor's pass for his vehicle.

"Sir, if you step out of the car. Please leave the pass in the car; it will be parked for you."

Karlton did as the guard asked and was handed a visitor's pass and parking ticket. Karlton was escorted to the elevator where the doorman met him asking what floor he was going to.

"Mr. Mince's office please."

The security guard tipped his hat at Karlton as he entered the elevator.

"Thank you sir, have a good day."

Karlton rode the elevator thinking how well organized the staff was. The elevator doors opened to the glass doors with golden knobs. The gold writing on the doors read 'D.Q. Enterprises'. He pushed open the doors and was greeted by Ms. Berry.

"Good morning Mr. Harris. If you'll be seated, Mr. Mince will be with you in a moment."

He was impressed. The professionalism was well above most companies he had dealt with. The office was immaculate. There was no doubt in his mind that D.Q. raised Darrell to fill his current position. The intercom interrupted his thoughts.

"Ms. Berry, please send in Mr. Harris."

"Mr. Harris if you would follow me sir."

Karlton followed Ms. Berry through another set of glass doors that lead to the other executive offices. At the end of the hall, she opened the door to Darrell's office. Darrell turned from the view in his large picture window as the door opened.

"Thank you Ms. Berry. Mr. Harris, welcome to D.Q. Enterprises. Have a seat here, unless you prefer to sit at the conference table. It has a better view."

"Whatever, it, it doesn't matter."

"Is there something wrong?"

There was something wrong but Karlton couldn't tell Darrell, unless he was willing to spoil the purpose of his visit. He looked at Darrell and saw D.Q. He was his father's twin. Karlton only had one confrontation with D.Q., and it wasn't pleasant. Tonya never knew about it and both men kept it that way. Karlton promised he wouldn't see Tonya again if D.Q. wouldn't see Nikki again. D.Q. punched him in the mouth and the fight lasted until the cops came.

"I knew your father. You look a lot like him. I guess old memories touched me for a moment."

"I see. Did the two of you have some business together?"

"No, no nothing like that. We had a mutual friend."

"Oh, well I've been told how much I resemble him, so I hope it doesn't bother you much."

"No, no, not at all. It just startled me, I guess."

"Well, what can D.Q. Enterprises do for you?"

"I'm interested in the vacation properties, particularly the ones listed by Ms. Nikki Robbins."

"Good choice, have you seen the latest views of the property?"

"I don't know. I have these brochures."

Karlton showed 'Rell the brochures that Tonya had given to him. 'Rell took them and looked at the customer code on the mailing label and immediately knew they were from Tonya. *"When is he going to tell me he knows Tonya? Was he sent here by her to see what they can get? That Bitch! Okay, I'll play the game Mrs. Mince. You'll be sorry that you included this new player."*

"These are a little old. Let me show you the better views. These shots were all taken this year. Not that the shots in that brochure are bad but these give you a better idea of the land and the surrounding properties."

'Rell handed Karlton a book and flipped to the pages where Nikki's properties began.

"Do you think these properties are the best for the Spring Season?"

"Any season, they are located where the weather changes early from winter to spring. The sites are beautiful."

"I see. What about exchanges with other sites or clients?"

"That isn't normally a problem. It can be done and has been done. We leave that between the clients. You look for the site you would like to vacation and the available weeks. You discuss it with the client or the owner and the arrangements are made accordingly."

"Just that easy."

"Just that easy. We're simple people here Mr. Harris. There's nothing that we won't try to accommodate."

"That's good to know."

"Which property interested you?"

"The Virginia Beach Site looks nice. Are these sites for lease or sale?"

"Some are both. They are leased out until they are sold. Some are units, multiple sites at the same location. Those are lease only."

"And Virginia Beach is?"

"Lease only."

"I see."

"Mr. Harris, why do I get the feeling that you don't really want to lease or buy? What exactly can I do for you? It has nothing to do with the properties, does it?"

"You are your father's son, very perceptive. Years ago I wanted to invest in stock with D.Q. Enterprises. Your father wouldn't budge for the price. I'm still interested."

"My father was a wise man when it came to business. When you wanted the vacation property, you had a better chance. There is no stock to be sold to you Mr. Harris."

"No stock to be sold? I would think you would want to hear the price and amount first."

"My father declining to let you buy years ago is enough for me to know. I echo his words. There is no sale here for you. Mr. Harris let me stop this game of cat and mouse with you. I have the feeling that you and I can guess why you're here and who sent you. I don't deal with Mrs. Mince when it comes to business. I let my associates handle it. I will refer you to the best associate here. However, you will not be offered anything other than property. You will not be a stock holder, or investor in D.Q. Enterprises."

"Mr. Mince, I really think you've misunderstood my intentions. I just came into town. Mrs. Mince, Tonya, is an old friend. She told me about the company and D.Q.'s death and the possible investment I could make since I intend on doing business in the city. I'm looking to make a sound investment in land or stocks, hopefully, with D.Q. Enterprises."

"Mr. Harris, that won't happen. My father's words and choices mean a lot to me. He chose not to do business with you. I respect his choice. Your intention means nothing to me."

"I don't know what to say. Tonya led me to believe that you would be receptive to my business. I guess she was wrong."

"Yeah, I guess she was. She doesn't know much about me. Let me call Mitchell Carter to help you with the properties, that is, if you're still interested. I'm sorry we can't talk much longer, but you'll be in good hands with Mr. Carter."

"Mr. Mince, I hope I haven't spoiled a relationship we would have had together."

"No not at all. There are lines I don't cross and my father's decisions are a part of those lines. You may lease one of the vacation properties for the time you will need but that is all D.Q. Enterprises can offer you at this time."

"Mr. Darrell Mince will not make an offer, even if it involves Derek and Shai."

'Rell's thoughts went immediately to the call he received from Derek earlier. *"Is this man linked to Derek's accident? How does he know Tonya?"*

'Rell walked to the window and took a deep breath.

"Mr. Harris, get to the point. What do Shai and Derek have to do with this?"

"Mr. Mince. Tonya and I are rekindling an old relationship, we were all friends. Your father, Tonya and I knew each other when your father first started in this business. He turned down my offer then. I think it was pride. He was raising money to open the company, and I offered it to him. His pride wouldn't let him take it. I saw his dream and I still see it. I'm still willing to invest. Derek has a new company. I understand your loyalty to D.Q. Enterprises, but what about Quintech?"

"Okay, that explains Tonya and Derek. How does this involve Shai?"

"Shai wants what's best for Derek. He'll need an investor after this courtroom drama unfolds. Shai won't want to hear how you didn't allow him to stand on his own."

"Mr. Harris, Tonya didn't give you correct information when she sent you here. I don't take threats lightly. Neither

Derek nor Shai needs you. My father, their father, left them with enough to live comfortably for years to come. He invested in all of us. I don't know what your next trick is, but if you've rekindled with Tonya Mince watch out for the poison droppings. Again, thank you. There will be no investing in D.Q. Enterprises or Quintech."

"Well, you leave me no choice but to visit them."

"Mr. Harris, they don't run D.Q. Enterprises or me. Good day sir."

'Rell turned walking toward his office door. He noticed Mr. Harris did not rise to his feet. He sat there as if he were waiting for something.

"Mr. Harris is there a problem?"

"Yes, Tonya is trying to redo all her wrongs. You know with Shai, Derek and you. She sent me here to feel you out. She told me if you let me invest that would be a sign that you had moved on without holding a grudge toward her. There needs to be peace for her, for Derek's sake."

"Hmm, there may be peace but there won't be any investments. Mr. Harris I don't know what this relationship you have with Ms. Mince is, but she needs to deal with Derek and Shai. I don't care about her, one way or the other. I respect her as their mother and that's it. That's the way it will be."

"But you could help her rekindle the relationship with Derek and Shai. That's really why I am here. We need your help. Shai and Derek think highly of you. You could make this period in their life special."

"I'm sorry Mr. Harris. Mrs. Mince leaves an ill taste in my mouth, a rumble in the pit of my stomach and other things I care not to mention. I will not interfere with their relationships. I'm not for it or against it. It's not my mother or my responsibility. If you have chosen to take this on, God bless you."

Karlton chuckled at the thought of his last comment. He stood from his chair and shook 'Rell's hand.

"Your father made a wise choice giving this Enterprise over to you. I wish you well."

"Thank you Mr. Harris. If you should truly want to lease any of our properties don't hesitate to call."

'Rell opened the door and escorted Karlton to the elevators. He got on the elevator without another word.

"Ms. Berry, make a note. Call Kenny, Mr. Karlton Harris is not to enter this building again."

Chapter 46

Mr. Simpson sat at his desk looking over the court documents that were faxed to him from Hudson and Hewitt the law firm hired by Carson Web Designs. The law firm received Mr. Simpson's letter informing them he would be representing Derek Mince. This would leave them representing the other four employees from Carson Web Designs who were involved. Derek was the only employee charged with Trademark Infringement that wasn't still an employee of Carson Web. The papers showed the transactions and sales of logos over the past four years. Most of the sales were made by Derek but were not commissioned sales. Mr. Simpson couldn't see where Derek was paid for the work he created. He was the artist and designer in all the questioned logos. Two European companies filed charges of infringement when the logos sold to their clients appeared on commercials ads for two American firms. Mr. Simpson carefully scanned through the paperwork for questions he needed to confront Darryl and Darrell with. The main question was why the prosecution would ask them to testify against Derek.

"Tracey, what time did Mr. Mince say he would be arriving this morning?"

"He asked to be penciled in for ten thirty Mr. Simpson. He called saying he was on his way, that was ten minutes ago."

"Well check my phone before sending him in the office. If I am on the line, please have him wait in the reception area."

"Sir, Mr. Mince just walked in."

Darryl smiled hearing his name. He didn't have time to wait for Mr. Simpson or anyone else this morning. He had a flight to catch at two o'clock and he wanted to see Simone before he left. He needed to go home for a week or two to check on his business and family. He still wasn't sure that his family wasn't in any danger from the gambling debts, he and Derek owed.

"Mr. Mince, I'm glad to see you were able to stop in before catching your flight out."

"Well, 'Rell said it was important that I see you first."

"Please be seated, I was going over the prosecution's documents. I'm trying to grasp what went on."

"When do you think the court proceedings will start?"

"Well, Derek is looking to be released from the hospital this week. It could be anytime after the judge feels is feasible for his recovery. I will try to put it off as long as I can. But the decision is ultimately the Judge's."

"So what are they claiming 'Rell and I know?"

"It's not clear. The charges state that Derek resold logo's he had clearly designed for the companies overseas. My guess is he could have gotten away with this if the clients never linked with the American companies. The European company found out that Carson Design or Derek was designing logos, setting up the ad campaigns, and selling the logo again to another company. The news spread internationally. They have hard evidence; contracts, checks for payments, ads, slogans and of course, the designs themselves."

"Mr. Simpson this has nothing to do with 'Rell and I. How do we fit in? Especially 'Rell, he didn't even know Derek when he worked at Carson Web."

"You're right but you did. Apparently, they know about your gambling with Derek. The money that Derek gambled with was company funds. You were a part of his gambling. 'Rell, on the other hand, cleaned up his bills, debts, and bought him a car and home. They don't know how much was inherited, but they are assuming it was extra money from 'Rell. This money was taken to the American competitors and Derek paid for their silence. They may only ask you two questions, and then again, they may ask you thirty. There is no limit. The two of you may be the hole in his story."

"What is his story? Why did he take the logos and sell them to another company? That sounds like he put the noose around his own neck."

"You're right. He did. But it's my job to see no one pulls that noose any tighter. So tell me what you know if anything."

"There were only a few occasions that I can recall that we paid off big debts or went to see someone to pay them. My outings with Derek were purely social not business. We would meet, go bet on the horses, bet on the weather, bet on the games for the night, simple shit. Nothing that would make them want to kill him."

"I'll need a few days to go over these papers. I'll write down what you have told me and speak to 'Rell.

Maybe it was an intimidating ploy to have you both subpoenaed. At this point, I don't know, but I wouldn't put it past them."

"So, when will you know the court date? I'm leaving for Detroit this afternoon."

"Have a safe trip. Believe me, if we need you, we will find you."

Darryl had to laugh. D.Q. used to send guys to search for him. They knew most of his old spots but things were different, since he was seeing Simone."

"Don't hesitate to call though Mr. Simpson. I want to know what's going on as you discover it."

"Sure, that's not a problem."

Both men got up to shake the other's hand. Mr. Simpson walked Darryl to the receptionist's desk.

"Thank you for stopping by. Hopefully, I won't have to call you. As the family lawyer, we need to get to know each other rather quickly."

"Yeah, Mr. Simpson, I hate to take up your time, but do you think these are the men who tried to kill Derek?"

"I don't know Darryl, that's what I will have to find out. If they are, there's more to it then infringement, and I'm quite sure it involves higher stakes."

"Well, I should be back within the next two weeks."

"Darryl, have a safe trip. Hopefully, I won't have to call you back sooner than you have planned."

Darryl took the elevator when the doors opened. He thought about Mr. Simpson's question. *"What do I know? I know that Derek has to explain this shit!"* It was eleven- thirty and Simone was meeting him at twelve. There was no time to stop at the hospital. He would have to rely on 'Rell asking Derek what was going on. Darryl dialed 'Rell's phone and found he had to leave a message. He asked 'Rell to call him as soon as possible. Darryl got in his rental car and drove off to meet Simone.

Chapter 47

Shai and 'Rell arrived at the hospital and waited in the family lounge for Derek to return from his whirlpool treatment. The nurse said he would be coming pass them soon.

"Rell do you think the treatments will restore the feelings in his legs?"

"Babe, how can I answer that? Didn't you ask the doctor the other day?"

"No, I asked about the test they were taking this week. I guess they will be able to determine with the results what progress he has made, if any."

"Shai, it's going to take time. We have to be patient and pray for the best. He's alive and that matters more."

"It's hard for me, so I know it must be hard on him."

"Well, he's coming around. I mean, he asked to see us, so he must have been thinking about this situation."

"Do you think that's what he wants to talk about?"

"Shai what else could it be? Maybe it's about his health, the arrangements for when he comes home, or the court thing."

"You gave this some thought huh?"

"Shai, I don't know what he wants. I'm just guessing."

"They've changed my visits for the doctor's. I'll be going every two weeks now. Do you think you'll be able to come with me to the next visit? I think we ought to talk to the doctor about our relationship then."

"Okay, if that's what you want. You're in your sixth month right. I get confused because you're still pretty small to be carrying twins."

"I don't feel small, that's for sure."

"Well you better think of when we're going to tell the rest of the family."

"Derek's coming home this weekend if all is okay. Let's have a dinner at my house, and we'll tell everyone then."

"You will have dinner at your house and tell everyone. I will be the invited uncle remember."

"Oh, yeah, you're right. I got excited and forgot."

"You can't forget."

"Forget what?" Derek wheeled into the waiting room with a smile on his face.

"Hey Derek, you look good." Shai greeted her brother with a kiss. She waited for him to adjust his wheelchair before returning to her seat.

"Good for a wheelchair jockey. I feel okay but this takes a little getting use to."

Derek put the brakes on the wheels parking his wheelchair across from Shai's chair.

"Are you tired? Do you want to go to your room?"

"No, this is the only time I'm out of the room. I get out twice a day for my therapy sessions. I'm a little sick of it all."

"Derek, be patient, it's for your own good."

"Shai, you sound like your mother. Anyway, that's what I called you guys here for. Maybe we should go into my room. It will be more private there."

Derek whipped his chair around and wheeled it down the hall towards his room. Shai and 'Rell followed him in silence. 'Rell entered the room last and closed the door behind him. Derek moved his chair close to the bed. He took his time and made his way out of the chair onto the bed. Shai watched his movements. It was as though Derek had been paralyzed for more than four weeks. He had adapted well and that worried

Shai. She didn't want him to be depressed, but she didn't want him to be content with things the way they were.

"Listen, you guys have to understand one thing. I'm paralyzed not crippled and I will not be treated as though I'm crippled. The doctors are saying that they're going to look at the test I take on Thursday, and if it shows that there's any possible way they can operate and repair the damage, they'll let me know. It was hard to see the damage with all the swelling and the other problems I had, mainly the bleeding in my head. I'm blessed and while I'm being blessed, I want them to repair whatever they can."

"What are the chances of you walking after the surgery?"

"Shai, I don't know but can it be any worse?"

Shai was getting upset. She didn't want Derek to go through unnecessary procedures hoping for a miracle. She looked at 'Rell for a supportive comment but didn't get one.

"Anyway, I called you guys here to get some help. Shai our mother is after my money. I know she is. I'm asking Mr. Simpson to draw up my papers for a living will. I'll be leaving everything to you if something should happen to me. If things should change and I live long enough to have a wife and family, I'll change the paperwork then and only then. 'Rell I need all the papers from Quintech Designs to be secured for your eyes only. I am leaving the business to you. I need these things in place before I undergo any other surgeries, and before I'm released from the hospital. I want it to look as though this all was in place since dad died. There will be no reason for mother to fight it in court if it is done that way."

"Derek, man, your mother can't get her hands on your business. It's protected under D.Q. Enterprises. I'll let Mr. Simpson explain the shares and holdings to you. You can leave it to Shai if you like, but it can't be left in my name. That's a conflict of interest."

"Well as long as my mother can't get it. She thinks I don't understand her motive. She's still after you 'Rell and D.Q. Enterprises. She talks over me, as though I'm in a coma, I've heard her intentions. She's told the hospital that I'll be coming home to live with her. I need my home wheelchair compatible. Is Uncle Darryl still in town?"

'Rell looked at his watch before answering.

"He's catching a flight out this afternoon. He said he would be back in two weeks."

"I need to talk with him too. Can you catch him before he leaves? Call him from this phone and tell him I need my home done and ask if can he recommend a contractor right away."

Shai picked up the phone and dialed Darryl's cell. 'Rell and Derek continued to talk as she explained Derek's request to her uncle.

"Derek, Mr. Simpson will probably call you or stop by later. We need to know who has it out for you man. What kind of shit are you caught up in?"

"Rell man, we owed a lot of money, after losing some serious bets. Uncle Darryl got his money from his company's profits and borrowing from Nana and Aunt Darlene. I didn't have it quite that easy. I had over extended myself with Shai, and Aunt Darlene was helping Uncle Darryl. We tried to keep family out of it. Anyway, I thought I could sell logos for the extra cash. I had sent a few samples overseas. I never got an answer from the clients, and I thought the logos went into the dead file. I didn't receive payment for them through the normal channels. I got paid by a salesman in Carson Web Design, who no longer worked for the company. He said he was doing business for an American competitor, and they would pay a high price to use the designs. I thought these were dead files anyway so I sold the work. It was legally mine."

"You never got paid by the Europeans?"

"No, never, it was a few weeks later when Mr. Carson came to me with the payment from the designs sold overseas. I thought it was for the new designs I was working on. When he told me which logos were being used for the campaign, I couldn't tell him I sold everything because the money was just that good. I sold the American competitor the campaign slogans, ads, everything, a duplicate of what was sent overseas. 'Rell I got paid a lot of money from both ends. When Mr. Carson found out, he fired me. He told me that if I told what went on, I would pay out my ass. He intended on keeping the money the companies share from the European sale. I never told. I had all but spent my share. Now here they come with the bullshit."

Shai turned around. She was about to speak when she noticed Derek looking at her with a puzzling look on his face.

"Shai, are you pregnant?"

"Derek, don't change the topic. You knew they would hurt you, and you didn't tell anyone?"

"No, I didn't tell. Are you pregnant?"

"Derek, do you know you jeopardized your life and others by not telling?"

"I didn't think they would do this shit okay? Are you fucking pregnant?"

"Yes, Yes!!"

"What the hell! Who is the father?"

"Derek, that's not the topic right now."

"Yes, it is! Who is he?"

"Derek, stop it! Your life is in danger. You're about to pay a hefty fine or do jail time. You can't be seriously thinking that the story you just told will hold up in court."

Shai was trying to keep the subject on Derek's problems. She looked at 'Rell for help. He didn't respond.

"I don't care if it does or not, it's the truth. Those guys know it, that's why they're trying to kill me. They committed the crime, not me. I didn't know the shit was sold. They tried not to pay me."

"Derek, you sold those logos. Was there a policy that said that the work you did for the company and submitted to the company was theirs?"

"Rell, I think so. That's the only reason I think they can bring me up on charges. But the punks thought I would rat them out so they tried to kill me."

"Shai, who's the father, or don't you know?"

"What the hell does that mean? You and your mother, I swear. I know who the father is. I will tell everyone at dinner on Sunday. Just wait until then."

"Shit, I have to wait until everyone is told. What's up with that?"

"Derek, I'm not in the mood for this shit. I came here to see you, not talk about me."

"Rell, who's the father?"

'Rell looked at Shai. He wanted to say it was him. He wasn't going to lie. 'Rell stood up and both Shai and Derek watched him walk to the window on the opposite side of the room.

"Rell, man who's the father?"

"He doesn't know Derek, let it go!" Rell kept his back to them as he prepared himself for an unwanted conversation.

"Shai wants to keep us all in suspense Derek. I've asked her and she didn't tell me either. We'll just have to wait. Listen, Mr. Simpson will be here either today or tomorrow to talk to you about the case. I'll get with the contractors about the renovations at the house. Shai, what did Uncle Darryl say?"

"He said he would call Derek later and make sure what he wants is done. He'll be back in two weeks, unless Mr. Simpson calls him."

"Alright, I'll talk to you later about the papers. Shai, I've got an appointment. Do you need a ride or are you staying awhile?"

"I better go with you 'Rell. My mom will be here shortly. Derek we'll talk. I love you."

"Not enough to tell me who the father is."

"You're right. I'll tell you when you come home."

"Do I know the punk?"

"I don't think so. Love you."

"Love you too, later 'Rell."

"Later."

A Different Kind of Love

'Rell walked ahead of Shai to the elevator. His silence told her he was angry. This was going to be harder than she imagined. 'Rell pushed the button for the lobby. They were on the elevator alone. When the doors closed, 'Rell turned and faced Shai. He looked into her eyes and let his face touch hers. 'Rell kissed her, letting her know he understood and loved her. She returned the kiss understanding and loving him more.

Chapter 48

Darryl thought about what Simone said before answering. They had been arguing since he arrived at the Courtyard Suites. Simone had spent the night there waiting for Darryl to show. He had no excuse for the evening and told her he had to be at the airport by one o'clock. She was no longer listening. It was her turn to talk, and she had been talking for the last five minutes, non stop.

"You don't understand, because you don't care. I've been waiting for this kind of shit to happen. Do you know why Darryl? Can you guess why? Can you? Because you swore to me, when we first started seeing each other, this wouldn't happen. Do you remember that Darryl?"

Simone paused as though she wanted Darryl to answer, but he knew better. He would let her vent. She was right, he did promise not to let his family life interfere with their relationship. Simone wasn't naïve. She knew the place of the "other" woman. She didn't think Darryl knew his place.

"You can't have it both ways Darryl. If you have your family to tend to you can't expect me to make reservations and put my life on hold. I expect to see you when you say you're available for me. I don't think that's unreasonable. It seems you think I'm at your disposal. Why would I get a room at a damn hotel to be in it by myself?

That's the bullshit that you don't understand. Just tell me why I shouldn't be mad as hell. Not only did you not show up last night, you didn't call. You didn't call this morning when you got up. You wait until midday to tell me you're going home to check on your family in an hour. Why shouldn't I be mad as hell? In all of your thoughts, did it cross your mind that you may be putting me in a situation that I wouldn't like? No hell no. I'm not your dizzy ass wife, Darryl. I know you don't give a damn about nobody but yourself. You're not going home to check on them. You're going home 'cause you're running scared."

"Simone, I think you've said enough. I get your point and I apologize, but you're not going to talk about Francine, my family or how I choose to manage my business. Look, I've got to handle this, and I have to leave today; now if you can't deal with it okay but that's it. I'm trying to handle all this without shutting anyone out. I've shut out my family. I need to go home."

"Darryl you do what you need to do. I need to do some things too."

"Aw girl, don't trip. I'm in some serious shit here. You don't understand. If they're trying to kill Derek, I could be next."

"Why are you tripping? You don't even know if they're after you. Have you been to see Derek or Mr. Simpson? What gave you the clue that they're looking for your ass?"

"Simone, please. I've seen Mr. Simpson."

"Well. Well, Darryl. What did he say?"

"He'll call me if it pertains to me; but Simone, who knows?"

"You know it doesn't. You don't need an excuse Darryl, just go. It was fun boo."

"Oh, it's like that!"

"Check your watch. It's time for you to catch your flight. I told you I won't stand between you and your family. I meant that. Francine's time is hers. I can wait for mine. If it's meant to be, it will be."

"So, that's it! What are you saying? We're through because trouble comes up?"

"No, I just don't want you using a situation to cover for you being down right inconsiderate. You knew last night that you weren't meeting me here, and you had a ticket for your flight well before this morning."

"Okay, I see your point."

"Well, then you should see that I'm not the friendly flyer stop over. It's bad enough that I have to keep the relationship we have a secret. Darryl you won't play me for your fool."

"Shit girl. Shit!"

"What's the problem? Take your ass home!"

Darryl pulled out his cell phone ignoring Simone's comment. He looked at his watch and shook his head. He couldn't make the flight if he tried. Francine would be upset but she wasn't there to express it. He dialed his home.

"Fran, listen, I'm going to have to talk with Derek before leaving here."

Simone kept quiet listening to his side of the conversation. She felt good about his decision to cancel his flight. Simone knew if she really was the reason for his delay, he wouldn't say when he was leaving.

"Yeah, he's doing okay. I talked to Mr. Simpson this morning."

Simone hoped he would stay the weekend. That would give her the rest of the week and the weekend to fulfill her pleasures. She was becoming accustomed to meeting him late at night and waking up in his arms.

"I don't know. I'll know tomorrow after I talk with him. No, I don't think he had his test done today. I think it will be later this week. I'll find that out too. Yeah, that's true. Okay, maybe I will. I'll call you tomorrow and let you know. You're right. I'll call you after I speak to him. Okay, you too. Later."

"So, you're staying until tomorrow?"

"No, I'm going to finish this business here. You were right about that. Leaving now will not settle anything. I do need to know if I'm involved at all. I haven't talked to Derek about it yet. I'm not satisfied with not knowing. The other thing is us. I'm not in any position to make claims or wants other than what you allow. I want to be with you as much as I can but you and I both know I'm married."

"I'm not trying to pull you out of your marriage Darryl. Just treat me with respect. Don't have me waiting all day and night when you know you have no intention of seeing me."

"Again, I'm sorry. You're right. I was thinking about me. Can I make it up to you?"

"I don't know, can you?"

Darryl knew what she wanted, but he wasn't sure anymore what he wanted. There were women he dealt with in the past that would have pulled the stunt that Simone pulled, and he would have been on the plane. By the time he called them again they would be glad to hear from him. Darryl stayed because he didn't want to lose Simone. He wasn't sure he wanted to go home. Francine didn't seem to care, one way or the other, and that didn't bother him either. She never did.

"Simone, can we spend the afternoon out? I want to breathe some fresh air, have some lunch and then relax with you."

"It sounds good."

Darryl took Simone's hand and kissed it. He pulled her to him and kissed her forehead softly.

"Thank you for understanding and helping me understand. Our relationship is different Simone. I'm learning to love all over again."

Chapter 49

Nana looked in the closet for the second time since D.Q. died. 'Rell called to say he would be going through his father's things within the next two weeks. She didn't really care when he did it. She wanted to be sure it was all together. It seemed as though he had more boxes than what was in the closet. The door bell rang as she remembered there were boxes of D.Q.'s on the back patio stacked neatly in a corner. *Now how many boxes are out there?*" The door bell sounded again.

"Alright, alright, I'm coming. Who is it?"

Nana opened the door to find Nikki bending down picking up the groceries that fell through the broken bag she was carrying.

"Child, you okay? Let me help you."

"Mama Mince, I have it. Thanks."

"Well, come on in. Put that stuff on the counter baby. What is all of this?"

"I was bringing you some snacks for the house. I know how we run in and out of here munching, so I brought over a few things."

"Thank you Nikki, how thoughtful."

Nana and Nikki put up the groceries. Nana poured two glasses of lemonade as they moved to the living room to sit and talk.

"How's Derek, Mama?"

"He's doing better. They're testing him this week. If everything is okay they'll release him Friday."

"That's good. How's his therapy coming?"

"He still doesn't feel a thing. He might have to have another surgery. The test will tell."

"Will the surgery help?"

"I believe it will. None of us really know though, Derek is willing to have the surgery if they say it may help. How's your business coming along?"

Nikki was glad Nana mentioned the business. It could lead into what Nikki stopped by to find out. She wanted to know if Nana suspected Darryl and Simone. Darlene didn't know if Nana knew and didn't care. She repeated over and over again that Darryl and Simone were grown and knew what they were doing. Nikki wasn't taking the blame for their mistakes.

"The business is picking up. We have customers up and down the east coast. Simone does most of the meetings, and I do the specs and pricing. We work well as a team."

"That's good. Is Simone thinking 'bout moving this way?"

"I don't think so, I offered my home to her, but she hasn't taken me up on my offer."

"Well, as long as you can manage with her being in New York. I guess it doesn't matter."

"It does cause her to travel a lot, but once we establish our customers it will slow down."

"I don't know baby, Darryl and 'Rell travel from time to time even though the business is established. Darryl travels more now than ever, spends a lot of time on the road. Francine is always telling me he's on the road."

"Hmmm, is Francine okay with that?"

"Francine don't say much about anything that Darryl does. He's been doing things his way, since they got married. I guess Darryl doesn't care much either."

"Francine's a strong woman. Mama I don't think I could do that mess all over again."

"What mess Nikki?"

"You know; the second woman thing. I sat waiting for D.Q. to make up his mind about our relationship. Now that I learned how D.Q. truly felt, it was worth it, but Lord knows I wouldn't do it again."

"Even if it was D.Q.?"

"Even if it was D.Q., Mama, I spent nights competing with Tonya for his attention. I always had his body but his mind would drift. He was devoted to the word marriage. I couldn't do it over again."

"So how does your relationship with D.Q. compare to Francine and Darryl?"

"She's been there too. I mean, with the kids he has had outside of the marriage. Darryl goes in and out of his marriage like it has a swinging door. I just feel for her."

"Darryl does what Francine allows. If he had a woman who would put her foot down, he would stop that foolishness. Francine is sweet and Darryl don't always need sweet. But that's their business. I don't get involved in that mess. He knows not to bring it around me."

"Mama, has he ever brought it around you?"

"I can't say he has. Francine usually calls me crying, and I listen. Darryl calls afterward and I listen. I don't get involved."

"Mama, is Darryl still gambling?"

"Gambling with his marriage? He probably is."

"No I meant betting and owing debts."

Nana chuckled. She didn't know what Nikki was implying, but she could tell Nikki was serious.

"I have no idea baby. If he's cheating again I don't want to know."

"Mama Mince, I think he is gambling."

Nikki couldn't bring herself to tell that she knew he was cheating and who the woman was. Nana would have to understand her reasons if and when she found out.

"Well if he is, it's on him. I ain't got no money to pay off any other debts he makes gambling."

"Did he go home?"

"I don't think so. He didn't call me and he will call before, and after he flies."

Nikki hadn't heard from Simone, since she left the night before. Nikki would talk to 'Rell and see what he thought about Darryl and Simone. He could advise her if she should say anything. Nikki looked at her watch, which read two fifteen. She wanted to be home when Simone got there.

"Mama, I'm going to get going. I just stopped by to say hello. Sam is meeting me at the church at three o'clock."

"How is Deacon Smalls?"

"He's fine. We're going to the movies this evening. I think we're eating out too."

"Well y'all have a good time."

Nikki put on her coat and walked toward the door.

"Mama, let me know about Derek and how he's coming along. Tell him he's in my prayers."

"I will. Thank you for the snacks. I'll talk with you soon."

Nana watched Nikki get into her car from the door. She stood in the door moments after Nikki pulled off. She thought about D.Q. telling her how much he loved Nikki. Nana had learned to love her too.

Chapter 50

onya waited for Karlton to come in the door with the news of his meeting with 'Rell. She banked on his ability to convince 'Rell that his investment would be a plus for D.Q. Enterprises. It was after six o'clock and he hadn't called. She was tempted to call him but prepared her third whiskey sour instead. The phone rang as she stirred the drink with her finger. She hurried to answer it as Karlton put his key in the door. Tonya looked at the phone confused but smiled when she saw his face as he entered the den.

"Hello."

"Hi Ma, how are you?"

"Derek?"

It was the first time since his accident that he called her. Tonya felt a surge of guilt knowing she hadn't visited him for the past three days.

"Yes, it's not Shai. Who else calls you Ma?"

Tonya laughed pretending his question was a deliberate joke. She took a drink from her glass waiting to answer any questions about her absence.

"Listen, I'm having my test done in the morning. The results should be ready early next week, but I will be released sometime on Friday."

"Friday, baby, that's day after tomorrow. The test won't be reviewed until next week. Why not wait to see what the results show?"

"They said I can go home Friday. I will start my outpatient care next week until they decide if I will need another surgery. I will be in counseling sessions, no physical therapy until they know more. So, I can come home."

"I don't' know Derek, maybe I should talk with the doctor."

"I made the decision to come home until they review the test."

"Your house is not equipped for you and a wheelchair. There will need to be renovations to accommodate you."

"Rell and Uncle Darryl are handling that. I don't want to complete the renovations until it's determined that this condition is permanent."

"What do you mean Derek? You're in a wheelchair for God's sake. You need your home to fit your needs."

"It will. It will be exactly as I want it."

"Why didn't you call me before you called them?"

"Ma, you're not a contractor, and you don't have the money or the space at your home. It's being handled. I just wanted you to know I was going home on Friday, just in case you decided to stop by. If not, call me at home after Friday."

"You're not thinking Derek. You're still under medical care. You should let me take care of you for a few weeks until you adapt to your home again."

"Shai said she'll help me. She's not banned from my house. Anyway I have to get used to this if I have to live this way."

Tonya was floored. Derek wasn't playing the depressed cripple. "I guess you're right. Shai can help you. Well, call me if you need your mother!"

Tonya slammed down the phone. Tears of anger rolled down her face. Then she remembered Karlton had walked in. She turned from the bar as she wiped her eyes and looked at Karlton sitting on the sofa holding his head in his hands.

"Derek's being released on Friday, he's going to his house. It's being renovated over the next few days to handle him and his wheelchair. He spoke to that damn 'Rell and Shai. I missed my chance."

"Rell is sharp. He peeped my card right away. He knew about me and D.Q., told me off the bat that my money was no good for investing, I can do the vacation thing and that's it."

"What kind of shit is that?"

Tonya turned back to the bar and poured herself another drink. She pointed the wine at Karlton. He nodded his acceptance and she filled a glass with wine for him. Karlton took the glass and sipped a little before he answered.

"I don't know, but the man is on point. D.Q. prepared him well. I was impressed with him and his staff. He knew what I wanted and shut me down. Tonya it's gonna take some work to get anything from him or the company."

"Karlton, he owns nothing. That company doesn't belong to that bastard! His mother has properties, money and whatever else D.Q. left her. Hell no, I refuse to let it go."

"Tonya, we have to look over your papers. Do you have them here?"

"I have them in the safe. I might as well burn them. I can't cash them in. One of the partners called saying that the papers were of no value, unless I had something they didn't have on file. My lawyer checked it out right after D.Q. died. Nothing! Shit! Now Derek's going home and he isn't even depressed."

"Listen let's look over the papers together. What do you know about 'Rell? Any dirt, anything to disgrace the company? What about his mother? Let me do some spying. Everyone has their secrets."

"Rell, Rell. He had a girlfriend. I think her name was Monica or Monique. I don't know if he still sees her. And there's a business associate named Craig. They should know something and they're no longer around so maybe there's some hidden dirt there."

"Tonya, you work on your relationship with Shai and Derek. If you're going after 'Rell, they're not going to like it. You've got to play the changed mother. Start with not hanging up on them when they talk to you. I'll deal with Mr. Mince."

"I don't know what you might find. Him and his Mama are too Godly for me. I know damn well D.Q. wasn't her only love she stole from someone's home, and for that bastard son of theirs, he squeaks he's so clean. It's sickening."

"Baby calm down, maybe his mother is looking for a new love since D.Q. is gone."

"Well it won't be you. Try something else."

"Scared you'll lose me?" Karlton teased. "Tonya, say it ain't so."

"It ain't. I just don't want to have to kill that winch."

"No, I'll make it my business to deal with her about the vacation homes personally. Let's see if she bites. That's all. 'Rell won't like it but hey, his momma is grown."

"I don't like it Karlton. Why does it have to be you? No, leave the bitch alone. Find out some dirt on her son. That will wreck the company. That's what I'm after. If we wreck his world her world will crumble.

<h1 style="text-align:center">Chapter 51</h1>

Shai got up rushing on Saturday morning. It seemed that the clock was determined to catch her unprepared for the guests she invited to dinner. Everyone agreed a dinner on Saturday was better than one on Sunday. It was perfect timing. She was showing and was well rounded. Mia and Mitch stayed with her late the night before setting up the nursery with the furniture, curtains and matching Winnie the Pooh décor.

The room was beautiful and Shai was proud that the job was completed. 'Rell had done all the shopping for the groceries and beverages. He skipped the decorating to pick up the items Shai would need for the twins to be comfortable out of their room. He got the car seats, the double stroller and the bouncy chairs, diapers, bottles and clothes. He promised Shai he would get there before the guest arrived so no one would suspect he was anyone other than the Uncle. Shai enjoyed watching him pick and choose but wasn't sure that everyone wouldn't think he was reacting like a father. She decided to say she shopped early if they asked about the items that were bought.

Shai invited the family members that mattered to her. She left a message inviting her mother on her answering machine, but didn't care if she came or not. Derek was home and 'Rell would be picking him up on his return trip to her house. Everything looked fine but she was behind in the cooking. It was almost eleven when she got up, and she blamed herself for not setting the alarm. She would need Marci to come over early to help with the salads. Shai told everyone to come around four o'clock, dinner would be served at five. She decided to call Marci and plead with her to get her to come earlier than planned.

"Marci hi, it's me." Shai tried to sound innocent but Marci knew better.

"So, you're just getting up and…." Marci filled in the words for her cousin, knowing she needed help for the afternoon.

"And I could use your help if you got here a little early. Please."

"I had planned on it. I'm picking up Mia at two thirty is that early enough? She wanted to come and help."

"Does she know I'm pregnant?"

"I don't know. I didn't ask her if she noticed. No, she would have said something."

"Okay, come then. I just won't tell her who the father is."

"Shai, what are you talking about. You're going to tell everyone who the father is?"

"No, I don't think I'm going to tell them at all.

I'm pregnant. The father and I did not have a serious relationship, and by the time I found out, I was pregnant, he had transferred to another hospital."

"Shai, I don't know if my Mom and Nana will let it ride at that. You know how they are. No, they won't let that ride girl."

"Well, 'Rell really gets upset with this boyfriend thing. They'll read his expressions. This way there is no one they can question me about and none of you will get tripped up in questions either."

"So does this guy know he's a father?"

"No. We dated for a while. He got notice that he would be interning, say, in Maryland. It was what he wanted. He wanted me to come, I told him no. We broke up, he left. I wasn't feeling well after, say, a couple of months, went to the doctor and babies up."

"Are you telling them you're having twins?"

"Yeah, I don't see why not. I'm not asking them to give me permission Marci. I'm having a dinner to let them know. I have two babies on the way. I've asked you and Mitch to be the Godparents and 'Rell will be their caretaker if something should ever happen to me."

"Wow, won't Derek freak about that. I mean, he's your brother too."

"Marci, I wish this was simple. I've got to give 'Rell a part in this. People will see him involved in the twin's lives and wonder why. Like where is his lady? Why hasn't he gotten married? It's hard to explain but for right now I have to validate our closeness."

"Girl, maybe you're digging a hole for you and him. If I was you, I'd do just what you planned and leave out what 'Rell's part may be. After all you are his only sister. He showers you because you've only known each other for what, not even a year. He wants you to have a good relationship. He showers Derek too. No one will think otherwise."

"You may be right. I'll think it over. Did I tell you we're going to talk with the doctor about our relationship, so she can tell us what to expect."

"The babies may be fine though. Like I said before, you don't have the same parents, just the same father. Mitch and I were talking about that the other night with 'Rell. I read up on it a little."

"Well I'll be glad to hear that from the doctor."

"Shai, that's my cell ringing. Girl, it's in my purse. It's probably Mia. I'll see you about two forty-five."

"Thanks, Marci, for everything."

"You're welcome girl. Love you."

"You too."

Chapter 52

Nana persuaded 'Rell to wait for another day before going through his father's belongings. They both agreed that the day would be interrupted with the dinner at Shai's place. He completed his shopping about twelve thirty and headed for his mother's house. He decided a visit with his mother would kill some time.

'Rell stuck his key in the door and immediately began shouting his arrival. "Ma, Simone, it's me. Is anybody here?"

"Yeah, 'Rell, I'm in the den. Your mother is in her room."

"What's up? How's the decorating business?"

Simone came into the living room where 'Rell was making himself comfortable. He grabbed the remote but put it down when he saw Simone entered the room to join him.

"It's going fine. We're picking up clients in what seems like a patterned area. It's making it easy for the orders to be filled."

"So once you design a place that's it for the client, or what?"

"Sometimes it's a one shot deal and then others have franchises or other business they are connected to. We're trying to get into hotel and restaurant chains."

"Wow, it sounds like you're busy."

"Do you want a beer? I think we have a few in the fridge."

"I'll get it Simone, do you want one?"

"Yeah, that will be good."

'Rell got up and went behind the bar and reached into the small refrigerator where they kept the beer. Nikki came into the room to join them. She smiled when she saw 'Rell.

"Hey, Mr. Mince."

"Mr. Mince was my father."

They all laughed. It was a line D.Q. would use all the time. Now and then Darryl and 'Rell would use it to mock him.

"What's up Ma? Simone was just telling me about your business perking up. I'm happy for you. Restaurants and hotels are a big venture. Maybe I should work for you."

"D.Q. Enterprises has enough to keep you busy."

Simone looked at her watch. She told Darryl she would be ready by two o'clock. Since he changed his mind about leaving, his attitude was different. Simone loved the affection he was giving her, but it wasn't the same Darryl she met, the family man. They agreed to lay the cards on the table before he left for Detroit the next day.

"How's your brother 'Rell?"

Simone asked the question when she realized Nikki and 'Rell were staring at her.

"He's home. He came home yesterday. Shai is having a family dinner tonight, and he'll be there. We're riding there together."

"Shai's having a family dinner? I thought it was just a dinner. She called to invite me, but I told her I wasn't certain about coming. 'Rell you can tell her for me, I'm sorry I'll miss this one. I don't want to bump heads with her mother." Nikki went to the kitchen to get napkins and snacks.

"Do either of you want anything special while I'm in the kitchen?"

"No Nikki, I'm leaving in a few. I thought you would be going to the dinner. I'm going to the movies."

"Simone, lately you've been going to the movies, the mall, window shopping, and who knows what other excuses you've been using. Cut the mess girl. I know you have a friend. I know that's where you go, and we can leave it at that."

"Okay then I'm going out."

Simone got up and went into the guest room to change her clothes and freshen up. 'Rell and Nikki watched her walk while mumbling to herself. Nikki forgot about going in the kitchen.

"That's better. So 'Rell, what's new on your plate?"

"What's that about?"

"Simone and her bull that's all. I've been tempted to tell her about it for a week or more. I couldn't hold out any longer."

"So who's she dating?"

Nikki didn't want to lie or answer that question she just put her fingers to her mouth as though to hush 'Rell. He looked at her confused.

"We'll talk when she leaves," whispered Nikki.

'Rell stood up and went to the bar to get a glass and ice for his beer. He knew his mother would want to talk awhile. He sat on the bar stool waiting for his mother to open the conversation. Simone closed the bedroom door. Nikki went to the far side of the room causing 'Rell to turn to face her. His mother kept her voice low as she spoke.

"Monique called me yesterday. She read about Derek in the paper and was wondering how you were doing. It was hard for me to believe you two hadn't been in touch with each other."

"Is she still dealing with Craig?"

"I didn't ask her and she didn't say. She said she would call again so we could get together."

"That should be a good day for you. You said you enjoyed her company."

"I just hope she doesn't think she can get back into your life through me."

"I hope she doesn't think that either. Monique is not stupid but..."

"But what?"

"Well Ma, your son is irresistible. I was a good catch for that girl." 'Rell's joke broke the serious moment they shared.

"Yeah, Mr. Mince."

They both laughed as Simone came into the room smiling pleased she didn't have to lie about having a date. Although she was casually dressed, her outfit and perfume would make anyone take notice. She had the glow of a woman with confidence.

"Since you know I have a date, how do I look?"

Nikki didn't answer, she knew who the date was with, and it was killing her not to tell Simone she was headed for a dead end road.

"You look good. I should be your date. You need a young man on your arm tonight."

"Rell, you're like a son. I wouldn't take you out."

"No, I would take you out. Wine you, dine you and…"

"Rell, I'm your older cousin, watch it boy."

'Rell started laughing. Nikki joined in with her own jokes.

"Simone couldn't handle someone your age 'Rell. Any of them would put it on her."

"So this date must be in her age category or older. Simone do we know him?"

"No, you don't. So don't start that guessing thing. Have a good time at the dinner you two."

"I'll be here, I'm not going. Tonya will probably be there or stopping by. What's the dinner for anyway 'Rell?"

"Shai's pregnant. She wanted to announce it to the family. You know get the questions answered all at once."

"Well, I've got to go. Tell her congrats. See you tomorrow Nikki." Nikki just shook her head and waved her hand. She got up from her seat to pour herself a glass of soda. 'Rell gave Simone a hug and tried to kiss her neck.

"Boy, that tickles, stop it."

"Yeah, that's what a young brother would do, make you say stop." Laughter filled the room again. Simone made her way to the door and waved goodbye.

"So Ma, you know who he is, don't you?"

"Rell, I know who it is, and I need your opinion about what I know."

"My opinion, what does that mean?"

"It means I don't agree with who it is, and you probably won't either."

"Okay who?"

"Your Uncle Darryl." Nikki felt a mental release. If she could just tell Simone she knew she would be mentally free of the feeling of guilt she held.

"Uncle Darryl. He stays in enough mess. How long has this been going on?"

"I'm not sure. I just figured it out by talking to your Aunt Darlene about his air flights and stopovers in New York. 'Rell your uncle is wrong, but so is Simone. It doesn't seem to bother her that he's married. She doesn't see the problems that it causes to love a married man."

"Ma, Simone is grown. So is Uncle Darryl. She has to see the problems. He knows the problems. I don't understand what he's doing. Aunt Francine accepts it all though. She's a strong woman to take all of that and still stay with him. Listen, don't you get all caught up in their affairs. They'll have to answer for that not you."

"I just don't want anybody thinking I condone what's going on. I didn't introduce them for them to start a relationship. You know people they'll think I was aware of their intentions."

"People are going to think what they want to anyway. Like I said, they're grown. Uncle Darryl is a trip though. You would think after two outside children he'd love to be a married man. Why be married if you live like you aren't? I guess it's a different kind of love."

"Thanks for listening. Your Aunt Darlene said the same thing, but for some reason it sounds different hearing it from you."

"Aunt Darlene knows?"

"Yeah, I told her about how I felt. I tried to tell your grandmother. They both said they didn't want to know. Darlene knows it's Simone though. Your Nana didn't even let me get to naming who I suspected."

"Take their advice, let it go. It's not your problem and they haven't asked you for your opinion or best wishes."

"So, again how are things with you?"

"Well, Derek's home is being renovated for him if he should still need a wheelchair after this next surgery."

"Another surgery and he'll still be paralyzed?"

"We hope not. The doctors will know better next week. Anyway, the house is being made ready just in case. Besides, even with the surgery he will need physical therapy to help him walk again. His house will be ready for him to move around."

"And Ms. Shai is pregnant. Who's the father?"

'Rell paused. This was important to him. He didn't want to lie to his mother, but he didn't know where to start or what to say.

"I don't know him. Ma, we need to talk seriously. I want to talk about this after I go through dad's belongings."

"What does that have to do with Shai? I don't understand."

"I don't either but Mr. Simpson said go through dad's belongings before Shai made her announcement. I know that sounds confusing. I'm confused. I'm mentally tired. But please can we talk about the pregnancy after next week."

"Sure baby."

"How's Deacon Smalls?"

"We're going out tonight, he's fine. I really enjoy his company. You would like him."

"Maybe we can get together sometime soon."

"Rell that would be good, he loves basketball and football."

"Maybe we can go to a game or two together."

'Rell felt better knowing Nikki was secure in her relationship with Deacon Smalls. She didn't push with any other questions about Shai or his father's belongings. They talked for another hour then 'Rell left to pick up Darryl. Nikki sent her congratulations to Shai apologizing for her need not to be present.

Chapter 53

The cars parked in the driveway and around the front lawn let 'Rell know the guests had arrived. Those parked in the driveway left room for him to pull up close to let Derek out of the car. Mitch came out of the garage when the car engine cut off.

"Man, your ESP is working great this evening."

"I was on my way to my car for a bag Marci thinks she left. Hang on let me get it, and I'll help you with the chair. What's up Derek?"

"Hey man, what's up with you?"

'Rell looked at the space to go into the house through the garage and decided it would be a tight squeeze with the wheelchair.

"Derek, I think it will be easier for you to enter from the front door."

"Whatever you say man."

'Rell sat the chair by the front door and returned to the car to help Mitch get Derek. Tonya's car pulled up behind 'Rell's. She stayed in the car watching them move her son to his chair. Tonya got out of her car but paused purposely wanting to make her own entrance into Shai's home. Derek was taken into the grand room where he could move around freely with the wheelchair. He immediately drew attention from those who hadn't seen him since his accident.

'Rell walked through the room greeting family and friends he hadn't seen for months. Others introduced themselves as cousins, aunts and uncles, who were related to Tonya. They all said they were glad to meet him, how much they had heard or read about him and welcomed him as an extended family member. 'Rell smiled and thanked all of them. He entered the family room and spotted his side of the family. Mia was the first to give him a hug and told him he was looking good in his black jeans. 'Rell laughed at her comments trying to ignore her deliberate flirting.

"Mia, you're my cousin."

"Damn shame boy. So who's your girl now?"

"Not dating. I'm still trying to get a grasp on being this big CEO. It takes up a lot of my time; little room for playing."

"But Mr. Mince, I know you, you do play. I just was wondering where."

"Nowhere for now, I hit the clubs every now and then. But I can't really deal with the club chicks. The executive chicks are after my money, so I'm laying low."

Mia pulled 'Rell's ear to her mouth so no one else could hear. "That's that bullshit, Mr. Mince. You and I both know it."

Mia walked off smiling. 'Rell shook his head. Certain she didn't know about his relationship with Shai, he realized her comment could only mean she heard gossip about his involvement with someone. Marci walked in the room and noticed 'Rell standing in the middle of the floor.

"You look confused."

"No, your sister is a trip. Have you seen Shai?"

"She's making Apple Martini's. I think she went to get ice from the kitchen. Everyone is having a good time, talking and mingling."

"Did she make her announcement yet?"

"No, you weren't here. She wanted to wait for you and Derek."

"Mitch is in the other room with Derek. They're talking with the other side of the family. This dinner is more than I expected Marci. Remind me to tell Shai the family will have to schedule visits to see the kids."

"Rell you're funny. You know how family is they call when they're a block away."

"You're right. Let me see if I can help this girl with anything. You said she was making the Martini's right?"

"Yeah, that's what she's been doing." 'Rell walked toward the kitchen when he heard Tonya calling Shai's name from the grand room.

"Shai sweetie, bring Derek something to drink; maybe a little juice."

"Shai, I got it." Mitch asked Derek what he wanted and Derek told him any juice would be fine. Tonya watched Mitch and got up leaving him standing there.

"I'll get it for him. I thought Shai was closer that's all. No need for you to help him."

Mitch shook his head and continued to talk with Derek letting Tonya wait on her son. Shai turned and noticed 'Rell watching her every move.

"Hey 'Rell, I'm glad you're here. Can you check the ice in the refrigerator behind the bar and restock it if needed?"

"Anything else?"

"Yes, the trays on the counter need to be in the dinning room."

"Okay, anything else?"

"Stop 'Rell. I know it's a lot, but it's turning out okay.

"Are you okay?"

Tonya walked between them. She didn't excuse herself, she just stepped between them. 'Rell walked away.

"What is it with him? Does he think you need him? And that damn Mitch, he's with Derek like a bodyguard."

Shai didn't answer and handed Tonya a tall glass of punch for Derek. Tonya gave her a pert smile. Shai walked away with a full container of Apple Martini's. 'Rell put the trays in the dining room where he saw Nana and his Aunt Darlene talking with Reverend Wilcox and another man he didn't know.

"Hey, baby. We were wondering when you would get here."

Nana gave him a kiss hello which was followed by his aunt's hug and the Reverend's handshake. 'Rell gave the other man a nod of recognition.

"I stopped to see my mother and pick up Derek."

"Rell, this is Shai's friend from her job, Richard."

'Rell froze. He didn't know what Shai had decided to do, but he knew that there was no mention of a person matching the name Richard. He needed to clarify what was going on. If this guy was to act out the part of her so called boyfriend 'Rell was determined to clear the house. Shai entered the room and saw 'Rell's look.

"Rell, can I talk with you a minute?"

"Yeah, excuse us please."

Darlene, Nana and Richard looked at each other wondering what went wrong. Shai and 'Rell walked to the back of the house into a guest room.

"Who is he Shai? Richard? Like the Richard who is supposed to be your boyfriend from the job?"

"No, he's actually here to meet Mia. I didn't get a chance to tell you. I guess when we were talking, I thought up the first name that came to me. Anyway, Richard and Mia are somewhat dating. 'Rell, you can't think I'm stupid enough to bring a man into your home."

"This is your home Shai. I'm sorry. I don't like this boyfriend thing."

"I'm not even going to go into the daddy is working thing. I'm just going to say we broke up before I knew I was pregnant. I don't have a boyfriend, and I'm having twins."

Marci came into the room.

"Sorry guys, but people are hungry. Are we doing buffet, grab a plate, or what?"

"Marci it's all set up in the dinning room. 'Rell just put the last trays in there. Darlene and Nana are in the dining room so no one can take any until it's blessed by Reverend Wilcox. He'll bless the food after I gather them together and make my announcement."

Chapter 54

Karlton went over the papers Tonya left for him. Everything was just as she described. There was no inheritance from D.Q. Enterprises. Her stocks were sold to another firm a month prior to D.Q.'s death. Although they were lucrative they were not D.Q. Enterprises stock. Tonya's only connection with the company was the payment they made for her home. It had been paid in full a week after D.Q. died. The company presented a written agreement to pay the taxes and insurance yearly. All repairs or renovations would be paid for by Tonya if needed. Her vehicles were paid off in the separation agreement. Tonya could not expect any other money coming from D.Q. Enterprises. Karlton couldn't believe she didn't see it coming. D.Q. gave her what she wanted in the separation agreement and dispersed anything she could claim after his death before he died. Tonya took a leave from her job to provide care for Derek. Now it looked as though she would be returning to work.

Karlton contacted the company he worked with and told them he would take them up on their offer to become a traveling representative. He would need to keep the job until he knew exactly what the future held for him. After looking at her papers it seemed Tonya would need him to take care of her. He had to find a way to get Tonya back in 'Rell's good graces. *"If 'Rell could see Tonya's anger as sincere hurt, he may help her for Shai's sake."*

Karlton thought about contacting Nikki but thought better of it. He would meet Derek and 'Rell together and explain Tonya's drinking came from the same hurt and anger. Making the phone call was nagging at him. *"What harm could it do? Just one phone call."* Karlton was curious, *"What type of woman was Nikki Robbins?"* Tonya warned him, as though she was scared. *"Maybe Nikki was the way into the company."*

Tonya was at the dinner and wouldn't be back for a couple of hours. Karlton picked up the address book and looked through it for Nikki Robbins number. Another brochure was on the table in the hall, he would find her contact number there. Karlton went to the hall and found the brochure. He was disappointed to find the contact number for Nikki Robbins was D.Q. Enterprises. He would have to wait for an opportunity to get it out of Tonya. He was sure she knew the number. In the meantime, he went through the brochure again looking for a loophole.

Chapter 55

The guests gathered in the dinning room waiting for the food to be blessed and Shai's announcement. She tried to make room for Derek to be closer to the table by asking other family members moved back to let the wheelchair through.

"Is everyone in the room? Aunt Carol where is Uncle Bill? I see him, okay. I am happy to see everyone is enjoying themselves. It's good to get together for good news sometimes."

Everyone nodded and made comments in agreement. Tonya looked around the room noticing none of these people had spoken to her in months other than her sister Carol. She shook her head with an expression of disgust.

"First I want to thank God, although I think he has heard from me more within the past few weeks than all my life. I am so glad he stayed with Derek, and brought him home to us. Even though he has a long road to total recovery I have faith that God didn't bring him this far to leave him. Derek I am proud of your courage. You have shown me what it means to beat the odds."

Everyone clapped their hands and chimed in with 'Amen' and 'Thank you Jesus'. Tonya smiled at Derek and tapped him on his shoulder.

"Secondly I wanted to give you all news that I have been keeping to myself for the last few months. I know some of you have been wondering about my weight gain. I have gained. It is an expected gain. I am six months pregnant. My due date is February twenty sixth. I'm expecting twins."

Someone said, "Did she say twins?"

"Shai, twins?"

"Yes, Aunt Carol, twins?"

"They're healthy and so am I. I wanted to have this dinner, bring you all together, and answer all your questions tonight. Reverend Wilcox, if you would please bless the food and our family."

"Sure Shai. Heavenly Father, we are united here together to share our love and understanding as a family, one unit. Father, you have been good to this family, and they want to say thank you, Father, for all you have done."

A voice in the midst shouted 'Thank you Father'.

"We want to thank you, Lord, for your mercy and everlasting grace you bestowed upon this family in its time of need. Father, bless this family bless their need to be one unit, their need to understand each other, their need to show each other love. Bless this food, Father, and the hands that prepared it. We ask for your blessing as we travel the roads going home this evening. We ask this in your name."

Everyone joined in saying "Amen".

The questions began right away. Shai answered them as they came. No more information was given than what was asked. 'Rell stood by and watched. Shai was glowing as she told of her doctor's visit and the surprise she had when she found out, she was pregnant with twins. Derek interrupted her asking Shai if he could speak with her a moment. They went into the kitchen with no one following them.

"Shai is 'Rell okay? He looks like he's not feeling well."

"I'll check on him. He may just be tired. He's been a big help to me. I don't know how he's been managing it all. D.Q. Enterprises, Quintech and helping me, he's probably real tired."

Shai thought about it as she said it. 'Rell was tired. Why hadn't she noticed it before now? It was a lot for anyone to take on. She would definitely talk to him to reassure him how much she loved him.

"Shai, I have a friend that I invited over. I just wanted to make sure it was okay for her to come here."

"Sure, why wouldn't it be? Do I know her?"

"You might. She was the morning nurse from the hospital. We exchanged numbers and I asked her to join me here for the evening. I'll be leaving with her."

"Well, I'll say, you are recovering well. I'm glad to know your accident hasn't spoiled your romantic side."

"I don't know about that yet. She's been a help for my mental state. She's aware of my condition, and we get along so far. I'm taking it a step at a time. Go ahead and enjoy your guest. I just wanted to make sure you were okay with her coming to your home, by the way, congratulations. Did Mom say anything?"

"No, you know she will. I really don't care. That's why I told her when I told everyone else. I didn't feel that she deserved to know what was going on with me, especially, after the way she treated me in the hospital."

"You're right. Maybe her knowing she'll be a grandmother will change her attitude."

"Derek, if her attitude changed, I would be worried."

"You and me both, it was just a thought."

They both left the kitchen laughing about their mother and her ill attitude. Shai went looking in the rooms for 'Rell and Derek returned to the grand room waiting for Leeza to arrive. 'Rell was at the bar pouring a drink when Nana walked up behind him.

"You okay Darrell? You look like you don't feel well."

"I'm okay Nana. I'm a little tired. I think I may be coming down with a cold."

'Rell told the lie hoping Nana would let it go as that. He didn't know how to hide his feelings. He needed a reason to leave.

"Well, if you feel the cold coming on you need to be taking a shot of medicine instead of a shot of vodka."

'Rell smiled. She knew he wasn't sick. He knew she would let it go.

"Thanks, I'll take your advice as usual."

"So, Shai is pregnant. How long have you known? Must've killed you not to tell; when you supposed to go through those things of your daddy's?"

"I'll get to them this week I hope. I need to get to them as soon as possible. It's just that different things keep coming up."

"Well it's a lot to go through. You could start this week and still not find what you're looking for."

'Rell looked into Nana's eyes. *Does she know something I need to know? This shit is ridiculous.*

"Nana, is there something I need to know?"

"You tell me. What would you need to know?"

"I need to be ahead of this guessing game. It seems since my father died, I've been guessing about everything. I just want to know what he was into. It all seems to tie in with my life in some way. I'm tired of surprises."

"You weren't too surprised when Shai said she was pregnant."

'Rell went to answer. He was willing to tell his grandmother he knew only because Shai shared the news with him. But he held his tongue. Shai approached them and the topic changed.

"Well Momma Shai, I knew you had gained weight."

"Yes Nana. I wanted to tell everyone finally. Did you have enough to eat?"

"Yes indeed. You cook well enough to be a mother. I didn't know you cooked like that. The macaroni and cheese was delicious. 'Rell did you get a plate?"

"No, I'll get one later to take home."

Shai looked at 'Rell puzzled about his answer. Nana saw the look and decided to leave them to talk. Nana didn't understand why Shai gave him the look, but she would finish her conversation with 'Rell later.

"Rell are you okay?"

"I'm fine Shai, just tired."

"Are you sure? I'll make your plate."

"No thanks. I don't have much of an appetite. I'll eat later."

"Why did you say you would take a plate home?"

"Shai, I think Nana would wonder if I said I would eat later, or I would get up in the middle of the night and fix a plate."

Shai smiled. She felt better knowing 'Rell intended to stay. They noticed Derek wheeling his way into the room with his friend.

"Leeza, this is my sister Shai and my brother 'Rell. Shai we're going to be leaving now."

"Did you introduce her to the other family members? Leeza did you want something to eat? My brother is so rude. Give her a chance to know some of us a little better. Shai took Leeza by the arm, and they left the room. 'Rell looked at Derek and shook his head.

"Are they starting to go home?"

"Yeah, most of the once a year family members have left. Nana and Aunt Darlene are cleaning up in the dining room and kitchen. I think Marci and Mia are helping. Man, this has been one dinner. I mean, I didn't think I would see another family dinner."

'Rell listened as Derek went on about Shai, the twins, his mother and the other family members. Derek's voice began to fade. His thoughts kept returning to Mr. Simpson saying; "Go through your father's belongings before announcing the pregnancy."

"Rell, did Shai tell you Marci and Mitch were going to be the Godparents?"

"Yeah, we talked about that. I think she told them last week. Marci knew all along. You know they're close man. Anyway she helped Shai deal with your mother while she got this dinner together. They're like sisters man, that's a good thing."

"Are you okay 'Rell?"

"Derek, I'll be fine. Have you heard from Mr. Simpson?"

"No, no news is good news."

Shai and Leeza returned with plates wrapped in aluminum foil. Shai told them to give her a minute to get a bag for the plates. 'Rell called Mitch to tell him they needed to lift Derek down the front steps. Shai returned with the bags for them. Derek and Leeza said their goodbyes as they went out the door.

It was another hour before the remaining guests began to leave. Everyone exchanged hugs and thanks for the invitation. They agreed they would see her soon for her baby shower. Shai told them twins were unpredictable, so she probably would have the shower after they were born.

Darlene, Nana and Tonya were in the kitchen. Darlene had started the dishes while Nana put up the leftovers. Marci, Mia and Mitch left shortly after Derek and Leeza. Reverend Wilcox and 'Rell were in the den watching the basketball game on ESPN.

"Tonya, you've been quiet. Are you okay?"

"Mrs. Mince, I'm fine. I guess I'm just a little shocked."

"Shocked about what?"

"Twins, isn't that shocking? Not to mention pregnant with no husband, boyfriend or father. I don't know what Shai was thinking."

"It don't take much thought. I don't know nobody that can tell you what they were thinking when they got pregnant. Do you Darlene?"

"No Ma'am. Shai's grown Tonya. She's got a good head on her shoulders, a home, and a job. What man could possibly compete with what she has? He probably felt intimidated knowing he couldn't do what she may have wanted."

"He could have stayed around Darlene. You and Mrs. Mince can't believe he didn't know he was a father. I think he just up and ran. I wish I knew who he was."

"Well if Shai said she didn't tell him that's it. There's no need to get into that. She's accepted he won't be a part of their life." Nana waited for Tonya to reply, but she didn't. Shai walked into the kitchen.

"Would you guys like to see the nursery? Marci, Mitch and 'Rell, helped me get it together. It's beautiful."

"Rell, what does he have to do with this? I'm sick of him and that Mitchell. Shai, they're men. They shouldn't even be this involved in your life."

"Ma, Mitchell is going to be the Godfather. 'Rell is my brother and just like Derek, he will be the uncle. They will all play an active role in my children's lives. Get used to it."

"I won't. I won't get used to it. They don't deserve this special treatment for being in your life less than a year. I don't understand you're head over heels concept of this so called brother and his friend. Derek is your brother, why wasn't he included?"

"Ma, where is your mind? Derek was in the hospital about to die! That's where he was. If you would stay off the bottle long enough for your memory to regenerate you would know that. 'Rell has been by my side even when you weren't. You can say what you want. Your opinion is just that, an opinion!"

"Well, show the damn room to Darlene and your grandmother. I don't need to see it. Did you call Nikki to decorate it too?"

"Ma! Good night! I've had enough of your sarcastic remarks for one evening. You don't really care, so why pretend?"

"I know you don't think you're putting me out."

"Just like you put me out of the hospital, only you don't have the same restrictions. You're welcomed to come back. I know you won't."

"You'll call me first little girl."

"Ma, once again good night and don't wait for my call. Nana, Aunt Darlene let me show you what I've done."

The three ladies left Tonya standing in the kitchen. Tonya thought about snatching Shai by the hair and shaking her until she apologized. She thought twice about it knowing Darlene and Nana would interfere. She was losing all around. Derek and Shai weren't any different toward her than they were when D.Q. was living. Reverend Wilcox entered the kitchen looking for Nana.

"Sister Tonya, are you okay? You look a little upset."

"No Reverend. I guess I'm shocked, I'll be a grandmother."

"They tell me being a grandparent is a blessing."

"I don't know about that. I had problems being a parent."

"Well Tonya, parenting doesn't come with a manual. All of us have difficulty with parenting."

"Do you have children Reverend?"

"Yes, I have two boys and a girl. They're grown, living in Philly. That's where I lived before I grew fond of Virginia."

"So you were married?"

"Yes, my wife died twelve years ago. I have grands and great-grands. It's a test of strength at times, but I wouldn't trade it for the world."

"Hmmm, well I don't know but sometimes the trade sounds good to me."

"Well Sister Tonya, prayer always helps. Sometimes we just have to leave the solutions in the hands of the Lord."

"Thank you for the words of advice Reverend. I'm going home now. I hear my bed calling me."

"Yes, I was looking for Jewels, I hear something calling me too."

"Jewels?"

"Yes, Sister Mince, Jewels for Julie."

"Oh, I didn't realize you were on those terms."

"Yes, she and I are engaged. We haven't set a date yet. We got engaged the day Derek was in the car accident. We haven't really got back to an official announcement. I thought you knew."

"No, well, wish you luck. She's a piece of work, like that Shai or should I say Shai is like her. Anyway I'll keep you in my prayers, and you do the same for me."

Tonya walked away leaving Reverend Wilcox in the kitchen by himself. She headed for the closet near the front door to get her coat and then went out the door without speaking to anyone else.

Chapter 56

Shai closed the door behind her last guest and sighed with relief. Although she enjoyed the company, she was tired. The preparations for the day and the anticipated problems drained her. She longed for a hot shower and her bed. She worried a little about 'Rell being upset throughout the evening. Shai didn't know what to say to him, but she needed him to understand she loved him for being there.

'Rell was cleaning the bar and restocking the refrigerator when Shai entered the room. She decided she would just hold him before speaking. They stood in the middle of the floor holding each other. The pressure of the day was at an end.

"Baby, I'm sorry. I didn't know I would feel this way. I'm trying this uncle thing, and maybe I can deal with it better in small groups. The family can tell my feelings without me speaking. The bad thing about it is the babies aren't even here."

"I know 'Rell. I wanted to get it done to avoid a call here and there. Now I think the calls would have been better."

"No, I don't know. You would have to answer all the calls from now until they're born. This was best. I'll survive. It just will take some getting used to."

"Well we've been okay so far. We must be doing something right."

'Rell held Shai's face and kissed her. "Our love is right. I love you Shai."

"I'm glad you do. Cause me loving you without you loving me would kill me."

"That won't happen. I know you're tired girl. Let me pamper you in the shower and massage your body with oil."

"Please do Mr. Mince."

They headed toward the master bedroom. 'Rell went into the bathroom and set the water valves. He lit the scented bathroom candles and dimmed the lights. Shai entered the shower in her robe and smiled knowing 'Rell would come out of his clothes. They stepped into the shower together. 'Rell bathed Shai tenderly kissing her neck and face as he poured the shower gel over her breasts. 'Rell continued to massage her shoulders as he stepped behind Shai in the shower. He bathed her back, buttocks, and thighs. He reached around her waist tenderly bathing her stomach in a circular motion. He reached below her waistline massaging her vaginal area. 'Rell turned Shai to face him.

Shai poured the shower gel down his body, watching small bubbles of soap appear on his chest and the walls of his abdomen. His penis stood erect as she touched him massaging him as she cleaned his body. 'Rell turned so his back faced Shai and the water touched his face, neck and chest. Shai slowly massaged his shoulders, and kissed his back as the suds fell to his feet. She reached around his waist massaging his penis slowly.

'Rell turned and faced Shai allowing the water to sprinkle in her face. He kissed her slowly as he rubbed her stomach as the water rinsed the soap from their bodies. He reached back and cut off the water as they continued to kiss. 'Rell stepped out of the shower and got Shai's robe and wrapped her in it. Shai took a large bath towel with her into the bedroom. 'Rell dried off and got the body oil from the shelf in the bathroom. The candles added a relaxing aroma to the air. 'Rell had preset the radio to their favorite midnight station and the music added the final touches of what was total pleasure for both of them. Shai was lying in the bed with her robe showing her thighs and her breast. 'Rell opened her robe fully and began to slowly massage her feet with the oils as he kissed her inner legs and thighs. 'Rell continued to massage Shai's body working his way up to her breast. He took his time as he sucked each nipple before applying the oil. Shai moaned in pleasure rubbing his body as he maneuvered to finish the full body massage. 'Rell slowly turned her from one side to the other and then massaged the back of her body down to her feet. Shai returned the pleasure giving him tantalizing kisses as she oiled and massaged him from head to toe. They laid together after the massage.

"Rell let me please you."

Shai knew by now they would have been on round two and 'Rell had not attempted to make love to her."

"Baby, we have plenty of time for that, relax and rest. I'm pleased right here in your arms."

Shai closed her eyes and dozed off. It was the best sleep she had in months.

Chapter 57

Another week passed without a word from the court regarding Derek's indictment. Mr. Simpson prepared all the appropriate paperwork to request a postponement if necessary. He was in his office early all week to make sure no courier deliveries were missed. It seemed odd that no correspondence had been sent. Derek gave him a call to inform him that he would be readmitted for his next surgery that morning. The phone rang for the second time that morning. The staff at Simpson and Simons had not arrived yet. Mr. Simpson answered the phone. It was the call he had been waiting for.

"Mr. Simpson, please."

"Yes, this is Mr. Simpson."

"Mr. Simpson this is Mr. Masters from the Clerk's Office in the Superior Court. You have submitted paperwork that you are representing Mr. Mince in his legal proceedings with the State."

"Yes."

"His case is scheduled to begin this Monday. We understand he has undergone extensive surgery. Is your client able to report to court?"

"No, he has been readmitted to the hospital this morning for another operation to repair damage to his spine."

"I see. Have you filed postponement papers with the court?"

"No, Sir I have not. I found out about his surgery last night."

"Well Mr. Simpson the prosecution is willing to get the preliminary hearing started without Mr. Mince being present. If you agree the scheduled date will stand."

"I will have to confer with my client. As you know I have just taken over the case and should have gotten all the documents by now. Nothing has arrived."

"In light of that Mr. Simpson we will contact the Prosecutors Office and allow you to get the documents you need to review the case. Please contact this office in writing to arrange your postponement and reschedule a date for the preliminary hearing. Again, this can be done without your client."

"Thank you Sir. I will get that to the court today."

"Mr. Simpson you might want to contact the Prosecutors Office if you are not in receipt of those papers by Monday."

"Thank you Mr. Masters, I will."

As he hung up the phone the other line rang. "Good morning, Stanley Simpson."

"Mr. Simpson this is Mr. Monroe. I am the lawyer representing Ms. Tonya Mince."

"Good morning Mr. Monroe. How are you?"

"I'm well sir. I'm calling regarding Ms. Mince. She is requesting all papers regarding her separation settlement be reviewed, as well as the documentation for the reading of her husband's will. Her concerns are she was not allowed to remain in your office for the complete reading of the will."

"Mr. Monroe, as a lawyer, I recognize your need to serve your client's best interest. However, there is nothing for your client to gain by insisting she has any financial link to D.Q. Enterprises. However, I will forward copies to your office. I do believe you have the documents there. I will update these with a cover letter dated with today's date. Mr. Monroe, I should warn you that if this continues, Mr. Mince will have no other choice but to file charges of harassment."

"Harassment?

Mr. Simpson I don't think you would have grounds for harassment simply because my client is seeking answers to her settlement."

"Mr. Monroe, anyone would agree that your client has had her questions answered, and her actions are to agitate Mr. Mince. I can't allow this to happen. I will send the papers, and if they do not suffice, we will see you in court."

"Thank you, have a good day."

"You do the same, Mr. Monroe."

Chapter 58

Nikki's suspicions about Simone and Darryl were confirmed within a week of Darryl leaving for Detroit. Simone didn't leave the house in the evenings. No dates, or over nights and Nikki wanted Simone to know she knew. Simone had given her the appointments for the next two weeks which proved she would be going back to New York soon. Nikki began to see the pattern. Simone usually left a week after Darryl, and they would be back in town at the same time. Until now Nikki had taken the advice of everyone regarding the hidden affair that Darryl and Simone had. It was true they were grown and their affair was their business. She still wanted to talk to Simone about it. Nikki waited most of the morning for Simone to wake up and tell her she would be leaving over the weekend.

"Good morning. Are you all packed?" Simone entered the living room with a pad and pencil.

"Packed? Packed for what?"

"Well you said there was a New York meeting Monday, so I wasn't sure if you would be leaving today or during the weekend."

"I hadn't made plans for either. The meeting is with the suppliers. That's your meeting. I don't think I know enough about the materials yet. I'll be glad to go with you though."

Nikki was totally caught off guard. She thought her questioning Simone about leaving would lead her to getting answers about her relationship with Darryl.

"So you planned on staying here while I went to the meeting?"

"Yeah, I figured I would handle the phones and set up the other appointments. After the New York meeting, there is one in Maryland and a possible appointment in Washington. They will call sometime today to confirm. I didn't want to go to New York just to fly back, but I will if we have to."

"Okay so the meeting in New York is with the suppliers?"

"Yes. Why are you questioning the meeting in New York? I wrote the information down for you to confirm it two days ago."

"Simone, we need to talk. I've had a lot on my mind, and I need to clear it with you now."

Simone sat back in the chair. She waited for Nikki to blame her for not handling the appointment in another way. She set her attitude at *"this is your fault not mine."*

"Simone, I'm going to just say this, and I hope you don't think I'm being nosy. But I don't think I should be a part of something where I can be blamed for it, and I wasn't involved."

"Say what? How can you be the blame for setting appointments? I set the appointments."

"This has to do with Darryl."

"Darryl who?"

"Darryl Mince. I know the two of you are seeing each other. It's really bothering me to know this and pretend I don't know. I don't want anyone thinking I introduced you to him knowing you would get involved."

"Nikki. Who is anyone? We're grown and discreet. The only reason you know is you've been watching my every move. I guess you've been watching when he comes into town and leaves too. Girl you're bugging. You dealt with a married man for thirty years. You didn't back up."

"His wife wasn't in my circle. There was no possibility of us being in the same place at the same time."

"Nikki, do you think you're the only woman who can deal with a married man? I know who his wife is, and I know when and when not to be around him. I won't be in her company, and he won't bring her in mine."

"Simone what about the fact that you're related to me, or even 'Rell for that matter? What about our feelings and reputation?"

"You had your married man. You did what you wanted with him as long as you wanted to. You even told him to go home to his wife and kids knowing you still loved him. Well, Nikki I did the same."

Simone began to cry. She stood up as her words broke up between the tears. "I did that Nikki. I haven't heard a word from him since he went to Detroit last week. I guess he's content being that married man. He didn't do what D.Q. did. He didn't decide to stay with his children's mother and hope I would understand that it wasn't his choice to be married. No Nikki, D.Q. loved you, and you turned your back on him. Well, I love Darryl and he's turned his back on me."

Simone walked away crying. Nikki could still hear her crying after Simone closed the guest room door. She didn't want to follow her. She had to digest her words. She understood Simone's pain. Nikki's feelings for D.Q. surfaced with the thought of Simone's love for Darryl. She sat in the recliner in the living room and cried.

The house had been abnormally silent for an hour after Simone and Nikki spoke. The silence was broken by the ringing of the phone. Nikki answered after the fourth ring.

"Hello."

"Ms. Mince?"

"Yes."

"This is Karlton Harris. You don't know me, but I was a friend of D.Q. and Tonya Mince."

"Yes."

"I came into town a few weeks ago seeking to invest in D.Q. Enterprises stock and property. Tonya referred me to your son Darrell. Well, I'm afraid we must have gotten off on the wrong foot. The young man told me I wouldn't be able to invest in anything other than the vacation homes."

"So why are you calling me, Mr. Harris, is it?"

"Yes, Harris. You see, I love the homes listed under your name, but I would love to have a stock option with D.Q. Enterprises. I knew D.Q. a while back, and I would love to add his stock to my marketing options."

"Well Mr. Harris. I don't handle that end of the business at D.Q. Enterprises. It is true that I have vacation homes that I sell and lease, but there is no connection to the homes and the stock. You really should contact the office and speak to one of the representatives there. They could assist you in purchasing available stock."

"Ms. Mince, my dear, we can cut through the red tape if you would just handle this transaction. I feel confident that you could sell me the stock and no one need be the wiser."

"That won't happen, Mr. Harris. I don't invest or buy any stocks. The buying, selling and investing is done by 'Rell's staff. They would find it strange if I took on this sale."

"I see. Did D.Q. leave you sitting well?"

"I beg your pardon. Mr. Harris, that has nothing to do with investments."

"Ah, but it does. You see Tonya has been left dry. No investments, no property other than the home she lives in, and no cash flow. I think you understand what I'm saying. You, on the other hand, have plenty. Your son is even the CEO. How fortunate you are, or was it your investment that paid off after D.Q.'s death?"

"Mr. Harris, speak to the representatives at D.Q. Enterprises for your interest in investments or any properties. As for my relationship with D.Q.; I won't honor that with an answer."

"I'm trying to stop Mrs. Mince, Tonya, from taking her story to the media, should do well for publicity, *"Ex- wife is left with nothing." "Mistress is living well."* Your son may not be able to stand up after the paparazzi gets this story."

"Mr. Harris what is your relationship in all this?"

"Tonya wants what's hers and let's say, just like you invested in D.Q. and reaped the reward, my investment in Tonya will have its benefits."

"Mr. Harris, Mrs. Mince's bottom fell long ago. Investing in her was and will always be a bad investment. I wish you luck but don't call my home again. I know why my son wouldn't deal with you."

"Do you now?"

"Yes Mr. Harris. I can smell your game through the phone and my lawn is already fertile. Have a good day Mr. Harris."

Nikki hung up the phone with an attitude. *"Damn that bitch won't quit. That name Karlton Harris rings a bell. Where do I know that name from?"* Nikki decided to mention it to 'Rell the next time he called.

Chapter 59

r. Pittman walked into the waiting area an hour after the surgery looking for the Mince family. Shai convinced Tonya a cup of coffee would calm her nerves. Shai, Tonya, 'Rell and Marci had been waiting for Derek to be moved to recovery after his surgery. Shai and her mother went to his bedside while 'Rell and Marci stayed behind.

"Dr. Pittman, how did everything go?"

'Rell didn't wait for the doctor to ask where Shai and Tonya were. She talked with them prior to surgery. The surgery was longer than expected, and she felt the need to explain the procedure that had become necessary to perform.

"Has your mother and sister left?"

'Rell ignored the comment about Tonya being his mother. He had been introduced as Derek's brother. It was a mistake anyone could have made.

"No, they went for coffee. They should be returning shortly."

"I'd prefer telling you all together, but I'm afraid I have another surgery to perform in twenty minutes. I need to do paperwork for Derek's after care prior to that surgery. If it's okay with you, I will give you the information and if either of them feels the need to call, please tell them to contact my pager later today. I should be free after one this afternoon."

"I can pass on the information, of course."

262

"Well, Derek's surgery was successful from a surgical point of view. We will not know if the nerve damage is permanent until some time has passed. If the damage is not permanent the nerves will regenerate, and he will have feeling where there is none now. The damage was not in the spine as we predicted. It was in the nerves and tissues surrounding the nerves. Time is what will be on our side. It is a slow healing process with a lot of therapy. Derek will have to work at making his lower extremities function. Because the procedure involved dealing with the nerves and tendons in his lower back and legs he will be in the hospital for two weeks before he will be allowed to begin therapy and outpatient care. He will be in recovery shortly and moved to a room. His visits can begin once he is in his room. Do you have any questions for me?"

"Dr. Pittman, will there be a need for more surgery? I'm sorry I'm Marci, Derek's cousin."

"I don't see a need for any further surgery at this time. We repaired the damage as we found it."

'Rell was numb. He didn't know what to ask. He was sure there were questions that needed to be answered, but he couldn't think at the moment.

"Again if you, your mother, or your sister, feel you need to talk about this procedure or his progress during the next few days, please don't hesitate to call my pager."

"Dr. Pittman, will Dr. Collins still be dealing with Derek's case?"

"Mr. Mince, I believe Dr. Collins is his regular physician. She should be checking on him during his stay at the hospital."

"Thank you again, Dr. Pittman. I will relay your message and tell them to contact you if they need to."

"Have a good day."

Dr. Pittman walked away leaving 'Rell and Marci to wait for Shai and Tonya. A few moments passed before Shai came through the double doors first with Tonya walking behind her.

"Shai, tell me I didn't leave my cell phone on the counter in that cafeteria."

"Ma, I didn't watch you. I don't remember you using your phone."

"I didn't say I used it. I can't find the damn thing."

Marci began telling Shai and Tonya what Dr. Pittman came to tell them. 'Rell was glad she was there. He really didn't want a reason to talk to Tonya. He took the opportunity to check his messages at the office and to call Mr. Simpson. He walked down the hall through the double doors where his conversations could not be heard. He called the lawyer's office after he checked all of his other messages.

"Mr. Simpson, this is 'Rell. Good morning."

"Good morning 'Rell. How are things going with Derek?"

"The surgery is over. He's in recovery. He will be here at least two weeks. Then he will begin his outpatient   therapy. If all goes well he should begin to get feeling in his legs. Time will heal him and he will be able to use his legs again if it's God's will."

"I'm glad there is hope for feeling. The courts called, we will be postponing the case until Derek can appear. But they will do all the preliminary hearings and other pretrial procedures that don't require his appearance."

"I see. What does that mean for me and my uncle?"

"You may be asked to testify at the grand jury."

"When will that be?"

"I've asked for a postponement until I can see what the lawyers at Carson Web have done and intend to do. I don't know who the other people from Carson Web are and exactly what their involvement is. 'Rell, the people who tried to kill Derek could be from Carson Web. I have not received any correspondence from them. It's odd, we are defending against the same companies, and they are not willing to join forces to defend Derek. That leads me to believe they didn't have any intentions for Derek to have a solid defense."

"Mr. Simpson, do you believe Derek could be fronting for the company?"

"It's a possibility. He could be the fall guy. At some point they may have thought that Derek decided to tell it all. They have until Monday. I will file papers with the courts and the Prosecutors Office on Tuesday."

"Thanks."

"Did you get to your father's belongings?"

"I have a doctor's appointment in the morning, and I will begin with my father's belongings when I return from that appointment."

"Doctor, are you okay?"

"Yes, it's for the twins. We're doing blood tests for possible problems. We decided to tell Dr. Kindell about Shai, and I, being sister and brother."

"I see. 'Rell it is imperative that you go through those papers. There are documents that could tie ends legally and financially for you, but I can't handle it without your father's documents."

"Have you got a list of documents you're looking for?"

"You'll know them when you see them. I believe he marked them and separated them. Your grandmother couldn't find them all."

"Look, Mr. Simpson. I believe Derek is in his room, they're calling for me to join them. I'll call you later today."

"That will be fine 'Rell."

Shai was waving to 'Rell from the other side of the doors. Tonya and Marci were waiting for them to catch up. They were waiting for the elevator to arrive. Shai opened the door for 'Rell to come through.

"Derek's on the next floor. The nurse came out to tell us he was moved."

Shai was smiling. 'Rell didn't understand why but it was good to see her smile in the presence of her mother.

"What's got you in such a good mood?"

"Marci said Dr. Pittman said there are hopes for Derek to regain movement of his legs."

"Well it's going to be a long recovery and a lot of therapy."

'Rell stopped talking so he wouldn't upset Tonya. The day was going smooth, and he didn't want to ruin it. Marci did well as a buffer for both Shai and 'Rell. She talked with Tonya keeping her focus on a separate conversation from time to time.

"Rell, are you going to visit Derek now?"

'Rell felt Tonya's words; they sent chills up his spine. *"This is it. She's going to start with me knowing I won't say anything to her here."* 'Rell decided to keep his answer positive to avoid conflict.

"If there's a limit on visitors, I can wait."

"Well if Shai, Marci and I are visiting, I would think that was enough for this morning."

"Mother, don't start. We can rotate so 'Rell can talk with Derek. There will be plenty of time when he can't get to the hospital to see him."

"Hmm why would you care Shai? You're being allowed to visit this time, so far."

"Rell and I will go in to see Derek for a few minutes than you can have the stage."

"The stage?"

The elevator door opened and the four of them got into the empty elevator. Marci pushed the button to the fifth floor without saying a word.

"The stage Shai, what stage?"

"Ma, the stage is wherever you choose to perform. I saw your hospital performance. Maybe Marci would like to see an encore today. I don't and neither does 'Rell. We'll leave. You can ride home with Marci."

"Shai please, don't start your shit!"

"I don't intend on it. I will see my brother and leave."

"And you 'Rell?"

"Mrs. Mince, I didn't come here to argue with you. I'm here to see that Derek is okay. Once I do, I'm out."

"Marci?"

"Aunt Tonya whenever you're ready, I'm ready."

"Shai tell your brother, I don't want to rain on his parade of well wishers. That's all you are. I will be back to care for him later. Marci push the lobby button after it stops at five. We can leave now."

"Aunt Tonya?"

Marci paused. Marci felt like 'Rell, it wasn't worth arguing with Tonya. She would take Tonya home and come back tomorrow by herself.

"Never mind, Shai, tell Derek I'll see him tomorrow."

The elevator stopped at five. Shai and 'Rell got off the elevator saying their goodbyes to Marci. Neither of them spoke to Tonya, and it didn't seem to bother her. Marci pushed L for the Lobby. She and her aunt rode on the elevator to the lobby in silence.

Chapter 60

The visit with Derek was short. He was still feeling the effects of the anesthesia. Shai held his hand and talked to him softly. 'Rell watched from distance thinking about what Mr. Simpson said about the Carson Web lawyers. 'Rell stepped into the hall and dialed his Uncle Darryl. He wanted to give him the information about testifying at the Grand Jury.

"Hello." Francine answered the phone at her home aware that it was 'Rell.

"Hey Aunt Francine, how are you?"

"I'm fine baby, how 'bout you?"

"I can't complain. Is my uncle around?"

"No, he left here two nights ago. I haven't seen him since. I thought he was on his way to Virginia. I don't have a clue where he went."

"Really, he didn't say where he was going?"

"Rell, things haven't been right between us, and he does little or nothing when he's here to correct it. I finally said something. He said I had a lot of nerve, like he was giving me something! 'Rell I don't want to give you all of this over the phone but to put it simply, I'm sick of your uncle's shit!"

"Okay, I hear you. You said you thought he was heading to Virginia. Where did he go?

"He told Michael and Alesha they could reach him by his cell phone. That's all I know. Oh well, he can go to hell. He's probably with some hoochie. It ain't worth it 'Rell. I run the business when he's out of town. I balance the books; pay the employees and the bills. It should be my business. When he runs it, we're in debt. I got it straight now, and I'm going to see a lawyer about what's rightfully mine or how to make it mine. It's too much. I don't know who she is this time, but I've had enough. He ain't gonna be satisfied until he fills another belly. Well, it ain't coming here."

'Rell didn't know what to say. His mother told him who the "hoochie" was. He didn't know what his uncle was thinking. Francine repeated her side of the story over and over each time adding another chorus of "It ain't worth it".

"Aunt Francine, did he mention to you, he might have to go to court regarding Derek?"

"Yes, he said something about that too. That was supposed to be his excuse for traveling to Virginia so much. But his cell phone says he does a lot of talking to someone in New York. I ain't stupid 'Rell. I know y'all think I'm naïve about a lot of things Darryl does. I ignored them because I truly thought he just got caught up. I thought he loved me like I love him. After all these years, Darryl throws himself out there to get caught. Well, this time he can stay right in her catcher's mitt. Trifling, that's what both of them are, trifling."

"Well the lawyer did call. If he calls can you tell him to call me please?"

"Honey, I ain't got no intentions on speaking to him. Call Michael or Alesha. They can give him the message. Try his cell phone. He may want to hear from you. He might be looking for a home if she ain't sharing hers with him."

'Rell was shocked. He wasn't shocked that his uncle tried the same game he had been playing for years, but to hear his aunt say she knew the game stunned him. She was right. The family always thought she was naïve. He tried Darryl's cell phone twice and left a message. He would have to call Michael or Alesha. 'Rell laughed to himself as he thought of the family secrets that kept unfolding.

Shai came out of Derek's room. She saw 'Rell down the hall near the window that overlooked the outdoor visiting area. It was a beautiful scenic park even in the winter. Although no one was in the area, there was a quiet calming effect as she looked out the window standing next to 'Rell.

"Are you ready to go? Our appointment with Dr. Kindell is in forty five minutes."

"I'm ready when you are. I was trying to reach Uncle Darryl. Seems like him and Aunt Francine are on the outs. He's left home."

"Left home? Is he crazy?"

"Yeah, pretty much. I don't understand him."

"I understand him. He's been doing her wrong for so long he expects her to accept any and everything he does. Women get tired of that mess. I don't know why men don't"

"Not all men are like that."

"Where is he then? Is he at Nana's?"

"No, that's just it. He's not at Nana's and he's not answering his cell phone. I'm trying to reach him about this court thing for Derek."

"It's postponed right?"

"Not the preliminary hearing and other proceedings where Derek is not needed to appear. Which means Uncle Darryl will have to testify at Grand Jury."

"When will that be?"

"Mr. Simpson doesn't know. We will have to testify though. Uncle Darryl needs to be in touch with somebody."

"Well, all you can do is keep trying to reach him. He knows there's a pending court case. He'll get in touch with you. Who's the woman his messing with this time?"

'Rell hadn't told Shai about his mother's suspicions and Shai hadn't been around Simone enough to have an opinion about her.

"You know her 'Rell? Tell me you didn't know about this. What is with the Mince family secrets?"

"I didn't know about it. My mother had suspicions about it and told me the other day. I advised her to mind her business. I guess her suspicions were right."

"Well, who is it?"

"My cousin Simone, I think you met her at my mother's house."

"Your cousin Simone, she's from New York right? Damn, another 'family romance."

"Well she's not his cousin. Anyway, it doesn't matter it was still too close for comfort. Now I understand what my mother was talking about. People are going to assume my mother, and I knew."

"Well you were right, it is their business. It's a shame he's going to lose out this time. Do you think that Francine is finished with him?"

"Shai if Uncle Darryl thought Francine would get over it, he would have stayed home. Either she's convinced him she's had enough, or maybe he really wants to be with Simone."

"I didn't even think of that. He's never left his home or business before. You may be right. He'll call you. He'll call somebody. He's probably taking time to think about what to do."

Shai went toward the elevator and pushed the button. "Come on baby. We'll be late for our appointment."

The elevator indicator light lit up. Shai and 'Rell left the hospital on their way to Dr. Kindell's office.

Chapter 61

Nana and Darlene sat at the kitchen table listening to Darryl's story. Nana shook her head in disbelief. Darlene was trying to understand her brother's intentions.

"Darryl, you have a business and a family. What is on your mind? You're not a young man, and you're married."

"Darlene, you think I don't know that. I'm trying to express my feelings; not explain them. Simone makes me feel different."

"Darryl, at one time or another they all made you feel different. You said the same thing about Michael and Alesha's mothers. Francine has raised those children right along with hers. She accepted them knowing they were from an extramarital fling. Do you really expect her to accept this?"

"She doesn't have to. I'm willing to leave. I want to have time to myself. I don't know why I always step outside my marriage. But Darlene, it don't change the fact that I am attracted to other women. Simone told me things that made me think about Darryl Mince, me. I need to know who I am, and what I want before I involve someone else."

Nana shook her head again before she spoke.

"You should have looked at yourself before you involved Francine in your life. But then again, everyone makes mistakes. Darryl I'd just like to know, when do you reflect on your mistakes to avoid making them again?"

"Mama, what are you saying?"

"I'm saying you've been down this road twice only to find there was no place like home. Now you're venturing again, for what? What are you looking for son? I agree you need time to think. It's just a shame that Francine is in all this mess. She's a good woman Darryl, she sure doesn't deserve this."

"Simone is a good woman too.

"Well if she is Darryl, she doesn't deserve this treatment either." Darlene couldn't imagine Simone wanting to take on Darryl's drama.

"What are you going to do then Darryl? What about Alesha?"

"Alesha ain't no baby Darlene. She's old enough to have her own friends and schedule."

"So what are you going to do Darryl?"

"Mama, I just want to get my thoughts together. I'll stay in town until I have to testify and then make up my mind. That should give me some time to sort things out."

"So you're coming to live with Mama until then and have your company here?"

"Who said that Darlene? I didn't say anything about staying here or company. Don't assume shit!"

"Alright now, Darryl you know you're welcome to stay but your entertaining is something different. You're still a married man in my eyes and the eyes of the Lord. If you want to entertain it won't be here."

"I've made arrangements already thank you Mama. I don't know if I will want to entertain. I'm still debating whether or not I will be going back home."

"Don't you think you need to talk with Francine about that? You can't just think the door will be open until you make up your mind."

"Darlene, I don't. I'll talk to her when I know what I want to do. I'll talk with both of them. I owe that to them. I just wanted to let you and Mama know what was going on. I didn't want you to hear it from Francine or anyone else."

Darlene thought about the conversation she had with Nikki. She was sure Nikki didn't know about Darryl leaving home, or she would have called her. She would call Nikki on her way home.

"Well, lunch is in here. I'm going to read my bible and wait for Wallace to come by before I eat."

"Is he at the church?"

"Yeah, the Deacon's board meeting is this evening. He's getting things together for that. He'll be here shortly."

"Thanks Mama for listening. I needed to talk with someone.

"That's what Mama's are for Darryl. Darlene have you heard from Shai? She was going to the doctor's today. Something about some blood work.

"No, she must be okay. She would have called."

"You're right. 'Rell ought to be here shortly. Darryl if you want to stay he could use your hand getting those boxes of D.Q.'s down out of the closet."

"He's finally going through D.Q.'s stuff."

"That's what he said, we'll see."

Darlene and Darryl fixed their plates with the left over fried chicken and potato salad Nana had prepared. Their conversation changed to talk about Derek and the case. Darlene called Marci and told her she would meet her in the mall. She said her farewells shortly after kissing her mother and brother.

The afternoon was more than comforting as Darryl took his place in the recliner in the living room for a nap while Nana read verses from Psalms.

Chapter 62

Dr. Kindell's office was filled with women and children. There was one man other than 'Rell in the waiting room. 'Rell and the other man acknowledged each other with a smile. 'Rell grabbed a parenting magazine and buried his face in it. Shai signed her name in at the front desk and took a seat across from him. Two women sitting next to 'Rell were talking about the fathers of the babies they expected. He tried ignoring their conversation by burying his head further into the magazine. He looked up as he heard the nurse asking a woman who walked in for her insurance card. As the woman went into her purse to get the card, she dropped her purse. As she bent to pick up her items that fell another nurse came to the waiting room door and called her name.

"Monique Davis."

The woman looked up from the floor where she was retrieving her lip gloss, lotion and other items. She smiled acknowledging her name. 'Rell watched as she stood thanking everyone for their help and walked into the door to the doctor's examination rooms. Monique was there for a doctor's appointment. 'Rell was glad she hadn't noticed he was there.

"Dershai Mince."

'Shai stood not noticing 'Rell's reaction to the woman who went in before them. He stood waiting for the nurse to beckon him into the door with Shai. They walked down the hall where the nurse asked them to have a seat outside of the office door adorned with a name plate that read Dr. Kindell. The nurse put the chart on the wall next to the doctor's name plate. She left the couple looking at the next chart in her hand. She politely called "Christine Smith" and waited for the patient to respond.

"Did you recognize the name of the woman who they called before you?"

"No, what name did they call? You're talking about the one that dropped her purse right?"

"Yeah, it was Monique."

"Wow, small world."

The nurse came back through leading another patient to the examination room next to the doctor's office.

The doctor's office door opened and Dr. Kindell greeted them with a smile. As they stood to enter the office Monique came out of the examining room two doors down. Shai went into the doctor's office first and 'Rell followed. He didn't see Monique, who noticed him as she left.

"Well Shai how are you feeling these days. You're coming around the bend now. In the seventh month and still quite small, you're carrying nicely."

"I'm fine Dr. Kindell. I wanted to see you to discuss possible genetic disorders. I probably should have brought this up earlier in the pregnancy."

"Shai you've only been here two months. Surprisingly you did well the first five months without prenatal care. What are your concerns? I haven't detected any abnormalities."

"This is Darrell Mince. Darrell is the father of my twins."

"Shai, did we neglect to mark you in your folder as married?"

"No Dr. Kindell, Darrell and I were friends and dating and of course having sex before we knew we were brother and sister. Our father died, and we found out we had the same father after I had conceived."

Dr. Kindell pushed her seat forward. Sitting closer to her desk she picked up her pen making notes on Shai's chart. She took a moment to get her thoughts together before speaking.

"Shai, Darrell, I don't know or care to know how this happened. We will have to watch the pregnancy closely. There may be difficulties that we are not aware of. I'll need you both to give blood and a DNA test, for the record. I usually do this procedure with all parents who may have concern for disorders. I didn't know what Shai's concerns could have been. I understand now. Let's do the blood work first. The results come from Quest an outside lab. I won't get the results back until, let's see, it should be early next week. I will have the nurse call you if there are any concerns when we receive the results. Are there any questions prior to getting the blood work or the DNA results back?"

"No, can you have the nurse call either way. I just want to be sure."

"Sure Shai that's not a problem. I'll mark the paperwork that way. Darrell any questions for you?"

"The records will be kept confidential won't they?"

"Yes, everything is done by code and then recorded on the patients chart. It will be kept confidential."

"Thank you. No one knows I am the father."

"Understood, well let's get the blood work done."

Shai and 'Rell were taken into separate rooms where the blood was drawn. Shai came out into the waiting area to find 'Rell was there ahead of her. They left the office without a second thought about Monique.

Chapter 63

Mitch and Marci sat comfortably on the sofa at Marci's apartment. They had made no particular plans for the rest of the day and had not heard from Shai or Darrell, which meant they were still in the doctor's office. Marci's phone rang and the caller ID told her it was Monique Davis. Monique and Marci had become friends after the death of 'Rell's father. Marci always felt Monique only wanted to be her friend to stay close to 'Rell. After she stopped pursuing 'Rell, she stopped calling Marci.

"Hey, Monique, how are you?"

"Hi Marci, I'm just fine. I heard about Derek's accident. How is he coming along?"

Marci could tell from the question something was up. Monique and Derek didn't get along. Derek wanted to date Monique at one time, long before anyone knew he was related to 'Rell, but she showed no interest. Derek thought she was conceited.

"He's recovering. He had another surgery. Hopefully, it will repair the nerve damage, and he will regain use of his legs. How have you been?"

"Busy. I moved closer to the business district. I found a nice apartment complex that I could afford. Other than that, not much is new."

"So, what made you decide to call me today?"

"Oh Marci, c'mon, it was nothing special. I was thinking about you and decided to call. I just got situated recently and thought I would invite you over to see my place."

"Are you having a house warming?"

"No, I just thought we could spend some time in the mall or something like that and then hang out at my place or yours."

"When?"

"Well it's still early, what are you doing this afternoon?"

"Actually, not much but I promised 'Rell, I would hang around until he came from the hospital."

Marci mentioned 'Rell and that gave Monique the opening she hoped for.

"I see. How is Mr. Mince these days?"

"He's fine. He stays busy though."

That's what you wanted to know from the beginning of this conversation. He said you were sneaky with your shit.

"How's Shai?"

"She's holding up. I think she's really worried about Derek. 'Rell's been keeping up with her. They went to the hospital together today."

"I saw them at Dr. Kindell's, the OB/GYN office."

Marci was stunned. She didn't know what to say. Since Shai had officially announced her pregnancy, she didn't see any harm in confirming Monique's suspicions. She would tell Shai and 'Rell about the conversation when they called.

"I didn't know Shai's appointment was today. She's expecting. They must have gone there after their visit with Derek."

"Shai's pregnant? When is she due?"

"Late February. She announced it last week to the family. 'Rell is helping her get things together. I guess he's playing the proud uncle."

"Wow! Who's the proud father? I would think he would want to go to the doctor with her."

"I don't think she told him. They broke up and he transferred his hospital residency to Maryland before she knew she was pregnant. Shai found out she was pregnant during her fourth or fifth month."

"So she's going to raise the baby with the help of a proud uncle."

"I don't know if that's her intention, but I do know Derek and Darrell are all in. They have hooked her up with all kinds of things preparing for the birth."

"So does she know if it's a girl or a boy yet?"

"No, I don't think she knows."

"Hmm, how does 'Rell's girl deal with him spending so much time with his sister?"

"She's pretty cool with it. "

Marci knew that answer would end the questions. She thought that was all Monique wanted to know.

Monique still wasn't satisfied with the answers Marci gave. She decided she would call Nana and Nikki, to get another reaction to her questions. *Well thank you Ms. Marci. I'll find out what I want to know before this is over.*

"She better watch her man Marci. That Darrell Mince is a good catch."

"I guess she knows that."

"What did you say her name was?"

"I didn't Monique. Listen there goes my cell phone. I'll call you later. Good hearing from you."

Marci hung up the phone before Monique could answer. Monique looked at the receiver and smiled.

"You know something you shouldn't know. I wonder what it is."

Marci returned to her position on the sofa and waited for Mitch to ask her what was the conversation about. He didn't. She pinched his leg and waited for his reaction. Mitch gave a simple grin.

"What is it babe? Monique got it out of you, didn't she?"

"No, you heard what I told her. I couldn't believe that she led me into that."

"She's good. 'Rell said she was slick. Anyway, what did she want to know, who 'Rell was involved with?"

"I think that was her intention. She saw them at the doctor's office. I think I handled it well. I even told her that 'Rell's girl was cool."

"Now there's a woman for 'Rell and a man for Shai that neither of us knows. This is really growing into a story."

"I don't think she believed me though."

"Monique has to see it to believe it. She'll probably call 'Rell herself."

"I thought she was dating Craig?"

"Maybe she cut him loose too."

"Yeah maybe, Mitch when is the grand opening for Quintech Design?"

"I don't know. I think it was cancelled due to Derek's surgery and the court case."

"What about the anniversary dance for D.Q. Enterprises?"

"I think it was postponed too. I'll ask 'Rell. I was looking forward to that dance."

"I was too. I guess it really hasn't been on 'Rell's mind."

"I think he wants to be firmly planted in his position before celebrating. All the brochures indicate the company is in its twenty fifth year. Maybe he'll wait until things are a little calmer. It still will be year twenty five."

"You have a point. That type of celebration adds to a night. Getting dressed, going out and mingling. It's always a beautiful night out."

"So, Marci wants a beautiful night out."

"In the midst of all this, yes, I could use one."

"I think I could use one too."

"Mitch, what does that mean?"

"You only have to ask. I thought you wouldn't want to go out with all this going on. I'll make reservations for dinner and a show. And your beautiful night can be tomorrow night.

"Thank you, hon."

"No, thank you. I didn't want to put too much on you. I mean with you wondering about Derek, Shai, and everything else I just didn't want you to think I was being pushy for our time."

"Thank you."

They sat watching movies, called 'Rell and Shai, and ordered pizza. Marci didn't tell Mitch but her beautiful night begun one day early.

Chapter 64

arrell thought he would have to postpone going through his father's belongings again. It was close to three o'clock when he and Shai left the doctor's office. They stopped at the mall to pick up items Shai selected from a catalogue. She told him once she picked up these items she felt that the twins would have all they needed for starters. 'Rell smiled, he heard her say that three times since the announcement dinner.

'Rell drove to Nana's after assuring Shai he would not be there all night. Shai had begun to fear being alone at night. After taking her home 'Rell pulled into Nana's driveway but thought twice about it. He backed out and parked curbside in front of her house. He didn't want to have to move his car if Reverend Wilcox came over to visit. There was another car parked behind Nana's car. He didn't recognize it and but hoped it was his Uncle Darryl's rental.

It wasn't really cold for an early December day. 'Rell walked around his grandmother's house to the back yard just to breathe in the crisp air. It was soothing standing in her huge yard listening to the winter birds and the wind rustling the leaves. As he heard the back door on the deck open, he turned to see his uncle watching him. They both smiled. Darryl stepped off the deck and joined 'Rell in the center of the yard. Neither spoke a word for what seemed to be five minutes.

Darryl put his arm around his nephew's shoulder as they went into the house.

"Mama, 'Rell was in the yard. You were right."

'Rell went into the kitchen to greet his grandmother. Nana was rinsing salad in the sink for dinner. He kissed her on her check as he reached across her for a glass out of the cabinet over her head.

"Boy, I saw your car out of the window. I knew it was you, but when you didn't come in the door shortly after I told Darryl you were in that yard just staring."

"And how did you know that, Nana?"

"You did the same thing as a child; just stood in the yard and stared at the wind. I guess it would clear your mind then too. So how are you son?"

"I'm good Nana. How are you and your Uncle Darryl? I've been leaving messages for you. You don't return calls these days or what?"

Darryl chuckled softly before answering.

"I needed to be in that yard clearing my mind."

Nana laughed. D.Q. and Darlene did the same thing. It soothed their soul that was the only reason Nana could think of.

"Well if it helps, the yard is always there. I'm glad you got here. I had Darryl pull down your father's boxes that I couldn't reach. So you can start when you feel like it."

'Rell handed his uncle a glass of lemonade and sat at the kitchen table.

"What do you think you'll find 'Rell? Did Mr. Simpson tell you anything else?"

"No other than you and I will have to testify before the Grand Jury. He's waiting for paperwork from the Prosecutor's Office. That's what I was calling you for."

"So what does all of this have to do with your father's belongings?"

"Oh, nothing, Mr. Simpson told me to finish going through his belongings before this court thing came up. I think he wants to make sure there are no lingering papers that need to be changed over to someone else in the family. Plus Nana can get rid of what isn't important."

"That's for sure. I got rid of most of his clothing and shoes. I took those things to the church. People were asking every week could they help me bring more from the house. The boxes and that old trunk is the last of it. I'll keep the trunk but if we can get rid of the boxes and all the papers that would be a blessing."

"I'll get started today. I know you'll help won't you Uncle Darryl?"

"I would but I'm going to meet Simone. I told her I would pick her up at seven."

'Rell gave his uncle a puzzled look. He had no idea that Darryl had told Nana about Simone. 'Rell's expression said he didn't want to discuss it any further. He kept his reply simple.

"Okay, I guess I'll see you later."

'Rell left his grandmother and uncle in the living room. He went into the bedroom where there were seven large boxes and one trunk stacked near the wall to wall closet. 'Rell decided to start with the boxes. He opened the first box and noticed the papers were separated in individual folders or envelopes each was marked as Mr. Simpson had said. *"This should be easier than I thought."*

'Rell had been going through folders and envelopes for more than two hours. Some of the envelopes required him to open them to read their contents. Once 'Rell knew the subject matter, he separated them in two piles. Nana peeked in on him every now and then asking did he need anything. 'Rell told her he could get whatever, he needed and reassured her, he was fine. He completed three boxes before he decided to call it quits for the day. He took the pile that was to be trashed and put in all in the same box.

"Nana, I have one box filled with papers that we won't need. I have to bring the shredder over to get rid of it. Is it okay to leave the box here on the deck?"

"I have a shredder 'Rell. Your father bought it for the house when he moved here. Come and get it from my room."

'Rell followed his grandmother into her bedroom. She went into the walk in closet. She came out with the shredder.

"If you want, I'll sit and shred those papers tonight while I watch my movies. It hums when it runs, real quiet like. Your father paid a lot just for it to hum. He had two others before this one and took them back because he said they made too much noise."

"I can shred that stuff next week when I come by."

"Rell it can be shredded by then I'll take my time when I'm just sitting and do it. You went through those papers good now didn't you? I don't want to be shredding nothing that we may need later. Mr. Simpson should have told us what you were looking for."

"I'll move the box to the living room for you. I checked it thoroughly. Most of it is outdated from at least ten to fifteen years ago. I think he kept most of the papers from the same years together."

"I wouldn't know. I hope you don't get down to the last box and that's where the papers are that Mr. Simpson is talking about."

"Doesn't matter Nana, I would have to go through them all anyway."

"So when did you say you would be back to go through a few more boxes?"

"Maybe the end of the week, I'll call you."

"I was just thinking you would want to get it done before you and Darryl have to go to court."

"You're right. I'll see how my schedule is during the week. I hope to be done by the weekend."

"Okay, suit yourself. It sure will be here until you get around to it."

'Rell took the box into the living room and thought about visiting his mother on the way to Shai's house.

"Oh 'Rell, why didn't you mention you saw Monique today?"

Nana came into the living room and sat in her recliner. 'Rell plugged in the shredder and positioned it near the box. He knew there was only one reason why Monique would call his grandmother after seeing him.

"Marci mentioned Monique had called her too, what did she say to you?"

"Just that she had seen you and Shai in the doctor's office, and she didn't know Shai was pregnant."

"Nana, Monique was looking for answers. She doesn't care about Shai being pregnant."

"Why do you say that?"

"She spoke to Marci earlier. Why would she have to call you to confirm Shai's pregnancy?"

"Well, now that you say that she did ask questions about you. I told her she needed to call you for those answers."

"Answers to what?"

"Answers to who was your girlfriend now, she didn't think you and Shai had just found out you were related, and some other mess."

"Yeah, she needs to call me, or maybe I'll call her before she calls my mother."

"Do you think she'll call your mother too?"

"Nana, Marci didn't give her the answers she wanted, and she called you. You didn't give her the answers she wanted. Monique will call my mother. She's picking."

"Picking for what? You and her aren't together."

"I guess she wants to know who I'm dealing with."

"I thought she was with Craig. I guess she's not happy with that relationship either. I can remember when she would complain about you."

"Yeah, I guess Craig didn't have the right size wallet either. She's not happy about Shai being my sister either. I'll call her and see exactly what she wants."

"I tell you, women don't change no matter what the age. She reminds me of that Tonya, always a hidden agenda."

"Nana, I guess there's one in every family."

"Well how did we get two?"

"Monique is not family."

"'Rell I think somebody needs to tell her that."

Chapter 65

arryl had time to go and see Derek before meeting Simone at seven. He pulled into the parking lot at Richmond Medical Center and headed toward the main lobby. Karlton Harris was at the visitor's desk. He asked the woman for a pass to see Derek Mince. Darryl looked at him trying to remember where he knew him from.

"Karlton Harris?"

Karlton turned to face Darryl. He backed up to get a better look at the man who called his name.

"Darryl?"

"Yes, Darryl. How are you man?"

Karlton was a little shaken. He thought he would visit Derek, and they would be alone. He knew once Derek was fully conscious it would be hard for him to sit with him without an explanation of who he was, and what he was to Tonya.

"I'm fine man. Long time no see. Have you been in town for a while?"

"A little over a month, I've been visiting Tonya."

"Hmm, some things don't die. Why are you here?"

"To see Derek and you?"

"The same, since he had surgery earlier today, I came to see how he was doing."

"Where's Tonya?"

"I haven't talked to her today. I thought I would visit him first and then call her."

"Well let's go, unless you have a reason not to want to share the visit."

Karlton thought about it. "No man, he's your nephew. Go and have a good visit. I'll wait and see him another time."

"He's probably sleeping. We both can visit, but if you choose not to, I will go to see him for a moment. Will you still be here?"

"I'll call Tonya to see if she's coming. If she is, I guess I'll wait here for her and we can visit together. Go on man, I'll see you when you come down."

Darryl proceeded to the elevator. He watched Karlton using his cell phone in the lobby. There was something strange about their encounter, but he couldn't put his finger on it. He would visit with Derek and call 'Rell from his phone.

The elevator stopped at the eighth floor and Darryl got off looking for the room numbers that matched his visitor pass. He entered the room to find Derek sleep. The nurse was in the room checking his vitals. Darryl waited outside the room. The nurse came out and said it was okay for him to enter.

"Has he been awake at all this afternoon?"

"Yes, if you shake him, he will awaken. He's been sleep for about thirty minutes or more. He was up prior to that eating his dinner. He's fine."

Darryl entered the room looking at the machinery that was surrounding the top of the bed. Derek's television was on but the volume very low. He decided to take the nurses' advice and shake him. Derek woke up upon feeling his uncle's touch.

"Hey Uncle Darryl."

Derek was squinting trying to open one eye than the other. He frowned as he used his arms to move over in the bed. Darryl stood over the bed to be of assistance if Derek needed it. His slow movement showed the signs of apparent pain.

"How are you feeling?"

"A little sore, I expected that though. I told my mother, I will probably feel worse in the morning. Stiffness seems to set in overnight."

"Your mother called?"

"No she was here. She came up right after the surgery. She said she will be back tomorrow."

Darryl suspicions heightened. *Why wouldn't Karlton know that Tonya was at the hospital right after the surgery? What is the purpose of his visit?*

"Derek, do you know Karlton Harris?"

"No, I don't think so. Should I?"

"I don't know. He knows your mother. I saw him downstairs. He said he was waiting for her to visit."

"Really? She said she wouldn't be back until tomorrow. I'm sure of that because she asked the nurses about Shai. They told her that Shai was here until I got out of recovery. My mother figured Shai would be back. She's not coming here again today."

"And you never met this guy?"

"No, I never met the guy."

"I'm just wondering why he would want to visit with you when no one is around. It doesn't make sense. Let me use your phone."

"Go ahead. Are you calling my mother about this guy?"

"No, 'Rell. I think he needs to know about this guy and see if anyone else has had any encounters with him. I'm not sure about his relationship with Tonya or his relationship with you."

"A relationship with me, I just told you I don't know the man."

"And I heard you, calm down. Rest, it's just precautions. We don't know how you wound up in that accident and this guy is a blast from a crooked past; I'm not trusting him. Mr. Simpson can put the boys on him before anything else goes wrong."

"Hello, 'Rell. This is your uncle. Listen…."

Darryl explained what was going on and his concerns. He told 'Rell what he knew about Karlton Harris and the fact that it seemed odd that he would be at the hospital without Tonya. After all Karlton didn't know Derek. He wanted him checked out thoroughly. Karlton Harris had been known to be tied to some shady operations. He didn't know if he had connections with Carson Web or still held a grudge for D.Q. Enterprises. Either way Darryl felt Karlton Harris didn't mean Derek any good.

Darryl hung up the phone after 'Rell told him of the visit he had with Karlton at the office. He agreed that Karlton needed to be checked out. He assured him he would call Mr. Simpson, as soon as they hung up.

Derek dozed, off and on, for fifteen minutes. When he opened his eyes Darryl told him he would be leaving shortly. Derek thanked his uncle for the visit and told him he would be home within two weeks. Darryl stood by the elevator with the thought of confronting Karlton if he was still in the lobby. When he got to the lobby Mitch and 'Rell were there waiting.

"What's up?"

"Mr. Simpson is sending one of the security men over for the night. He felt it was necessary until he finds out what Karlton Harris wants."

Darryl looked at Mitch and 'Rell realizing the seriousness of the situation. 'Rell continued to explain what Mr. Simpson had conveyed to him.

"Karlton Harris is obviously working with Tonya in her quest to obtain D.Q. Enterprises' stocks. I think that is only part of his quest. He called my mother telling her that she should think about the media and the drama that could be caused for D.Q. Enterprises if the public knew Tonya Mince was left nothing and the mistress got it all. He's seeking to destroy the company either from within or through publicity."

Mitch added his thoughts. "The man wants D.Q. Enterprises to fall."

"So what does Simpson propose?"

"He took your advice. He's running a background check on Karlton Harris from the time he was last in town until now."

"So what does he think about him working for Carson Design or anyone connected to the accident? This man had it bad for your father 'Rell. He wanted Tonya to be his as well as D.Q. Enterprises lot, stock and barrel."

"Why did he have it bad for my father? What did my father do to him?"

"He whipped his ass for one. They argued about a business deal and D.Q. didn't let him in on it. Some kind of way D.Q. found out Tonya was feeding information to Karlton, and he confronted Karlton about it. D.Q. told him stay away from Tonya. Karlton mentioned something about D.Q. and your mother and your father flipped. He whipped the man until the cops came."

"He mentioned they didn't see eye to eye on a business deal. He claimed that's why he was coming to see me."

"Rell you can't trust him. You know if your father didn't trust him, it wasn't a good business deal."

Mitch tapped 'Rell and nodded toward the front doors of the lobby. Mr. Simpson and two men were coming toward them.

"Hello, this is Vance and I believe you all know Kenny."

They all shook hands acknowledging each other.

"Mr. Mince I brought Kenny because I knew you would be comfortable with him in this situation. Derek has met him and that makes things easy. I have already cleared their presence with the hospital. Vance will alternate with one of our other officers but Kenny will be our primary contact, if that is okay with you and Mr. Carter."

Mitch looked to 'Rell for him to agree. Vance and Kenny worked with him daily he had no problems with their assignments.

"Uncle Darryl, are you comfortable with this arrangement?"

"I feel better knowing someone will be here."

"What floor is he on Mr. Mince?"

"He's on the eighth floor. I forgot the room number."

"I think it's eight eighteen, you better check first." 'Rell couldn't remember the number either.

Kenny went to the information desk and inquired. He then proceeded to the security desk and waved for Vance to come over. They pulled out their credentials and were logged in.

"Mr. Simpson, how long will it be before we know about this Harris guy?" Mitch needed to know how long Kenny and Vance would be at the hospital.

Mitch was usually the liaison for Mr. Simpson and 'Rell when they had special security on duty or investigating. It had been an assignment of Mr. Scott's when his father was the CEO but 'Rell felt his father picked who he was close to, and he was closer to Mitch. It was a smooth transition for Mitch, but it sometimes meant working after hours.

"Mr. Carter I can't say, but I have people working on it as we speak. We should know something by this time tomorrow."

Kenny and Vance returned to say they were going to the eighth floor and would check in with Mitch later. Everyone told them thanks. Mitch told Kenny he could reach him on his cell if he needed to. Darryl looked at his watch, which read six-thirty and told 'Rell, he had to go. 'Rell shook everyone's hand and they all agreed they would talk with him later if necessary. Everyone left going their separate ways.

Chapter 66

Simone sat at the table that Darryl reserved for dinner. She looked at her watch wondering if he had said eight o'clock instead of seven. Darryl wasn't usually late for their dates without calling. Simone couldn't help but think about her reservations at the hotel and him not showing. She had second thoughts about coming and now as she looked at her watch for the third time she wanted to leave. The waiter came to the table with a bottle of champagne on ice in a bucket. Simone was puzzled.

"Excuse me. Did someone order this champagne? I think you have the wrong table?"

"It's okay sir, the champagne is for this table."

The waiter walked away as Darryl took his seat across from Simone.

"I'm sorry for keeping you waiting. I stopped at the hospital to see Derek. The visit turned into a problem which threw my timing off. I thought I would be here a little after seven. I do apologize."

"What's wrong with Derek?"

"There was someone we're suspicious of trying to visit him."

"Oh my God, he wasn't one of the men who tried to kill him?"

"Simone, we don't know. I don't want to say it is and I hope to God that it isn't. As a precaution I called 'Rell, and they've got private security staying with Derek."

"Did the man try anything with you?"

"No, as a matter of a fact, I know the man."

"You know him? Someone you know is involved with trying to kill Derek?"

The waiter interrupted placing a basket of baked bread on the table. "Would you like to order now? Ma'am, Sir?"

"Simone, do you want an appetizer or a salad?"

"A salad, I'll have the garden salad with Caesar dressing please."

"I'll have the same."

"And would you like a drink?"

Simone didn't want a drink. The champagne would be enough for her. She ordered a coke and Darryl order a Miller Beer on tap.

"I'll bring your salads and drinks right out."

"Simone, I don't know if this man is involved. It's just that he and D.Q. didn't get along back in the day, and he doesn't know Derek. It just seemed strange to me that he would be visiting so I called to have him checked out. While the background check is being done, Derek will be under some sort of protection."

"Damn. This is more serious than I thought. I didn't really believe the thing about someone intentionally pushing his car in the other lane. Have you been okay? I mean no one has shown signs of wanting to hurt you have they?"

"No, I really don't know where this attempt came from now. It could be the court case, which involves Derek's old job or now this guy having a lifelong grudge against D.Q."

"What happened to the possibility of the gambling debts?"

"Oh, you heard about them too huh? They've been paid. They were all paid before Quintech Designs was constructed. At least that's what Derek led me to believe. I don't owe anyone else. I haven't gambled like that since either."

"So you're not in danger?"

"I don't think so. I went home and made sure all those loose ends were tied. I didn't want to drag any old dirt into a new situation."

"What new situation?"

"Simone, that's what I wanted to talk to you about. I went home this last time thinking for the first time about what you said to me when we were together. You struck some nerves, nerves that hadn't been touched in years."

"Darryl, I said some things that I shouldn't have said. I was hurt and angry, and I was venting."

"No, you said things that needed to be said between two adults that are trying to get their act together. That's what I meant about striking nerves. I love you Simone and if you love someone you just don't neglect to respect their feelings or understand their needs or wants."

"What about your wife?"

"That's the other part. If I could see what I was doing to you, why didn't I see what I was doing to Francine? You're not the first woman that I have stepped outside of my marriage with, but I never cared. I never cared about her feelings at all, yet I love her. It's a different kind of love Simone. She's the mother of my children, she's cared for those she didn't birth, but I'm not in love with her."

"Darryl, what are you trying to say?"

"I left home Simone. I'm not saying I want us to live together after dinner and get married next month, but I want us to resume our relationship."

The waiter came with the salads and the drinks.

"Are you ready to order now?"

Simone looked at Darryl and smiled. Neither of them had looked at the menu.

"We'll have the chef's choice."

Simone had no idea what the chef's choice was. She smiled at the waiter and nodded her head in agreement. He left the table without giving her a clue what her dinner would be.

"Darryl, you left your home? Maybe you needed more time to think about this. You have a wife, children and a business."

"I'll handle that. I've thought about it off and on throughout the years, I just didn't have a force or reason to leave. My love for you has become my force and reason. I don't want to live in a relationship because it's what's expected if I'm not in love, and don't respect the love I receive in return. Again, that's not fair to Francine. She deserves better than that. I don't want to love you and have to hide it. You're not a woman of the street nor should you be treated or loved as such. I want our relationship to be respected. People don't have to accept it, but they will respect it. I've told my mother, sister and 'Rell. Right now, that's all they need to know."

"Have you told Francine, your children or your business associates?"

"Francine knows there's someone else, I don't think it matters who. I'll talk to the children separate. I'll work the business from here until I sit with Mr. Simpson to settle everything through a divorce."

"Are you sure about this Darryl? As you said you've stepped out before. Like I said this may just be another fling to you. You may need time to digest the fact that I won't let it be that way."

"If you won't let it be that way then it won't. You and your opinion matters to me, it never mattered in the other affairs I had. I'd go home, get comfortable and be on the hunt again. I can't do that this time. My love for you won't let me. I can't make you understand. I just want to take it day by day. I still have a lot of ends to tie up. I don't want us sleeping around. I want us to love each other and be together as long as our love lasts. I don't want to die like D.Q. without the woman that I love. You do love me, don't you Simone?"

"Of course I do Darryl. Where are you staying?"

"I've got a room at the Radisson on Route 95. I've been looking for a condo unit. I was hesitant because I wanted to be where I could still manage my company. I think I'll open a division here or just start with a new crew altogether. Those are things I still have to work out."

"So you're moving here to Virginia."

"I've moved to Virginia, yes. Simone, is there a chance we can make this work? Can you take this day by day journey with me?"

"Yes, Darryl. Yes I can."

The waiter arrived at the table with a plate of vegetables, a baked potato and lobster. Simone smiled, she loved lobster.

Darryl asked the waiter to open the champagne. The evening ended with Darryl and Simone taking a ride to the pier and walking until they decided the weather would have both of them sick in the morning. They returned to the car and Darryl drove Simone to Nikki's house for the first time, since they began dating.

"Simone, I want to say thank you for a lovely evening, one of many to come."

"No, thank you. I thought I lost you, and if I had, it was my fault for wanting too much."

"Why did you think you were wanting too much?"

"Darryl, you're a married man. If you wanted to go home to your wife and family, that was a fact that I had to accept. I wanted what was taboo, a married man."

"Well, you got what you wanted, this married man. I'll be talking with Mr. Simpson on Monday to discuss the divorce papers."

"You don't have to rush things Darryl. You have your business to set up, and you have to find a place."

"Yeah, do you think Nikki would help you decorate?"

"I sure hope so. Darryl thanks again for such a beautiful evening."

"I'll call you tomorrow."

The two kissed and Simone got out of the car waving good bye.

Chapter 67

Simone entered the house and hung her coat in the hall closet. She could hear Nikki talking from the front hall.

"Monique, I wouldn't say that they spend a lot of time together just because you saw them once. I don't understand the purpose of your call. You said you were wondering about 'Rell and how his new relationship is working out. If it's working what difference does it make to you? Yes, Yes. I understand, sure I'll be here. Goodbye."

Simone watched Nikki hang up the phone and throw up her hands.

"Simone, I guess young love today is a lot different than when we were their age. That was Monique she's worried about 'Rell's new girlfriend liking the relationship he has with Shai."

"Sounds like she's worried; who's 'Rell's girlfriend anyway?"

"I don't know. And that was another thing she wanted to know, did I know her, and what I thought about not knowing her."

"Rell said she had changed since D.Q. died. Maybe she felt that she had a chance with no girlfriend or sister in the picture."

"Could be, she said she really needed to talk about this, and she was stopping by."

"Isn't 'Rell coming over?"

"He said he was. He hasn't called to say any different. The two of them can talk right here. She can say what she needs to say to him."

"She's got nerve."

"Simone, that's the new woman. Claim your man, even if he doesn't want you. Let 'Rell deal with her. He has before so it won't be new to him. I really didn't think she was that bad. She even asked me if I thought him and Shai were too close."

'Too close for what, sister and brother? They have missed so many years. I think they get along fine, Derek too. I don't think Tonya has a liking for 'Rell but then that's expected. I guess Monique sees what she lost. I mean 'Rell has grown into a fine businessman. Any woman would want him."

"And you know I don't know the lady in his life these days. That's odd, 'Rell usually will talk about one or two, even if they're just dating. He hasn't talked about dating anyone since his father died."

"He's been real busy though, cleaning up everyone else's mess and his own. He'll get back to dating again soon Nikki, you'll see."

"Speaking of which, how was your date with Darryl? Did the two of you clear the air?"

"We did. He's decided to live here in Virginia. He's leaving Francine. He said he was filing for a divorce and looking to have a division of his company here or start a new one."

"Simone, where is he staying?"

"For now at the Radisson Hotel on Route 95, he was looking for a condo and decided he better straighten out his business first."

"What about you and him?"

"He wants us to stay together, not sneaking around. He told Darlene, his mother and 'Rell about us. He's going to talk with his children too."

"Darryl told Francine he was seeing you?"

"No, he said he didn't think it would make a difference who I was. She's aware he's seeing someone."

"Simone that's a touchy situation; be careful you may get hurt. Darryl may love you today and forget he loves you when the next woman comes along. He's been known for that over the years."

"I don't need you to tell me that Nikki. He admitted it. He also said he never thought once about Francine. This time he did. He decided it wasn't fair to her or me. He chose to clear his head and take it day by day loving me."

"That's okay Simone when it makes you feel good. But there's going to be some bad days in between. Let's just pray the love lives through those bad days."

"Thanks for the words of wisdom. Save some for Monique. She'll need them cause' your son sure don't love her."

Simone left Nikki sitting at the kitchen table waiting for 'Rell to call or visit.

<h1 style="text-align:center">Chapter 68</h1>

arrell parked behind his mother's Navigator. He never noticed Monique's car parked in front of the house. As he put his key in the door, he heard Monique's voice and knew this would be a day he would remember.

"Hey 'Rell, Monique stopped by to see me, and I told her to wait to see you."

"Have you been waiting long?"

'Rell knew the longer she had waited, the more questions she had asked. He just didn't know why.

"Well Darrell, I must say your busy schedule doesn't show on you physically. You look good for a brother that's always on the go."

Monique stood from her seat attempting to get a friendly hug as a greeting. 'Rell gave her a smile and pointed to the couch where he took a seat. Nikki noticed the change in 'Rell's behavior and waited to hear the beginning of their conversation. Although she and Monique had been close she wanted to see how 'Rell would be handling her questions.

"What are you talking about Monique?"

"I've called your office several times, and you're always busy with a client or out of the office. Seems I never can catch you and then today I see you at Dr. Kindell's office with Shai."

"I thought that was you."

"You couldn't speak?"

"No, we were on our way into the office, and I wasn't sure it was you."

Nikki went into the den and left them in the living room to talk. She had held Monique at bay long enough. After 'Rell told her what he wanted her to understand, she would be letting her know that this matter wouldn't be coming up again.

"Rell, you had to have heard them call my name. I was in the waiting area picking up everything that had fallen from my purse when the nurse called me in."

"And your point Monique?"

"Oh, now your mother is gone, and you can say what you want."

"No now my mother is gone, and you can ask what you want. You've spent a lot of time tracking me today. First Marci, then Nana and now my mom, what's up Monique? What do you want? Or should I say what do you want to know?"

"Shai's pretty close to you. I mean for you to go to the G-Y-N with her. What's up with that? Where's the baby's daddy?"

"What difference does it make to you? No one owes you an explanation?"

"Rell, I think you do. Shai was calling you and you were calling her when we were dating, when you lived in College Park. I have one of your cell bills with her number on it. Mr. Mince I do believe you knew her before you found out, she was your dear, dear sister."

"And?"

"And you tell me."

"We knew each other. What does that have to do with today or you?"

"So what's the game 'Rell?"

"What game Monique? I knew Shai two years before I found out she was my sister. What game? I know a lot of women. If you checked that bill, you have checked others. There are more women on the bill than just Shai. Do you want me to name them? It doesn't mean a thing. I had other female friends. I didn't fuck them though Monique. I didn't lie and tell you I loved you and loved them too. I didn't break down and tell you that I wanted to be with only you and move to where you were only to be with one of your girlfriends, so what damn game!"

"You sound like a man that's full of guilt."

"Guilty of what, being your fool for so long? Guilty of not seeing that you were sleeping with Craig? Okay, I'm guilty."

"I guess I deserved that. I wasn't sleeping with Craig throughout our entire relationship."

"Monique, I didn't ask you when. I don't care when. It doesn't matter. You did. You did it while we were dating. You knew we were still seeing each other, and you dated my friend. You knew he was my friend and that didn't make a difference either. It really doesn't matter if you slept with four more men during our relationship. That was one you shouldn't have slept with."

"Darrell what are you saying, that I slept around on you. Don't turn this over. You knew Shai before you knew she was your sister and your closeness proves there was something there."

"Again I ask, and?"

"Rell she's your so called sister."

"What are you implying? Say it Monique. Cut through the shit and say it."

"Are you fucking Shai?"

"No, and even if I was, it ain't none of your damn business. We're done, forever!"

"Forever, that's it, huh? You and I split because you said you need space and it becomes forever."

"Baby, you made it forever by sleeping with Craig."

"You don't even like Craig."

"I did then. I trusted him like I trusted you. Good thing you both weren't snakes."

"So why the brotherly love act with sister girl; if you knew her before, why play the over caring brother now? If she was just a friend would you still be up under her?"

"Are you following us around? I mean, I would hate to find out that you're stalking me or her. What I do or with whom I do it, is none of your business Monique. Get a life. How is Craig? Does he know you're here?"

"Drop it 'Rell. I'm trying to save your reputation. It looks like you and her were an item. That baby is yours and…"

"And what Monique; if that were true who would it affect? Certainly not the Davis family; your reputation will not be marred by my indiscretions. I'm a grown man. What I do, I can handle."

"You may need a friend in your corner."

'Rell laughed. He couldn't believe his ears. Although Monique had the story exactly right he knew he wouldn't want her around when the truth unveiled itself.

"It's not funny 'Rell. It could ruin your business."

"Monique, I knew there was a reason for you being here, my money, again. You're not worried about my welfare only that I maintain my status. I don't give two shits about that business if my life is in shambles. That's how my father died. My life, my happiness and my family will always be first and foremost. Monique you were a part of my life for five years. If you knew me, you would understand that. Listen, I came to visit my mother, update her on my brother's condition and go home. I've spent enough time with you. As a matter of a fact, more time than I cared to spend with you.

'Rell got up without waiting for Monique to follow. She stood and walked toward the front hall. 'Rell passed Monique her coat. He unlocked the door in preparation to let her out.

"Rell you don't have to be nasty. It's not in your character."

"Well you being nosy isn't in yours. Things change. Tell Craig I said call me. Maybe we could get together for dinner sometime."

"Oh, yes, I'd love to meet your girlfriend."

"No, I was talking about Bryon, Mitch, Keith, Craig and I. It would be like old times."

"So you're not dating."

"Give up Monique it's none of your business."

"Rell you like sex too much not to have a girl."

"Baby, I'm doing like you, just sleeping around."

'Rell opened the door as Nikki came out of the den.

"Monique wait, I'll walk you to your car. I want to say something to you before you go."

'Rell went into the living room leaving them at the front door. Monique turned to face Nikki on the step of the porch.

"Monique, I just wanted you to know I really didn't appreciate you using me to find out information about 'Rell. That won't happen again Monique."

"You're right Mrs. Mince. 'Rell can go to hell."

Monique turned and walked to her car without waiting for Nikki to respond. Nikki came in out of the cold air and returned to the living room where 'Rell had cut on the television.

"I'm sorry you had to go through that Ma."

"I'm sorry I didn't believe you. She's a bit much."

Simone came in the room and looked around.

"She left? Whew, she was not satisfied until you put her out."

"Simone, I told you both, she had changed. Maybe she didn't change her true colors just began to shine."

"Rell what was she trying to imply?"

"I guess that I cheated on her with Shai. My mother told you I knew Shai before we found out we were brother and sister right?"

"She mentioned it."

"Well I think Monique was trying to justify our splitting up by implying that Shai and I had some dealing in the past. She tried to say by me being with her so much people could think that the baby is mine and the rumors would ruin me."

"What kind of mess is that? Her background is what could ruin you. After all she was dealing with Craig. Simone you know Craig, 'Rell's friend from college?"

"The light, bright, good looking boy?"

"Simone, that's some description."

Their laughter released the tension 'Rell was feeling.

"Rell, me and your mother used to have a description for all your college friends. Didn't we Nikki?"

"I plead the fifth."

Laughter filled the air again. Soon the conversation swayed from Monique and 'Rell's college friends to the security coverage at the hospital for Derek.

"Ma do you know a man named Karlton Harris?"

"Karlton Harris? That man called here the other night looking to invest in stocks and property at D.Q. Enterprises. I said then I knew that name. I just can't remember where I know him from."

'Rell told Nikki and Simone about the call he received from Darryl at the hospital. Simone heard Darryl's version of the story but 'Rell's version included Karlton coming to the office and inquiring about the stock and property. 'Rell told them both about the fight that Karlton and D.Q. had.

"I know who he is now!"

Nikki jumped up from her seat. "That's the man that confronted your father about me. Yes, I remember the name now. I never met him before. Your father was questioned by the police a few days later. Nothing ever came from it, but they said the man had been assaulted. He didn't press charges but a witness said your father was the assailant."

"Nikki what happened that D.Q. beat the man in the street like that?"

"Simone, D.Q. and I had been out two weeks prior at a restaurant in D.C. D.Q. ordered a drink after we ate and then told the waiter to cancel the order. I didn't find out until after the police came that D.Q. saw Tonya and this man Karlton at the same restaurant. Well, the night of their fight this Karlton

Harris told D.Q. he would leave Tonya alone if D.Q. left me alone."

"Karlton knew about you and D.Q.?"

"I guess Tonya told him about us. I wouldn't have known who Tonya was. I had never met her well you both know that, until after the funeral."

"So Tonya was cheating on dad?"

"Rell I don't know. I thought so. Your father said she was doing it to get this man to buy him out, something to do with investments. Tonya told Karlton about all the stocks, investments and properties that D.Q. was interested in order to increase profit margins at D.Q. Enterprises. Karlton Harris would get it sold or get it bought before D.Q. could even talk to the owners. It was as though he had a competitor living in his home. Anyway, Tonya must have told him about us and Karlton used it when they were arguing."

"What did he tell D.Q. Nikki?"

"D.Q. told him something about leaving his wife alone. Karlton replied, 'I'll leave her alone when you leave Nikki Robbins alone'. D.Q. beat him down."

"That's what Uncle Darryl said."

"So what does this guy want now?"

"Simone, he told me if I didn't cooperate he would go to the media about me getting the money D.Q.'s widow should have."

"You're joking."

"No, the joke is this guy told Uncle Darryl he was visiting Tonya and wanted to visit Derek. Derek doesn't even know the man."

"He wouldn't know him, you were babies then. How many years do you have on Derek?"

"Two, maybe three."

"You had just turned three then. I think that's right. He was a baby then."

"How long did he stay around?"

"I don't know. Your dad never mentioned him again. The police spoke to your father that night and that was it. I never heard about him again until he called the other day. I didn't remember who he was."

"Rell do you think he wanted to visit Derek to harm him?"

"Simone, I don't know. People are attacking from all angles. Carson Web Designs, the gamblers, Karlton Harris, Tonya Mince, and Monique Davis, who knows which is more dangerous."

"Well baby it's a good thing you have your father's genes."

"No, it's a good thing I have his business sense. Nana was right when she said it would be hard to fill his shoes. Listen, I promised her I would check on Shai on my way home. I also have to check in with Mitch and Mr. Simpson. I'm going to bid you ladies a good night."

"Rell watch out for peeping eyes."

Simone pretended to be spying from behind the sofa.

"Who is peeping?"

"Monique Davis for one."

"Oh, my mother's girl."

"Something's wrong with that chick. Young or not, she violated the rules of a woman."

'Rell gave his mother a questioning look.

"Yeah, she did. A good woman never sinks low enough to show a man she cares that he moved on. We cry like hell behind closed doors but never show concern or go to his mother and ask questions."

"I know that's right," chimed in Simone.

'Rell laughed understanding what they meant. He kissed them both good night and got in his car heading for Shai's house.

Chapter 69

The week went by quickly and for 'Rell the lack of major events made it peaceful. Mr. Simpson didn't receive any paperwork from Carson Web Designs lawyers and filed the appropriate postponement papers with the courts.

Derek was able to move with more comfort in and out of his bed and wheelchair. There still was no feeling in his lower extremities. Kenny and Vance remained posted at the hospital. Karlton Harris had not returned to visit.

Shai was still attending classes at the University, but she cut her work hours down to four hours a day. She was enjoying her pregnancy and the attention 'Rell gave her daily. 'Rell told her about Monique and Shai's response was, "And?"

Tonya's lawsuit against D.Q. Enterprises claiming she was entitled to profit sharing hit 'Rell's desk Tuesday morning. She found documents that she thought would prove she was enrolled in the profit sharing plan ten years prior to D.Q.'s death, and she claimed she was not terminated as a member. Byron and Keith were assigned to disputing her claims and checking the old records.

It was Thursday and 'Rell decided that he would leave work early to look through more of his father's paperwork. Now that Tonya had presented paperwork, there was a need to find her profit sharing payout or documents to prove she was no longer entitled to any profits.

The intercom sounded as 'Rell was packing his briefcase to leave. "Hey, 'Rell it's Mitch man. Stop by my office on your way out."

"Your office is not on the way out. Come on down I'm still here."

"On my way."

Mitch opened the door to 'Rell's office two minutes later.

"What's up man?"

"You got a minute?"

"Yeah, what's up?"

"I need your opinion. I want to propose to Marci. I wanted to do it at the anniversary celebration. But looks like that's postponed, for the moment, so I need a time or place that would be memorable."

"Hmm. Proposing, wow. I didn't know. You're serious huh?"

"Yeah, I'm serious. I know she's going to want Shai in the wedding so the wedding may be more than a year away, but I want her to know I'm serious about us. I think it's time to make a commitment."

"What about a nice dinner?"

"That's typical though. I wanted something unusual."

"Give me a day to think man. I'll come up with something."

"Okay, hey, by the way, I want you to be my best man."

"You couldn't get married if I wasn't."

"Thanks."

Mitch shook 'Rell's hand as they hugged each other.

"Listen, I'll be at Nana's if you need me. I'm going through the rest of my father's belongings today."

"Alright, I'm going to the jewelers, and then I'll be home."

"Okay later man."

Mitch left the office. 'Rell looked at a picture on his desk of Mitch and Marci and smiled at the thought of the wedding. He left the office on his way to Nana's.

Chapter 70

Reverend Wilcox was standing at the front door of Nana's house looking around the porch when 'Rell pulled up. 'Rell watched him from the car wondering what he was looking for. As he got out of his car the Reverend closed the door, he never saw 'Rell. 'Rell walked up the slate patterned flagstone path to the door and used his key to unlock it. Reverend Wilcox was standing at the door's opening holding his chest.

"Rell, did you ring the bell son? I was just out there looking for who was ringing that bell."

"Wallace, I told you I didn't think I heard no bell. 'Rell has a key. Why would he ring the bell?"

"Jewels, I tell you I heard a bell ring. Boy, you sure scared me though, how you?"

"I'm fine Reverend. How are you?"

"I don't know since your grandmother said she didn't hear no bell ringing." Nana walked past them both shaking her head as she took 'Rell's coat.

"Baby don't pay him no mind. He's been hearing that same bell for the past hour or so. I'm going to put your coat in my room. I was moving some things out of this closet here for the church folks. I didn't know your father still had some clothes in here."

"Okay, how are you doing Nana?" 'Rell leaned to kiss his grandmother's cheek. Nana didn't stop taking his coat and cutting her eyes teasingly at the Reverend. The two men followed her into the living room.

"I'm just fine baby. Did that girl call you this week?"

"No, Nana I think she's done with me for sure now."

"Ain't no telling with Ms. Monique, she has nerve though, I have to hand it to her."

"Rell, did she call your mother?"

Nana must have shared the news of Monique calling with Reverend Wilcox. He seemed to know the problem she caused and knew she said she would be calling Nikki.

"Rev, she called my mother right after she called Nana. I don't understand her motive though. We haven't talked in months, and then she feels it's her business what I do now."

Nana picked up a few things as they continued into the den where Nana and Wallace were working on crossword puzzles.

"We were doing today's crossword puzzle. You can go in there and start when you're ready. I left everything like you had it. I shredded those papers and Wallace put the bags out yesterday. If you want anything, juice or iced tea, just call me. I'll bring it to you."

"I'll take the break and come and get it."

Reverend Wallace laughed.

"Your grandmother will have you in there all night. You better come out every now and then. I was working on that closet out front there all day yesterday; then she told me about the shredded papers. I took them out and just stood in the yard."

"In the cold air? That's probably why your ears are ringing today."

Nana and Wallace laughed together. 'Rell looked at them and said a silent prayer. He thanked God that Reverend Wallace brought his grandmother happiness in her later years. 'Rell went into the bedroom assuring Nana he would put his coat in her room. He was determined to complete his search through the rest of the boxes.

'Rell came across a photo album with pictures of his family in their younger years. He recognized Nana and his grandfather, Randall. The album was full of pictures of family members 'Rell knew. Darlene, Darryl and his father D.Q. when they were children. The album was well preserved and 'Rell was glad to see his father had held on to the memories. There were papers in envelopes marked cards. 'Rell opened the envelopes to find the papers were report cards Nana had kept of her children from grammar school. There were also Father's and Mother's Day cards, Valentine Cards, and Christmas Cards. They were all handmade and 'Rell was certain if he looked through them all, every holiday for at least their grammar school years would have a card.

'Rell decided to take his first break and noticed he had gone through the bulk of what was left. He stood and stretched while looking at his watch, which told him three hours had passed. He decided to walk into the den to stretch his legs.

"You done for tonight?"

Nana was watching the television while Reverend Wilcox was snoring in the recliner. They both smiled as he paused at the sound of Nana's voice but returned to his snoring without losing a beat.

"No, I have the trunk left. I still didn't find the papers that Tonya is talking about. I don't even see the paperwork that she sent Mr. Simpson."

"You said it was profit sharing right?"

"We offer it to our employees, not the spouse. Why would dad let her invest separately like that?"

"Well if it's not right Mr. Simpson will sure find out. How packed is that trunk? Is it full?"

"It looks full but it could be things that are too old or just things that have sentimental value."

'Rell went into the kitchen and filled a glass with iced tea. It was eight o'clock. He would have to call Shai and tell her he would be there late or wait until tomorrow to finish the trunk.

"Rell, is this your phone ringing?"

"I guess so Nana, I thought I had it on me."

'Rell took the phone with him back into the bedroom. He hoped it was Shai and not another problem.

"Hello"

"Rell, its Shai. I know you can't talk. Listen I'm with Marci. She's going to spend the night with me. We're looking at wedding gowns on-line."

"So, you have company for the evening. That's good. Have fun, I'm going through the last of the boxes. I should be finished with them all tonight if I stay a little longer."

"The doctor's office called and said to call them tomorrow, I'll call them in the morning.

"Not a problem. I'll talk to you then."

"Love you."

"You too." 'Rell hung up the phone and sighed. He hoped whatever Mr. Simpson wanted 'Rell to see was in this trunk and not something that was mysteriously missing. He returned to his place in front of the large closet. There were a few packets marked confidential and 'Rell put them aside to go through last. He came across another photo album, which would now be the sixth or seventh one he browsed through. He put it to the side and then decided he would glance through it anyway.

The opening pages had his father's military paperwork, all his pens and accolades. There was a wedding photo of Tonya and D.Q. followed by pictures of the ceremony, reception and their guests. 'Rell thought about skipping the rest of the book. He didn't want to know much about that part of D.Q.'s life. Thoughts about Shai's younger years surfaced. 'Rell wondered what she looked like as a girl and how her childhood was in comparison to his. He continued to flip through the pages. There were pictures of D.Q. with Derek and Shai throughout their school years, birthday parties, graduations, family celebrations and what appeared to be yearly family portraits that included Tonya. 'Rell picked up the next album. Tonya and Shai were on the first picture in the book. 'Rell changed his mind about looking through another album and put the book to the side. A paper fell from the book.

The paper had Karlton Harris's name and address.
'Rell looked at the paper turning it over to see if there was any more information than what he read on the one side. He picked up the album the paper fell from and looked through the balance of the book. There was nothing unusual.

Pictures of Shai and Derek in their childhood activities, his father had been in all the photos. 'Rell began to wonder how his father lived in two households. D.Q. had attended all his activities, as well, and if he wasn't there from the start of the event he would arrive late. D.Q. was a major part of 'Rell, Derek and Dershai's life.

There were other papers in the trunk that pertained to Darryl's business at its onset. The incorporation documents, the blueprints of the building and other important papers. 'Rell would make sure Darryl got the papers and filed them where he wanted them. He repacked the trunk with the papers and the photo albums. He picked up the first envelope he had put to the side that was marked confidential.

The envelope was not just closed it was sealed. He tore open the end. The envelope was an outer envelope for an inner envelope which was marked 'Darrell Mince'.

"Shit. What is this now dad, what?"

Chapter 71

s 'Rell looked at the other three envelopes also marked confidential he knew they were packed the same. He took a deep breath and tore the end of the inner envelope. There was an 8 x 10 photo of Karlton Harris. He looked much younger than the man 'Rell met in his office. A note was clipped to the picture with his name written on it. There was a second photo of him that resembled the Karlton Harris that 'Rell had met. That picture let 'Rell know his father had updated the photo before he sealed the package. There was a hand written letter for 'Rell clipped to the second photo.

"Rell, by now you have gotten over the fact that I didn't marry your mother. In these envelopes, I have explained all the reasons why. It would have been difficult to divulge these facts in your younger years. You weren't old enough to understand the business aspects or handle it emotionally. I realized when it was too late that I would not live long enough to put things in order. I know you have enough knowledge, and I left you with the right people to keep what I started at D.Q. Enterprises going throughout your life. Who knows maybe you can pass it on to your son. It would then be a third generation company. Three generations in business, that's rare for a black family. If you are searching through these packages and found this letter that means that Karlton Harris has found you or Stanley thought you needed the guidance these papers will provide. In either case, these three envelopes will help you. I wasn't sure how to tell you that Karlton Harris and Tonya would be a thorn in your side. But these envelopes will take the steam out of their sail.

318

'Rell, remember I loved you first. I loved you before there was a Derek or Dershai. I loved you through it all. And if I had my way, I would do it again just to love you and your mother again."

'Rell held his head back, fighting the tears that were beginning to fall. He took a deep breath and continued. He flipped the letter and went on to the next item in the envelope. There was a folder with documents from D.Q. Enterprises. 'Rell shook the folder in front of him and smiled. D.Q. had thought of everything. The document was regarding shares of D.Q. Enterprises stock. The name on the document was not Tonya Mince, it was Karlton Harris. 'Rell froze; he had no idea that Karlton Harris had owned stock in D.Q. Enterprises.

The document entitled the holder to ten percent per share of D.Q. Enterprises stock. There was also a court document in the same folder that named Filmore Inc. as the purchaser of the said stock. That court transaction had taken place five years later after Karlton Harris had purchased his shares. The year would have made 'Rell about three maybe four years old. *"Just about the time that dad and Karlton had that fight."* It was a mystery unraveling and 'Rell was putting it together quickly. *'Karlton purchased company stock and then slept with the CEO's wife. He must have given a copy of the purchase to Tonya saying he bought it and transferred it to her name. Karlton never told her the stock was later purchased by Filmore Inc. Tonya owned Filmore Inc. stock not D.Q. Enterprises. It was obvious that Karlton never told Tonya about the sale to Filmore Inc."* 'Rell would need to check the date on the document Tonya presented to her lawyer to be sure, but he was certain Karlton had tricked her into believing he had stock in the company.

'Rell made a mental note to talk to Mr. Simpson about the purchase. They would definitely need her copy of the original documents and her statement, should Tonya insist on pursuing the lawsuit. There were other documents that 'Rell had seen copies of at the reading of the will. 'Rell closed the envelope and pick up the next one.

Again the envelope was an outer envelope with folders and paperwork in it. 'Rell cringed when he found more pictures wrapped in sheer sheets. He sighed, thinking it was another "family" walk down memory lane album. These pictures were different because they left 'Rell sitting with a devil's grin.

The pictures were of Tonya and Karlton, together at restaurants, in cars, entering and exiting hotels, at the airport and kissing at the front door of what 'Rell assumed was Karlton's house. Each picture was dated with the exact address written on the back. 'Rell knew the pictures had been taken by a private investigator. He looked through them again before opening the folder that was in the same envelope.

Derek's birth certificate was the next document 'Rell came across. Everything seemed to be in order but 'Rell looked over the document carefully. He realized that if there wasn't something his father wanted him to know about this certificate it would have been packed with the other documents in a different box. He recognized Dershai's birth certificate and smiled. 'Rell's curiosity peaked wondering why the birth certificates were separated from the other documents his father kept from their youth. Attached to each birth certificate were the results from blood and DNA test done at Richmond Medical Center. 'Rell read the attached sheets over twice not believing his eyes. He quickly turned to the letter hoping it would explain the coded results.

'Rell read the letter aloud after reading it a third time. *"Dear Mr. Mince, The results of the blood work and DNA tests taken on both, Derek Quinton Mince, age five and Dershai Quinelle Mince, age two and yourself prove that you are not the biological father of either of the children. If you have any further questions regarding this matter, please contact our office."*

'Rell sat in a trance letting the information settle in his mind. He looked at his watch it was eleven thirty. He was sure Nana was in the bed. There was nothing else in the second envelope to go through. He looked at the third. 'Rell was hesitant about opening it. He had enough for one night. 'Rell's thought was to call Mitch and have him be his bartender for the next couple of hours as he told him of his findings.

'Rell reached for the third envelope. Again he tore the end. The folder held contracts from Carson Web Design. 'Rell thumbed through the first couple of pages but his mind kept drifting back to Derek and Dershai not being D.Q.'s children. That meant Shai and 'Rell could get on with their life as a loving couple.

'Rell tried to focus on the third envelope. He put the contracts to the side and decided Mr. Simpson could go through the papers. If they were contracts and papers that could help Derek he would know. As he put the contracts back into the envelope he noticed an envelope marked 'Nikki' on the floor. It was in his father's writing. He would have to speak to his mother and Nana in the morning. Right now he needed that drink and conversation with Mitch.

Chapter 72

$\mathcal{T}$he conversation was turning into an argument and Karlton wasn't getting his point across. Tonya was determined to conquer D.Q. Enterprises and Karlton was telling her it had become a losing battle.

"Tonya, why would you file a lawsuit against D.Q. Enterprises with that stock?"

"Because it's mine; you gave it to me, and it shows my investment in D.Q. Enterprises."

"Baby, it's not what you think."

"Karlton it has to be. That stock is over twenty years old. I told Mr. Monroe to check the current price of the stock and what the shares would be worth."

"It's not worth anything Tonya. Not in D.Q. Enterprises."

"What are you saying Karlton?"

"D.Q. Enterprises no longer owns that stock. It was sold to Filmore Inc. Haven't they contacted you with monthly statements?"

"Wait Karlton; you're telling me that Filmore Inc. is the company that owns that stock, not D.Q. Enterprises?"

"Yes, you should have gotten monthly statements or a payoff check."

"You said you had stock in D.Q. Enterprises! Isn't it some sort of profit sharing?"

"No it was an investment in stock that D.Q. Enterprises owned. I never got into D.Q. Enterprises Property

Investments. The growth of that stock at the time would have made money to invest in the properties but D.Q. sold it some time after. I received one letter from Filmore Inc. and then I didn't hear from them anymore. You and I were no longer communicating, and I just assumed they would be sending you the information on your stock."

"Why would I want their damn stock? I thought you gave me what I couldn't get from D.Q.. What was that, some shit you just threw my way?"

"Tonya, it's in the past. I've saved up money and I have stock in the company I'm with. We can live with what I have. You don't need shit from your dead husband."

"Don't tell me what I don't need Karlton! I stayed with that bastard to get what I deserved! I could have gone with your dead ass after I had *your kids* if I wanted you!"

"My kids?"

"Your damn kids! Derek and Dershai! I know you didn't think they were D.Q.'s? I didn't want his kids. I had those children as leverage for his ass to give me what I deserved. I deserve part of that company, and I'll fight for it. I was his wife, and then your ass held the kids and my marriage against me."

"I never threatened you about those kids. I wanted to tell D.Q. about us. Why didn't you tell me they were mine?"

"Yes, they're yours. Now you know! What the hell is the difference?"

"Tonya, you wait thirty years to tell me I have two children. I loved you and you claimed you loved me. This game you played with D.Q. ruined your life. He didn't leave you shit Tonya. You don't have the money, your family, your peace of mind, or me. I was there for you when you said you were caught in a trap. I loved you and…."

Karlton cut his own sentence off. He got up pacing the floor as his anger built. Tonya went to the bar and made a drink. She drank the glass down and made another.

"Put that shit down! That's what's wrong with your ass. Face the shit Tonya. Stop drowning the problems you created in liquor!"

"Problems I created? You don't know what you're talking about."

"Tonya, I was with you for seven years. You married D.Q. for all the wrong reasons; the desire to be what, miserable? You married him for his money. You didn't love him. You had Derek and Dershai for his money. He's dead and you still want his money. You don't even love yourself."

"You don't know what or who I love. I want what I lived my life for."

"And then what Tonya, if you got the money, then what; would you stop living? Your children will find out D.Q. wasn't their father, then what?"

"Who's going to tell them? No one else knows."

"I do. The lies will stop here. You used me and them in your grand scheme. I will be introducing myself."

"They don't know you, they won't believe you."

"They will know me."

Karlton walked into the bedroom and gathered his clothes and his garment bag. He began packing his clothes.

"What the hell is this Karlton? You can't possibly expect me to believe after all we've been through you're hurt."

"Just for the record Tonya, this is not the first time you hurt me, but it will be the last. I loved you all my life. I had other women. I even have had thoughts of marrying, but I always held on to the possibility of being with you. You led me to believe that you loved me and your situation held you trapped. I came back Tonya because I thought D.Q.'s death released you. I can't love you, I realize that. You need help. I can't help you."

"While you're keeping record, note that I did what I needed to do. I raised those damn kids and kept his ass looking good. I'm not letting what's rightfully mine go to his bitch and that damn 'Rell."

"Tonya, what gives you the right to even want it. You deceived two men so you could get money? You're sick! Do me a favor, give me ten minutes to pack my shit and get the hell away from you before I black out!"

"I'm not stopping you, take your shit and go. Why you so mad anyway? You lived off that same money that I took from D.Q. For some reason, you seem to skip that part."

"Tonya, you paid me to simply stay away. I should have. I was stupid, stupid to love you. I thought that money would always link us together. I should have told D.Q. when I had the chance."

"When was that?"

"I should have told him when he told me to stay away from you, and I guess in a way I did tell him."

"You told him what?"

"He told me to stay away from you, and I told him I would, when he stayed away from Nikki. We fought, the cops came, and that was it. Everyone plays life to their advantage. He had the advantage and he won."

"What the hell are you talking about?"

Tonya sat on the bed. For the first time, she was listening to what Karlton had to say. Karlton stopped packing and pulled up the chair in the bedroom to talk with her face to face.

"Sweetie, I believe D.Q. peeped your card."

"What the hell?"

"Let me finish. D.Q. started messing with Nikki you said about four years into your marriage right? Listen, don't say anything; just listen. They had 'Rell. Why? Did you ever wonder why? Because D.Q. knew you didn't want kids. I think you knew that. You knew he had a child with Nikki, and he probably wanted to leave you then. You fought him on it, and he stayed. I met you that year we got together, did our thing, and you got pregnant with Derek. You told D.Q. you were pregnant, and he became the family man. He still was dealing with Nikki. Your plan was another child, and he would be too involved with "your family" to stay with Nikki.

We were still seeing each other, and you got pregnant with Dershai. D.Q. definitely took care of home, the children, but he still didn't want you. It didn't matter though, your hand was set. You knew you had a winner. You were the loving wife and mother raising "his" two lovely children."

"Okay, how did he peep my cards?"

"Tonya, you turned your hand over. How would D.Q. know to tell me to leave you alone? Did you argue about stocks? Did you tell him I gave you that stock? Did you throw it in his face that he wasn't the only one who had someone else? Think about it Tonya. What did you tell your husband in your arguments about our relationship? Something you said put him on to me. He knew, Tonya, D.Q. knew your every move."

"You can believe that shit if you want to. D.Q. was too wrapped up in that damn business and Nikki to follow me around."

"Tonya, I don't think he followed you. He had someone follow me. How else did he know? How did he know who I was or where to find me? I bought that stock through a broker."

"So, D.Q. knew about us?"

"And he cut your ass off. Slowly, but surely he got rid of everything that linked you to him. How many times did he tell you he wanted to leave? How did you get him to stay Tonya? You even used Derek and Dershai."

"I did what any other wife with children would do."

"Your husband was able to find out more than you think. He worked on leaving you nothing for years. D.Q. methodically planned to leave you broke. You played into his hands. He was a step ahead of you. Baby it's over, you lost."

"That's your bullshit story. I still have Derek and Dershai and…."

"And what Tonya, what are you going to tell them when they find out what you did?"

Tonya began to cry. Karlton got up and pushed the chair back and continued to pack. He went into the bathroom and got his razor and other items. Tonya wasn't in the room when he returned. Karlton knew she was headed to the bar to make another drink. He shook his head and got his shoes from the closet. While Karlton was putting his shoes in the bag, he heard a crash, the sound of glass breaking. Karlton ran into the living room. Tonya was lying on the coffee table in the center of the room. The glasses that they used were shattered on the rug. A knife was on the table with blood on it. Tonya's wrists were bleeding. Karlton picked up the phone and dialed 911.

Chapter 73

itch and 'Rell woke up to hangovers and Alka Seltzer. 'Rell called Nikki to tell her he needed to talk to her and Nana together. Nikki told him she had two meetings, but if it was important she would cancel them. 'Rell told her cancel them, he needed to see them both around nine thirty. 'Rell planned to see Mr. Simpson around eleven, and then he would go and see Shai. Mitch agreed that was the best way. 'Rell would have all the information before going to see Shai. She would have plenty of questions.

"Man, I know you're glad this shit is over. Now you and Shai can move on with your lives. I guess people will understand it as time goes on. They'll still look at you as sister and brother."

"I just want the family to know. The media will get hold of the story through the gossip at the office. It's okay though I can deal with that."

"Do you want some orange juice?"

"Yeah man, I'm going to get cleaned up."

'Rell picked up his overnight bag, one that he kept in the car, just in case he made a crash landing at any of his friend's house. He stepped into the bathroom longing to be refreshed by the water of the shower hitting his skin. The shower relieved the tension he had since his father's death. He took his time as the water took his thoughts down the drain mixed with his tears. 'Rell finally understood his father; he knew there

328

couldn't have been another way. D.Q. didn't know how to tell anyone what he knew, not even Nikki. Nana was right he didn't have enough time. 'Rell got dressed and returned to the kitchen for his orange juice.

"Hey Mitch man, it's just seven o'clock. Let's go for breakfast, man, at the diner."

Mitch was in the master bedroom getting dressed. The door was closed and 'Rell's voice was muffled. He opened the door to the room and yelled back at 'Rell.

"Say what, 'Rell did you say something?"

"Yeah man, let's go to the diner. I could go for their pancakes."

"Man, I don't know if food will stay on my stomach."

"Take another Alka Seltzer. You'll be fine. Are you going to the office early?"

Mitch came into the kitchen with his shoes in his hand. "I have some contracts to finalize but nothing's pressing. What did you have in mind?"

"Maybe we'll hook up later. Shit, that depends on how Shai takes this shit. I just thought about it. I tell her D.Q. Mince is not her father and then what? I don't know for sure who is."

"What do you mean for sure? Who do you think the father is?"

"I think it's Karlton Harris. I think my father thought that too. I didn't bring the pictures for you to see, but he had them followed. I think Karlton and Tonya had it going on for a while."

"Oh, shit. That could be why he was trying to visit Derek."

"Yeah, but if that's the case Mr. Simpson knew."

"I don't think so 'Rell. He would have told you when we were thinking about the security for Derek."

"You may be right. He didn't mention it when Karlton visited the offices either. I'll know after I talk with him. So man you want breakfast or not? My treat, c'mon, you'll be fine."

Chapter 74

ana was up early doing house work and laundry. She called Reverend Wilcox and told him she would be meeting with Nikki and 'Rell and it seemed to be a serious matter. She agreed to call him when they were done. The church was preparing for the Christmas season and Nana promised she would pick the floral arrangement for Sunday. The Reverend reminded her that the senior choir was rehearsing and she needed to get their sizes to order the celebration's choir robes. She told him she would get 'Rell or Nikki to drop her off at the church.

Nikki said she would be arriving between nine and nine thirty. Nana still had time to put the boxes that Darrell had gone through in her storage closet. She walked in the room wondering why 'Rell had left such a mess. She couldn't tell what papers were being kept or shredded. Since he was on his way to her house, she decided that he would clean up the mess he left. The door bell rang which told Nana that Nikki had arrived. She opened the door smiling. The two greeted each other in the doorway and entered. Nikki welcomed the warmth of Nana's home.

"It's a little cold today, Mama Mince. I didn't know it was that cold."

"You have this nice heavy coat and you're still cold? Then it ain't a little cold, it's cold."

"I guess you're right. It's cold. Did 'Rell get here yet?"

"No, not yet, c'mon let's get comfortable."

The two went into the den. Nana moved her crossword puzzles from the recliner and sat down, while Nikki sat across from her on the love seat. They discussed the progress of Nikki's business and how excited she was about it.

"Mama Mince, how is Francine?"

"She hasn't called. I don't know what was or is on Darryl's mind. But you know what Nikki; I'm not going to worry about Darryl's love life. I am a little concerned about the family and how they'll adjust after his leaving. Although in the past few months he hasn't been there much. Nikki, I don't know if it will make you feel better but this is not the first time Darryl left home. Simone is not the first woman that Darryl thought he would have a better life with. That's how Michael and Alesha were born."

Nikki heard Nana say the very words that she wanted to say to Simone. Simone was in her glory and Nikki couldn't spoil her happiness with facts. She wanted to know how Nana really felt about Simone.

"I don't understand Simone. She knows about Darryl's past discretions. It doesn't seem to bother her. I think that would have made me stop."

"Everyone has their limits, except Darryl. I don't know why he even got married. Take my word Nikki if Simone puts her foot down and tries to make him responsible for what he says or does, he'll go back to Francine. I know my son Nikki, he loves himself. He's not like D.Q. was."

There was a sound of keys and then the front door opening. 'Rell stepped inside and hung up his coat. He heard the voices of his mother and grandmother and went into the den to join them.

"Good morning, ladies."

"Morning, 'Rell."

Both his mother and grandmother greeted him speaking together. He leaned over the recliner and kissed Nana on her cheek. He went to the love seat and sat next to his mother. He kissed her and gave her an affectionate hug. 'Rell laid an envelope on the table, but got up hurriedly and went into his father's room to get the other envelopes he needed. Nikki and Nana watched him leave and return in silence.

"We've got, or maybe I should say I've got problems. Problems that started around the time that dad died. I didn't tell either of you about them. I guess I may have been embarrassed about not being able to handle the problems the way that dad would or just feeling I put myself into the situations. At any rate the solutions are in these envelopes with other information I need to share with you."

"Your father knew you would have these problems?"

"Nana, he knew there were problems that would need explaining. I think he was preparing for them to be taken care of when he found out he was sick. He left the information in these envelopes to clear up the problems he knew about."

'Rell didn't know where to start but he thought it over while driving to his grandmother's. He would start with telling them how he really met Shai. The two year friendship they had, their off and on conversations, emails, and cards. He told them about their plans to meet each other before the funeral. 'Rell told them how he fell in love. Nikki listened as 'Rell explained the twinge of pain he felt as he sat across the conference table during the reading of his father's will staring at the woman he loved who was being introduced as his sister.

'Rell reminded them that he and Shai stepped into Mr. Simpson's office to talk. He looked at both of them and paused.

"Rell, are you okay?"

"Nana, I'm fine. I'm better now that this mess is over. Shai and I decided to live on secretly. She got her house, I built my home and we lived in love separately. Mitchell, Marci and Mr. Simpson are the only ones who knew about our relationship. We've been together, as a couple, since the week before dad died. I love her, I truly do. She's pregnant with my twins. I'm the father."

"Lawd have mercy." Nana gave Nikki a look of concern and mumbled her thought again. "Jesus, Lawd have mercy."

Nikki and Nana sat back in their seats. 'Rell knew from their reactions they had no idea about the paper work he was getting ready to present. 'Rell opened the envelope with the birth certificates and the letter written to his father. He handed the papers to Nana first. As she read them he watched her reaction. Tears began to flow down her face as she handed the papers to Nikki. 'Rell gave Nikki the envelope that was marked with her name. She took the envelope and opened it after she read the birth certificates and the letter that was attached to them. After reading her letter she sat in silence.

"Rell, I didn't know baby, I didn't know. I always thought it but I didn't know. D.Q. never once told me those children weren't his. He took care of them like he took care of you. I always asked him why he didn't press Tonya to make them visit me more and he would bring them by the next day. He never pushed for me to be real close to them like I am to you, Marci, Mia and the rest. I knew it was a reason but I didn't know what it was."

"Mama Mince. D.Q. didn't want anyone to know. He never told me about the children. He told me about Tonya about one or two months after we got together. He constantly complained that she would ruin him if he walked out of the marriage. She told him he was the father. He says that in this letter he left for me. He didn't believe they were his and that's why he had these tests done. He found out his suspicions were right, but he took care of them and stayed with them because he knew Tonya wouldn't."

"Nikki, Tonya used those kids to keep D.Q. He always wanted children. Tonya always wanted to live better and she used those kids for D.Q.'s money. That's why he didn't leave her anything in the will, he knew those kids weren't his."

"Rell, did you find anything that says when he found out?"

Nana wanted to know just how long D.Q. was aware of this deception. Nikki added her own question.

"Rell, did you find out who their father is?"

"I can't really answer those questions. I can show you what I found and you come to your own conclusions."

'Rell passed Nana the pictures. She turned them over and read the date and location for each one. As she passed the pictures to Nikki she just shook her head. The door bell rang as Darlene put her key in the door.

"Mama, you home?"

"We're in the den. Girl, hurry up; c'mon in here."

Darlene came in and sat in the recliner opposite her mother's. She spoke to 'Rell and Nikki as Nikki handed her the papers and the pictures.

"Stop playing. Ma, you've been saying all these years that you didn't think Shai and Derek belonged to D.Q. I'll be damn. This joker in the pictures is the father?"

"Looks that way don't it. 'Rell said come to your own conclusion. 'Rell tell your aunt about you and Shai."

"Rell and Shai? What's wrong with Shai? Wait, how did all of this come about?"

"Rell's been going through D.Q.'s things you know I wanted to get rid of what we didn't need to keep. Well all of this came from those boxes; D.Q.'s personal stuff."

"Rell tell me. Let me sit back."

'Rell told Darlene the story from the beginning bringing her up to speed on why he was meeting with his grandmother and mother.

"Well, the problem is solved, you're not her brother. Does she know yet?" Darlene's thoughts had drifted to how Shai would feel.

"No, I wanted to talk to Nana and my mother first."

"Boy, this is a mess. They've been a part of this family all their life."

"Darlene they still will be a part of it. 'Rell just needed to tell us the truth because he's the father of Shai's babies."

"Boy, this is a mess. Go ahead 'Rell, tell us."

'Rell told them about Karlton and the stock, the stock that Tonya based her lawsuit on. He passed around the papers that showed the stock had been sold.

"Tonya doesn't have a lawsuit if this is the same stock she's claiming."

Nikki was frowning in deep thought.

"Rell, your father met this man Karlton and sold him stock in D.Q. Enterprises?"

"Ma, I don't think dad sold it to him. I think a broker sold it. After dad found out about Karlton and Tonya he sold the stock to Filmore Inc. I think the fight was the beginning of Tonya's downfall. She wouldn't divorce him.

I guess as hard as he fought to leave her, Tonya fought to keep him. Dad loved Dershai and Derek even though they weren't his and he didn't trust their care to Tonya. He stayed with her but knew he wouldn't leave her with anything."

"Those kids loved the ground D.Q. walked on. They never were close to their mother. That may be the reason why. I knew they weren't his though."

They passed the papers regarding the stock around but Darlene read it longer than anyone else.

"What's wrong Aunt Darlene?"

"I remember talking to D.Q. about this stock. I just can't remember exactly what the conversation was. I wish I could remember. He mentioned he had to get rid of it and I asked him why. I can't remember what he told me."

'Rell picked up the last envelope. He passed the paperwork around again. Nana looked at the papers and passed them to Nikki quickly.

"Rell, you'll have to explain those papers. Whose contract is that?"

"That's a contract from Carson Web Design. It looks like dad got a hold of it two, maybe three, years ago.

I really didn't read it in detail. I'll take it to Mr. Simpson later this afternoon. I'm certain, that if in these envelopes, is a solution to something that's going on or something that's going to come up. Maybe it will help Derek with this court case. That could be why Mr. Simpson said for me to look for things that needed to be finished."

Nikki was passing the papers on to Darlene. Darlene didn't even look at them she sat them on the table.

"Let's hope they do. Well, nephew, what's next?"

"I don't know. I'm taking it one step at a time. I've got to see Shai and Mr. Simpson. Then whatever comes, I'll be ready for it."

"Well, Tonya won't be ready for me. I'm sure going to call her and ask her what is on her mind. Dershai and Derek don't deserve this. She's going to explain this mess to me. I will be talking with her today."

'Rell put all the papers back into the envelopes. He was taking them with him to show them to Shai and Mr. Simpson. He left the ladies sitting in the den as he went into the bedroom to sort through the mess he left the night before. Darlene waited a moment and then went in the bedroom to talk to 'Rell alone.

"Rell, are you okay?"

"Yeah," 'Rell sighed, "You know if you had asked me that same question last night I think I would have broke up some things. It's been mixed emotions. So far I'm okay. I can't say how I'll feel later."

"If you need to vent, I'm always willing to listen."

"Thanks, I think Shai may need you and Marci though. I don't know how she'll take this."

"Are you going to see her when you leave here?"

"I think I should. I was going to Mr. Simpson's first, but I want her and Derek to see these documents. I'll meet her at Derek's. They need to hear this information while they're together."

"That may be best. Call me and tell me how you're making out through the day. Do you need help in here?"

"I was putting the papers to be shredded in this box. The rest is packed and Nana can put the boxes and that trunk where she wants. If Mr. Simpson doesn't need this contract or the papers on the stock, I will file them in my personal belongings."

"Okay, it sounds like you've got it all worked out."

Nikki entered the room. She looked around as a chill ran down her spine. The thought of D.Q. caused her emotions to heighten. Although Nana had changed the look of the room so it didn't reflect D.Q.'s image, Nikki could feel his spirit.

"Rell, are you done? Do you have more papers to sort through?"

"No, Ma that was it. These papers are to be shredded and Nana can put the rest of these up."

"I'll stay with Darlene and your grandmother. We'll clean up this mess. You go talk to Shai and Derek."

'Rell kissed Nikki and Darlene goodbye and went back into the den. Nana was sitting in the recliner where he left her. She stood when she saw him coming toward her.

"I knew your father was living in pain. 'Rell, he died in emotional and physical pain. You tell Shai and Derek even though he wasn't their father, he loved them. He cared for them all his life. You bring Shai by here when you get through talking. I should be home from the church by then. I'll cook dinner for everyone. What are Nikki and Darlene doing in that room?"

"They're putting those papers in the box to be shredded I told them which ones were to be packed. If you want I'll put the boxes up when I come back."

"Don't worry about those boxes. Darryl or Wallace will put them up. Go on now. I'll see you this evening."

'Rell hugged her and kissed her whispering, "I love you."

"I love you too. Call if you need me now."

"I will."

<h1 style="text-align:center">Chapter 75</h1>

Shai hadn't heard from 'Rell. She called his cell leaving two messages. She called Mitch to see if they were together and Mitch told her he went to talk with Nana and his mother. She decided to wait for him to call back. Dr. Kindell's office opened at nine o'clock, and she wanted to call the office before the doctor got busy with her daily appointments. The clock read ten-thirty and Shai didn't want to wait any longer. She would tell 'Rell about the conversation when he called.

"Good Morning, Richmond G-Y-N Group."

"Good Morning, I'm Dershai Mince, and I received a message to call the office regarding my DNA test results."

"Hold on please."

Soft jazz played while Dershai remained on the line. It wasn't as long as she expected before she heard a voice replacing the silence on the other end."

"May I help you?"

"Yes, I'm calling regarding my DNA test results, this is Dershai Mince."

"Yes, Ms. Mince. Hold on for Dr. Kindell."

The music started again and Shai took a seat on her couch.

"Good morning Ms. Mince. How are you feeling this morning?"

"I'm okay I guess Dr. Kindell. I'm calling to find out the results on the DNA test."

338

"Dershai, where's Darrell?"

"I don't know where he is this morning. I think he had a meeting. He'll call me shortly though."

"Good. You said he was your brother correct?"

"Yes, that's why we're concerned about the health of the babies."

"Dershai, he's the father of the babies, but he is not your brother."

Shai heard the doctor but couldn't reply. She was speechless.

"Dershai?"

"Yes, yes, I'm here. What do you mean he's not my brother?"

"The DNA test shows you're not related. I don't know what to tell you. Darrell Mince is not your brother. The problems you thought would be genetic would not be attributed to you both having the same parent."

"We don't have the same parents. Our father was the only common parent. He was his father and mine."

"I'm afraid not Dershai. I don't know whose father he was but one of you is not a Mince."

"Dr. Kindell, I know you're reading what the test results show, but something is wrong."

"The test results are ninety eight percent guaranteed. There are very few mistakes with this test. You may want to look further on your end."

"Our father is dead. How would I find out if he was my father?"

"I wish I could help you Dershai. Your twins are fine. The father is not your brother. That problem is solved. You will have to seek the answer to your question through your relatives. Is there anything else I can help you with?"

"No, Dr. Kindell. You have solved one problem. I will have to find the solution to the other. Thank you for your time."

"Did you make an appointment for your next office visit?"

"Yes I'll see you then. Have a good day doctor."

"You too Dershai."

Shai sat back on the sofa. She couldn't believe her ears. *"Why would my father claim 'Rell if he knew he wasn't his child? Is that what Nikki held over his head, that this outside child was his?"* Shai began to cry. She didn't know what to do. She picked up the phone and dialed her mother's house. After her mother's recorded voice cut in, she hung up the phone. She got her cell phone and used the speed dial to call her mother's cell. There was no answer. Shai began to cry again. 'Rell hadn't called and she had no idea where he was. Shai needed to talk with someone. She called Derek's cell number.

"Hey baby sis. We're on our way to your house."

"We who?"

"Chill girl, what's wrong? You don't sound right."

"Who are you with Derek?"

"Rell, that's all."

"Rell? Why is he with you?"

"Shai are you okay?"

"Rell was supposed to be with Nana and his mother! Why didn't he answer his cell?"

Derek handed 'Rell the phone. He knew Shai was angry, and he wasn't the target.

"Hey lady, what's up?"

"Why didn't you return my call 'Rell?"

"I didn't have the phone on me Shai it was in the car. When you called Derek was the first time I looked at the phone. What's wrong?"

"Are you on your way here?"

"Yes, I went through dad's belongings like I told you, and I've got some news about the three of us that we need to talk about. I went to get Derek so you wouldn't have to drive to his house."

"Information about the three of us; how long before you get here?

"I'm about ten minutes away."

"Good, we can exchange information."

Shai hung up the phone. *"Information about the three of us? Oh, my God. If I'm not a Mince, Derek's not a Mince."* Did daddy's belongings include him telling who isn't a Mince? Then 'Rell knows.

<h1 style="text-align:center">Chapter 76</h1>

erek waited in the car while 'Rell opened the garage entrance for him. Shai came to meet them. 'Rell put Derek in his wheelchair and they both entered as Shai held the door open.

"Hey sis."

"Hey Derek, you're in a good mood."

"Things are getting better for me. I'm doing better with my therapy. Dr. Pittman told me it would be a while before I would master some of the exercises and to be honest I've done better than she predicted. I decided that if I don't regain my mobility within the prescribed period I would get extra therapy for my legs. I'm doing better dealing with it Shai, thanks to Leeza. I really like her company and her advice. I don't think my handicap bothers her. I think we'll do well as a couple."

"I'm glad to hear it. We all need love, true love."

"Well, 'Rell what do you have for Shai and I to look over or understand. I forgot what you said."

"I said we need to understand what I have found in dad's belongings. Shai are you okay? Are you still mad at me for not returning your call? Seriously, I had just got your message."

"Rell you've got to do better than that. Suppose I was in labor or something was wrong?"

"You're right. I'm sorry. Are you okay?"

"Yes. I have news for the two of you too. But you go first. I want to hear what you have to say first."

342

Shai decided her news could wait. If 'Rell knew that they weren't related already it would help her explain the truth of the pregnancy to Derek.

"Let's go to the dining room where we have the table to lay these papers out." 'Rell stopped Shai as she went to walk in front of them. Derek maneuvered his chair without them.

"Baby, are you okay?"

"I'll be alright. Let's get through this."

'Rell didn't like that answer, and he couldn't imagine what was wrong. He followed Shai and Derek and took a seat at the table. 'Rell placed the envelopes marked confidential beside him.

"I finished looking through dad's belongings late last night. I wanted to call you Shai, but I was stunned and didn't know quite what to say. I wanted to find out if Nana and my mother knew about the information in these envelopes, but they didn't. I don't think anyone knew including Mr. Simpson. He only knew there was unfinished business to be handled."

"So what's in the envelopes?" Derek was anxious, Shai wasn't sure she wanted to know what the information was.

"I need you to promise me that we will look at all the information before jumping to conclusions."

Neither Shai nor Derek answered 'Rell, they just stared at the envelopes. He placed them on the table to explain them the way he explained them to Nana, Darlene and Nikki. He passed the birth certificates first with the DNA result letter attached.

"Rell, I have to say something before we go on."

"Shai, can we put all the cards on the table before we go into assumptions and questions."

"This is not an assumption. I was calling you to tell you Dr. Kindell's office called and gave me this same information. Not in the same terms but they told me one of us is not a Mince. I guess this answers the question which one."

"What the hell are you talking about Shai?"

"I'm sorry Derek. I guess we can tell you and everyone else now."

"I'll tell him Shai." 'Rell started from meeting Shai at the mall, their relationship, love and the expected birth of their children. He told him why they were taking a test at the doctor's office.

"I thought the two of you were rather close. Hey, it's good you're not related. But Shai, your mother owes us an explanation at least."

"My mother, shit, is she our mother?"

'Rell shook his head. He knew from the responses they gave, they would be able to handle what the envelopes revealed.

"Why didn't dad say something? I'm sorry 'Rell, I don't think I will get used to not referring to him as my father. I loved the man as my father, and he loved me as his son. I know he did. He loved Shai more though. She was spoiled rotten by that man. Anyway, I wonder what kept him from telling us when we became adults. He knew we weren't getting along well with Mom."

"I guess he didn't want us to feel different toward him. And you're right Derek. He loved us, as though we were his children. We had a father in him. I will always remember him as my father. But I'm glad 'Rell and I are not related."

'Rell was silent. He listened as Shai and Derek reminisced about good times with their father and the thoughts they carried throughout the years about their mother.

"I see why he wanted to leave her."

"I think this will explain that a little more." 'Rell passed the pictures of Karlton and Tonya to Derek. Derek took the pictures and looking at them slowly pointed to Karlton's face.

"This is that man that came by a few times when we were younger. Don't you remember him Shai?"

"How young is younger? No, I don't remember him."

"I don't know, we were kids, I remember his face."

"That's the guy, Derek that was trying to visit you in the hospital."

"No shit 'Rell? This is the guy that you wanted to know about? Damn! That means he's in town."

"I wonder if he's our father; do we even have the same father?"

"For someone who didn't want kids, Mom went out of her marriage to have us? I don't understand this at all."

"Shai there's no telling why she did this other than for dad's money. If this guy is in town, he might have come to see us since dad is gone. 'Rell didn't you say they fought?"

"Yeah, some years ago; I guess that was when dad found out or began to suspect something was going on. I think he had Karlton followed. Those are the dates and locations. He must have kept a record of it and then approached him."

"So Mom played them both, and she lost it all in the end."

"Looks that way because the lawsuit she filed will fall through too."

'Rell passed the next envelope to Derek. "The stock is not D.Q. Enterprises stock. I'm going to take these papers to Mr. Simpson to get them clarified. Her lawyer will contact her with the news."

"Why don't you tell her 'Rell? She's given you enough trouble these past months. You should enjoy giving it back to her."

"Derek, I'm not out to get your mother. She hasn't liked me from the start, and I guess in a way I can understand why. I was always the threat to her. I do want to confront her but not about this stock. It's on a more personal note."

"I want to confront her ass too. I've always been the one telling Derek to talk with her, show her love and compassion and all along, she knew we weren't Mince children. That's why she would tell us to get all we could from daddy. I can remember her saying he owes it to you for not wanting to be around. She's a sick, selfish woman. I definitely want to give her a piece of my mind. I can't wait to tell her I'm in love with D.Q. Mince's son. I'm having his children. They are Mince children."

"Shai calm down baby."

Shai was angry. Tears were in her eyes as she went on about her mother.

"No 'Rell. You and Nana defend this woman all the time. What she has done is not right! Who does that? Live a lie and pass it on. Have your children believe in a lie? I've loved you for more than a year, and we've had to hide it believing this lie. If daddy hadn't died leaving these papers, would she have told us?"

"Well now we know. You'll get your chance to confront her." Derek held his head in his hands. 'Rell noticed he was crying. He didn't know if it was anger or sadness, but he felt his emotions.

"Derek, this last envelope I believe is for you." 'Rell passed the envelope to Derek and waited while Derek thumbed through the contents.

"Man, our father, and I will continue to see him as my father, was something else. This is the original contract with the foreign company. It has all the logistics of the sale spelled out. I don't know how much it will help me but my name is not on this contract as the artist or designer."

"But you still resold a logo that was in use by a client of the design company you worked for."

"Mr. Simpson can work wonders with this."

"If you say so my brother, we'll see."

"Look 'Rell, a fine in court is a lot better than jail time. Trust me. I'm good with this."

"That's between you and your lawyer. I'll take all these papers to Mr. Simpson, so he can handle what needs to be taken care of."

"Rell what about what was left to us by D.Q.?"

"Derek, whatever he left you is yours. He loved you man. I love you too. I must admit I love your sister more, but this doesn't change a thing. Quintech is yours. It's a part of D.Q. Enterprises, and I want to see you do well with it. As for your sister, I've got other plans for her."

'Rell leaned toward Shai and kissed her.
"Shai have you tried to call your mother?"
"My mother? I didn't get an answer."
"I wonder where she is."

Chapter 77

Karlton was still at the hospital answering doctors questions and talking to the police. According to the doctors report Tonya would have died if Karlton had not been there. He applied pressure to her wrists and waited for the ambulance to arrive. When they got there her pulse was faint, and she had lost a lot of blood. They rushed her into the emergency room and reported it to the police as an attempted suicide. Karlton stayed at her side until the doctors told him he needed to talk with the admitting nurse and the police. That was at eleven thirty that night. It was now twelve hours later and Tonya had not opened her eyes. The doctors told him she had just missed cutting the major arteries in her wrist. When the EMT's arrived at the house, they found tranquilizers she had taken prior to cutting herself. That mixed with the alcohol she was drinking had put her in a comatose state. Tonya was in critical condition. Karlton answered all the questions he could.

"Mr. Harris, who is her next of kin?"

The nurse had asked him this question more than once and each time Karlton was hesitant about answering. He knew the answer but he was at a lost. He didn't know how to contact any of her family members including Shai and Derek. He would have to go to D.Q. Enterprises and speak to 'Rell. He didn't have a clue where Derek or Shai lived or how to reach them.

"I think I can contact a family member. Un- fortunately, I would have to leave the hospital to contact them. Can I leave you with my cell number just in case she turns for the worst while I'm gone? It should take less than an hour to get in touch with her daughter or son."

The nurse told him she thought it was best, although Karlton had brought her insurance cards and identification, the hospital needed to talk to a family member. He understood and left the hospital en route to D.Q. Enterprises. Karlton drove at a moderated pace, although his nerves were rattled. *"After all these years, what do I say to Derek and Shai? Your mother tried to kill herself after she told me you were my children?"* Questions repeated over and over in his head. He arrived at D.Q. Enterprises with no answers.

Karlton parked his car in the visitor's lot and approached the entrance to the building. The guard at the security desk asked for Karlton's identification and who he wanted to see.

Karlton handed him his driver's license and replied, "Darrell Mince, please."

"Is he expecting you?"

"No, it's rather important."

"I don't think he came in this morning."

The guard dialed three digits and waited for an answer on the other end.

"I have a Mr. Karlton Harris here for Mr. Mince. He says it's important that he see him."

He nodded his head and said, "Thank you."

The guard hung up the phone and handed Karlton his driver's license.

"He's not coming in today sir. Is there anyone else who would be able to help you?"

"No, thank you."

Karlton went back to his car. He had no idea what to do next. He drove out of the parking lot and stopped at the next corner as the light turned red. A car behind him had to blow its horn to get him to drive on when the light turned green. He was in deep thought. He decided to go by Tonya's house and look for Tonya's phonebook hoping to find someone's phone number that could help him reach Derek and Shai. His hope was that Tonya had 'Rell's personal numbers in her phone book. He didn't want to call Derek or Shai direct; to them, he was a stranger. Tonya had 'Rell's home number and his cell number listed. He dialed the home number and as it went into 'Rell's voice mail he hung up. Karlton sat on the couch and prayed that 'Rell would answer the cell phone number.

"Hello."

"Hello, who's this?"

'Rell asked the question seeing that the number registered Tonya Mince, but he heard a man's voice.

"Rell, this is Karlton Harris."

"Mr. Harris, what can I do for you?"

"Rell, man, there's been a terrible accident. Do you know how to reach Derek or Shai?"

"What type of accident?"

"Do you know how to reach Derek or Shai?"

"Yeah, what kind of accident!"

"Their mother…"

"What happened to her?"

"She tried to kill herself. She's at Richmond Medical Center; they need to get there as soon as possible."

"What the hell did you do to her?"

"I didn't do anything man. She cut her wrists. I'll explain it to them when they get there."

"They're on the way."

"Thank you, 'Rell."

Chapter 78

*T*here was an eerie silence in the car as they drove to the hospital. No one asked 'Rell any questions after he said Tonya tried to commit suicide. He told them Karlton Harris called looking for the two of them. 'Rell made a call to Mr. Simpson after speaking to Shai, he told him he had papers that he would need on the drive to the hospital. He wanted to get the papers to him before Monday. Mr. Simpson told him he would have a courier pick up the papers at the hospital. 'Rell agreed that would be best.

"Rell don't you think those papers could wait?" Shai was irritated about the call. She couldn't believe 'Rell was carrying on with business as usual.

"Babe, Derek has a court case pending. Mr. Simpson may need these papers to clear it up or get it reduced to a fine. I don't want to sit on it while the Prosecutor's office pursues it and he has to do jail time and wait to appeal."

"Oh, I thought you were giving him those other papers too."

"Shai, I'm giving them all to him. Mr. Simpson handles my legal affairs. I told those I wanted to tell, and he can file whatever, he needs to protect us. That includes you and Derek. If either of you want copies I can have them made. I don't know what your mother filed but the courts thought it had credibility. Mr. Simpson needs these papers to wrap up the last of dad's loose ends."

351

"I just thought that it could wait."

"Shai, it will be alright. 'Rell, is this Karlton guy going to meet us at the hospital?"

"He said he would be there."

"Do you think this guy knows we're his children?"

"I don't know Derek. If it were me and I knew, I think I would have made myself known. I don't think I would still be trying to get with my ex if I knew she kept our children a secret from me. But Derek I don't know."

"It doesn't matter Derek."

"What do you mean Shai? This guy shows up and all hell breaks lose. Just as we find out, we're not in the Mince family, our mother tries to kill herself. Karlton Harris just happened to be there? It sounds strange to me."

"It was timing Derek. It was time we knew. It was time 'Rell and I knew. And she knew it. Tonya Mince gave up. She finally realized she lost. She lost a love she could have had with D.Q., with Karlton and with us. She couldn't get the money she wanted and with Karlton back in the picture she couldn't trust that he wouldn't want to tell us. She lost everything Derek. So she tried to kill herself."

"That's your story. I want to hear hers. I think she did what she's done all her life. She wants attention. You have a life ahead of you and so do I, she doesn't. Having just Karlton wasn't enough. She wants someone to know she's in charge. This is another one of her games."

"Derek, how could you say that? Suicide is no game. She may die."

"Will you miss her shit, Shai? Will you miss her lies, her secrets; her love? I can answer that, no. Shai she saw me as a way to conquer D.Q. Enterprises. She doesn't even see us, and she could give two shits how we would feel about not being D.Q.'s children. Otherwise she would have been a mother Shai and told us regardless who our father was. She would have been our mother. But you know what Shai, being a mother takes a different kind of love. I told you over and over again, Tonya Mince loves Tonya Mince."

They pulled into the emergency room parking lot. Shai went in ahead of them not waiting for 'Rell to take Derek out of the car.

"Derek, you're probably right but take it easy man, she's your mother regardless." 'Rell maneuvered the wheelchair and pushed it through the double wide entrance.

"I hear you 'Rell but the reality is, she needs to remember we're her children. I know who she is."

Shai was at the triage station waiting for a nurse to come to the window. 'Rell and Derek joined her just as Karlton Harris walked up to them from behind.

"Hello, Shai, Derek, 'Rell. Follow me, she's been admitted."

Shai and Derek stared at the man who spoke to them and followed him to the elevator. 'Rell walked slightly behind them. Shai tried to find a resemblance in her and Derek to this man who could be their father. It was a strange feeling to think of someone other than D.Q. Mince possibly being a father to her. Although he was quite handsome and refined, he wasn't what she expected. Shai looked at Derek for his reaction to this man and found none.

"I'm Karlton Harris. I'm a friend of your mother's."

"How did this happen? I mean, what was going on before she did this to herself?"

"Shai, I'll answer all of your questions. Can we please check on her condition first? I left the hospital to get in touch with 'Rell, so he could contact both of you. I haven't checked on her, since I got back."

They rode the elevator to the fourth floor in silence. The elevator doors opened to what the signs said was the psychiatric unit. There was a desk at the entrance of the floor next to the elevators. The nurse asked for everyone's identification and their relationship to Tonya. She recognized 'Rell from the business magazine she had been reading. She showed him his picture in the magazine and complimented him on his success. She never asked for his identification or his relationship to Tonya. When Karlton handed her his identification she looked at it and repeated her question.

"Sir, what is your relationship to Mrs. Mince?"

"He's our father," replied Derek.

"Oh, I'm sorry. You know I have to check, for the record. Now you go through these doors and follow the yellow arrow until you get to the Urgent Care Unit. You'll see the signs. They will make you sign in again there. The nurse at that end will give you directions about your visit."

Shai didn't say anything but she gave Derek a questioning look when she caught his eye. Derek ignored her. The four of them signed in a second time and went into a waiting area. A nurse came and greeted them.

"The doctor will be right out to talk to you."

"Will we be able to visit her?" Shai's question was on everyone's mind, but they were afraid to ask.

"I'm afraid she's still not responding. She won't know you're here. The doctor will explain it to you."

The nurse left them in the room waiting for the attending physician.

"Mr. Harris. Why haven't we met you?" Derek's question hit the air like a blow from a hammer. Karlton felt it hit him and he paused, feeling his emotions knotting up before he answered.

"Derek, I don't want to answer for your mother. I can only give you the information as I know it. Your mother and I had a seven year affair while she was married to D.Q. During that time although I wanted her to leave D.Q. and marry me she had you and Dershai. Shortly after Shai was born, I asked her to bring the two of you with her, so we could live as a family. She told me D.Q. wouldn't give her what she wanted if she left him."

Karlton stood up and walked over to the window and looked out at nothing particular. Derek, Shai, and 'Rell listened intently as Karlton continued the story.

"I never thought you were my children, I thought that was why D.Q. insisted she stayed. I didn't know he told her she could go. She told me that last night. She told me that she never wanted children and she had you as leverage for him to stay with her. Tonya didn't think D.Q. knew the two of you weren't his. Your mother wanted D.Q. Enterprises. I threatened her from the time I found out her love for D.Q. Enterprises was more than her love for me. I was willing to tell D.Q. about us. She paid me monthly not to tell. But she thought I was threatening to tell him about you being my children. How could I tell him something I didn't know? I was going to tell D.Q. about the love I had for her and the fact that I knew they didn't love each other. I found out D.Q. loved your mother 'Rell. I watched your father for months. He was always a family man and he played the role in two houses. When he approached me about the stocks that I gave Tonya I told him I would leave her alone when he left Nikki alone. We fought. That told me he loved Nikki. He loved his business and he tolerated Tonya. I told Tonya what happened and she laughed. She told me D.Q. stayed with her because of the children. It all came out last night."

Karlton sat down in the seat close to Derek and sighed before he spoke again.

"She told me she still wanted D.Q. Enterprises. She didn't care about my love for her. She told me that I was your father and she did what she had to do to get what she felt she deserved. I told her I was leaving. I started to pack. I told her that I deserved to know my children. We argued about me telling the two of you who I was. She started screaming and crying. I continued to pack. She went in the living room and after a few minutes I heard a crash. She had slit her wrists. I called 911."

"So our mother didn't tell you we were your children?"

"No, she didn't Derek. Not until last night."

"Then why did you try to visit me at the hospital?"

"I was there to meet your mother. I didn't know she came to visit you that morning. I wanted to talk with you and maybe get to know you as Tonya's son, not my son; a man whose mother I loved. I knew she would be spending a lot of time with you because of your condition. I thought it would be easier for us to get to know one another if you knew I was close to your mother before the accident."

"Just in case she got my money you would be there already in the mix huh?"

"Derek, I have my own money. Have 'Rell and his boys check me out. This wasn't about your money."

Karlton lied but there was no need to tell Derek how his anger over the years changed and that when he first came into town he could have taken the money and been satisfied. Things were different now.

"Mr. Harris."Why didn't you call us, like you called 'Rell?"

"I realize I'm a stranger to you. I don't want to be. I realize our situation though. 'Rell and I have spoken. I trusted he would not hang up the phone."

The doctor entered the waiting area. He had a somber look on his face that gave the indications that Tonya wasn't doing well at all.

"Hello, I'm Dr. Stern. I'm the attending physician on the unit. Are you here for Mrs. Tonya Mince?"

Rell, Shai stood with Karlton to greet the doctor.

"Yes, is she going to be alright?" Shai asked the question and braced herself in 'Rell's arms.

"We can't make an educated guess on that. It appears she has taken a high dosage of tranquilizers and mixed it with a high level of alcohol. She didn't take them right before cutting her wrist as the EMT's believed. She had been taking them and drinking for hours. We don't know if she'll make it through the night. She has lost a tremendous amount of blood. There will be several tests she may need to take for us to see if there is any brain activity. Again at this point we don't know."

Shai cried softly and sat in the seat next to Derek's wheelchair. Derek put his hand on her shoulder.

"We have her resting and that is the best for her. You can peek in on her but do not stay long. Do we have contact numbers for you?"

"You have my number. Shai and Derek you may want to leave your number."

"They can call you Mr. Harris."

Shai answered for both her and Derek.

"That will be fine Dr. Stern."

The doctor continued down the hall as they looked on in silence. Karlton extended his hand to Shai. She accepted his hand and he put his arm around her. Karlton waved Derek on as a sign for him to join them. The three of them went through the double doors. 'Rell dialed Mr. Simpson's number and told him he would drop the papers off after the visit.

Three Years

The phone rang and Nana yelled from her bedroom. "Somebody answer that phone. Michael, you or Alesha answer that. It might be your brother calling from the airport."

"Nana, its Reverend Wilcox."

"Darryl, can you get that for me, I'm looking for my slip. I know I laid everything out last night."

Darryl came to Nana's room. He peeked into her bedroom door. Nana was looking in her dresser and stopped and shook her head.

"Mama you alright? Rev said don't forget his tie clip in his top drawer."

"Darryl, come on in and get it. I swear I can't find my slip. I can't wear that dress without the proper under garments."

Darryl smiled as he walked past his mother looking into her dresser again. Her slip was on the floor next to the chair with her other garments. Darryl opened the top drawer and noticed the tie clip was on the top of the chest drawers. Darryl laughed to himself.

"I don't know which of you is more nervous. You didn't act like this on your wedding day. Your slip is here my dear and his tie clip is on the dresser not in it."

"Thank you. There was no need for me to be nervous at my wedding. The Reverend and I both knew all our guests. 'Rell is a big CEO, who knows who will show up."

"Mama, they can't come if they're not invited."

"The media ain't invited and they sure will be there. They call it news. Black folks call it gossip. There will be some of them there too."

"Everything will be fine. Did Darlene call?"

"Darryl, call her. I don't know if everything is alright over there. I should have went over there myself. Did the rest of your crew call?"

"Francine called saying they would meet the family at the church."

"I sure wish Francine wouldn't separate herself like she does."

"Well, it works for us. She'll be fine at the reception. She knows Simone will be there, they're cordial with each other."

"It is what it is." They both laughed. Darryl left his mother to get dressed.

'Rell stood in the yard gazing into the sun. It was eighty degrees and the temperature was climbing. The soft breeze was refreshing as 'Rell let the thoughts of his father cross his mind. He was at peace knowing he and Shai would be married at one o'clock. Mitch came into the yard holding Bryce, 'Rell and Shai's three year old son.

"Hey man, are you missing Mommy and your sister?"

'Rell reached for Bryce, who stretched his arms out for his father's embrace smiling. He took his son in his arms and gave him a kiss on the forehead.

"I think he's bored."

"Well he won't be in another two hours. There will be plenty of people to keep him busy, plus Brianna will be in his sight."

"Yeah, you can tell they're twins, always together."

"How did Marci make out with her dress?"

"She got it back yesterday, they took it out again?"

"Is she showing now?"

"She has a pouch. Marci is self conscious about it though. She's four months and people ask her how far along she is."

"Do that many people know she's pregnant?"

"No, some are just finding out we're married. What time did you tell Byron, Keith and Craig to get here?"

"They're going to meet us at the church. That way they can be with their dates before the ceremony."

"Did you know Craig was still with Monique?"

"No, but she called and said she hoped I was happy."

"She's giving you well wishes."

Mitch laughed and Bryce laughed along with him hoping for a moment to play.

"Yeah man your dad's player days are officially over. Listen I'm going to put his tux on him. Everyone should be ready by then."

'Rell watched Mitch and Bryce walk into the house. He looked for his watch and noticed he didn't have it on.

Chapter 79

onya and Karlton arrived at Shai's house as the photographer was taking pictures in the living room. Darlene opened the door and Brianna ran to the door behind her.

"Hey little lady, look how pretty you are."

Karlton picked up Brianna as he and Tonya entered the door.

"How are you Karlton, Tonya? They're taking the last pictures, and then we'll be heading to the church."

"Ladies, if you could just step in closer. I think we have our last photo here." The photographer waved his hand to indicate which way he wanted them to move.

"Thank God. I'm burning up. Mama cut the air on higher."

"Mia, we're leaving after this shot, now get ready to smile."

The women got closer together and smiled for the last house photo. They agreed that they wouldn't take pictures on the lawn at the house. Each of them was scared of the heat ruining their hairdos. Shai asked the photographer if he could take another picture for her. She walked over to where Karlton was still holding Brianna. Tonya was talking to Darlene. She was getting her corsage and Karlton's boutonnière.

"Hi Karlton, how is she feeling?"

"Today seems to be a good day. She hasn't had any seizures for the past two weeks. I think it's the new medicine she's on. I don't know if it's me but her speech seems to be improving. The therapist says she is stubborn but who doesn't know that about your mother. Shai, she's coming along."

"I'm glad of that. Can you bring Brianna and get my mother for a picture?"

"Sure."

The four of them took a few pictures in chosen spots of the house. Darlene told them it was getting close to the time for them to leave so they would get to the church on time. Shai told her she would be there in a moment. She stopped Karlton as he was going out of the door. Brianna pulled at Karlton's hand.

"C'mon Granddaddy, c'mon."

"Wait baby, mommy wants me, go with Marci."

Brianna obeyed, happy to be with Marci and Mia.

"Shai, what's wrong?"

"Nothing, I wanted to thank you before the afternoon got too emotional for me to remember. I don't know how this day would have been without my mother, and the man I knew all my life as my father. You came into my life when I needed that other shoulder. My mother was slipping away from me, and you saved her. My love for D.Q. Mince will never fade, but I have learned in these past three years, you're a good man Karlton Harris and I'm proud that if D.Q. wasn't my father, you are. I know it's been hard for you too, but thank you. I don't know if any other man would have stayed with a woman who denied him access to his children. Thank you for being there and giving her back to me and my brother."

Karlton reached out and hugged her. The three years had been trying. Tonya didn't remember much about the attempt she made to take her life. She lived from day to day as though it was her first. Karlton transferred to Virginia and lived with Tonya in her home. Although her recovery was slow she did show her love for Karlton. He was in the driver's seat and his direction was now Tonya's. He remained distant but close enough to Shai and Derek where they trusted him. His path was laid all he had to do was follow it. Shai was closer to him than Derek and he allowed her to be. He kissed her on her cheek. They both walked out her door as Darlene was coming in to get them.

"Girl you better come on you have a man waiting to marry you."

Chapter 80

Cameras flashed as the couple walked into the reception hall. Shai couldn't believe all the tables were filled. Although she had a guest list of one-hundred-fifty people she couldn't believe that all of them actually showed. The ceremony was beautiful and Shai hoped the video reflected it all. Marci cried more than any of the other females in the bridal party, and they teased her that it was due to her pregnancy. Bryce and Brianna walked down the aisle together, one with the pillow and the other with the flowers. They had rehearsed for what seem like months with Bryce walking first, but he froze in the middle of the church aisle. Brianna being the more sociable of the two walked up to him and held his hand until he saw 'Rell and walked to the front of the church on his own.

Karlton escorted Shai down the aisle and tears flowed from all that knew the significance of the entrance. Tonya blew a kiss as her daughter passed her aisle and Nana said a soft, "Thank you, Father." Nikki and 'Rell lit a candle at the start of the ceremony in memory of D.Q. Reverend Wilcox performed the ceremony with a beautiful solo by one of the choir members.

At the reception, there was plenty of food, music and those who had questions. Monique made her way to speak to 'Rell, who was saying thank you to his employees from D.Q. Enterprises for attending and bringing gifts. She waited until they noticed that she had not joined them to congratulate the groom. The subtle hint said she wanted to speak with him alone. They told 'Rell they thought the ceremony was lovely, repeated their well wishes and quickly walked away.

"So Mr. Mince, should I say I told you so."

"About what?"

"About you and your so called sister. Why would one marry their sister?"

"Cute, you're still cute. I found out, oh, shortly after you saw us at the doctor's office that we weren't related. She's not my father's child."

"I always said your family could be on Jerry Springer or one of those shows. So she hit it rich both ways. She was left money and married money, how lucky!"

"Some girls have all the luck. I see you're still with Craig."

"It's off and on."

"Well if you ever want to take me up on that date for the four of us…. "

"I don't think I could stomach it."

"C'mon Monique, you love drama."

"No thanks. Congrats, just keep my number in case you want to pick up where we left off."

'Rell watched Monique walk off. He sighed deeply glad he chose a new relationship when he did. He walked through the crowd of guests saying thank you while looking for Shai. Mr. Simpson stood at the end of the bar watching as 'Rell came toward him.

"Stanley, how are you?"

"Rell, life is good. I see Ms. Davis has not given up."

"You see more than I do. How's Derek?"

"He's fine. He's upset, he couldn't be here for the festivities."

"Well, his leaving the country was his choice."

"Rell, they would have killed him. It would have been ugly."

"Did you ever find out what was involved? It wasn't just trade infringement was it?"

"Rell let's just say it was imported trade."

"Well said Stan well said. Is Leeza still with him?"

"Yes, they're in her native land. I don't know if he'll come back other than to visit."

"Well Shai misses him but you're right he's better off out of the country."

"When do you and Shai leave?"

"Tonight, we'll be in Hawaii for two weeks."

"Be safe."

"We'll be in touch."

"I'm sure you will 'Rell. I'm sure you will."

Shai walked up behind 'Rell and put her arms around his waist. They went on the dance floor and danced. 'Rell kissed Shai passionately as the glasses in the reception hall sounded simultaneously. The guests repeated the tapping of their glasses until 'Rell and Shai parted laughing. Bryce and Brianna ran onto the floor playing around their parent's feet.

Monique watched from the bridal party's table. She took another drink from the waiter's tray as he passed. After having few drinks, she distanced herself from Craig and the other guest. She was beginning to feel left out although Craig checked on her by bringing drinks to the table. She definitely wasn't the main attraction, and she didn't care to mingle with any of the other guests. She left her seat and found a table with a few empty chairs and a better view. Monique watched 'Rell and Shai as they danced drinking slowly from her Martini glass. The woman next to her took a picture of the couple and looked at Monique afterward smiling.

"They make a beautiful couple."

"Yes, they look like the couple from the fairy tales."

Monique was being sarcastic but the woman, a reporter, was looking for inside news. She spoke hoping Monique would give her good gossip.

"Well I guess you're right, she found her Prince Charming."

"Are you a relative or friend?"

Monique wanted to know who she was talking to. Not that she would remember if she was asked the next day. The woman answered trying not to reveal her purpose.

"I guess you can say I'm just a friend of theirs."

"Well, the new Mrs. Mince better hold on to her fairy tale Prince 'cause there's a lot of women here today that want to live happily ever after."

Other Novels by Nanette M. Buchanan

Family Secrets Lies and Alibi's

Bruised Love

Purchase Your Copy Today

www.ipendesigns.net
www.amazon.com

Rising Sonz Books
Willingboro, New Jersey
Urban Knowledge Bookstores – Maryland

www.ingramcontent.com/pod-product-compliance
Lightning Source LLC
Chambersburg PA
CBHW051601100726
47898CB00001B/181